Pamela Evans was born and brought up in Ealing, London. She lives in Wales but goes to England regularly to see her family and five beautiful grandchildren.

Her previous novels include *Second Chance of Sunshine*, *The Sparrows of Sycamore Road* and *In The Dark Streets Shining*.

WHEN THE BOYS COME HOME

As German bombs wreak havoc on West London, Megan Stubbs' father, Dai Morgan, is killed in an air raid. Coping with her loss, Megan takes over her father's milk round, and she and her mother, Dolly, brave the ravaged streets with the horse and cart. Comforted that her twin girls have been safely evacuated to Wales with her sister Hetty, Megan worries about her husband, Will, fighting abroad. And when Will's life-long friend, Doug Reynolds, returns, wounded and disfigured, she takes him in. However, Doug is not the man she thinks he is . . . When peace is declared in 1945 the boys come home. But the reunion for Megan and Hetty with their husbands brings heartache, especially for Megan, who is nursing her own battle scars . . .

Books by Pamela Evans
Published by The House of Ulverscroft:

A BARROW IN THE BROADWAY
MAGGIE OF MOSS STREET
STAR QUALITY
THE WILLOW GIRLS
A SONG IN YOUR HEART
THE CAROUSEL KEEPS TURNING
CLOSE TO HOME
SECOND CHANCE OF SUNSHINE
THE SPARROWS OF SYCAMORE ROAD
LAMPLIGHT ON THE THAMES
IN THE DARK STREETS SHINING

PAMELA EVANS

WHEN THE BOYS COME HOME

Complete and Unabridged

CHARNWOOD
Leicester

First published in Great Britain in 2007 by
Headline Publishing Group, London

First Charnwood Edition
published 2008
by arrangement with
Headline Publishing Group, London

The moral right of the author has been asserted

British Library CIP Data

Evans, Pamela
When the boys come home.—Large print ed.—
Charnwood library series
1. World War, *1939 – 1945*—Social aspects—
Great Britain—Fiction 2. World War, *1939 – 1945*
—Evacuation of civilians—Wales—Fiction
3. London (England)—Social life and customs—
Fiction 4. Wales—Social life and customs—Fiction
5. Large type books
I. Title
823.9'14 [F]

ISBN 978–1–84782–121–8

Published by
F. A. Thorpe (Publishing)
Anstey, Leicestershire

Set by Words & Graphics Ltd.
Anstey, Leicestershire
Printed and bound in Great Britain by
T. J. International Ltd., Padstow, Cornwall

This book is printed on acid-free paper

To all my friends and neighbours
in Swansea who have been so kind
and supportive.

1

Tucked away among the serried ranks of terraced houses in the back streets of Hammersmith stood Morgan's Dairy, on the corner of Blossom Road. Like most parts of wartime London, the landscape of this riverside area was battered and depleted, the bomb sites a permanent reminder to the neighbourhood of the friends and loved ones they had lost.

Although the dairy building was run down and in need of redecoration — which it wouldn't get until after the war, when materials became available again — it was a fine Edwardian construction with elegant pillars flanking the entrance to the shop, which had an imposing corner frontage. This small family business was at the heart of the community, delivering fresh milk to its customers each morning, and incorporating a general store where people could obtain most of life's necessities, including a chat or a shoulder to cry on. There was an adjoining house in which the owner, Dai Morgan, lived with his wife, children and grandchildren.

As it happened, he was out on his milk round one morning in June 1944 when the eight o'clock news on the wireless caused a dramatic hush to descend upon the family over breakfast.

'Oh, good God alive! D-Day has come at last,' cried Dai's wife Dolly when the bulletin ended. Imbued with patriotic emotion, she stood up with shoulders straight and head held high and added in a respectful tone, 'God save the King.'

'Hear, hear,' whooped her elder daughter Megan. 'Our troops are back in France, yippee! It's been so long in coming, I can hardly believe it's true.'

'It didn't sound very official, though, did it?' observed her sister Hetty warily.

'That's probably because the news has only just come in and the newsreader doesn't have any more details about it,' their mother suggested brightly. 'He said there have been Allied landings in Normandy. In other words, it's D-Day. It'll be officially confirmed later on, most likely.'

'We don't need to wait for that, though,' decided Megan, rising with a purposeful air, the last precious vestiges of porridge in her bowl abandoned in the excitement. 'Let's go outside and see the boys of the air force on their way. Come on, kids.'

They all trooped into the small sunlit back garden, the children infected by the sudden buoyancy in the air even though they didn't know what it was all about.

'There they go,' said Dolly, squinting up at the clear blue sky where great fleets of planes roared overhead, as they had done intermittently since the early hours, presumably heading for the coast to give support to the ground troops involved in the invasion. 'Good luck, boys. You're heroes, every one of you.'

'Is the war over then?' asked Megan's daughter Netta; it was a reasonable assumption for a six-year-old to make, given the sudden upbeat atmosphere.

'Are we going to have a party in the street with jelly and cake and that?' added her identical twin sister Poppy, eyes shining with hope. Both children were adorably pretty, with dark wavy hair like their father and the same sloe-black eyes.

'And flags to wave?' This was Hetty's son George, a thin, brown-haired lad with solemn, shandy-coloured eyes and a rather pasty look about him.

'Afraid not, kids. Not yet anyway,' replied twenty-six-year-old Megan, her joy fading slightly as she wondered how many more servicemen would die before victory was finally achieved. Her husband had been sent abroad in the war's early stages and she hadn't seen him for almost four years. For security reasons, all communications from him were censored by the army, so he wasn't able to let her know exactly where he was. She knew it was somewhere in the region of the Far East, though, which meant that he was too far away to be involved in today's landings.

Now there were wails of disappointment from the children, who had grown up with the promise of huge celebrations after the war.

'It won't be long, though,' assured their grandmother, a cheerful, warm-hearted soul with an endless capacity for optimism. In her mid-fifties, she was still easy on the eye in a homely, mumsy sort of way, being slight of build with greying blond hair and sparkling blue eyes.

3

In direct contrast to her husband, who was of a rather serious nature and often affectionately teased for his Celtic melancholy, she was comical and light-hearted. 'You'll have plenty of jelly and cake, and bunting strung across the street, when the time comes. We'll make sure of that, don't you worry. It'll be the best party you've ever been to, but you'll have to wait a bit longer for it.'

'How much longer?' enquired Netta.

'Nobody knows, love,' replied Dolly with a gusty sigh. 'We'll just have to be patient and wait until they get it sorted.' She paused, looking at her grandchildren. 'In the mean time, today is a very important day. When you're grown up with children of your own, you'll be proud to tell 'em that you remember D-Day.'

'Why can't we have a party if it's such a special day?' Poppy was nothing if not persistent.

'Because it isn't the sort of special that involves parties,' explained her mother.

'Not fair,' she pouted.

'It certainly isn't, love,' agreed Megan, who could understand her daughter's eagerness for some sort of merry-making. Today's children had so few treats: no ice cream or oranges or fancy food; just meagre portions of plain fare, and their precious sweet ration, which was a mere paucity compared to what had been available in peacetime. All this and the absence of their fathers too: it was hard on them even though they remembered nothing else. Megan poured all her energies into making them feel loved and secure. She wanted their childhood to be a

4

happy one, despite everything. 'But it's much worse for Daddy and Uncle Ken. At least we're at home all together.'

'Dad won't be coming home yet then, Mum?' said George, who was just a few months younger than his cousins but much less exuberant, and permanently in thrall to them. He didn't remember his father but his homecoming was synonymous with the end of the war, which everything seemed to hinge on from the viewpoint of a child.

'No, not yet, George.' Sighing wistfully, his mother put a comforting arm around him. Twenty-five-year-old Hetty had been notified back in 1940 that her husband was in a prison camp, having been captured at Dunkirk, so there was no chance of his return until after the hostilities ended. 'But he'll get back to us as soon as he possibly can. And when he does come home we'll give him such a smashing welcome, he'll wonder what's hit him.'

The boy nodded, seeming satisfied with this.

'Cheer up, Hetty,' urged Dolly, observing her daughter's flagging spirits. 'All right, so the war isn't over yet, but it's the best news we've had in ages.'

'I'll say it is.' Megan was petite like her mother, with the same blue eyes and blond hair, though Megan's hair was lush with youth and she wore it in a simple shoulder-length bob. 'But for now, come on, kiddy-winks, let's go back indoors to finish your breakfast, or you'll be late for school.'

In the general rush for the door, the

high-spirited twins elbowed George aside.

'Oi, you two, not so rough,' admonished their mother sternly, because George was a delicate, sensitive boy. If there was anything going around, George would catch it. Coughs, sore throats, bilious attacks and colds made a beeline for him. Not so her beloved and boisterous twin daughters, who were always in robust health and often known as 'the terrible two' because of their tendency towards mischief. Being so complete in themselves, they didn't often need other playmates, which meant, inevitably, that George was sometimes excluded. That upset Megan, because he was such a sweet child and always seemed rather lonely. She constantly urged them not to leave him out, and they did as she asked up to a point, but neither she nor they could do anything about the special bond that existed between them as twins. 'Move out of the way and let George go inside first. He was in front of you.'

'Yeah, watch where you're going,' added Hetty firmly. 'There's no need for pushing and shoving.'

'Sorry,' they chorused and moved back to let George through.

Her sister's intervention hadn't been strictly necessary since Megan had already reprimanded the twins, but she didn't allow herself to be rattled by it. Living in the same house, a certain amount of communal discipline was inevitable. If Hetty were ever to step over the line and take liberties, she would find herself at war with

Megan in defence of her children. But it was unlikely to happen. Megan and Hetty were friends as well as sisters, and understood each other.

Megan did sometimes have cause to worry about Hetty, though, in that she tended to be overly protective of George. It was understandable in a way as he was such a sickly child, but she did seem to fret excessively. Although rational in other areas of her life, she was almost paranoid when it came to her son, which couldn't be good for either of them.

Although the children had picked up on the excitement, they weren't old enough to understand the significance of today. Questions about victory parties and the return of their fathers from the war was just a habit to them, having been brought up in the anticipation of glorious peace and all that went with it. The twins had no emotional ties with their dad, as they had been so little when he went away. But Megan did what she could to keep Will's presence alive by talking about him and making sure his photograph was in a prominent place in the bedroom the three of them shared.

Now they all settled back at the big round table in the homely parlour next to the kitchen and continued with breakfast, the adults falling into silence, each engrossed in their own thoughts.

'I wonder if your dad has heard the news yet,' mentioned Dolly eventually.

'I'll be surprised if he hasn't,' responded Megan, smiling at the thought of her father. 'Can you imagine Dad's customers keeping quiet about something as big as this? Everybody will be full of it.'

'Yeah, that's true,' said Dolly with a chuckle. Her husband was hugely popular in the area, despite the fact that he wasn't a sharp talker full of cockney banter like some of the London milkmen. People liked him because he was kind and reliable. 'Someone will have told him and given him a cuppa tea while they're at it, I expect.'

'Knowing Dad, he'll make sure of the cuppa,' put in Hetty. The younger woman wasn't at all like her sister to look at. Less pretty than Megan, but attractive in her own way, she was tall and angular, with the look of her father about her; she had the same striking combination of greyish-blue eyes and dark hair.

Just then the shop bell tinkled.

'Aye aye. Duty calls,' said Dolly, taking a quick sip of her tea before rising.

'Do we have to open the shop quite so early, Mum?' enquired Hetty, not for the first time. 'At least we could have our breakfast in peace if we opened up a little bit later, instead of having to get up and down to the bell.'

'How many more times must I tell you? People rely on us for bits and pieces on the way to work, and the customers are our bread and butter; never forget that,' lectured Dolly. 'Anyway, I don't mind an early start and there's never much of a rush until later on.'

'I'll go and see to this customer, Mum. You

finish your tea,' offered Megan, reaching over and putting a restraining hand on her mother's arm.

'No, love, you stay and finish your breakfast and get the kids off to school,' Dolly said, moving away and leaving the room before there could be further argument.

To live in the Morgan home was to be involved in the family business. It was a way of life Megan and Hetty had grown up with. Having flown the nest after their respective marriages, they had returned when their husbands went away to war. It had seemed the only sensible thing to do, with the housing shortage so acute in London.

More important was the fact that their parents had needed their help in the dairy, with staff being called up for the services and war work. Living on the job meant they were always on hand. The war had caused the turnover of the business to drop: food had been rationed, and the demand for milk was reduced by a massive civilian evacuation from London, with men away on active service and milk deliveries being cut to one a day as part of government restrictions. When their father's roundsman had been called up for the army, Dad had decided to save on his outgoings by doing the job himself, so the business was now staffed by just the four of them.

Megan and Hetty worked as a team with their mother, doing their share of the household tasks, taking their turn in the shop and helping in the dairy. While their mother

9

ran the shop, their father was in charge of the milk side of the business.

Although it was a relatively small business, there was a huge amount of work to be done behind the scenes: bottle-washing, sterilisation, filling and sealing the milk bottles, making sure the dairy was kept spotlessly clean and hygienic at all times, as well as keeping the shop stocked and the customers happy. There was also increased paperwork with the coming of ration books for shop goods, and as milk distributors, they were accountable to the Ministry of Food so daren't be dilatory in the task. The nature of their trade meant that it was seven days a week, but although they delivered milk every day, they only opened the shop for a few hours on a Sunday morning. At the end of each week either Megan or Hetty would go out on the round with their father to help collect the milk money.

A proud Welshman, their father lived by rules that were somewhat out of touch with modern times. Although he was happy for his wife and daughters to work with him in the business, he wouldn't allow them to actually do the milk round unless there was some dire emergency. He didn't think it fitting for a woman, despite the fact that milk-women had become a familiar sight on the streets of London since war broke out. Women were definitely the weaker sex in his opinion, never mind that they had been doing an excellent job of men's work throughout the war.

Dai was a good sort, though, a solid tower of a man, reliable to the core and able to take a joke despite his sombre nature. Megan smiled at the

10

thought of how the family joshed with him when he was a bit too effusive on the subject of his beloved Wales. There was no stopping him once he got on to that subject.

'Come on then, you two,' she said to the twins now. 'If you've finished your breakfast you can go and get your things together for school.'

'You too, George,' added her sister.

Chattering and giggling over something between themselves, as usual, the twins had to be told several more times before they finally did as their mother asked, while George got up immediately and headed for the stairs.

★ ★ ★

'Thanks for the tea, bach,' said Dai Morgan, emerging from a small terraced house. 'There's kind you are.'

'A pleasure, Dai,' said a large, smiling middle-aged woman who had been a customer of his for years. 'I wouldn't be much of a person if I didn't give my regular milkman a cuppa on a day like today, would I? It's been long enough coming.'

'Aye, it has,' he agreed, the lilt of West Wales still prominent even after so many years away. 'Let's hope they don't take as long to finish the job.'

'Ooh, don't say that, for goodness' sake, Dai,' she said in a tone of mild admonition.

'I didn't mean it literally,' he said, noticing her worried look.

'I should hope you didn't, especially on a day

11

like today.' Wearing an apron over her summer frock, and carpet slippers on her feet, she poked her index finger under the front of her turban and scratched her scalp between the curlers, looking thoughtful. 'I don't think we'll have to wait too long, myself. Those damned Jerries don't stand a chance now that our boys are back on French soil. The war's all over bar the shouting.'

'There's optimistic you are and I hope you're right,' he said. 'My trouble is that I'm a realist and I can't help wondering what's happening to our boys now that they're back in France.'

Her face tightened and she shook her head slowly, her lips pushed together in a grim line. 'I think we're all worried about that. There's more blood to be shed yet, and that's a fact. But at least there's been progress now, so we have to keep hoping for the best.' She paused, looking at him. 'Are your girls' husbands involved in the invasion?'

'No. One of them is a POW, the poor dab, and the other is further afield somewhere.'

'Maybe now that the second front has started, you'll have 'em both home soon.'

'I hope so.' Humour wasn't his forte but he decided to give it a try to lighten the mood, especially as this customer enjoyed a joke. 'Apart from anything else, I need them here to give me some back-up support against all those damned women. Now that my daughters have come back home to live, there's five o' them including the twins. There's bossy they are.'

'You poor thing. My heart bleeds for you,' she

chortled. 'I'm sure a big strong boy from the valleys is more than a match for a few women about the place. They are the backbone of this country, you know.'

He gave a wry grin. 'So they tell me, on a regular basis,' he said. 'So don't you start.'

She loved this sort of banter. 'You know we're right,' was her spirited response.

'Aye, maybe I do, but I shan't tell them that or they'll make my life hell.'

'You thrive on it.'

'Course I do. I wouldn't be without them and they know it.'

'That's what I like to hear.'

'Anyway, I'd better be on my way.' He turned to go. 'So long, bach. Thanks again for the tea. You look after yourself now.'

'Ta-ta, Dai. Mind how you go.'

A big-built man with rugged features, Dai was tall and thick around the middle. He had dark hair peppered with white, and grey-blue eyes that made him look every inch a Celt. Whistling softly to the tune of 'Bless 'Em All', he walked to his milk cart parked at the kerb, loaded a crate of empty bottles on to it and paused for a breather, feeding his black shire horse with a carrot.

'There's a good pal you are, Chips.' He fondled the horse's head, the whiteness of the blaze down the front of the animal's face gleaming in the sunshine. 'You're a good worker too. We're partners, you and me. I couldn't do without you and that's a fact.'

A strong believer in communication between man and beast, and extremely fond of his horse, he stood with him for a few minutes longer then led him to the next block of houses in the narrow London street, pausing on the way at a horse trough for him to drink some water.

It was a fine, sunny morning and it felt good to be out in the open air. He'd been forced by wartime economics to go back on the round himself but he was very glad he had; he enjoyed being at the grass roots of the business again.

With the shortages and limitations of wartime, things were hard in the dairy trade, but working together as a family they were managing to keep the business ticking over. At least he had his own reserved territory now, so he was safe from competition from the big dairies that would monopolise milk distribution in the capital given half the chance. Some small dairy owners he knew of had already sold out to them. But not Dai! Never! He'd worked too hard to build his business to hand it over to someone else.

London had been kind to him, he reflected, as he made his way from house to house, leaving the full milk bottles on the doorstep and collecting the empties, cursing those customers who hadn't put theirs out. It wasn't good enough, especially as it was generally known that there was a serious bottle shortage.

The streets here hadn't exactly been paved with gold when he'd been forced to leave his beloved Wales in search of employment at the beginning of the century. He hadn't been much more than a boy at the time.

But at least he'd found work, which there was precious little of in rural Wales in those days.

He'd got a job as a milk roundsman initially, turning his hand to other things in his spare time to put a few extra quid in his pocket: labouring; painting and decorating; delivering groceries to posh people in the big houses. Anything as long as it came up with the dosh and was legal. His hard work and determination had paid off and he'd eventually been able to open his own dairy, by which time he'd married his lovely Dolly, whom he had met when she'd been working as a kitchen maid in one of the big houses he delivered to. The poor dab had been brought up in an orphanage and put into service as soon as she was old enough.

In those days the milk had been fresh straight from the cow, and very tasty it was too. Nowadays pasteurisation was all the rage, in London anyway, so he purchased his milk from the wholesaler ready treated rather than invest money in the equipment to do it himself. He'd managed to get some basic machinery when times had been good for various other routine dairy tasks.

Despite the war, and all the heartache and misery it caused, he was happy with his lot. Even, he thought affectionately, if he did live in a house overrun by the opposite sex, with their women's talk, mania for tidiness and lack of interest in football or the inner workings of an automobile engine. Dai was a man's man. He'd grown up in a world where men provided, women ran the home and Father was most definitely the boss.

He grinned to himself. He wouldn't fancy his

chances if he tried to introduce that regime into his house; they all had plenty to say for themselves. He loved the bones of them all, but a spot of male company wouldn't go amiss. There was George, bless him, but it would be a long time before he was old enough to assert his presence and be an ally to his grandfather.

Dai thought the world of all his grandchildren, but although he tried never to show it, there was a special place in his heart for his grandson, maybe because he hadn't had any sons of his own. There's lovely it was, to have a boy in the family. But if the poor lad wasn't being teased and tormented by his cousins, his mother was fussing over him like flaming Florence Nightingale. True, he wasn't a robust child and had had a lot of illness in his life so far, but he didn't need to be smothered. He was a boy; he needed a bit of rough and tumble.

Although there was plenty of Welshness in Dai's heart, there was precious little of it in his home, which was inevitable as his wife was a Londoner through and through and his daughters had been born and raised here. His elder daughter Megan had been named after her grandmother on his side, so at least there was a touch of Cymru in that.

But Dai hadn't kept up with the customs like some of his compatriots, who went to the Welsh chapels here and conducted their social life in their mother tongue. It wasn't that he hadn't wanted to exactly; just that he'd drifted away from it over the years and had allowed himself to mingle into the metropolis. He'd become a part of the way of life here, especially after he'd married Dolly. But he would always be Welsh at heart and still had a passion for his homeland.

Oh well, press on and count your blessings, boy, he thought, as he neared the end of his round.

★ ★ ★

The news of D-Day was officially confirmed just after half past nine that morning by the well-known broadcaster John Snagge. The King spoke to the nation on the wireless in the evening. Megan reflected on his broadcast as she lay in bed listening to the even breathing of her sleeping daughters. She had found his obvious sincerity profoundly moving. He had matched her mood completely, and she thought most other people would have felt the same. Her thoughts turned to her dear husband Will and she was besieged by a plethora of emotions: fear for his life and dread that he might never return, turmoil at the memory of his complex personality, and above all love for him so deep, it hurt just to think about it. She hadn't heard from him for a while so had no idea whether he was alive or dead, and was hardly able to even consider the latter. Twenty-six was no age to die.

Although Will was everything to her, theirs wasn't an easy marriage. But she vowed that if he was spared she would try even harder to understand him.

Her stomach churned at the thought that she

must find the time to visit his mother. The fact that she wasn't easy to get along with didn't alter the fact that Will was her son and she would be as worried about him as Megan was.

Megan could hardly bear to imagine how her mother-in-law would cope if Will didn't come back from the war. That would be one blow too many for a woman who had already had more than her fair share of anguish and was filled with bitterness and resentment as a result. As disagreeable as she so often was, she was still Will's mother and as such would be treated with respect by Megan. Somewhere beneath the older woman's prickly persona there beat a warm heart, Megan was sure of it.

★   ★   ★

'I thought I'd just pop over to see how you are,' said Megan to Audrey Stubbs.

'I'll put the kettle on,' responded Audrey indifferently. According to people who had known her for a long time, she had once been strikingly beautiful, smartly dressed and extremely gregarious. Now she was almost white-haired, dowdy and very unsociable, her attractive features distorted by a permanently harsh expression as she exuded aggression towards the world in general. She was tall and overly thin, with a hopeless stoop about her, and she looked much older than her fifty-odd years.

'Thank you, that'll be lovely,' said Megan politely, sitting down at the kitchen table while the other woman filled the kettle and put it on the gas stove to boil. It was the following afternoon and they were in the kitchen of Megan's in-laws' small house on the borders of Hammersmith and Chiswick. Audrey lived here with her husband Jack, an amiable, unassuming man who worked as a welder in an engineering factory. Will was their only child — now.

'D-Day came at last then,' commented Megan sociably.

Audrey shrugged. 'About bloomin' time an' all,' she stated with disapproval. 'I don't know what took them so long. The people who run the military must be nothing short of useless, every damned one o' them.'

'I suppose they do their best,' responded Megan patiently. 'The invasion must have been a massive thing to organise, and they would have had to wait until the time was right. There's a lot to it that we don't know about, I think.'

'Yeah, maybe there is, but those who are running it should have made it their business to get it done before,' Audrey grumbled. 'This war has gone on for far too long. It isn't right, people having to put up with so much pain and suffering.'

'Most people seem to think the end won't be long now, though,' mentioned Megan, determined not to get into an argument about the logistics of the war.

'Time will tell,' Audrey said gloomily.

'It was good news, though, about D-Day.'

'Mm, no doubt about that,' she replied without much interest. 'But there's still a lot of

19

fighting to be done before it's over.' She looked at Megan. 'Have you heard from Will lately?'

Megan shook her head.

'Neither have we.'

'Will's a survivor,' Megan tried to reassure her. 'If anyone will come through the war, it's him.'

'I know that,' Audrey said sharply. 'There's not much point in worrying about it anyway; there's nothing we can do except wait and work our fingers to the bone for the war effort.'

'How's the job going?' Audrey worked a morning shift on war work in a factory nearby.

'It's bloomin' hard work,' she replied. 'But I'm glad to get out of the house, to tell you the truth. It's better than being indoors all day, thinking about things.'

Will's twin brother Ron had died in a drowning accident when the boys were fourteen. From what Megan had heard, it had had a disastrous effect on both Will and his mother. Will and Ron had had the special closeness that was common in identical twins and had been inseparable, which meant that one was lost without the other. Apparently the grief had sent Will off the rails for a while, and his parents had had a hard time with him when he'd started to hang out with yobs and got into trouble with the police for rowdiness on the streets. Although the yobbish behaviour had proved to be just a phase, Megan believed that he had never got over his brother's death. Sadly, though, he never opened up to her on the subject.

As for Audrey, she'd been broken by it and left angry and belligerent towards everyone, in particular Will, who had been with Ron at the time of the accident. Sometimes it seemed to Megan as if Audrey resented Will for being alive when Ron wasn't. Will had never spoken to her about it but she guessed he must be very hurt.

Will had been almost nineteen when Megan met him, so the trauma had been in the past, though the effects of it had been very much in the present. He was handsome, caring and full of down-to-earth humour and charm, which was why she'd fallen in love with him and married him. But even though there was tremendous chemistry between them, she never felt emotionally close to him. A part of him held back and that distressed her.

There was a darkness within him that seemed to go beyond grief somehow, and wasn't apparent to other people. On the surface he was sociable and funny. Everyone liked Will Stubbs. Only Megan and possibly his mother — if she could see beyond her own misery — knew about the other side of him. He never raised a hand to her but he built a wall between them as solid as bricks and mortar.

'How's Jack?' Megan asked dutifully now.

'He's all right; plodding on the same as ever,' Audrey replied, sounding bored. 'How's everybody with you? Are the kids behaving themselves?'

'They're up to all sorts, as usual,' said Megan, pride and love unmistakable in her voice. 'There's never a dull moment when those two are around. They certainly keep me on my toes.'

'It's with there being two of them,' suggested

21

Audrey wistfully. 'My boys were the same.'

'Twins, eh, who'd have 'em,' joked Megan. Realising immediately that her light-hearted remark might prod at Audrey's wounds, she opted for a swift change of subject. 'The children thought the war was over yesterday when the news came through about the invasion, with us all rushing into the garden like mad things. They thought perhaps we'd be having a victory party.'

'Huh! Chance would be a fine thing,' said Audrey tartly, pouring the tea and putting two cups on the table before she sat down herself. 'God only knows how long they'll have to wait for that.'

Getting a dialogue flowing with this unhappy woman was nigh on impossible. Megan stayed just long enough to be polite, then left feeling depressed. Audrey always had that effect on her. But at the same time she was filled with compassion for her mother-in-law, and couldn't bear to think how she herself would cope if she lost one of her children. She doubted if she would get over it either. It was a dreadful burden for Audrey to have to live with, so Megan would continue to visit no matter how cold the welcome.

★ ★ ★

'How do you make someone like you, Grandad?' George enquired in a serious tone.

Considering the matter for a few moments, Dai looked down at the skinny scrap of a boy with freckles on his nose and solemn pale brown eyes. 'I'm not sure I know the answer to that, boy. Treat them decently, I suppose.'

'I do, but they still don't seem to like me.'

'In that case they must be a bit *twp*,' he said, using the Welsh word for stupid. 'Who is it, anyway, who doesn't like you?'

'I can't tell you that.'

'Some boy at school, is it?'

George shook his head,

'Only your mum will be up that school like lightning to get it put right if some bully is getting at you,' Dai told him gravely. 'No doubt about it. So speak up if that's what it is.'

'It's nothing to do with school.'

It was the following Saturday, just after midday, and they were in the dairy yard. Dai had finished his round and was unloading the crates of empty bottles from the cart and stacking them in the dairy ready for washing and sterilisation. The horse was still coupled to the cart prior to being taken back to the communal stables used by local tradespeople, having finished his work for the day.

'Why can't you tell me who it is then?' Dai asked.

'Because it would be telling tales.'

'Mm, there is that, I suppose.' He considered the matter some more. 'Still, if it stays between us it wouldn't matter. It's only if the other person gets into trouble over it that it would be tale-telling, and they won't if no one else knows about it.'

'You promise not to tell anyone?'

'When have I ever let you down?' said Dai

'You know our little chats never go any further.'

George looked pensive. 'Well, all right, I'll tell you,' he said, still reluctant.

'Spit it out then, George, before I grow old waiting.'

'It's the twins,' he blurted out, looking as though he wished he hadn't.

Dai tutted loudly. 'I might have known those little monkeys would be behind it.' He shook his head slowly. 'High spirits, it is. I'm sure they don't mean to be unkind.'

'Yes they do. They're always mean to me. They're always taking the mick, saying I'm a sissy boy just because I'm not as daring as they are.' He paused then became vehement. 'They hate me.' Another pause and his mouth tightened. 'And I hate them back.'

'You just said you wanted them to like you.'

'Well I do, but as they're never gonna like me, I might as well hate them too.'

'Now you're talking twp,' Dai admonished. 'Your cousins are twins and they don't really need anyone else. It isn't that they don't like you in particular; just that they have each other. They're probably the same with everybody.'

'I wish I had a brother or sister,' sighed George. 'Then I'd have someone of my own as well.'

'You have pals in the street and at school, don't you?'

'I s'pose so.'

Dai suspected that they might be a little thin on the ground but he wasn't going to cause the boy more pain by mentioning it. The harsh

24

reality was that the school playground could be hell on earth for a boy like George, who wasn't as physically strong as the others.

'I could have a word with your Auntie Megan about the twins, if it'll help,' suggested Dai. 'Ask her to tell them to be a bit kinder to you, is it?'

George was horrified at the suggestion. 'You promised you wouldn't say anything,' he said, a scarlet flush suffusing his face and neck. 'If you do that it really would mean I'd been telling tales and the twins will hate me even more.'

'All right, boyo, don't get yourself into a state about it,' Dai said kindly. 'My lips are sealed. But can you try to stand up to those cousins of yours a bit more? That might help.'

'I try to but it doesn't work. They just laugh at me; they're always giggling.'

'It's in their nature, son,' Dai told him. 'You're like a brother to them, and all sisters and brothers tease each other.'

'It wouldn't be so bad if they were boys. But girls . . . ' George looked disgusted and emitted an eloquent sigh. 'They like playing stupid girls' games: mothers and fathers and that. They want me to join in when they're playing that because I have to be their flippin' kid. And if they're playing skipping I always have to turn the rope.' He reached up and patted the horse gently, as though drawing comfort from the animal. 'I hardly ever get a turn at skipping. It doesn't matter how much I argue with them about it. They think they're the boss of everything, just because they're twins.'

'As you won't let me say anything, I can't do

much to help you as regards your cousins, but I tell you what I *can* do to cheer you up,' said Dai, removing the last crate from the cart, uncoupling the horse and putting the cart against the whitewashed wall of the dairy. 'I can take you with me to take Chips back to the stable. You can have a ride on his back if you like.'

The boy's eyes lit up. 'Ooh, could I, Grandad?'

'Yeah, I don't see why not.' For the boy's sake he chose not to remind himself of his daughter's disapproval of such things. Hetty was over at the house so with a bit of luck she'd be none the wiser and no harm done. 'Come on then, young 'un. Up you go.' He helped him up and George sat astride, smiling broadly. 'Hold on to the horse's mane,' Dai said as the animal moved forward. 'Slowly does it.'

Before they could progress further, there was a sudden violent interruption.

'What on earth do you think you're doing, Dad?' shrieked Hetty, running across the yard towards them, a look of terror in her eyes, her face scarlet and blotchy.

'Taking him to the stables to take Chips back,' he explained, knowing that he was in big trouble but standing his ground and staying between her and the horse. 'I'm letting him have a ride as it's only a few minutes' walk down the road.'

'You know I don't allow it.'

'There's no harm in it, love.'

'Are you trying to kill my son or something?'

'Look at me, Mum,' chirped the boy gleefully. 'I'm up here, ever so high.'

But Hetty was far too upset to pay any

26

attention to her son's obvious pleasure. 'Get him down at once, Dad,' she demanded, her voice quivering. 'He'll break his neck if he falls off.'

'But he won't fall off,' her father assured her. 'I'll make damned sure of that.'

'Get him down,' she shouted, her voice distorted with desperation as she moved towards the horse. 'Quick, before he falls off. Don't worry, George; we'll soon have you down from there.'

'I don't want to come down, Mum,' the boy told her, his smile fading. 'I like it up here. I'm going for a ride with Grandad.'

'You're far too young to be on horseback. There isn't even a saddle,' she disapproved hotly.

'We're only going down the road. He'll be all right — '

'You're really out of order this time, Dad,' Hetty interrupted furiously. 'You're encouraging him to do things he's far too young for. Now get him off that horse or get out of my way so that I can do it.'

'Leave the boy alone, love,' requested Dai in a tone of quiet persuasion. 'It's only a bit of fun.'

'For you maybe,' she ranted, almost beside herself now. 'You're the kid around here, not George. It's high time you grew up and started acting your age.'

'Don't you talk to me like — '

'You've no sense of responsibility whatsoever,' she butted in rudely. 'You are not fit to be a grandfather. Now get him off that horse this instant.'

'Dad won't let him come to any harm, Hetty,'

reassured Megan, having heard all the shouting from the house and come to see what was going on.

'He's my child, not yours, so keep your big nose out of it,' Hetty blasted at her sister. 'I want him off of that horse — *now*.'

Looking both angry and hurt, Dai reached up and lifted the boy down.

'Go inside, George,' ordered his mother solemnly. 'I'll be in to see you in a minute.'

Disappointed and near to tears, the boy did as his mother asked with his head down.

'I'd rather you didn't speak to me like that, especially in front of my grandchild,' Dai rebuked. 'You could at least show some respect for your father.'

'If you behaved like an adult, maybe I would.'

Megan saw him wince but he said, 'Why did you have to spoil it for him? The boy was enjoying himself.'

'And why did you put me in a position where I had to,' Hetty came back at him on the verge of tears. 'You know George isn't a strong child. He has enough trouble with his health as it is, without adding a broken neck to it.'

'As if I would let that happen.'

'Not deliberately, no,' she was forced to agree. 'But you get carried away and danger doesn't seem to occur to you. He's your grandson; you ought to look out for him.'

'You think I don't — '

'Calm down, the pair of you,' Megan intervened. 'You're both getting het up and saying things you don't mean.'

'I do mean it,' shrieked Hetty. 'He's taking risks with my child's safety, and it has to stop.'

'He's a little boy,' her father pointed out tersely. 'It's only natural he wants to have some fun. Chips is the most docile of horses, you know that. A babe in arms would be safe with him.'

'Rubbish,' she ranted. 'He's an animal and as such can't be trusted. Why do none of you try to understand the extra worry that comes with having an ailing child?'

'We do understand — ' began Megan.

'You've got a damned funny way of showing it then, that's all I can say. Anyway, I'm going inside to George,' snapped Hetty, tears running unchecked down her cheeks now. 'He's probably seriously traumatised, having been sat on the back of a damned great carthorse.'

And with that she turned on her heel and marched across the yard to the house.

'I wouldn't harm a hair on that boy's head,' Dai confided to Megan, obviously very hurt by Hetty's accusations. 'I've never thought of myself as an irresponsible man.'

'You're not, Dad, and Hetty knows that in her heart,' Megan tried to reassure him. 'She doesn't mean what she said. She was just lashing out because she's all strung up. You know how nervous she is about George.'

'How could I not know? And most of it's unnecessary.'

'He does fall ill more than most kids of his age,' she pointed out, defensive of her sister but wanting to support her father too.

'I know that, but she doesn't have to wrap him in cotton wool when he's well.'

'I think she's got a lot on her mind, what with Ken being shut up in a prison camp, and George falling sick a lot,' Megan said. 'She takes it out on us.'

'You're just making excuses for her and I'm not sure that she deserves it,' Dai admonished. 'I mean, your husband is away too, and we don't have all this malarkey with you.'

'My children are fit and healthy,' Megan reminded him. 'So at least I don't have that to worry about. Keeping them out of mischief is my problem, as you very well know.'

He chuckled affectionately. 'They are a bit on the lively side,' he was forced to admit.

She smiled. 'Try not to be too upset about what Hetty said, Dad,' she advised him. 'She's oversensitive about George and gets herself into a state about nothing.'

'Too often in my opinion,' he said. 'She never used to be so highly strung.'

'She isn't over other things,' Megan pointed out. 'It's only when it comes to George.'

'The poor dab. He was so disappointed when she made him get off the horse.'

She nodded. 'Anyway, I'll just go and see what the twins are up to, then I'll come and make a start on the bottles.' Washing and sterilising the bottles was one of her regular jobs.

'What would I do without you, *cariad*?' he said, smiling at her and warming her heart.

'You'd manage.' Megan adored her dad and had always been close to him.

'Poor old Dad's still smarting from that trouncing you gave him over at the dairy,' Megan told Hetty back at the house, having made a point of speaking to her about the incident.

They were in the parlour, which overlooked the small rear garden adjacent to the dairy yard. Leading off from the kitchen, it was the most versatile and well-used room in the house and was unstylish and comfy with a pleasant outlook over the vegetable patch. The room had well-worn armchairs and sofas as well as dining furniture, and a big fireplace with a cast-iron surround.

'Is he?' Hetty looked sheepish.

'Of course he is,' Megan confirmed. 'Naturally he was hurt by what you said. I know you had George's interests at heart, but you didn't half go on at Dad. I don't think you were at all fair to him.'

Hetty brushed a tired hand over her brow. 'Oh God, was I really that hard on him?'

'Yes, you were,' her sister confirmed. 'That's no way to treat your father. The family is everything to him and he doesn't deserve that sort of a roasting.'

'It was just that I was so scared when I saw George up there on the horse's back.'

'But why?' asked Megan. 'Dad can be trusted to see that no harm comes to him. He wouldn't put any of his grandchildren at risk. You must know that. He's devoted to them.'

'He wouldn't mean to, I admit that,' Hetty

31

conceded. 'But I ask you, fancy putting a young, delicate child up on a horse of that size.'

'Most children enjoy a ride on the milkman's horse,' Megan reminded her. 'I let the twins have a go, as you know.'

'That's quite different,' insisted Hetty. 'Your kids are a lot stronger than George. Honestly, Megan, you haven't got a clue how much I worry about him.'

'I've seen how much you worry and I don't think you need to do nearly so much of it,' Megan advised in a kindly manner. 'Sure, he gets more coughs and colds than the others, but he always comes through, and he's fine at the moment.'

'He wouldn't have been if he'd fallen off that horse.'

'Dad wouldn't have let it happen,' Megan insisted, clinging to her patience by a thread. 'He's a strong man, he knows how to deal with horses and he's not the slightest bit irresponsible.'

Hetty didn't say anything.

'Anyway, you can't protect a child from every single thing in life,' Megan continued. 'They have to live and have fun; they have to have a childhood. You'll spoil his and make yourself ill if you don't calm down and get things into perspective.'

Her sister sighed. 'It goes with the territory, I suppose, when you're a mother,' she said. 'I don't know how you can take it all so much in your stride.'

'It's a question of getting it into proportion.' Megan looked at her sister. 'You seem especially tense at the moment. Is there anything I can do to help?'

'Thanks but no. It's just the way I am.'

'At least we can look forward to the end of the war now,' said Megan cheerily.

'Yeah, I know,' agreed Hetty. 'But I still feel on edge.'

'Maybe you'll feel better if you apologise to Dad,' suggested Megan, ever the family peace-maker. 'He might be a bit overenthusiastic at times but he does his best for us all. There can't be a more devoted father and grandfather on the face of the earth.'

'Now I feel awful,' Hetty admitted, 'but I still say he shouldn't have put George up on that horse.'

'Dad was brought up in the country, remember, and things are different there. I think he was probably on and off horses at a very early age himself so doesn't regard it as dangerous. And he really does think the world of George, you know. He would never admit it but I think George is his favourite grandchild. So he's understandably hurt at your lack of trust in him.'

'Yeah, all right, Megan, don't go on about it,' Hetty said irritably. 'I will go over and patch things up with him.' She gave her sister a determined look. 'But whether you like it or not, I shall tell him not to do anything like that again.'

'I shouldn't think he'd dare after the wigging you've just given him.' Megan grinned and tried to make light of it for her sister's sake. 'Anyway, I'm going to make a start on the bottles. The twins are playing out but they know where to find me.'

'I'm taking over from Mum in the shop until we close for dinner,' Hetty told her. 'She's got things to do in the kitchen. I'll go over and make my peace with Dad first.'

'That's my girl,' said Megan.

★ ★ ★

The dairy shop had black and white tiles on the floor, and dark, solid polished wooden counters with shelving behind. Along the front of the counters were square open tins of biscuits, some of them being sold cheap because they were broken, as well as loose sugar, sacks of flour and various other provisions.

Behind the counter, Hetty's fingers were trembling as she worked at the bacon slicer, cutting the meat thinly so that the customer's ration would go further. Apologising to her father had eased her conscience but not her nervous system. The sight of George on that horse had frightened her to such an extent she had felt physically sick, and the effects still lingered on.

The world seemed beset with peril for her son, and it didn't get any easier for Hetty when there were no air raids, as was the case at the moment. Apart from the little blitzes early in the year after three years of relative tranquillity, the raids were few and far between. The fact of the matter was that it was her job to protect George, and she always felt inadequate to the task, with him being

34

so sickly. He was her pride and joy, her adored Ken's son, and it was her duty to keep him safe from harm at all times.

Hetty had never been particularly lacking in self-confidence until she'd had George, but the minute he was born, she knew she'd changed and would never be the same again. She found the responsibility of motherhood all-consuming, terrifying and quite beyond her capabilities, even now, six years on.

She couldn't talk to anyone about it — not even her sister, to whom she usually bared her soul about everything. How could she admit that she was actually frightened of being a mother, that she didn't feel up to the job, and blamed herself every time George got sick?

His being poorly seemed to symbolise her failure. Motherhood was supposed to come naturally. She'd been brought up to believe that it was women's purpose in life, and that everything they needed for their child's health and well-being would come to them with the birth.

It hadn't come to Hetty, and she didn't know how other women were so calm, even casual about it. She felt like a freak, and tried to convince herself that her feelings of nervousness and inadequacy were caused by George's tendency to fall ill. But she had a horrible suspicion that she would feel like this even if he was as tough as an old boot. It was something inside her that had been there since the instant he had come into the world.

People probably thought she was a 'smother

mother'. But she'd sooner be one of those than not do the job properly. George was her life, and she was afraid that if she didn't give him the ultimate in protection, he would be taken from her.

'Are you all right, love?' asked the customer, who had an apron over her clothes and a cigarette in her mouth.

Recalled to the present with a start, Hetty turned to the woman on the other side of the counter and said, 'Yeah, I'm fine. Why wouldn't I be?'

'You look a bit pale and preoccupied, that's all.' The woman emitted a throaty laugh. 'I thought for a minute there that you were gonna slice your fingers off.'

Hetty arranged her features into a smile. She'd been brought up to be cheerful and friendly towards the customers at all times, regardless of her own feelings. 'I've been at it too long to do something like that,' she assured the woman.

'That's a relief. I wouldn't want to be here if you had an accident like that,' she chuckled. 'I'd pass out cold.'

'I don't suppose I'd be feeling any too chirpy either,' said Hetty with a forced grin, putting the rashers in paper.

The customer cackled, removed the cigarette from her mouth while she coughed raucously, concluded her purchases by asking for this week's tea ration, then put the family's ration books back into her shopping bag. She handed Hetty a shilling piece and moved aside to let a waiting customer get to the counter, whereupon they struck up a conversation and everyone in the shop joined in.

The all-female gathering launched into a lively discussion about the latest news from abroad and the war news generally, since everyone kept themselves informed by means of the wireless and the newspapers. They then moved to lighter topics, such as some spicy neighbourhood gossip concerning a local girl and a GI, different ways to make the rations go further, and what was on at the pictures.

As she worked behind the counter, with the shop full of friendly chatter, Hetty's trembling finally began to abate.

★　★　★

'Are you still upset about that ding-dong you had with Hetty, Dai?' enquired Dolly that night. Wearing a high-necked, ankle-length, winceyette nightdress, she was sitting at the old-fashioned mahogany dressing table putting her curlers in in front of the mirror. Her husband was already in bed, lying with his hands linked behind his head. They never stayed up late because they had to get up so early. 'You've got that troubled, brooding look about you.'

'I'm all right, love.'

'I don't think you are, you know,' she persisted.

'Oh yeah, and what makes you think you can read my mind?' he wanted to know.

'Years of experience, I suppose,' she said in a matter-of-fact tone. 'I've been married to you for a long time. I probably know you better than you know yourself, if the truth be told. So come on: tell me what's eating you.'

'Can a man not keep his thoughts to himself?'

'Not when he's my husband and he's worried about something. Come on, out with it.'

'Well, it isn't a nice thing to be told by my daughter that I can't be trusted to look after my own grandson.'

'No, it isn't, but I'm sure Hetty doesn't really think that and she knows she was well out of order,' said Dolly, who had been told what had happened. 'She's apologised to you and you accepted it, so I should forget all about it now.'

'She shouldn't have said those things in the first place, then she wouldn't have had to apologise.'

'You're quite right, Dai, she shouldn't, and she knows that now.'

'But she's told me not to let George go near Chips again,' he went on miserably. 'Does she really think I don't have the sense to look after the boy?'

'She doesn't think anyone can look after him except herself. So it's nothing against you personally, love,' Dolly tried to reassure him. 'You know what's she like about that boy of hers, and anyway it's over and done with, so don't you go upsetting yourself about it.'

'Well . . . ' He still looked peeved.

'If you've got one fault, Dai Morgan,' she cut in, fixing her last curler in place, turning off the light at the switch by the door and feeling her way over to the bed, 'it's that you don't let things go. You let them rankle on in that head of yours and get yourself all upset.'

'Must be because I'm a Celt,' he said. 'We're very deep and passionate about things.'

'It's because you're a daft old sod, more like,' she said, climbing into the high bed beside him, chuckling.

'Trust you to reduce it to ground level.'

'You know me. Down-to-earth is my middle name.'

'You're telling me.'

'Go on with you,' she joshed as she settled herself. 'You know you wouldn't want me any other way.'

'Stop fishing for compliments.'

'It's the only way I'll ever get any from you.'

'You know how I feel.'

'Course I do.'

He thought for a moment. 'I notice you said I only had one fault,' he said eventually. 'That's nice to know.'

'I said, *if* you had one fault; I didn't say you only had one,' she corrected. 'We've all got plenty of those. I'll point yours out to you if you like.'

'No thanks. That won't be necessary.'

'You'll do for me, though, faults and all,' she said brightly.

'Are you after something with your soft talk, woman?' Although he was an uxorious man, he wasn't at all comfortable with sentimental talk.

'If I wanted something, I'd come right out and ask,' she said. 'You know me.'

'Aye, I do. You're not exactly a shrinking violet. You Londoners are all the same. Full of front.'

'You're a Londoner yourself after all these years.'

'Only in part,' he reminded her.

'And the rest is pure Welsh, I know.'

'Don't you forget it.'

'As if any of us could, Dai bach, when you're always on about it,' she giggled, wriggling about and sighing with pleasure. 'Ooh, it's so lovely to be in bed. It's been such a long day and I'm worn out. I must have walked miles today, in and out of that shop. I've got corns like marbles on my feet. This is sheer bliss, especially now old Adolf's boys have stopped coming over.'

'Do you always have to be so bloomin' cheerful?' he said in a tone of fond admonition.

'I don't have to, but I prefer it that way,' she came back at him. 'We've got a lot to be thankful for, you and I. We have each other, a smashing family, a good business, and . . . ' she paused, 'the war's nearly over. So stop worrying about Hetty and give us a cuddle.'

'You're right,' he said, putting his arm around her. 'We're winning the war and the future's bright. What would I do without your endless cheerfulness?'

'Be a miserable old git, I expect,' she quipped.

'Oh, charming, I must say.'

'Just joking. You should know that by now.'

'If I don't after all these years, I never will.' He

40

yawned. 'Still, as you say, things are looking better than they have in ages. We'll soon see the end of this damned war.'

'That's what I like to hear,' she approved heartily. 'Optimism, and plenty of it.'

2

The mood of buoyancy generated by D-Day was somewhat diminished a few days later when Londoners once again found themselves under fire from above.

In the early hours of the thirteenth of June, some curious flying objects scudded across the sky, flame spurting from their tails before they crashed to earth, leading eye witnesses to believe, jubilantly, that an enemy bomber had been shot down. But on the sixteenth the government announced that pilotless aircraft were now being used by the enemy against the British Isles.

Having felt as though the war was finally drawing to a close, it was a bitter blow for the Morgan family, as well as the rest of the population of southern England, to find that they were back in the front line, especially as these bombs came down at all hours of the day when people were going about their business. After a few weeks the alert was in force so often many people ignored it, finding that the most effective warning system was their own ears. When the grating roar of an approaching bomb turned to a splutter before the engine finally cut out, that was the time to dive for cover.

'Honestly, Megan, I'm beginning to think this ruddy war will never end,' moaned Hetty early one Saturday morning as they stood in a queue outside a greengrocer's shop in King Street.

Word had gone round that the shopkeeper would have some onions for sale, and queuing was to start from six o'clock. They had been there on the dot and had already been waiting for an hour and a half. The children were in bed at home with their grandmother.

'Yeah, I know what you mean but it *will* end, obviously. It can't go on for ever,' Megan pointed out wisely. 'It does feel as though we've had a setback with this new spate of bombings, but it'll probably just be a short-lived thing. After all, being bombed again doesn't mean we are not winning the war. Some people say the doodlebugs are a last desperate attempt by Hitler because he knows that time is running out for him. The word is that the war is in its final stages.'

'That doesn't make the bombs any the less deadly,' Hetty told her gravely. 'God knows how many people have been killed these past few weeks.'

'It's awful, I agree. We've been lucky.'

'Don't tempt fate, kid. We're not out of the woods yet.' She sighed. 'I know I mustn't complain when there are people worse off. It's just that, well . . . it's so long since I've seen Ken, it feels as though he'll never come home.'

'I know the feeling.'

'Yeah, course you do. There's me whingeing on and it's just as bad for you, with Will away.'

'He does seem to have been gone for ever, I must admit,' Megan said. 'It's surprising how you get used to things, though. It must be nature's way of getting us through; that and the

43

fact that we are so busy looking after things here we don't have time to mope.' She paused thoughtfully. 'I wonder if everything will be the same when the boys do finally get back.'

'Of course it will,' Hetty stated categorically. 'What a strange thing to say, Megan. I haven't even thought past getting my hands on him after all this time.'

Megan laughed. 'I've given that plenty of thought too, don't worry,' she said.

'What's all this about things not being the same, then?'

'I didn't say they wouldn't be the same; not at all. I sometimes wonder what it'll be like at first, that's all. I mean, they've been away for a heck of a time and people change as they progress through life. It might feel a bit awkward in the beginning, especially for them, having been away so long, and been through so much.'

'It might be tricky for some couples, but not Ken and me,' declared Hetty, who was wearing a faded cotton summer dress and sandals, her dark hair clipped back to the side with hair grips. 'We go back such a long way and know each other inside out, I'm expecting us just to carry on where we left off.'

'I'm sure you will too.' Megan thought her sister probably had the closest thing you could get to a marriage made in heaven. Ken was a local man whom Hetty had known since she was a schoolgirl, so they had made the journey from adolescence to adulthood together. He was an unassuming sort of person: amiable, reliable, honest and uncomplicated. It was obvious to anyone who saw them together that they were devoted to each other.

'You think it might be a bit strained between you and Will, then, do you?' Hetty enquired.

'No, not necessarily, but I do wonder if it might take a while to adjust,' replied Megan. 'After all, none of us can be certain how it will be when we see each other again after such a long separation. He's been away a long time and seen other worlds. His horizons will have broadened. His feelings for me might have changed.'

'You trust him, though, don't you?'

'Of course I do.' She could have added 'but I don't really know him', but that was something she preferred to keep to herself. It wasn't a subject she felt able to discuss with anyone without seeming to betray him. 'It isn't a question of trust. I'm talking about human nature and the passing of time.'

'Well I don't have any doubts about my feelings for Ken or his for me,' claimed Hetty with seemingly unshakeable confidence. 'It'll take more than a war and a long separation to come between us.'

At last the queue started to move slowly, and news came down the line that the greengrocer was only allowing one onion per person. Nobody complained because an onion was such a rare thing these days, and just one used sparingly could add flavour to a great many family meals.

'I hope they don't run out before we get to the front,' said Hetty, peering at the legions of women ahead of them.

'It won't be the first time, but maybe we'll be lucky.'

They were as it happened and left the shop beaming, with one onion each to take home for the family food cupboard.

They were walking away with the treasured items when the siren shrieked across the town. There was a general groan. A few of the women still queuing hurried away, but the majority stayed where they were because the chance of an onion for the stew was worth taking a risk for.

'That was a bit of luck,' remarked Hetty, as they hurried across Hammersmith Broadway. 'At least we got served before Moaning Minnie started to wail.'

'Let's hope we manage to get home before the bomb comes,' said Megan.

But it wasn't to be. A roar from above drew their gaze heavenwards and they both turned ashen, eyes wide with fear as the flying bomb clattered in their direction.

'Blimey,' gasped Megan, staring up at the missile with its flaming tail which was approaching fast, apparently unhindered by the ubiquitous barrage balloons filling the skies. 'It's creepy.'

'And it's coming our way,' observed Hetty nervously.

Glued to the ground in terror, they stood transfixed; this was the first of the unmanned aircraft they'd actually seen, though they'd heard plenty about them and seen the damage they caused. Along with everyone else out on the streets, they stared up at the sky over

46

Hammersmith Broadway, holding their breath and praying that the engine wouldn't stop. It seemed to be passing over and there was a general sigh of relief. Then the engine made a coughing sound and cut out.

People dived into doorways and shops; others lay on their stomachs on the pavement. The sisters threw themselves face downwards on the ground. So hard and fast were Megan's heartbeats, she thought her end would come without any help from the bomb. Rigid with fear and clenching her fists so tight her fingernails cut into her flesh, she waited for fate to do its worst.

When the explosion did happen, it sounded so close they were both surprised that when they scrambled to their feet they could see no evidence of it — at first. Then they caught sight of a cloud of smoke rising into the sky above the buildings in the direction of home.

'Oh my God,' gasped Hetty.

'Don't panic.'

But Megan was doing exactly that herself. As though of one mind, they tore across the Broadway and into the side streets towards Blossom Road.

★ ★ ★

The air raids terrified horses. So when Dai was out on his milk round and the siren sounded, he didn't follow the official procedure, which was to take the horse out of the shafts and turn it around with its head between them to stop it running away in terror. At that point the owner was supposed to leave the animal and go to take shelter. But Dai couldn't bring himself to do that and always stayed with Chips, talking to him and trying to keep him calm.

So he was with the horse in a street not far from home when he saw the flying bomb clatter across the sky. Stroking his beloved Chips and speaking to him in a soft tone, he heard the engine splutter and stop, saw the tail light go out and watched helplessly as the doodlebug crashed to the ground at the end of the road, crushing the houses as though they were made of cardboard.

'Steady, boy. Shush now,' he soothed as the horse started to rear and snort, hoofs scrabbling against the ground as his instincts urged him to run. 'It's all over now. We're going to be all right. There, there.' Dai held him close, putting his head against him and patting him lightly until he was quieter. Then he gave him a carrot. 'Good boy, Chips. I'm proud of you.'

People were running; there were screams and the sound of women crying. Dai's natural impulse was to go and offer help, but his horse needed him here. As the reassuring sound of ambulance and fire engine bells echoed into the morning air and the all-clear sounded, he continued on his round.

But the proximity of the explosion had brought him to a decision about something he had been mulling over ever since the beginning of the V-1 attacks.

★ ★ ★

48

They were a subdued group of adults around the table at lunchtime in the Morgan house; everyone was shaken by the nearness of the bomb. They'd had a good few close shaves during the Blitz, but at least the raids then had usually been at night, not when people were out and about doing everyday things. They had finished eating and the children had gone to play.

'I suppose we'll eventually get used to the damned doodlebugs as we have with every other horror the Germans have thrown at us,' suggested Megan.

'We won't be beaten by them, that much I am sure of,' declared Dolly.

'Oh no, that'll never happen,' agreed Megan, 'but these things are really evil coming over in broad daylight. None of us can take shelter all the time because there are things to be done.'

Her father had been noticeably silent throughout the lunch period. When he did speak he shocked them all.

'I want you all to go away to stay with my sister Dilys in Wales until the bombing stops, and that includes you, Dolly,' he announced in a firm tone.

'You'll be lucky,' was Dolly's spirited response.

'I'm not asking you, I'm telling you,' he said firmly, throwing her a look. 'I've been thinking about it for a while and made my mind up for definite after I saw that bomb drop this morning. It's far too dangerous here for you now, with these doodlebugs falling on our doorstep day and night.'

They all stared at him in silence, realising that he was deadly serious.

'If you think I'd go away and leave you here on your own during the bombing, you must need your head testing,' snorted Dolly at last.

'There's stubborn you are,' he reproached. 'I might have known you'd quarrel with me about it.'

'When you come out with a suggestion like that, of course I'll quarrel with you,' she retorted.

'So you'd stop me doing my duty, which is to look after the women and children of this family?' he persisted.

'On the subject of duty, it's mine to stay here with you, and I'm going nowhere.' Dolly turned and looked at her daughters. 'But I think you two and the children should go. I agree with your dad about that. It is too dangerous here.'

'We can't go away and leave you.' Megan was adamant. 'It just wouldn't be right.'

'You've the children to consider, love,' her mother pointed out, 'and it would be better than sending them away on the government scheme to stay with strangers. You'd be with them and you'd be with relatives. It will be nice for you.'

'Nice for us, yeah, but what about you two? You need us here,' declared Megan. 'Even apart from the personal side of it, there's too much work for the pair of you in the business.'

'You went to Wales when the Blitz was at its worst,' Dolly reminded her. 'We managed then.'

'There is that.' Megan couldn't deny it. 'But you had some outside help then; there were

50

more staff available because not so many people had been called up for the services. Be realistic, Mum. How would you keep this place going without us? You'd be run ragged, and make yourselves ill from overwork.'

'Will no one listen to me?' boomed Dai. 'I have decided to send my family to safety. I made the decision when a bomb dropped not fifty yards away from me, so I don't think I'm being unreasonable. But all I am getting is opposition. Do my wishes count for nothing in this house?'

'I'm not going away and leaving you, Dai,' announced Dolly, equally as determined, 'and that's my last word on the subject.'

He pondered on this for a moment. 'All right, if that's what you really want, I'll accept it. You and I have had a good chunk of our lives, but the others are only just beginning.'

'We're grown women, Dad. Well past the stage when you can tell us what to do,' Hetty reminded him.

'Well I'm not going and that's definite,' declared Megan. 'Running off to Wales and leaving you two here to manage this place on your own with bombs dropping all around? Not bloomin' likely.'

'We'll be all right,' her mother insisted. 'We'll get someone in to help in the business. I'll go to the labour exchange. They'll find us someone. Not everyone is away in the services.'

'Lots are working in factories, though, so you'll probably have to wait ages,' Megan pointed out.

'Not if I stress the essential nature of our

business. People can't go without milk and food.'

'You'll have all the extra expense of paying wages,' said Megan. 'Anyway, we're a family and we'll stick together and take what comes.' She turned to her sister. 'What about you? Do you want to take George to Wales?'

'I'd like to, of course. Who wouldn't rather be in the safety of the country with their children than here in the thick of the bombing? But I don't want to leave Mum and Dad here on their own. Either we all go or none of us do.'

'Don't be so soft, Hetty. Obviously your father and I can't go,' Dolly made clear. 'But I really do think that you two girls should do what your father says. It's the kiddies, love. We've got to do what's best for them, whatever our own feelings.'

'It's best for them not to be uprooted, and to stay here where their grandparents are,' Megan put in. 'It's bad enough for them having no dad around while they're growing up.'

'All this damned fuss,' grumbled Dai. 'It isn't even as if you'd be going to strangers. Your Auntie Dil and Uncle Owen will welcome you with open arms and look after you well.'

'We know that, and we love them both to bits,' Megan told him. 'But we also happen to think the world of you and Mum, and we're not prepared to leave you and go swanning off.'

'You wouldn't be swanning off,' corrected her mother. 'You'd be doing the sensible thing.'

'Why does no one do as I ask in this family any more?' asked Dai, spreading his big hands helplessly.

'Because we're adults with minds of our own,'

replied Megan, going over and giving him a hug. 'We appreciate your concern for us. But we have a sense of duty too, to you and Mum. We must have inherited it from you.'

'I don't know what things are coming to when a man isn't master in his own house,' he complained.

'I'll make you a nice cup o' tea,' said Megan, hoping to placate him, 'and you can take it with you when you go for your forty winks.' She thought for a moment. 'If we were to go away, you wouldn't have time for a nap in the afternoon. You'd be far too busy.'

'I'd sleep better at night, though, bombs or no bombs, because I'd know you were safe,' he informed her. 'So I wouldn't need a nap during the day.'

'At the hour of the morning you get up, of course you would.' Megan gave him a grateful, affectionate look. 'We appreciate your concern for us, but we're staying put, and that's that.'

Dai heaved a sigh of resignation, and Megan went to the kitchen to put the kettle on.

★ ★ ★

The Morgan family were not regular churchgoers, but they were believers and attended often enough for the children to be allowed to go to Sunday school in the church hall in the afternoon.

It was only a few minutes' walk from the dairy, and the children liked to go along with all the other neighbourhood youngsters. So the next day

Megan and Hetty sent them off in their Sunday best, faces washed and hair combed, waving to them until they turned the corner.

'Lovely. Now we can have a bit of peace and quiet for an hour or so.' Hetty was smiling as she and Megan went back into the house.

'Nice to know that they're in good hands while we take a break,' said Megan.

★ ★ ★

Sunday afternoon was the only daytime period of the week when the family was able to relax without interruption, because the shop wasn't open. With the clearing up done after Sunday lunch, the children out at Sunday school, and no customers to attend to, they sat in the parlour listening to the wireless, which was broadcasting solemn organ music. Dolly was darning socks and Dai was snoozing in his armchair. Their daughters were busy with their knitting needles.

'What we need is some dance music to liven things up a bit,' remarked Megan. 'There's nothing as dead and dismal as a Sunday afternoon. It's enough to give you the creeps.'

'I suppose the BBC like to respect the fact that it's the Sabbath,' said Dolly. 'There will be something more cheerful on later.'

'It's a bit too dreary for me, I'm afraid,' remarked Megan.

Just then the siren sounded.

'Is that lively enough for you?' smiled Dolly.

'I'd sooner have the dismal music, thanks,'

Megan said, rising quickly. 'I'm going to collect the kids.'

'The Sunday school teacher will take them to the shelter,' Dolly pointed out. 'There's no need to panic.'

'I'd sooner go and get them and have them at home with us,' Megan told her. 'It's bad enough having to leave them at school during a raid. As the church hall is only down the road, they can come home.'

Hetty was of the same mind, so together they rushed out of the house and ran down the street to find mothers pouring into the church hall to collect their offspring. The sisters were about to go in when George appeared in the doorway on his own.

'Be a love, George, and pop back in and tell Netta and Poppy to hurry up,' requested Megan.

He gave her an odd look and didn't move.

'Go on, son, chop chop,' urged his mother quickly. 'There's an air raid on. We've got to go home and take shelter down in the cellar.'

Still there was no movement.

'George, for goodness' sake, what *is* the matter with you? Don't just stand there,' admonished Hetty. 'Do as you're told and go and get the twins.'

'They're not in there,' he said sheepishly at last.

'Not in there,' cried Megan, puzzled. 'Of course they're in there. You all went to Sunday school together.'

He made no comment; just stood there biting his lip.

'So if they're not in there, where in God's name are they?' demanded Megan, worried now.

'I'm not allowed to say,' he said solemnly.

Megan put her hand to her head. 'Oh no! What are those two up to now?' She gave her nephew a serious look. 'Look, George, I have to know where they are so that I can go and find them. The siren's gone so the bombs will be over in a minute. I need to get them to safety. This is very serious.'

'Tell us where they are,' said his mother firmly. 'Come on now, George. Tell us and be quick about it.'

'I can't. I promised I wouldn't, and I'll be in real trouble with them if I do,' he told her.

Megan was getting panicky now. 'George, sweetheart, you have my word that I won't let them have a go at you. Just please tell me where they are.'

'They've gone to the park,' he mumbled miserably at last. 'They think Sunday school is boring.'

'Do they now? I'll give them boring. You wait till I get my hands on those little perishers,' declared Megan, her fear for them exacerbating her anger. She made a move to go. 'I'll see you back at home, Hetty. Shan't be long.'

'I'll come with you.'

'No, no, you get George home; there's no point you taking risks because my children can't behave themselves,' she told her, and hared off in the direction of the park.

People were hurrying out of the park as she reached the entrance, tears now pricking at the back of her eyes, mouth dry and stomach churning. There was no sign of her daughters and she couldn't remember ever having been this frightened before. Where were they? Someone could have gone off with them. It was all her fault. She should have taken them to Sunday school and made sure they went in. It wasn't as though she didn't know about their highly developed sense of adventure, which meant they couldn't always be trusted to do what they were told.

Skin suffused with cold sweat, she thought her heart would stop when she heard the ominous sound of a bomb approaching. When she did see the twins, her relief was so great it initially diminished her anger. They were with an elderly man who was holding their hands and coming in her direction. As she ran towards them, the twins spotted her and waved in greeting.

'I found them wandering,' the man explained, and Megan sensed criticism in his tone, as though he was wondering what sort of a mother let her children out alone during a time of intense bombing. 'I was going to take them to a shelter.'

She thanked him, grabbed the twins by the hands and led them out of the park, praying that the flying bomb would pass over, because the nearest shelter was quite a distance away.

'You are both in deep trouble,' she warned them breathlessly as she hurried them along, anger now returning at the thought of the danger they'd put themselves in. 'How dare you go to the park when you're supposed to be at Sunday school?'

'We wanted to see the ducks,' explained Poppy.

'To make sure they were still there and hadn't got bombed,' added her sister.

'When you want to go to the park, you ask me and I'll take you,' Megan lectured, knowing she must stay firm. 'You don't skip off Sunday school to go there. You are six years old, not sixteen, so you are not big enough to go that far on your own.'

'It isn't that far, Mum,' said Poppy.

'Don't answer me back.' She could hardly hold back the tears of joy that she'd found them safe, and secretly wanted to cuddle them. But she had to maintain discipline because they needed it all the more from her in the absence of their father. 'You've been naughty girls and I am extremely angry with you.'

'We didn't know the siren was gonna go and you'd come to fetch us,' said Netta naively, incriminating herself further.

'You thought you'd go back to the church hall and come home with George and I'd be none the wiser about the park, did you?'

'That's what we usually do,' said Poppy.

'So this is a regular habit?'

'We do sometimes do it, if it's sunny out,' admitted Poppy breezily. 'We don't like Sunday school.'

'What you like and don't like doesn't come into it, my girl. If I send you to Sunday school then that's where you go.'

'Sorry, Mum,' said Netta.

'Yeah, sorry, Mum,' added her sister, finally seeming to realise that she'd done wrong. 'We won't do it again, honest.'

'You won't do it again because you're not going to get the chance,' stated Megan. 'As I can't trust you, I won't let you out of my sight. Apart from going to school, you'll stay home until I decide otherwise. No playing out in the street. No fun and games. You'll stay indoors where I can keep an eye on you.'

The sound of another enemy aircraft stopped her in her tracks. She watched it, willing it to pass over. For a while it seemed that it would, but then the engine cut out and the twins dived to the ground on their stomachs as they had been taught and Megan lay on top of them protectively. As the explosion shook the earth beneath them, and the grating sound of another doodlebug could be heard in the ensuing silence, she knew she wasn't being fair to her children by keeping them in London when there was an alternative. She had no right to risk their lives.

★   ★   ★

'Thank goodness they saw sense after all,' said Dai early the next morning after he and Dolly had watched their daughters walk down the road with their suitcases, children skipping along beside them. They had been heading for the tube station to catch the train to Paddington, where they would take the train to Wales.

'Yeah, it's the best thing for them,' sniffed Dolly.

'Keep your pecker up, love,' he said, putting his arm around her. 'They'll be back before we know it. This latest crop of raids won't last long. Once it's eased off they can come home. Meanwhile, at least we know they're safe. The little ones will love it down at Dil's, with all that lovely countryside and fresh air. Dil will make a proper fuss of them too, bless her. She loves having kiddies about.'

'I know, Dai,' Dolly sighed. 'But I miss them already. The place will seem empty without them.'

'At least we know we've done the right thing.'

Dolly blew her nose and composed herself. 'Right, so we'd better get cracking. You need to get off on the round and I need to clear up indoors then get the shop sorted before I open up. I'll have to close up for half an hour or so later on while I go to the labour exchange. I don't know if they'll be open when we shut for dinner. We need someone who'll help in the shop and the dairy, and we need them fast.'

Dai nodded.

'Do you fancy a cuppa before you go?' she asked.

'That's a really good idea.' He would much rather get straight to work, but he knew how upset she was and thought perhaps a little of his company might help. 'I'm late already, with waiting to see the girls off, and I haven't finished loading the cart yet, so another ten minutes or so won't hurt.'

'I'll put the kettle on, then.'

The children were all very excited about their holiday in the country and couldn't wait to get there.

'You two are still in my bad books,' Megan reminded the twins as they waited for the train to Paddington. 'Just because we're going away doesn't mean I've forgotten it.'

'We'll be good, Mum,' said Netta.

'We'll be very good,' added her sister.

Megan didn't believe that for a minute but just said, 'You'd better be, girls, and I mean it. You're going to be living in someone else's house and you have to respect that and not cause any trouble. No mischief; no running off without permission.'

'Will there be cows in the fields like in my story book?' asked George. The children had been too little to remember much about their previous visit.

'Yeah, I should think they'll be outside as it's summer,' Megan replied.

Ostensibly her normal self, Megan was actually feeling terrible. Leaving her parents to face the bombing alone had cut deep with her. She'd felt as though she was deserting them. They'd seemed older somehow, and very precious, standing outside the dairy when she'd turned and given them a final wave before going round the corner.

But when the train came in and they moved with the crowd surging towards the doors, and she held the twins close to her to keep them safe from the throngs of people, she could feel their little bodies through their summer frocks and knew that her first duty was to them. She was overcome with love for them but she still felt an ache of sadness at leaving her parents and had to remind herself that it wouldn't be long before they were all together again.

★ ★ ★

The siren was already sounding by the time Dai and Dolly finished drinking their tea.

'I think you'd better wait for the all-clear before you go out on the round, Dai,' suggested Dolly, looking worried. She was used to him being out working during the raids, but it seemed more frightening somehow without the others around.

'It'll only start up again soon after. The siren is in force so often lately I'll never get the milk delivered if I wait for a gap between raids,' he pointed out. 'People need their milk, love, so I'd better make a start. I've still got to finish loading up.'

'I suppose you're right,' she conceded, collecting the cups and taking them to the sink to wash, along with the breakfast things that had been left in the rush of getting the others off to Wales. 'Ta-ta, then. See you later.'

He'd only been gone a few seconds when she heard a distant explosion, then the sound of him shouting and cursing.

'Chips has got out,' he told her when she ran outside to see what was going on. 'The bloody horse has bolted. Upset by the explosion, the poor dab.'

'At least he wasn't coupled to the cart,' she said, seeing the vehicle still in the yard.

'No. I like to leave him free for as long as I can,' he explained edgily. 'I thought he was safe as the gates were shut but he's gone right through them. That's what comes of not having decent gates. The wooden ones aren't a patch on the iron ones they took away for the war effort. I'll have to go after him.'

'It's dangerous,' she reminded him as bangs and crashes echoed all around.

'Exactly,' he said, pale and anxious. 'I can't just leave him. He'll go crazy and get himself hurt, or hurt someone else, if I let him run wild through the streets.'

'What about your safety?'

'I'll be all right,' he assured her, more worried about the horse than himself. 'He can't have got far. Anyway, I'm used to being out during raids.'

'I'm coming with you.'

'No, Dolly. It'll be best if you stay here.'

'You might need help with him,' she said.

'I'll manage. Now go back inside, for goodness' sake, woman,' he said hoarsely. 'There's no point in both of us staying out here. I won't be long.'

But she went after him anyway; followed him as he ran down the street. She was almost oblivious now to the ominous roar overhead. She was out of breath and had a painful stitch in her side. As she turned the corner she saw a woman further down the street trying to shoo Chips out of her front garden. She'll need some pacifying, thought Dolly, but was too relieved to have located the horse to worry about that. Dai was already taking the brunt of the woman's tongue by the look of it. She'd soon calm down once his Welsh charm got to work.

Dolly was so intent on the situation ahead, she didn't notice the sudden silence above and was knocked off her feet by an explosion so violent it lifted her off her feet and sent her crashing to the ground.

'Oh God help us,' she muttered, scrambling up in a daze to see chaos ahead. Some houses were in ruins and people were screaming and running around. Through the dust and smoke she could see Chips, safe and sound. But on the heels of relief came horror, as she spotted Dai lying on the ground beside him. Sobbing her husband's name, she ran towards him.

★ ★ ★

The journey to Wales was horrendous. The incoming train was delayed on its journey to Paddington, so they had to wait more than two hours on the station. When it finally arrived, the crowds were so dense it was suffocatingly overcrowded and they had only one seat between them, which meant taking turns and sitting on laps. There were several unexplained delays on the way, so by the time they finally pulled into St Clears station, it was evening and they were exhausted.

When they came out of the station, Uncle Owen was waiting for them with a farm truck.

'It's so good of you to collect us, Uncle,' said Megan. 'You must have been waiting ages.'

'The boss gave me the time off, like, seeing as you were coming, so it didn't matter.' Owen was probably about sixty. He had a tanned, weather-beaten look about him and was wearing overalls and a cap. 'You'd have a long wait for a bus, because they only run out to Cwmcae twice a week and there was one yesterday.'

He went on to remark how the children had grown since he'd last seen them, then helped them all into the truck. The children thought it was great fun riding in the back, while Megan and Hetty sat in the front bench seat with Owen. Although he was a shy, quiet man by nature, he was friendly towards them, talking about the war mostly. But Megan perceived a tenseness about him and wondered if they were the cause. It was, after all, a bit much suddenly having five Londoners descend upon his household.

'It's very good of you to let us stay with you, Uncle,' she said. 'We do appreciate it.'

'There's pleased we are to have you,' he said, sounding genuinely glad. 'Things are bad in London, so we've heard.'

'Pretty awful, yeah,' Megan confirmed.

'You'll be safe enough with us.'

He still seemed preoccupied, but Megan was so struck with the beauty of the place as the truck made its way through the West Wales countryside, it slipped to the back of her mind.

There was a verdant expanse of green hills

rising from either side of the main road, with cattle-dotted fields and occasional farmhouses set in the folds of the hills, everything bathed in the evening sunlight. It was so perfect it didn't look real; more like a beautifully painted picture. So different to the war-torn urban landscape they were used to.

'Gorgeous, innit?' said Hetty.

'I'd forgotten just how lovely it is down here,' her sister agreed. 'It takes your breath away.'

'It's like in the picture books,' observed George. 'All those toy cows in the fields.'

'They're not toys, you dozy twerp,' said Poppy. 'I saw one of 'em move. How can toys move about?'

'Real ones would be bigger than that,' claimed George. 'They would, wouldn't they, Mum?'

'They are real, love,' said his mother. 'They look small because they're so far away.'

'Cor,' said the awestruck George. 'I wish we could see them up close.'

'I expect you'll see plenty of them while we're staying here,' said Megan. 'Uncle Owen works on a farm, so I expect he'll arrange something.'

'Plenty of cows around our way, boy,' said Owen. 'It feels like a damned sight too many at milking time.'

Turning off the main road, they bumped down a lane flanked with hedgerows through which fields could be glimpsed. Then, sitting in the valley, just as Megan remembered it, glistening in the setting sun, was Cwmcae. There was a church, a chapel, a post office and general shop, the school and the pub. In the centre were a

66

telephone box and a scattering of grey stone-built houses surrounding the village green.

The children were beside themselves with excitement, and now Megan began to look forward to their stay too. Since they'd been forced into coming, they might as well make the most of it and enjoy the lovely countryside.

As they clambered out of the van outside the row of cottages where Dilys and Owen lived, Auntie Dil came out to meet them. She was a plump woman with pure white wavy hair framing a round face with the bloom of country living about it.

Megan knew immediately that something was wrong. Dilys's eyes were puffy and red from crying.

'Auntie,' said Megan, going over to her. 'What's the matter?'

'What is it, Auntie Dil?' echoed Hetty.

Dilys nodded towards Owen, who took the children inside the house.

'Oh girls. There's awful it is that I have to greet you with bad news,' she said, her voice tremulous and tears streaming down her cheeks. 'I'm so sorry to have to do it to you.'

'What bad news?' asked Megan shakily.

'It's your dad,' Dilys said thickly in her soft Carmarthenshire accent, her English precise and carefully spoken because it wasn't her first language.

'Dad. What's happened to him?' asked Hetty, while Megan stared anxiously at her aunt, mouth parched, legs turning to jelly.

Dilys took a handkerchief out of her apron

pocket and dabbed at her eyes. 'He's been injured by a bomb blast,' she blurted out.

'Is he . . . ' Megan couldn't finish the sentence.

'He's in a bad way,' her aunt informed them gently. 'Your mam phoned the pub and they came to get me.' She paused, having difficulty continuing. 'She doesn't . . . know if he'll make it.'

'Oh my God,' whispered Megan. 'We'll have to go back to London straight away.'

'There are no trains tonight, love,' her aunt sniffed. 'Owen will take you to the station first thing in the morning.'

'But Mum needs us,' sobbed Megan. 'We should be there with her and Dad.'

'We'll ring her up,' suggested Hetty.

'Yeah, we'll do it right away,' said Megan, eager for contact with her mother.

'You can't love. She'll be at the hospital with your dad; she told me to tell you that,' she explained. 'She knows you can't get back there tonight so she won't be expecting you. She said she'll telephone you at the pub if there's any news before tomorrow.'

'Oh, Auntie, what can we do to help her when we're two hundred miles away?'

'There isn't anything,' wept Hetty.

'There is, as it happens,' Dilys corrected.

'What?' asked Megan.

'You can come indoors and have some food, even though you don't feel as though you can swallow a morsel,' said Dilys.

'I couldn't eat a thing.'

68

'Nor me,' added Hetty.

'Your mam made me promise to make sure that you both eat something to keep your strength up, even if it's just a little,' said their aunt. 'You've the children to look after, so you must try to eat for their sakes.'

Then she held out her arms to them and the three of them stood outside the cottage in a huddle, drawing support from each other and letting their tears flow as the sun slipped behind the velvet green hills around Cwmcae.

3

In the event, Megan travelled back to London
alone the next morning after a highly emotional
departure from Cwmcae.

Reflecting on it on the train — squashed
between a continual pipesmoker with a rasping
wheeze and a woman with stifling body odour
— she could have wept as she recalled last night
and the twins' bewildered little faces when she'd
told them she had to go back to London without
them.

'We want to come with you, Mum,' they'd
chorused.

'I want you to come too, my darlings, but it's
far too dangerous for you there.'

'I don't wanna stay here without you,' Netta
had declared.

'Nor do I,' Poppy had added. 'I hate it here.'

'Me too,' her sister chimed in.

'Now you know that isn't true, both of you,'
Megan had told them in a tone of gentle
persuasion. 'You've been ever so excited about
your holiday in the country, and you'll still have
a lovely time here with Auntie Dil and Uncle
Owen even though I won't be with you. I
wouldn't go if I didn't have to, you know that,
but Grandad isn't well and both he and Granny
need me. So be good girls for them as well as for
me. I'm relying on you.'

They'd eventually accepted it, though there

70

had been copious tears, and not all of them shed by the twins.

Although Netta and Poppy were more or less sufficient in themselves as playmates, they still needed their mother, which was only natural at their age. This morning she'd left before they were awake, aching with love for them and unable to suppress the feeling that she was deserting them.

Now she thought back on the other drama of last night when Hetty, in floods of tears but absolutely determined to pursue her course, had told Megan that she wasn't prepared to leave George in a strange place so soon, when he hadn't even had a chance to settle in, so she wouldn't be returning to London with her. She was very sorry and she felt awful about letting their mother down, but George had to come first.

Megan had understood only too well how she was feeling, because she felt the same about leaving her own children, but unlike her sister she couldn't ignore her filial duty, no matter how painful the parting with the twins. Her parents were much too dear to her.

But now the train was pulling into Paddington and tension drew tight at the thought of what she was about to face.

★ ★ ★

There was an air raid in progress when she emerged from Hammersmith station, and the hospital entrance was a hive of activity with ambulances drawing up and stretcher-bearers bringing in the injured.

Sick with nerves and her legs shaking, she finally located the crowded ward her father was in. Judging by the number of bandaged heads and limbs she could see, they were mostly bomb victims. One poor man's pyjama jacket sleeve hung emptily at one side as he sat up in bed. Others had legs and arms in plaster of Paris; some were unconscious. People were moaning in pain.

Much to Megan's relief, her father was conscious, though his head was in bandages. He looked awful: blank-eyed and strange. What she could see of his face was tinged with a waxen pallor.

Dolly got up from her seat by the bed to greet her daughter. Observing her mother's anguish and exhaustion — her eyes were bloodshot and shadowed almost to the colour of charcoal, her skin pale with red anxiety blotches — Megan was glad she'd come, even though it had meant upsetting the twins. It was obvious how much her presence was needed here.

'Am I glad to see you, love,' cried Dolly tearfully, clutching her daughter in an embrace of gratitude and relief. She looked around. 'Where's Hetty?'

'Er . . . she didn't come,' Megan explained, hoping her mother wouldn't be too hurt by Hetty's decision. 'She told me to tell you she's really sorry not to be with you but she couldn't bring herself to leave George with strangers so soon after arriving, being that he's so delicate.'

'Oh . . . Oh, I see.' Dolly was visibly surprised and disappointed. 'Well, I can see her point. It's probably the best thing, with the children having only just got to Wales.'

Megan went over to the bed. 'Hello, Dad,' she said, putting her hand on his arm gently. 'How are you feeling?'

He didn't reply and looked vague, as though he didn't recognise her. His eyes weren't focusing properly.

'He's acting very peculiar but at least he's come round; he was unconscious for ages,' Dolly informed her. 'He isn't himself at all. He's very confused.'

'It's probably just shock,' Megan suggested, hoping to lift her mother's spirits.

'Yeah, he did have a nasty blow to his head. Enough to knock anyone out.'

'Have they told you what the damage is?'

'You know what doctors are like; they're always a bit on the secretive side,' Dolly told her. 'But they have mentioned concussion. It does make people confused apparently. It's quite common when someone has had a blow to the head.'

'What actually happened, Mum?' Megan asked.

'He was hit by flying debris when a bomb came down on a house,' Dolly explained. 'His poor head is a real mess under those bandages.' She shook her head gravely, remembering. 'He was unconscious when I got to him and there was blood everywhere.' Her hand flew to her brow and her breathing became rapid. 'Oh God,

73

it was awful, Megan. I thought I was going to lose him.'

'Don't upset yourself, Mum,' said Megan, taking her hand. 'He's being well looked after now.'

Dolly nodded.

'So what are they doing for him in the way of treatment?' Megan asked.

'I'm not sure, apart from keeping a close eye on him to make sure there are no complications. Any head injury can be serious but usually the concussion clears up within a few days, so they say. That's what they're hoping will happen with him. He'll need plenty of rest when he does get back to normal, though.' Dolly raised her eyes. 'The doctors and nurses here could do with some of that. The poor things are overworked; dead on their feet, most of 'em.'

'So are you, by the look of you,' observed Megan. 'Why don't you go home and have a sleep? I'll stay with Dad. You look all in. You need a break.'

'While he's lying there not knowing what day of the week it is? Not likely.'

'You'll have to sleep sometime.'

'Oh, Megan love, sleep is the least of my problems,' Dolly said, her voice quivering with emotion. 'I ought to go home and see to things at the dairy. Your dad will be very cross if I don't keep the business running properly while he's laid up. The milk wasn't delivered yesterday and there would have been nobody there when the delivery came today, let alone anyone to bottle it and get it out to the customers. It's all happened so sudden, I haven't had a chance to make any arrangements.'

'I'll see to everything,' said Megan.

'You're needed here for the moment.'

'Perhaps one of the other dairies will look after our customers just until things have calmed down here,' she suggested.

'Your dad will never forgive me if I were to let that happen,' she said. 'He wouldn't want anyone from the opposition involved in his dairy, even though they're no longer a threat.' Dolly rubbed her eyes. 'You know how hard he's worked to build the business, and how proud he is of it. When he starts to feel better, the first thing he'll want to know is who's looking after things, and he'll want it to be family. At least the milk is still in the cool room, because your dad hadn't loaded the cart, so it might be all right if we get it out to the customers soon.'

'I'll make sure it's sorted as soon as I can get away from here, don't you worry,' said Megan. 'Leave everything to me. I'll get the milk out to the customers.'

Her father was saying something.

'Megan. What are you doing here?' he asked in a tired, slurred voice. 'You're supposed to be in Wales.'

'I came back to see you, Dad,' she told him, relieved that he sounded normal.

'Why?' He looked around as though suddenly realising that he was in strange surroundings. 'What the hell is going on?'

'You got knocked out by a doodlebug,' she explained.

'Did I? Well, there's awful.' He stared at her. 'I hope you haven't brought those nippers back here with all the bombs about.'

'Don't worry. They're safe with Auntie Dil.'

'Make sure they stay there until the bombing has stopped for good.' His eyes widened and he grabbed her hand. 'You promise me now.'

'Of course I promise, Dad.'

'Much too risky,' he mumbled. 'You must keep the little ones safe. Make sure she does, Dolly. Dolly, where are you?'

'I'm here, love,' she said, gently taking his other hand, delighted that he seemed to be rallying. 'I'm not going anywhere. I'll see if I can get you a cup of tea in a minute.'

Her presence calmed him and he closed his eyes, seeming peaceful. Megan was moved to tears by her parents' obvious devotion. Then his head fell to one side. Megan shouted for help and two nurses came rushing down the ward to him.

But even before they reached his bed, Megan knew with dreadful certainty that there was nothing anyone could do for him now. The war had claimed another victim.

★   ★   ★

Megan felt dreamlike — distanced from events — in the awful aftermath of her father's death, which they were told was most likely due to a burst blood vessel beneath his skull, causing massive damage to the brain, though a post-mortem would confirm this for definite.

76

Whatever the official verdict, it was a direct result of his head injuries caused by the bomb.

Her own feelings, however, were pushed to the back of her mind as she concentrated on her mother, who was struggling so hard to be brave.

'The doctor said he would have been paralysed if he'd lived,' she said when they finally got back to the house.

'He wouldn't have wanted that,' said Megan.

'Neither would he have wanted to die before his time. Bloody war!' Dolly looked at Megan, her tired eyes brimming with tears, and her face crumpled. 'Oh love, what are we going to do without him? How can we carry on?'

'Shush, Mum, there, there. We'll get through it somehow,' Megan said, cradling her tiny mother in her arms. 'You won't be on your own. I'll be with you every step of the way.'

'I must pull myself together and be strong, because that's what he would expect of me,' Dolly decided, sounding determined suddenly. Megan felt her body stiffen with resolution. 'The last thing I want is to let him down.'

'You'll never let anyone down, Mum,' Megan said gently. 'You're a fighter.'

'There's such a lot to do: the funeral to arrange; the dairy to see to,' muttered Dolly worriedly, moving back and brushing her brow with a tired hand. 'I'd better get started. I mustn't sit around crying and moping.'

'The only thing you are going to do for the moment is get some rest,' said Megan in a tone of caring authority. 'I'll take care of everything.'

Her mother wouldn't go to bed but dozed in

the chair. Megan went to the telephone in the shop and asked the operator for a long-distance call. When she eventually got through to the pub in Cwmcae — against the noisy hiss and crackle of interference on the line — she asked if they would be kind enough to bring her sister and her aunt to the telephone.

★ ★ ★

Megan went out that same night delivering the backlog of milk. The next day Uncle Owen came to the rescue when he arrived in London with Hetty, who had known she must come home now under the dreadful circumstances.

Having managed at short notice to take some time off that was owing to him, Owen took over completely in the dairy so that Dolly and her daughters could get the funeral organised and reopen the shop. It was Dolly's livelihood, so she couldn't afford to let things slip no matter how bad she was feeling. One thing was for sure: there was no time for any of them to sit around nursing their grief.

Although Dilys would have liked to attend her brother's funeral, she stayed in Cwmcae to look after the children. It was generally thought best not to bring them back for the sad occasion because it would be far too distressing and dangerous for them. Although funerals were mostly low key these days, with fatalities at such a high level, there was a big turnout at the cemetery for Dai because he had been such a well-known local figure.

Standing beside her mother at the graveside with a supportive arm around her, Megan's whole body ached with grief. Nothing would ever be the same again without Dad; how could it be when he had been at the heart of the family? It was the end of an era, come a good few years too early. But what about her poor mother? Life would eventually move on for Megan and Hetty, but Mum's world had changed for ever.

It was up to her daughters to help her through this; to be there for her in every way, at both an emotional and a practical level. Auntie Dil had offered to look after the children in the long term, until it was safe for them to come home, because as they all agreed, Megan and Hetty needed to be with their mother. Uncle Owen had agreed to stay on in London for a day or two to help Dolly while the sisters went to Wales to see their children and explain to them that they had to stay in Cwmcae with Auntie Dil and Uncle Owen without their mothers for a while. Then Megan and Hetty were coming straight back to London to help their mother run the business and to give her personal support at this sad time.

At least that was the plan. But when the funeral wake was drawing to a close, and Uncle Owen and Dolly were busy with the remaining guests, Hetty got Megan on her own in the kitchen.

'When I go back to Wales tomorrow, I'm staying there until it's safe for the children to come home,' she announced with an air of tearful defiance. 'I won't be coming back until they do.'

'But you're needed here,' pointed out her shocked sister. 'You and I have to help Mum run the business. We can't manage on our own; there's far too much work for two people. There was more than enough to do when there were four of us. Anyway, Mum needs us for moral support. It isn't as if she has any family besides us to turn to. She's alone in the world apart from us.'

'I'm sorry, Megan, and I know this makes me seem like a selfish cow, but I just can't leave George.' Hetty felt terrible about letting her mother and sister down. She was also full of remorse for not saying goodbye to her dear dad. But she was ruled by her feelings for George.

'I'm none too happy about leaving the twins, but I'll just have to put up with it, and they'll be absolutely fine with Auntie,' Megan informed her. 'Dad has died and Mum needs us like never before. She's our mother, for goodness' sake. She's always done her best for us. Now it's our turn to do something for her.'

'I know all that. But I'm not leaving George with strangers for God knows how long, and that's all there is to it,' Hetty insisted. 'I can't do it, Megan.'

'Won't, you mean.'

'All right, won't then, if it makes you happy to hear me say that,' she snapped.

'Of course it doesn't make me happy,' Megan said angrily. 'I think you are being selfish. I mean, it isn't as if Auntie and Uncle are strangers.'

'They are to the children.'

'By now they won't be,' she argued. 'No one could be kinder than they are. They both have hearts of gold. The children will all be well looked after. In fact they'll probably have a whale of a time in that lovely countryside once they get over missing us.'

'Yours might. George won't.'

'He probably would if he was given the chance,' Megan said.

'I'm not prepared to risk it.'

'Look, be realistic, Hetty. Auntie Dil would let you know if he really didn't settle, and if that did happen you could go down and join him then. At least you would have given it a try,' Megan suggested. 'It isn't as if he's being billeted with people we've never heard of, like the kids who have to go away on the evacuation scheme. We're very lucky to have such good relatives in Wales.'

'The twins have each other,' Hetty reminded her. 'George is on his own, and he needs me.'

'And you think the twins don't need me?' Megan was furious now. 'They're six years old, for heaven's sake.'

'But they are fit and healthy,' argued Hetty. 'George isn't a strong child, as you very well know.'

'All six-year-old children need their mothers.'

'In that case you stay down in Wales with them.'

'And leave Mum here alone? Not on your life!'

'We can arrange for her to have help in the

dairy,' suggested Hetty. 'If she has some staff, she'll manage. A mother's first duty is to her children after all.'

'Oh, so now I'm neglecting the needs of my children, am I?' Megan responded sharply.

'I didn't say that.'

'That was the implication,' said Megan, torn between her duty towards her mother and her children. 'Mum is bereaved and broken apart. Even aside from the business, she needs people of her own around her at the moment. You might feel able to desert her but I don't.'

'It seems to me as if you'll be only too glad to get shot of the twins,' accused Hetty spitefully, lashing out because she felt so guilty. 'We all know what a handful they are. I reckon you'll be glad to have a break from them. Let someone else put up with their mischievousness for a while.'

Megan's hand cracked across her sister's face almost of its own volition.

Hetty held her cheek, staring at her sister with venom. 'You spiteful cow.'

'You asked for it.'

They were standing staring at each other in shock when their mother came in.

'Are you girls getting on all right out here?' she asked, looking pale and tired and far too preoccupied to notice the aggression in the air.

'Yeah, we're fine,' Megan replied.

'I just came to tell you that Audrey and Jack Stubbs are going now,' Dolly informed them. 'They both have to get back to work. Are you coming to see them off?'

Megan nodded.

'Yeah, we're coming,' added Hetty.

They followed Dolly into the other room in a stony silence. But their mother had far too much on her mind to pay attention to the fact that her daughters seemed more than a little angry with each other.

★ ★ ★

'Thanks ever so much for coming,' said Megan warmly to her husband's parents in the hall by the front door. 'It's very good of you to take the trouble.'

'Not at all,' responded Audrey in an expressionless tone.

'It's the least we could do,' said Jack, who was like an older version of Will. He had the same dark eyes and swarthy complexion but his once black hair was now almost white. He was a nice man, friendlier and more easy-going than his wife, and Megan liked him a lot. 'Your dad was a good bloke. He'll be much missed. A good man gone before his time, thanks to the perishing war!'

'I'll second that,' said Dolly.

'Anyway, we'd better get going,' he went on. 'Work calls and all that. Take care of yourselves now. Anything we can do, you know where we are.'

'Thanks, Jack,' said Dolly 'That's very kind of you.'

'Ta-ta,' said Megan, seeing them off at the front door. 'I'll let you know if I hear from Will.'

As soon as Audrey and Jack got outside, Audrey turned on her husband.

'A good man gone before his time, my arse,' she snapped. 'He had a damned sight more years than our Ron.'

'True,' agreed Jack as they headed towards the bus stop. 'But his life still ended prematurely, didn't it? It wasn't allowed to run its natural course.'

'They don't know the meaning of grief,' she went on, ignoring his comments, her anger growing with every syllable. 'They haven't even scratched the surface.'

'Oh, I don't know about that. Dolly has just lost her husband of many years and Megan and Hetty have lost their father,' he pointed out in a reasonable tone. 'I think that qualifies them to know what grief feels like.'

'Not like we did. It isn't like losing a child.'

'Grief isn't graded, Audrey; it doesn't come mild, medium or strong,' he reminded her drily. 'It will feel just as bad to them as it did to us when we lost Ron.'

'I don't agree with that,' she snapped. 'Dai Morgan had seen something of life. Not like our poor Ron, struck down before he'd even tasted adulthood.'

'You have to let it go, Audrey love,' Jack said with a heavy sigh. 'It's a long time ago. Let the boy rest in peace.'

'You're saying I should forget my son just because he died a long time ago?'

'Don't deliberately misunderstand what I say,' he urged, tired of her endless carping. 'You know perfectly well that isn't what I meant. Ron will never be forgotten. But this anger you have towards the world and everyone in it is spoiling your life, and mine too. It's time to start living again.'

'You don't care that Ron died,' she accused. 'You don't give a damn. It's all Will with you.'

'Now stop it, love,' he said, halting in his step, turning towards her and taking her arm gently, his eyes resting on her face with the affection he still felt for her, despite everything. 'You know that isn't true.'

'It's Will this and Will that — '

'Because he's alive, and he's our son too,' Jack reminded her. 'You haven't wanted to give him the time of day since Ron died. So I make sure that I do.'

'That's right, turn on me,' Audrey accused sulkily. 'It's a fine thing when a wife can't even rely on her husband for support.'

'That's a two-way street. What about you giving me some support?' he came back at her. 'Ron was my son too, and I felt his loss just as much as you did. I still do.'

'I've never said you didn't.'

'You've never accepted that I did either. You're far too wrapped up in your own sense of injustice to notice anyone else's pain,' he went on in a tone of weary resignation. 'Your daughter-in-law has just lost her father and I didn't see much sympathy towards her or her family coming from your direction.'

'Oh shut up,' she snapped. 'You're just like all the others. You don't understand how I feel.'

'No. I don't suppose I do,' he said sadly, walking on.

When Jack had lost his son when the boy had been only fourteen, he'd lost his wife too. The beautiful, gregarious and warm-hearted woman he'd married had changed overnight into an embittered nag with a grudge against the world and everyone in it. He'd thought, at first, it would be a passing thing, but now, thirteen years on, there was no sign of an improvement. Being miserable had become such a habit to her, she didn't seem able to change, and their marriage had suffered because of it.

There was nothing but rows and indifference now between them. She didn't seem to have any affection left in her; not for him or anyone, and certainly not for their remaining son. She used to be such a jolly, kind person too. It made him feel so sad.

★ ★ ★

Megan sat alone on a bench outside Cwmcae chapel in the afternoon sun, looking out over the surrounding hills: green and lush, a feast for the eye. She'd sneaked out of the house, needing to be on her own for a few minutes to clear her head. The air was pure and quiet, soothing to her shredded nerves. Soon one of the local farmers would come to take her to the station in his truck. It was that sort of a village. Owen wasn't available to do it so someone else automatically stepped into the breach.

When she'd explained to the twins that she would be going back to London without them, they'd been very subdued; had hardly said a word. It was a double blow for them so soon after learning that their grandfather had died, though George had been more upset about that than they had. There had always been a special bond between him and his grandfather.

Unlike last time, when they'd made a fuss about her leaving, they had just listened to what she'd had to say, holding hands with tears meandering down their cheeks; it was almost as though they knew somehow that her going was unavoidable and had been given maturity beyond their years to cope with it. Somehow that was more painful to Megan than if they'd been their usual vociferous selves. She was so proud of them.

Of great comfort to her was the fact that they had each other. It was a huge blessing for them. Hetty had been right about that making all the difference. Thinking of her sister pierced her heart. They hadn't spoken to each other since the altercation at the funeral, except when their mother was present, and then they behaved normally so as not to upset her.

Megan knew she shouldn't have slapped Hetty, and felt ashamed. Of course Hetty shouldn't have said what she'd said, but people blurted out all sorts when they were angry. She hadn't meant it any more than Megan had meant to hit her.

Mulling it over, Megan could see that

although Hetty was being unfair in a way, staying on here and leaving her sister to cope at home, it wasn't really selfishness but more a question of personal priorities. Maybe Megan herself had her own priorities wrong in feeling that her first duty lay towards her mother at this time, rather than her children. This wasn't a black-and-white issue; it was an individual decision. She herself was confident that the twins would be well looked after by Auntie Dil, so Mum's need of her seemed greater at this traumatic time, and somehow she had to find the strength to fulfil that need and do what was right. After all, she wasn't the only woman whose children had been evacuated.

Megan had always been the stronger of the two sisters. When they were growing up, she had always been there for Hetty, getting her out of scrapes and listening to her problems. They'd each had friends of their own but had always been best pals to each other.

Suddenly Megan found herself very glad that Hetty was staying on here in Wales, because it meant that the twins would have an adult around they were used to; someone from close family.

She couldn't go away leaving things as they were. She would go and find her sister and try to patch things up. She was about to get up when someone joined her.

'Mind if I sit here?' asked Hetty, settling down beside her.

'I was just coming to find you,' said Megan, turning and giving her a wary smile.

'Sorry I said those awful things,' said Hetty.

'Forget it.'

'I suppose it was my guilty conscience talking. I know I'm letting you down, and I was trying to defend myself.'

'Sorry I hit you.'

'I deserved it,' Hetty told her. 'It was a hell of a whack, though. I didn't know you had it in you.'

'Neither did I,' grinned Megan. 'I think I must have hidden strengths.'

'You certainly have. I'll remember that before I fall out with you again.'

They both laughed.

'Seriously, though, now that I've cooled down and thought about it, I realise that I had no right to judge you,' Megan admitted. 'We all have to make our own decisions about something like that. Anyway, it doesn't matter about your not coming back to London. Mum and I will manage.'

'Thanks, sis. I'm sorry I won't be there with you. I do feel bad about it.'

'Well don't. I also got to thinking how much better I shall feel knowing that the twins have you around,' confessed Megan.

'It would be a bit too much for Auntie Dil, having the three to look after on her own.'

'I agree, though she doesn't seem to mind. In fact, she seems to thrive on it,' observed Megan. 'I wonder if it's because having the children around takes her mind off things.'

'Losing Gareth at Dunkirk, you mean?' said Hetty, referring to their aunt and uncle's son, who'd been killed in action.

Megan nodded. 'She keeps busy; she does a lot of work for the war effort and for the village, but having the kids around will bring some young life into the house. Helping you out with them will take her out of herself.'

'She's a good sort; so is Uncle,' said Hetty. 'It's a pity we only see them when there are bombs around.'

'Still, if they lived nearer we wouldn't have anywhere safe to go to with the kids.'

Hetty nodded. 'Anyway, you can rest assured that the twins will be fine. I shall keep a special eye out for them. Between the three of us, they won't lack for love and attention.'

'Oh, come here, you,' said Megan, and the two women hugged each other.

★ ★ ★

Ten minutes or so later, Megan had said her goodbyes and was in the passenger seat of a farmer's truck, looking out of the window through a blur of tears. There was a small gathering outside her aunt and uncle's house, waving her off. Auntie Dil stood in between the twins, who were holding her hands. Hetty was next to them with George.

It was as though a camera clicked in her mind, and Megan knew she would never forget that scene or how she felt at this moment. It had been bad enough leaving them when she'd come back to London the last time. This time, she didn't know when she would see them again. The awful thought occurred to her that maybe she never would, given the number of people meeting their end in bomb-ridden London at present.

A sudden longing for Will overwhelmed her. She wanted him here by her side, sharing the moment, giving her strength and easing the pain. Inevitably, over the years she'd grown accustomed to his being away, but she still missed him to an agonising degree at times. He might not always have been the perfect husband, but he was her man and he meant the world to her. She needed him so much now in the aftermath of leaving the twins, his absence was all-consuming. All she could do was to write to him as soon as she got the chance; that would make her feel better, even though she couldn't be sure he would receive her letter.

Please spare me for my children's sake, she prayed silently. Please look after them, and let me see them again soon. She cried all the way to the station, and the farmer was far too much of a gentleman to comment. Instead, he silently offered her the use of his handkerchief.

⋆   ⋆   ⋆

The Burmese heat was intense and relentless on the dusty track, the ground hard and painful underfoot as Will Stubbs and the rest of his platoon marched on, uniforms soaked with sweat, feet blistered inside their heavy army boots, throats parched with thirst. Some of the men had passed out cold along the way but they'd still had to get up and move on as soon as they came round. 'March or die' was the motto of the sergeant, a power-crazy tyrant who behaved as though his handful of men were solely responsible for pushing the Japanese army out of Burma.

It was true that there were Japs omnipresent in the area — up the trees in the surrounding jungle, behind the hills; everywhere — so it made sense to get through this danger zone with all possible speed, but if they didn't stop for a rest soon, the whole platoon would drop to the ground in a communal faint.

Along with his comrades in this treacherous terrain, Will was weary of steamy jungles, muddy rivers, dysentery, scorpions and gigantic spiders that crawled over the bodies of dead soldiers. Malaria was prevalent among the men too, despite the daily tablets they were issued with. Up till now, Will had managed to escape the disease, so considered himself lucky. That wasn't a word that sprang to mind easily under these ghastly circumstances, but at least he was alive, which was more than you could say for the thousands of men who'd perished in this campaign.

Thank God for that, he thought, as the order came down the line that they were to take a short break. The men sank gratefully to the ground and swigged at their water bottles, rifles close at hand. Thirst quenched, Will mopped the sweat from his face with a khaki handkerchief, lit a cigarette and drew from the breast pocket of his jungle uniform his most treasured possession: a snapshot of his wife that he kept with him at all times. Through all the years of active service in various war areas in the Far East, he'd managed to keep it intact.

Long-lashed dark eyes fixed on the black-and-white image, he added the colour to it in his mind: blue eyes, golden hair, a bloom to the cheeks and lustrous pink lips. Megan wasn't a big woman, but she was very strong in character and physically beautiful, although she would be the last person to agree with him about that, because vanity wasn't in her nature.

If he made it home, he was going to tell her more often how gorgeous she was and how much he loved her. Just looking at the picture made him want to weep with longing for her. If he imagined her hard enough, he felt as if he could touch her and hear her voice. Oh, how he longed to do those things again.

He wasn't an easy man to be married to. He knew that he could be uncommunicative at times. It was something he had no control over, as hard as he tried. But he was going to make more of an effort if he was spared; he was determined about that.

Megan loved him for all his faults, he thought warmly. That wasn't to say that she didn't go on at him about his moodiness, because she could be extremely vocal on the subject when she was of a mind, and she was entitled to be. Not that he ever admitted that to her at the time, of course. He always told her to give over nagging and they would have a flaming row. There had been far too many of those in their marriage.

It was entirely his fault; there was no doubt in his mind about that. Sometimes he thought he should never have got married, given the demons that tormented him. He didn't deserve to be happy and he certainly wasn't worthy of someone as wonderful as Megan. How could he be entitled to any of the good things of life after what he'd done? Megan knew nothing about that; she had no idea of what it was that gave him bad dreams and turned him in on himself. Only one person besides himself knew about that.

The event of his youth still weighed heavily on him and shadowed his life, all these years later. Even the horror of fighting a war only dulled it temporarily when he was concentrating on staying alive. But it was always there, lurking in a dark corner of his mind, waiting to come to the fore at the slightest opportunity. When he was in combat or larking about with his army pals it faded, but not for long; it always returned eventually, a constant torment.

How Megan put up with him he'd never know. One thing he did know for certain. She wouldn't be so keen to do so if she ever found out the truth about him.

'Are you still drooling over that missus of yours?' asked the soldier sitting on the ground beside him.

Will turned and looked at him with a half-smile, his skin deeply tanned and smudged with dirt from the rough track. 'That's right, mate,' he replied. 'She's the only thing around here worth looking at, I reckon.'

'We only have to sit down for five minutes and out comes her picture,' the soldier joshed.

'You're obsessed, you are.'

'I am, I admit it. Anyway, I'd sooner look at her than you,' Will joked. 'She's much better-looking.'

Some of the lads laughed; others were too exhausted to join in and just listened without comment. Most of them were smoking; some were lying flat on their backs on the ground at the side of the track with their eyes closed.

The brief respite came to an abrupt end when shots rang out and a bullet skimmed the ground nearby. The men dived on to their stomachs, aiming their rifles towards the gunfire that was coming from behind a small hill ahead of them.

As the air resounded with the whistle and crack of bullets, Will hastily put the photograph back in his pocket where it belonged, close to his heart, and concentrated on the job in hand. They had to win this local battle so that they could proceed onwards to the next one . . . and the one after that, until this God-awful war was finally over and done with.

4

'There's awful, that you call the twins the terrible two,' Dilys remarked to Hetty when they were washing the breakfast dishes together one morning a week or so later. 'They don't seem terrible at all to me.'

'It's only meant in fun; just a nickname, you know,' explained Hetty. 'But you wait until you get to know them better. Then you'll understand how it came about.'

'Good as gold they've been since they've been here,' Dilys pointed out.

'Yeah, they have been well behaved, now you come to mention it,' agreed Hetty, giving the matter more thought. 'It isn't like them. They're usually much more boisterous.'

'From what I'd heard, I was expecting trouble, but they're such quiet little things, you'd hardly know they were here,' observed Dilys. 'They seem sad to me.'

'Missing their mum, I expect. Either that or they're sickening for something,' chuckled Hetty.

'There's mean you are.'

'Just joking, Auntie. I love them to bits really.'

'I know you do.'

'Anyway, we might as well make the most of their subdued mood,' suggested Hetty. 'When they get into their stride, we'll need our wits about us, I can tell you.'

'But I want them to be happy and at home

here,' Dilys told her with feeling. 'If that means being noisy, so be it. The poor dabs, having to live in a strange place without their mam. It must be hard for them.'

'Yeah, I'm sure it is,' Hetty agreed. 'But they're doing very well. I shall write to Megan while it's on my mind and tell her how good they're being. That'll cheer her up.'

Dilys emptied the washing-up bowl, wiped the sink around with a cloth and dried her hands with the kitchen towel, while Hetty finished drying the dishes and putting them away.

'Busy I am today,' she said with a purposeful air.

'What are you up to?'

'I'm running a 'knitting for soldiers' circle in the village hall this morning, then there's the 'make-do and mend' class this afternoon.' She paused momentarily as though remembering something. 'I mustn't forget that it's my turn to clean the chapel, and I've got to go out collecting for the Red Cross Penny a Week fund to raise money for comforts for the forces. So I've plenty to keep me occupied until the children come home from school needing their tea.'

'I can see to their tea, Auntie,' Hetty told her. 'I didn't come here to be waited on. You've got enough to do with all your good works.'

Indeed, coming to Cwmcae had been a real eye-opener for Hetty on her first visit to Wales during the Blitz. Contrary to popular belief that nothing much happened in a village miles from anywhere in the heart of the Welsh countryside, there was a wealth of activities, many of them organised by her aunt: Brownies, youth club, the village choir, and a host of events to raise money to help the war effort, including jumble sales, home-made cake sales, raffles, and social evenings in the village hall.

Being so far from the nearest town, and having only the limited stock of the village shop for groceries, Cwmcae residents relied on mobile traders to meet the rest of their needs. The greengrocer, the baker, the butcher, the fishmonger all travelled by horse and cart around the outlying villages. There was even a man who came round selling clothes.

Welsh was the first language of most of the residents, but some were bilingual and spoke English for the benefit of visitors. A few hardliners refused to, but in the main the people were friendly and welcoming.

'So what are you going to do with yourself today?' her aunt was asking.

'I'm not really sure,' Hetty told her. 'I shall have to keep myself busy somehow. I'm used to being on the go.'

'There are some other evacuees from England and their mothers staying at farms outside the village,' Dilys informed her. 'Maybe you could get together with them for a chat. They're a bit of a way out, but someone in the village will have a bike you could borrow.'

Hetty nodded.

'Homesick, are you?' asked Dilys.

'I am a bit,' Hetty confessed.

'Aah, you poor dab,' her aunt sympathised. 'You could have stayed in London with the others, you know. I was quite happy to look after the three children, and they would have been safe with me. I do have a lot on, but I would have made a point of being at home when they weren't at school. Anyway, everything I do is in the village. They would always know where to find me.'

'Oh, Auntie, I know that,' Hetty said, putting her hand on Dilys's arm. 'You're the kindest, most capable person I've ever met. It's just me. George has always been a sickly child and I just couldn't bear to leave him.'

'I understand,' Dilys said.

'I'm used to working, though,' Hetty explained. 'I'm not accustomed to having time on my hands.'

'We must make sure we keep you busy then,' said her aunt with a smile. 'We can always do with a helping hand with local events for the war effort. Why not make a start by coming over to the village hall and joining in the knitting circle?'

'I'll just drop a line home to let Megan know that the girls are being so good, and get it in the post, then I'll come over.'

'That's the spirit,' approved Dilys.

★ ★ ★

Hetty finished her letter and headed over to the post office to get a stamp. Knitting circles and the like weren't really her sort of thing, because she was used to working in a commercial environment, but she couldn't sit about the house all day, so she would give it a try. She was a fast knitter, and had produced a lot of socks, gloves and scarves for the soldiers in her spare time at home.

It was a fine sunny day, and when she arrived at the village shop in which the post office was incorporated there was a group of women talking outside.

'In a hurry, are you?' one of them asked.

'No, not especially.'

'That's just as well.'

Hetty looked towards the shop. 'Why? Are there a lot of people waiting?'

The woman nodded. 'We had to wait ages. Mrs Lloyd's assistant hasn't turned up again and people have come for their rations. Everybody's turned up at once.'

'It's too much for her on her own, the poor dab,' said another woman sympathetically. 'With having the post office to look after as well as the shop.'

'Does her assistant often let her down?' enquired Hetty.

'All the time,' replied the first woman. 'She's no use when she is there either. She's a bit *twp*, if you ask me. She can't add up to save her life. I'd give her notice if she worked for me.'

'It's finding someone else, though, isn't it?' said the other woman. 'If she can't get a replacement we'll have to wait all day to get served, with all the surrounding farms using the village shop as well as everyone in Cwmcae. Most people are on war work now.'

'Round here?' said Hetty. There was no industry in the area that she knew of.

'They're either employed on farms or working

100

over at Pendine at the Experimental Establishment,' the woman informed her. 'They employ people from all the outlying villages, checking the armaments before they're sent to the forces to be used.'

'But Pendine is quite a distance from here, isn't it?'

'They're taken and brought back by bus,' she was told. 'They get good money, too. More than Mrs Lloyd can afford to pay.'

Hetty stayed chatting until the women went on their way, then entered the shop and waited in the queue. When her turn came she asked for her stamp, paid for it, then said, 'I understand your assistant hasn't come in today?'

'You're quite right,' said the shopkeeper, a small, anxious-looking woman of about fifty in an overall with tidy grey hair worn close to her head and a scrubbed pink sort of complexion. None of the village women seemed to wear make-up, Hetty had noticed. 'There's unreliable she is.'

'I'm staying with my Aunt Dilys in the village and I'm experienced in shop work,' Hetty informed her. 'I can give you a hand until she turns up if it'll help.'

'How kind,' said the shopkeeper, looking relieved. 'When could you start?'

'Will when I've posted this letter suit you?'

'Thank you, bach, thank you,' the older woman said, smiling and lifting the counter flap to let Hetty through when she'd put her letter in the box outside.

It was evening, and Ken was standing in the yard in a queue for food, or what passed for food here at the prison camp: a bowl of thin, tasteless barley soup and a piece of bread; one small loaf between six men.

'Aye, aye, there's a row starting up at the front of the queue,' said the man behind him, peering ahead. 'I suppose the lad with the job of sharing out the bread hasn't got it quite even.'

'They should supply the poor sod with a ruler to save him getting a punch in the mouth,' suggested Ken with irony. 'No one can get every portion the same.'

'That's what hunger does to you,' his mate remarked. 'Everyone wants every last morsel of their share. People get childish when they're starving.'

'It beats me how we keep going on what barely passes for soup and a bit of bread,' said Ken, who, with the others, had been labouring in a quarry all day.

'They keep us weak so we can't give 'em trouble.'

'We still manage to annoy them by keeping our spirits up, though, and that takes some doing in this hellhole.'

'We've got good mates. We keep each other going.'

Ken nodded in agreement. The companionship among the prisoners was a lifeline here in this soulless enclosure of shed-like living quarters surrounded by barbed wire and watch towers manned by armed guards. Even with the late sun bathing the German landscape, everything looked bleak and grim. The hardship and inhumanity Ken had experienced here would have been unimaginable to him in peacetime. It was a common bond among the prisoners. Some of the guards were all right, but there were a few who were downright evil and disregarded the rules of the Geneva Convention altogether, their sole purpose in life being to make the prisoners feel worthless for allowing themselves to be captured.

The thing that really saved Ken's sanity was the thought of going home to Hetty and George. His longing for them was a constant ache, and he had to keep believing that one day he would get there, no matter how bad things got.

'They've sorted it out up the front and we're moving at last,' said the other man.

'Thank Gawd for that.' Sick with hunger, Ken moved along slowly with the rest of the emaciated men towards the kitchens.

★   ★   ★

'You mustn't do it,' George told the twins as the three of them walked through the village on their way home from school. 'It's really bad, the worst thing you've ever thought of doing, and you'll get into terrible trouble over it.'

'We don't care,' said Poppy.

'You wouldn't dare to run away,' he challenged.

'We would and we're going to,' Netta

103

informed him. 'And don't you tell anyone.'

'But what's the point of going when you don't even know the way to the railway station,' he pointed out. 'You'll only get lost.'

'No we won't. We'll go the way the truck went when it took Mum to the station.'

'The station is miles away,' he pointed out. 'It took us ages to get here.'

'That doesn't matter.' Poppy wasn't to be deterred. 'We'll keep going until we do get there. If we start off the right way we'll get there in the end. Mum gave us some pocket money before she went. We'll use that for the train fare.'

George's soft heart meant that he couldn't bear the thought of his cousins being lost and alone out in the countryside, or the trouncing they would get from the adults when they were found. 'I don't think that'll be enough,' he said.

'We're still going,' Netta told him determinedly. 'We'll get home somehow. We're not staying here in this dump without Mum.'

'It isn't a dump,' he disagreed. 'I think it's lovely here.'

'Well we don't,' Poppy made clear. 'The people speak funny. We don't know what they're talking about.'

'Some of them are nice,' he pointed out. 'Auntie Dil and Uncle Owen are lovely.'

'Yeah, they're all right,' agreed Poppy, 'but we'd still rather be at home with our mum, and if we get ourselves there they'll have to let us stay.'

'It's all right for you, George,' said Netta. 'You've got your mum here with you.'

He couldn't argue with that, so just said, 'When are you doing it?'

'Tomorrow, probably,' she replied. 'You just pretend you know nothing about it. That's all you've got to do.'

'They'll ask and ask . . . they'll keep on at me.'

'You mustn't give in to them,' Netta instructed him firmly. 'Not until you think we'll have had time to get on the train anyway. They can't do anything about it then.'

'You might get to like it here if you stay a bit longer,' he suggested in a last bid to put a stop to their daring scheme. 'You could leave it for a week or somethin'.'

'We're going tomorrow and that's that, and if you tell on us and they stop us going, you'll be sorry.'

'I won't say anything,' he said worriedly.

'You'd better not,' they chorused.

★   ★   ★

The next morning Megan had finished the milk round and was driving the cart home with the empties. It was pouring with rain, which was trickling down her neck under the collar of her waterproof coat and drenching her right down to the waist. Her soaked trousers were clinging to her, and her feet were wet.

'Come on, boy,' she said to Chips, pulling on the reins as they rolled homewards, the empty bottles rattling in the crates. 'I need to get home and dried off.'

She couldn't remember ever feeling this

exhausted. Even in the Blitz, when they'd had very little sleep, she hadn't felt as physically and mentally drained as she did now. It wasn't only the doodlebugs keeping them awake at night. It was the fact that she and her mother were doing the work of four people with very little break during the day to renew their energy.

While her mother looked after the shop without assistance, Megan had taken over from her father, operating the dairy side of the business single-handed. She'd been up at four this morning to load up for the round, and both she and her mother had been working until ten last night to finish the bottling and get all the milk into the cold room ready for today's deliveries.

None of it was a problem for her. She was young and fit; she could take it. But she was concerned about her mother. Megan did what she could to help in the shop, but she was so tied up in the dairy, she only had the time to be of limited assistance.

Dolly didn't admit to being overworked, and was being very brave in her bereavement, but she was looking tired and strained. She'd had no time to sit around feeling sorry for herself, which was probably a good thing. But on the other hand, there had been no time for her to be still and quiet with her grief; to let the thoughts and memories come.

They couldn't go on as they were indefinitely, that was obvious. They had to have help or the standard of service would inevitably drop, because they were both only human and there was only so much overwork their systems could take.

But with so many employment opportunities around, no one, it seemed, wanted to work as a general helper in a corner shop and dairy. The labour exchange had them on their books; they themselves had placed a card in the shop window and put an advertisement in the local paper. But so far there had been no response.

Still, at least there were no doodlebugs about this morning. The siren was in force but people had become even more blasé now that it was so commonplace. Imminent danger was often warned of by a car hooter in short, sharp blasts; the taxi-drivers in Hammersmith Broadway were good about that. But most people still relied on their own ears. The area had been badly hit, though. Megan saw it every morning while out on her round: wrecked houses and rubble everywhere.

Her darling twins were always on her mind. She'd had a letter from her sister to say that they were well and behaving themselves. Megan had no doubt that they were being well looked after, but that didn't lessen the misery of missing them. They were her children and should be with her. She comforted herself in the knowledge that they were in the best place, far away from the danger here.

This thought was confirmed by the ominous roar from above, growing louder by the second. She stopped the cart and jumped down. Following her father's example, she stayed with the horse, talking to him, stroking his head, and holding him firm when the explosion came and he struggled to get away.

She was just climbing back on the cart — relieved that she was still in one piece and almost home, where she could get out of her clinging wet clothes — when an elderly man ran out of a house nearby.

'Milkie!' he called, sounding panicky. 'Can you 'elp me, love?'

'Of course. What's the matter?'

'My missus is ever so poorly.' He was pale with terror and his voice was shaking. 'She's been ill for a few days but she's got worse and needs a doctor right away. She's burning up and her chest hurts. I think it might be pneumonia and you know what that means. She's in such a bad way I can't leave her on her own, so could you call at the doctor's and ask him to come? I'd be ever so grateful.'

It was well out of her way but she said, 'Certainly. Is there anything else I can do to help?'

'No, love, ta,' he said breathlessly. 'Just ask the doc if he can come to number five Oswald Road — sharpish.'

'Will do.'

'Ta, Milkie.'

'You're welcome,' she said, and went on her way, turning off at the end of the street towards the doctor's surgery. The poor old boy, she thought, her own discomfort and weariness seeming insignificant now. He really was in a sorry state.

★ ★ ★

Because Dolly couldn't bear to be an object of pity, there were two things she tried never to do when she was serving in the shop. One was to look sad; the other was to seem tired, no matter how grief-stricken or worn-out she was feeling. This morning she failed miserably on the latter. The volume of work was taking its toll and she just couldn't stop yawning.

'You look tired, dear,' observed one of her regulars, a middle-aged woman called Mrs Barker, who was a well-known gossip and busybody.

'I'm all right,' said Dolly, stifling a yawn and trying to look cheerful. 'We're all feeling a bit bushed with the bombs coming over night and day, aren't we?'

The woman nodded in agreement. 'It can't be easy for you now, being on your own,' she went on, her caring manner failing to hide a hint of condescension. 'With no hubby by your side, giving you support.'

'I miss him terribly, of course,' Dolly responded patiently.

'You need your family around you at a time like this,' stated the woman, criticism implicit in her tone.

'Megan's still out on the round,' said Dolly, as though she needed to explain. Losing Dai had made her vulnerable. He had loved and understood her; he'd been essential to her life, and she felt weak and lost without him. As well as the constant ache of missing him, she was struggling against a loss of confidence. She hadn't even come to terms with being a widow

109

yet; she hated the word. It set her apart; made her feel different to other people; lesser somehow, a victim with no status in society. The suggestion that she was helpless and uncared for, implied by Mrs Barker's manner, exacerbated these negative feelings, but at the same time it annoyed her and made her want to fight back. Diplomacy was essential when she was behind this counter, though, so she held her tongue.

'What about your other daughter?' asked the customer. 'She's in the country in Wales somewhere staying with relatives, so I've heard.'

'That's right,' Dolly confirmed.

'Her place is here with you,' stated Mrs Barker, sounding irate on Dolly's behalf.

'She's with the children,' Dolly explained, holding firmly on to her temper. 'It's too dangerous for them here.'

'Of course it is,' agreed the woman with sweeping authority, 'but they'd be perfectly all right in the country without her if they're staying with relatives. She should be here helping her mother, you poor thing.'

Like every good shopkeeper, Dolly adhered to the maxim that the customer was always right. But right now she wanted to throttle this one.

'It's good of you to worry about me, but I'm managing very well, and am absolutely fine, Mrs Barker,' she told her through gritted teeth, staying in control because the woman was a good customer.

'Well you don't look it to me,' declared the other woman. 'Kids, eh, they grow up and don't bother about the people who brought them up.

It's a damned disgrace that your other daughter isn't here with you at this bad time.'

Now Dolly had been pushed too far; she would have to break her rules and put the woman in her place. But before she had the chance to say anything, there was an unexpected interruption.

'It ain't your place to comment on the lady's private business,' said a young voice from behind Mrs Barker. 'Where her daughter is or isn't has got nothing to do with anybody else. So keep your trap shut.'

The silence was electric. Mrs Barker swung round and moved aside to reveal a young girl of about seventeen; slim and ordinary-looking except for her eyes, which were a greenish brown and lit with spirit.

'Who asked you?' demanded Mrs Barker.

'No one.'

'Well keep your opinions to yourself then.'

'That's what you need to do, mate,' the girl responded. 'You've no right to make personal remarks about someone else's private affair. That's a dead liberty, that is. Bloomin' cheek.'

'How dare you speak to me like that?' said the astounded Mrs Barker; being a bully, she didn't take kindly to opposition.

'Why shouldn't I?' the girl wanted to know. 'What's so special about you that makes you think you can say what you like to other people and get away with it but not have the same thing done to you?'

'You cheeky young article,' admonished Mrs Barker, who was clearly shocked and bewildered by the temerity of the stranger.

Watching this exchange with a certain amount of relish, Dolly thought she ought to intervene before the two came to blows.

'Will that be all for now, Mrs Barker?' she asked politely. 'Or is there something else I can get you?'

'Nothing else, thank you,' was the sharp reply.

While Dolly totalled her items and dealt with the ration books, Mrs Barker turned back to the girl. 'You want to watch your manners, my girl, and respect your elders.'

'I do when they deserve it,' was her response.

This was apparently the last straw for Mrs Barker, who practically threw her groceries into her shopping bag along with her ration books, said, 'Good day to you, Mrs Morgan,' and marched from the shop.

Dolly looked intently at the girl.

'Thanks for speaking up for me, but there was no need. I'm quite able to defend myself.' She paused, liking the stranger despite her outspokenness.

'She seemed to think she could say what she liked because you are that side of the counter,' said the girl. 'I couldn't just stand by and let her get away with it.'

Deeming it wise not to speak ill of one customer to another, Dolly just said, 'What can I do for you?'

'I've come about the job. Saw it advertised in the paper. My name is Mabel White and I'm seventeen.'

'Oh!' Dolly was taken aback. The girl was first

class as a champion on the other side of the counter, but if she spoke her mind to all of the difficult customers from where Dolly was standing, they'd have none left inside a week.

'I've bin working in a factory,' Mabel went on, 'but I've got a weak chest and the chemicals have aggravated it. The doctor says I've got to do something else for a living. I'd go in the forces but they don't want you if you've got anything wrong with you. So here I am, ready, willing and able.'

'The thing is,' Dolly began, 'shop work requires a certain amount of tact.'

Mabel looked at her, mulling the remark over.

'Oh, you mean that old crab just now,' she said.

'Exactly.'

'Don't worry about that. I won't frighten your customers away. I can keep a still tongue in my head if I have to.' She paused and added with a twinkle in her eye, 'Especially if I'm that side of the counter.'

'You'd better come through to the back for a chat then,' Dolly heard herself say, much against her better judgement. 'Before the shop gets busy again.'

★ ★ ★

Hetty went into the twins' bedroom to tuck them in and say good night and found that their beds were empty. She went next door to the bedroom she herself shared with George, expecting to find them there, because the

113

children often crept into each other's rooms when they were supposed to have settled down. She was ready to give them all a good trouncing when she realised the girls weren't there. Her son was lying on his side with the covers pulled up around him as though he was asleep, but she could tell that he wasn't.

'Where are the twins, George?' she asked.

Silence.

'I know you're not asleep, so you might as well stop pretending and tell me where your cousins are.'

Still no response.

Hetty pulled the covers down to find her son looking at her, wide awake and worried.

'Where are the girls, George?'

'Aren't they in bed?' he said innocently.

'You know very well that they're not.'

'Perhaps they've gone downstairs to the lav.'

'I'd have seen them,' she said, because the lavatory was in the back garden and to reach it they had to go through the kitchen, from where she had just come. 'Don't play the innocent with me. Tell me where they are. Where are they hiding? It's far too late for games like hide and seek.'

'How would I know where they are?'

'Because they would have told you. What prank are they up to now? You're all supposed to be in bed, not playing.'

He stared at her, keeping his mouth firmly closed.

'George, stop messing me about and tell me where they are hiding so that I can bring them back to bed and settle them down for the night.' She clicked her tongue against the roof of her mouth irritably. 'I thought it was too good to last, their being quiet and well behaved.'

'They're not hiding,' he said miserably.

'What are they doing then?'

'They've gone.'

'Gone? Where to?'

'Home to their mum.'

'Don't be so silly, son, their mother is in London.'

'That's what I told them.'

'You mean they've run away?' she said, anger and fear rising in equal proportions. 'To London?'

George nodded, thinking that his cousins were probably on the train by now. 'They've gone to the station,' he informed her.

'Those bloody girls,' Hetty cursed. 'I'll swing for them one of these days.'

'Don't be angry with them,' he entreated, sitting up and looking at her earnestly. 'They want to be with their own mum. You're always getting cross with them and telling them off.'

Hetty was in far too much of a state for his remarks to register. Those girls were her responsibility while they were in Wales. If something happened to them, it would be her fault. Her sister was going to go mad, especially as Hetty had promised to look out for them.

'When did they go?' she asked George.

'After tea,' he replied. 'They slipped out while you were all listening to the wireless.'

She rushed from the room.

'Auntie Dil!' she shrieked as she tore down the stairs. 'Auntie Dil!'

* * *

'Now calm down and tell me exactly what's happened,' said Dilys as Hetty burst into the living room, where her aunt was sitting in the armchair darning socks.

'The twins have gone off,' she blurted out, her voice trembling. 'They've run away. They're trying to walk to the station to get the London train, apparently, and it's much too far so they'll be lost by now. Oh Auntie, someone could have gone off with them by now. We'll have to get the police. I'll go to the phone box or the pub and call them.'

Dilys stood up and took her niece by the arms. 'Calm down, girl,' she said in a kind but authoritative tone. 'You're not in London now, you know. No one would have gone off with them so you can forget that right away.'

'They have perverts and murderers everywhere.'

'Not here,' Dilys said.

'We're wasting time; we have to get the police.'

'There'll be no need for that at this stage,' her aunt assured her calmly. 'The men of the village will organise a search party. The twins will be back here safe and sound before you know it.' She turned towards the door. 'Owen has popped next door. I'll go and fetch him. He'll soon get things underway.'

116

★ ★ ★

Hetty could hardly believe the speed with which a search party was organised. All the men of the village turned out; mostly the older generation, because the young men were away at war. Fortunately a lot of them had been in the pub when the word went out, which saved a lot of time. They gathered outside with torches turned down in accordance with the regulations, then went off in different directions to scour the countryside.

Standing outside the house, Hetty watched them go through a blur of tears.

'It's very good of them to turn out like this, Auntie Dil,' she said emotionally.

'They always rally round when there's an emergency. We look after our own here.'

'But we're outsiders,' Hetty reminded her.

'You're staying here, so you're one of us,' Dilys informed her. 'Though the twins obviously don't feel at home, or they wouldn't have run away.'

'The little perishers,' said Hetty. 'God knows what Megan's going to say.'

'I'm not sure that there's any need to tell her,' suggested Dilys. 'No point in worrying her unless we have to, is there? We'll think about that when we've found them.'

'Oh, Auntie,' said Hetty, looking out to see inky blackness lit only by a slice of moon intermittently appearing through the clouds. 'How are the men going to find them in the dark?'

'They'll find them, don't worry.' Dilys felt

something cold drop on her arm. 'The sooner the better too, because it's just started to rain.'

★ ★ ★

'I don't know why we haven't found the train station,' said Poppy as she and her sister stumbled on, clinging together, hardly able to see where they were going as clouds blotted out the light from the moon and the rain began to fall. 'We should have found it by now. We went in the right direction.'

'We shouldn't have come off the main road,' said Netta.

'That's your fault.'

'I thought it would be quicker across the fields. I forgot about it getting dark,' said her sister, close to tears. 'I'm sorry.'

''S all right,' assured Poppy, clutching her hand. 'I wish Mum was here.'

'So do I,' said Netta

'We'll never get to see her now we've gone and got ourselves lost.'

'I wish we were back at Auntie Dil's,' said Netta. 'At least it would be better than this.'

'We won't half cop it.'

'Auntie Hetty will go mad.'

Poppy shivered. 'I'm cold and wet now,' she said. 'I wanna go home.'

Netta started to cry. 'I'm scared, Pops,' she sobbed. 'I don't like the dark.'

'We'll be all right,' her sister consoled her. 'We've got each other.'

'I wonder if George has told them yet.'

'He said he would when he thinks we're on the train,' said Poppy. 'Then someone will come looking for us.'

'How will they find us in the dark?'

'They're grown-ups,' said her sister. 'They know how to do things.'

'I'm tired,' said Netta. 'I'm gonna sit down.'

The ground was slippery beneath them as the rain became heavier. They were holding hands for comfort. As they went to sit down, Netta felt her sister's hand slip from her grasp and there was a loud scream, then silence.

'Poppy,' called Netta. 'Poppy, where are you?' There wasn't a sound. Together the twins were invincible; apart they were just frightened little children. 'Poppy,' she called again, her voice echoing across the silent fields. 'Please answer me.'

Sitting on the wet grass, Netta was soaking wet and shivering. 'I want my sister,' she wept. 'I want my mummy.' Over and over again she repeated her cries. But there was no one to hear them. The only sound was the rain beating on the grass, and the rustle and scrape of some unknown creature in the bushes nearby.

★　★　★

'I'll have to get new lino if you don't stop pacing about,' Dilys told her niece. 'You're upsetting George as well as wearing the floor down to the boards.'

'Sorry, Auntie; sorry, George,' Hetty said.

George had been allowed downstairs under

119

the circumstances and was curled up in the armchair by the hearth, almost asleep despite his concern for his cousins.

' 'S all right,' he said sleepily, his lids drooping.

'I can't sit still, Auntie,' explained Hetty. 'I can't stop thinking that I should have seen it coming. The girls have been quieter than usual, as you mentioned, and I know that isn't normal. I should have read the signs and known they were homesick. I know them as well as I know George; I should have guessed they were feeling wretched and tried to cheer them up. The whole thing is my fault.'

'When we get them back we shall all have to try and make them feel happier here,' said her aunt gravely.

Hetty remembered something. 'George said I'm always telling them off,' she said miserably. 'I'm not, am I?'

'You do tend to be a bit sharp with them at times,' Dilys was forced to admit. 'I couldn't help noticing.'

'Am I? Oh dear, how awful!'

'Compared to how lenient you are with George, you do come down on them rather often.'

'I suppose we're all different with our own without even realising it,' Hetty said, biting her lip. 'And those two do try your patience. You never know what they're going to get up to next.'

'Perhaps you could try to be a bit kinder when we get them back,' suggested Dilys.

'Yes, yes, I will,' Hetty said distractedly. '*If we*

120

get them back.' She started to pace up and down again, wringing her hands. 'Oh, where are they?'

There was one thing that neither Dilys nor anyone else had mentioned to Hetty: the fact that there was an old disused quarry a few miles from the village. It was deep and rocky, and if the children stumbled into it, Dilys dreaded to think what sort of a state they'd be in. But there was no point in Hetty knowing about it at this stage, so Dilys said reassuringly, 'The men will find them, don't you worry. They know the land around here inside out.'

Hetty perched on the edge of an armchair, her head in her hands. 'If anything has happened to those two, I'll never forgive myself. I promised my sister I'd look out for them.'

'You're not responsible for the war, bach,' her aunt pointed out softly. 'It isn't your fault they had to be evacuated. There are thousands of poor dabs separated from their mams. None of that is your fault.'

'Maybe not,' she conceded. 'But I still feel really bad. They'll be frightened out there in the dark. I know they're as bold as brass most of the time, but the fact of the matter is, they are just little girls, and for all their confidence they will be frightened.'

Dilys wished she could get that damned quarry out of her mind. 'All we can do for the moment is wait,' she said. 'I'm sure there'll be some news soon.'

★ ★ ★

121

The men in the search party were only too aware of the quarry, and were heading towards it, having split up into groups with the arrangement that they would blow a whistle if anyone found anything relevant.

'They were heading for the station, apparently, the poor little things. Missing their mam, like,' said Owen. 'But they wouldn't have a clue where it was. So they could have gone around in circles once it got dark. It's easy done when you don't know the area. They wouldn't know where the hell they are.'

The rain had settled into a steady drizzle and the moon was now entirely obscured by cloud. The only light was from the thin beams of their torches, held towards the ground. The land was extremely hilly, which didn't help.

'What was that?' said one of the men.

They all stopped and listened.

'I thought I heard something,' the man said. 'I must have been imagining things.'

They walked on until Owen heard a noise and brought the party to a halt. 'It sounds like someone crying,' he said, listening again. 'Seems quite close, too.

'Netta, Poppy!' he shouted, his voice echoing across the hills. 'This is Uncle Owen. Where are you?'

At first the response was so muffled they could barely make it out.

He shouted again.

At last they heard a tiny voice saying, 'Here, Uncle Owen. I'm here.'

'Oh, thank God for that,' he said, and blew his whistle into the damp air.

They found Netta sitting on top of a grassy bank on the edge of a steep slope. She was soaked to the skin and shivering.

'Poppy's gone,' she sobbed. 'I don't know where she is. She doesn't answer when I call. I think she fell down the slope or something. She just let go of my hand and was gone.'

'Look . . . how about you go on home with one of the boys, like, and I'll go down there and find her,' Owen suggested kindly.

'I don't want to go home without her,' she said, shivering so much her teeth were chattering. 'I'm not leaving her here on her own in the dark. She'll be so scared.'

'In that case you stay here with Evans the post, and the rest of us will go and find her,' he said, trying not to show how worried he was. This land was full of dips and steep banks, and the quarry was nearby. Anything could have happened to the little girl.

★ ★ ★

'We'll use the whole of the tea ration up if we carry on like this,' observed Hetty as Dilys said she was going to make yet another pot.

'We'll worry about that when the time comes,' said Dilys, filling the kettle and putting it on the hob on the black range. The room was a kitchen and parlour combined, a cosy place with brass pots and pans on the walls, and little rugs dotted about the floor to add a homely touch. 'We'd have something a bit stronger to steady our nerves if I had anything in.'

'Ooh, Auntie, and you a chapel-going countrywoman,' said Hetty, teasing her in an effort to lift the mood to get them through the agony of waiting for news.

'It isn't only you town people who know how to enjoy yourselves, you know,' Dilys said, trying to smile.

'So I've noticed.' As well as all the work for the war effort, Hetty had been surprised at the amount of socialising that went on within the village. Nobody need be lonely unless they chose to be in this community.

'George has settled down, that's something,' mentioned Dilys. He'd dozed off in the chair and Hetty had just carried him upstairs to bed.

Hetty nodded. She felt absolutely dreadful. It was one thing after another. First Ken had had to go away, then Dad had died, and now her nieces had gone missing. As time passed without news, she became more and more frightened. Surely if the twins had been found alive and well, they would have heard by now.

As though reading her thoughts Dilys said, 'It would take them a good time to find anyone in this weather with no moon. It doesn't necessarily mean bad news.'

'No, I suppose not,' agreed Hetty, wishing she had her aunt's ability to stay calm. There was a kind of serenity about both her and Uncle Owen, yet they had had their own share of tragedy with the death of their son. 'Thanks for being so good to us, Auntie. Taking us into your home and looking after us.'

'I love having you,' Dilys told her. 'It's good to have my brother's family here.'

'Were you and Dad close?'

'When we were children, indeed we were,' she replied. 'But he went away when he wasn't much more than a boy. He had to, see. There was nothing for him around here.'

'He was always talking about Wales and Cwmcae,' said Hetty, remembering with affection. 'We used to tease him something awful for going on about it. But now I can see why he loved it so much.'

'You can take the boy out of Wales but you can't take Wales out of the boy, so they say,' Dilys said.

'They say that about Londoners too,' Hetty mentioned. 'I think it's probably true of anywhere and anyone. Roots go deep.'

'I couldn't imagine being anywhere else but here,' Dilys said. 'I'd like to see other places, though. The furthest I've been is Cardiff on a chapel outing.'

'The furthest I've ever been outside of London is here,' Hetty said. 'Before we came here, the limit of our travels was Southend.' She paused. 'It's a seaside place near London.'

'We go to Tenby for the seaside,' said Dilys.

The conversation petered out. They were both too exhausted from worry to continue with it. The terrible silence outside the house tore at Hetty's heart.

Climbing down the slope was tricky for Owen because the ground was so slippery with mud. He slid most of the way, landing by a clump of bushes at the bottom. Luckily he didn't lose his torch when he fell, and as soon as he got his bearings he shone it around, his heart lifting as the beam landed on a small, muddy, tear-stained face, eyes wide with fear.

'I want to see Netta,' sobbed Poppy. 'I want my sister.'

'And you shall have her, *cariad*, in just a few minutes,' he assured her gently, far too relieved to find her alive to reprimand her for running away. 'She's waiting for you at the top of the hill. I'll give you a piggyback, is it?'

'Yes please, Uncle Owen.'

'Come on then,' he said, lifting her on to his back and beginning the climb back up the hill, thanking God the girls hadn't wandered as far as the quarry.

★ ★ ★

'Do you realise the worry you've caused with your latest prank?' said Hetty the next morning.

'Sorry,' said Poppy, looking sheepish.

'We won't do it again,' added her sister.

'You could have killed yourselves out there on your own, if you'd fallen down the quarry.' Hetty had only been told about the quarry after the girls were safely tucked up in bed.

'Sorry,' Poppy said again.

126

Hetty chewed her lip and took a deep breath. She was determined to stay calm now and be more patient with them in the future, though she knew it wouldn't be easy.

'I'm not cross with you, just concerned about you,' she explained. 'It's very important that you know how dangerous your little escapade was. I promised your mum I would look after you, and she would be very upset to know that you ran away, especially when she's explained to you that she has to stay in London to help Grandma.'

Last night hadn't been the time for recriminations. The men had brought the girls home soaked to the skin and exhausted. Dilys had heated some water on the stove and Hetty had put them in the tin bath in the parlour, then straight to bed.

'What is it you don't like about being here?' enquired Dilys now. She and Hetty had agreed that this should be a joint exercise since it was Dilys's roof the girls were living under. George had gone to school as usual. The twins were having the day off to recover.

Neither of them replied.

'I only want to know so that I can try to make it better,' Dilys explained.

'It isn't that we don't like you or your house,' said Poppy.

'Your house is nice,' added Netta.

'It's when we're outside of here; at school and that. That's when we don't like it. It's all different here to home and it makes us feel funny inside,' explained Poppy.

'It's like a pain and it makes us feel sad,' added Netta, a look of desolation in her big dark eyes.

'We can't understand what the people are saying,' said Poppy.

'We want to be at home with Mum.'

'It's only natural,' said Dilys. 'Anyone would rather be with their own mam.'

'The fact of the matter is, girls,' began Hetty, 'it just isn't possible for you to go home to your mum at the moment because of the bombs. So do you think you could give Cwmcae a bit more of a try? It might not be for long.'

'You'll soon get used to our ways,' said Dilys.

'Will we?'

'Of course you will,' she said. 'George has already.'

'We'll try, then,' said Poppy, the miserable experience of last night still vivid in her mind.

'Can we trust you not to run off again?' asked Hetty.

'We won't be doing that again,' said Poppy.

'No fear,' added her twin.

'Go on then, off you go and play,' said Hetty. 'You'd better stay in the garden as you've not gone to school. We don't want to get into any trouble for letting you stay home.'

When they'd gone Hetty said, 'I suppose I'd better write and tell their mother all about it.'

'I'm not so sure about that.'

'She's got a right to know,' Hetty told her aunt. 'They are her children, after all.'

'But they weren't hurt, and all's well that ends well,' Dilys reminded her.

'That's true.'

'What can she do apart from worry herself half to death and feel she'll have to have them home, bombs or no bombs?' said her aunt. 'She'll feel she ought to come rushing down here to sort things out, and that will leave your poor mother on her own with the business.'

'Mm, there is that,' agreed Hetty.

'Let's see what happens over the next week or two,' suggested Dilys. 'If they really don't begin to settle, we'll have to tell her. Maybe she'll want to have them back home if that's the case. But for now, I think we should keep quiet. It isn't as if they are likely to run off again. I think they learnt their lesson.'

'All right then,' agreed Hetty.

She could see the sense of what her aunt said. She herself could help her nieces to feel better about being away from their mother. She wasn't the most patient of women when it came to other people's children, but she would definitely do her best.

5

Despite Dolly's initial reservations, Mabel proved to be a valuable asset to the dairy. Not as socially inept as she had at first seemed, she was quick to learn, industrious, willing to turn her hand to anything and a constant source of entertainment with her anecdotes of life as the only girl in a family of five boys. She was also amusingly forthcoming about her social life, in which the Hammersmith Palais was a major feature, with a night out at the pictures a very close second.

She fitted into the working routine of the dairy perfectly. Sensitive to the feelings of others and an ardent champion of the underdog — as had already been illustrated by means of the Mrs Barker episode — she had a seemingly endless capacity to listen and empathise with customers' grumbles, and could usually raise a smile from even the gloomiest soul.

True to her word, she managed to curb her wayward tongue, though the clenching of teeth could sometimes be perceived on the staff side of the counter. Megan enjoyed her company and valued her contribution to the workload, especially as she was so versatile.

'I didn't realise there was so much to selling milk,' Mabel confessed one day when she was working with Megan in the dairy. 'Before I came to work here I'd never given a thought to what

130

happens to the milk in between leaving the cow and arriving on the doorstep in the morning.'

'I don't suppose many people have. You wouldn't have cause to unless you were involved in it in some way, would you?' Megan pointed out, pressing her foot on the pedal of the small machine which filled the bottles and subsequently sealed and capped them with waxed cardboard discs.

'No, you certainly wouldn't. Milk isn't a thing you can get so excited about that you'd want to know more,' said Mabel, removing the filled bottles, wiping them with a clean cloth and placing them in the cold store ready for delivery. 'It's just there; not much taste to it. Not a thing you'd ever yearn for, like egg and bacon or chocolate.'

'Some people love it. I'm one of them as it happens.'

'Get away. I thought it was just one of those things you take for granted.'

'It's the same with anything else that's always around,' said Megan, who, like Mabel, was wearing a white coat and an elastic-edged cap to cover her hair. The dairy was a large, cool room with black-and-white tiles on the floor, and whitewashed walls. There was a workbench along one side and a large sink on the other, as well as a small bottle-washing machine and steam sterilising unit. 'Though there isn't as much of it around as before the war, of course.'

'It's the same with everything, innit?' responded Mabel with a wry grin. 'It's a wonder we haven't all died of starvation, considering the miserable amount we get to eat.'

'It isn't that bad,' said Megan. 'We have enough to live on.'

'Only just.'

'We're managing to stay healthy on it anyway,' Megan observed. 'I can put up with not having much to eat. It's being parted from my children that really gets me down.'

'Yeah, that must be rotten,' Mabel sympathised. 'The bloomin' war has ripped families apart: little kids being separated from their mums; men away fighting. My older brothers are in action overseas. Mum misses 'em and worries about 'em something awful, even though they're grown up and married. I do as well, truth be told.' She made a face. 'Don't get me wrong — we're not the sort of family to be soppy over one another, and my brothers pull my leg something shocking, but I hate not having 'em around. And there's always the worry that they might not come back.'

'That must be a constant fear for your mum,' said Megan. 'I'm lucky in comparison. At least I know my kids are safe.'

'They reckon that more people have been evacuated since the start of the doodlebugs than back in the Blitz,' Mabel mentioned. 'They're pouring out of London in their thousands, apparently.'

'I heard about that too,' nodded Megan, 'and there was us thinking it would all be over with the coming of D-Day.'

'Instead of victory we got the doodles.' Mabel looked grim, remembering. 'I nearly wet myself when I saw one for the first time; plain as day overhead. It came down quite near an' all. I thought I'd had my lot.'

'I've had a few of those moments too.'

'The Pavilion cinema down at Shepherd's Bush was hit the other day,' Mabel went on.

'So I heard,' said Megan. 'It's badly damaged so they say.'

'It's gonna be closed for an indefinite period; that's the official word on the subject,' Mabel informed her. 'I was proper choked when I heard that the Jerries had got that, because me and my mates often go there. There won't be any cinemas left down that way soon. The Silver caught it back in the Blitz and has been closed ever since.'

'There are still a good few about around here, so we can't complain,' Megan pointed out.

'Mm, I suppose not. Anyway, we've got the best dance hall in London. There's nowhere to touch Hammersmith Palais and I'm going there on Saturday night,' Mabel continued cheerily.

'Are you hoping to meet a nice boy?'

'Not half. I could do with a boyfriend. The way I'm going, I'll end up an old maid.'

'Come off it,' smiled Megan. 'You've got years before you need worry about that.'

'I don't know,' Mabel said in all seriousness. 'I'm seventeen. It's time I had a regular bloke and some prospect of marriage in view so I can get out from under my mum's feet. Trouble is, they all go for the pretty girls.'

A stunning beauty Mabel was not, but she did have a certain appeal, with her brilliant green eyes and air of vitality.

'There's nothing wrong with the way you look,' said Megan, hoping to reassure the girl without patronising her by overstating the case.

'Maybe I don't look like the back of a bus, but I ain't nothin' special neither. I ain't got blond hair or a big chest. That's the sort the boys go for.'

'Not all of them,' Megan said. 'If they did, no one else would get fixed up.'

Mabel shrugged. For all her outward show of confidence, Megan could see that she was as sensitive about her looks as any other young girl.

'Anyway, getting married and getting out from under your mother's feet don't necessarily go together these days,' Megan pointed out. 'My sister and I are both married but still living at home.'

'And very glad of it your mum is too, I reckon,' suggested Mabel. 'You can tell it's a comfort to her, having you about, with her losing your dad, I mean.'

'Yeah, I'm glad to be here with her,' said Megan. 'She needs someone.'

'Do you get to see your children very often?' Mabel enquired chattily.

'Not at all. It's too far to go to Wales without at least one overnight stay,' Megan explained. 'I couldn't leave Mum to look after things on her own.'

'She wouldn't be on her own now that I'm working here,' Mabel pointed out. 'I wouldn't mind putting in more hours, and coming in early to do the round, if you want to go away. I could

134

get my little brother to come and help out. He's thirteen, and still at school.'

'It's very kind of you to offer,' said Megan, 'but I couldn't expect you to do that. You work hard enough as it is.'

'A bit more won't hurt me and it would only be for a couple of days,' Mabel reminded her. 'But if you think I'm not capable of standing in for you . . . '

'It isn't that . . . of course not.' The thought of seeing her daughters filled Megan with such joy she began to wonder if it might really be possible to pay them a visit. 'It's just that it would mean a lot of work for the two of you.'

'I don't mind, and I'm sure your mum and I will manage,' Mabel assured her. 'Anyway, the offer is there if you fancy going to Wales at any time.'

'I'll have a word with Mum and see what she thinks,' Megan told her. 'Meanwhile we're just about finished here, so if you could go to the shop to give Mum a break, I'll finish off and get the machine washed and sterilised.'

'Okey doke,' Mabel said, moving away and taking off her white coat and hat.

★ ★ ★

'I think it's a very good idea,' was the way Dolly responded to the suggestion. 'It'll do you the world of good to see those twins of yours, and vice versa.'

'It'll mean a lot of extra work for you, though, Mum, even though Mabel is willing to work

135

longer hours and do the round,' Megan pointed out. 'You know what it was like for us before she came.'

'Nothing we can't cope with, as it would only be for a couple of days,' Dolly assured her. 'If it was longer I might not be so willing. But you go with my blessing, and give those kids a big hug from me. It'll be a load off my mind if you get to see them. It worries me that you have to stay here to help me out.'

Megan hadn't been this happy in ages. 'If I go at the weekend, at least you'll have Sunday afternoon to yourself.'

'Good idea,' Dolly agreed. 'So go ahead and organise it straight away. You'd better let Dilys know you're coming so she can sort out somewhere for you to sleep. You could leave a message for her at the pub.'

'Yeah, I'll do that,' smiled Megan, bursting with exuberance.

★ ★ ★

Megan was in high spirits all day Friday at the thought of seeing the twins and was doing everything she could to make it easier for her mother and Mabel while she was away: filling the shelves in the shop and checking the stock; cleaning the dairy from top to bottom after she'd got the milk bottled and ready for Mabel to deliver in the morning; leaving a list of instructions to assist her.

'Anyone would think you were going for a month,' said her mother over their evening meal.

'You'll be too worn out to enjoy the weekend the way you're carrying on.'

'Just want to do what I can to help.'

'You seem to forget that I was helping your dad run this place when you were still in your pram, and it isn't going to fall apart just because you're not going to be here for a couple of days. Try to relax and enjoy your weekend off.'

'I intend to, don't worry.'

★ ★ ★

Awake very early on Saturday morning in all the excitement, Megan decided to get up and make herself useful as she had time to spare. She went to get Chips from the stables then loaded all the bottled milk from the cold room into crates and on to the cart ready for Mabel.

'I thought we were supposed to be doing that,' Mabel said when she arrived with her brother Eric, a skinny, bright-eyed youngster with a look of his sister about him.

'I was up early so I thought I might as well make it that bit easier for you.'

'Thanks but you shouldn't have. I was expecting to do it, and he'd have helped,' Mabel said, looking towards her brother. 'That's what I brought him for. I'm not having him standing about idle.'

'Did she drag you out of bed, Eric?' smiled Megan.

'Yeah, she's cruel.' He made a face. 'She put a wet flannel on my face and threatened to wring it out on me if I wasn't up by the time she'd counted to ten.'

'Aah, that's mean,' said Megan.

'I'm used to her, don't worry,' the boy assured her. 'She's not so bad really.'

'I'll leave you to it then and go and get ready.'

'Ta-ta, have a nice time.'

'I'll do my best.'

Megan hurried into the house, got changed out of her working clothes into a summer frock, dusted her face with powder and brushed her hair, keeping the small amount of lipstick she had left in the tube until after she'd eaten her breakfast.

'I've made you some sandwiches for the train,' said her mother when Megan appeared in the kitchen. Dolly was stirring porridge in the saucepan on the stove. 'And make sure you have a good breakfast before you go. It's a long journey.'

Excitement had diminished Megan's appetite, but she sat down at the table in the parlour with the intention of making an effort with the porridge her mother served into a bowl for her.

'It'll be nice to have a weekend away from the damned doodlebugs,' she said as an ominous roar became audible from above.

'It'll pass over, I expect,' said her mother as the noise got louder.

'Course it will,' agreed Megan with feigned casualness. She always felt jittery when there was a flying bomb in the vicinity, but it had become a matter of principle with most people not to show it.

138

'I'll go in the garden and see where the bugger is,' said Dolly, heading for the back door via the kitchen. 'Then we can have our breakfast in peace.'

'No, Mum, don't do that. It's dangerous.'

'I'll just have a quick peep; shan't be a tick,' Dolly said, and left the room.

Megan had her spoon in mid-air when she heard the engine cut out. 'Mum, get down!' she shrieked, diving under the table. 'Take cover.'

If Dolly replied Megan didn't hear her, because there was an almighty crash that shook the house and must have blown the windows in, because she could hear the tinkle of broken glass. In the ensuing silence she could feel the beat of her heart throbbing throughout her body.

Scrambling out shakily from under the table, careful of the broken glass all over the floor, she got up and called out to her mother. There was no reply.

'Mum!' she yelled again, her shoes crunching on glass as she made for the back door in a hurry. 'Mum.'

Her mother was lying on her back on the kitchen floor with the door on top of her, hiding her face. It must have been one heck of a blast to blow it clean off its hinges, thought Megan.

'Mum, are you all right?' she asked, carefully trying to lift the door away to free her. 'I'll have this off you in no time. It's a hell of a weight, though. It must be squashing you half to death.'

All was silent. As Megan finally managed to remove the door and laid it on the floor, she could see that her mother's eyes were closed.

Her skirt was up around her waist and her knickers were on full view. Megan pulled the skirt down. 'We don't want you showing your drawers, do we?' she said with false levity as she struggled not to panic. 'Come on now, Mum, let me help you up. You can't stay down there all day.'

Dolly remained motionless.

'Oh no, please God, no. Not Mum as well,' Megan muttered, her voice breaking. 'Mum, please wake up . . . please please speak to me.'

But there wasn't a sound in the kitchen.

★ ★ ★

The twins had been out picking wild flowers to give to their mother when she arrived for her visit later on.

'Do you think Mum will like these?' Poppy asked as she came in the back kitchen door clutching a colourful assortment.

'I'm sure she'll love them,' said Dilys.

'Particularly as you picked them for her specially,' added Hetty. 'She'll be thrilled.'

'Mine are best, look,' said Netta proudly, holding up a straggly assortment of vegetation that contained rather a large proportion of weeds.

'Yours aren't better than mine,' argued her sister hotly, the air rife with sibling rivalry 'You've got loads of dandelions in yours.'

'It don't matter because they're a nice colour, so there. My bunch are lovely.'

'Now now, don't spoil things by falling out

140

with each other when you've been such good girls,' warned Dilys. 'Give the flowers to me and I'll put them all in water so that they'll still be nice and fresh when your mam gets here.'

'When will that be?' asked Netta, her dark eyes shining in blissful anticipation.

'It'll be a little while yet,' Hetty explained. 'It's a long journey from London.'

'Will she have got on the train by now?' Poppy wanted to know.

Hetty looked at the kitchen clock. 'Yeah, she'll be on the train I should think. While you're waiting for her to get here, why don't you two go out to play to help the time pass? George is playing with some of the village children.'

The two little girls trotted out of the back door, muttering something to the effect that they'd play on their own as they weren't going to hang around with a lot of rough boys.

'Bless their hearts,' said Dilys affectionately, watching them from the kitchen window. 'They're so excited about seeing their mam.'

'I bet she's just as keyed up about seeing them,' smiled Hetty. 'I'm excited myself at the thought of seeing her.'

There was a knock at the front door.

'I'll go,' said Dilys.

Hetty busied herself peeling and chopping some cabbage for lunch. When her aunt came back into the room, she didn't even look up.

'I won't do enough vegetables for Megan, as she can't possibly get here in time for lunch,' she said.

'She won't be here at all,' Dilys said sadly.

141

'That was Dewi from the pub with a message.'

Now Hetty looked up sharply. 'Why? What's happened?' she asked anxiously.

'There's been a bomb incident at the dairy . . . ' Dilys began shakily.

Hetty dropped the cabbage into the bowl, her breath catching in her throat. 'Oh Auntie, no. What . . . '

'I don't know any more than that,' Dilys said, brushing her hand across her furrowed brow. 'Megan wants you to ring her straight away and she'll tell you all about it. She probably didn't want to go into it too much with Dewi.'

Trembling and close to tears, Hetty went to get her purse and rushed off to the pub.

★   ★   ★

Breaking the news to the twins that their mother wouldn't be coming to see them after all was one of the most difficult things Hetty had ever had to do.

They stared at her, both looking equally crestfallen, after she'd dealt the blow.

'She isn't coming at all, you mean?' said Poppy, her eyes bright with tears.

'Not for a while anyway,' Hetty replied. 'I'm ever so sorry, girls. It isn't your mum's fault. There's been a bomb.'

'Is she . . . is she dead?' asked Netta fearfully.

'No, she isn't dead, love,' Hetty assured her.

'Has she been hurt?'

'No. Your mum is fine.'

'Is Gran all right?' asked Poppy

'She's been hurt but she's all right,' said Hetty so as not to worry the girl unduly.

'Oh.' It was all there in the child's eyes: the stinging disappointment, the sense of betrayal. Poppy was six years old and unable to see beyond her own hurt feelings to enquire about the details, and Hetty wasn't about to enlighten her. 'So Mum's all right but she's still not coming?'

'She will come, another time,' Hetty assured her. 'But no, love, I'm afraid it won't be today.'

'Doesn't she want to see us?' asked Poppy.

'Of course she does,' Hetty made clear. 'She's as disappointed as you are that she can't get away.'

Poppy just stared at Hetty, her eyes brimming with tears, then she went to the windowsill, picked up the vase in which Dilys had put the flowers she'd picked, took them out and threw them viciously into the rubbish bin.

'Don't take on, love,' said Hetty, holding her arms out to her. 'You'll see her again soon. Come here.'

The little girl stood still, her whole body seeming leaden with disappointment. 'I want my own mum,' she said, her voice quivering. 'Not George's.'

George, watching the scene in silence, went over to Poppy and put his hand on her arm.

'You can have my sweet coupons if you like.'

Hetty almost choked on the lump in her throat at this, the ultimate sacrifice, from her son.

'It's all right, George, you keep 'em,' said Poppy in a manner of friendliness that seemed to

143

exclude the adults. 'But thanks for offerin' anyway.'

With that she rushed out into the garden and her sister followed.

George went to go after them but his mother said, 'Leave them for a few minutes, son. Give them some time to cool down by themselves.'

He shrugged and went into the other room.

The cottage that had been so vibrant with joy and excitement just a little while earlier was now leaden with gloom.

'There are times,' began Dilys, sighing, 'when you wish you could go through something for someone else.'

'You're telling me,' agreed Hetty, 'and this is definitely one of them.'

★ ★ ★

That same evening, Megan walked alone by the Thames, the muddy water tinted olive green in patches in the late sun. The air was filled with the toot of tugboats and the seagulls' cries, the river busy with commercial craft: barges transporting coal and oily steamers loaded with industrial goods.

She'd felt compelled to get out of the house; to get away and let her feelings come to the surface, having been stifling them in front of her poor mother. Dolly was still badly shaken after being knocked unconscious this morning when the door was blown in. She had her foot in plaster and her arm in a sling, having fallen awkwardly and broken her ankle and sprained

144

her wrist. There were also several cuts on her body from the flying glass. The bomb had actually exploded in the next street but the blast had spread over a wide area, though the dairy part of the building had been unaffected, so Mabel and her brother were unhurt.

Megan wanted to scream with disappointment and rage because she'd been thwarted in her plans to see her children. Selfish? Undoubtedly, but that was how she felt and no amount of self-castigation made any difference. She didn't want to be here in London, looking after her mother and running the dairy. She wanted to be in Wales with her children.

There was no question of her being able to get away for at least six weeks. That was the minimum time her mother would have her foot in plaster. The twins would probably have forgotten all about her by the time she did get to see them again.

She was fully aware of the fact that it was worse for her mother, who was not only in physical pain but riddled with guilt because Megan had had to postpone her trip to Wales. And here was Megan feeling sorry for herself when she should be on her knees thanking God that her mother was alive. But for all her moral wrangling she still felt angry and frustrated. Sod the war; sod the Germans, she raged silently. Why can't there be an end to it now? Five years was enough for anyone.

There was an ache in her heart as she imagined how disappointed the twins would have been. They would probably never trust her again. They were too young to understand how things worked. They would simply think she'd let them down.

The evening sun was going down over Hammersmith Bridge in front of her, its green-and-gold-painted lines etched against the dusky-pink-tinted sky. The bridge was not to everyone's taste, with its elaborate ornamentation, flowing swirls and fancy towers, but Megan had always considered it to be rather lovely. A beautiful sight marred by the bomb damage in the area surrounding it. The Lead Mills, a boathouse and a couple of the wharfs were now in ruins; factories and some of the houses were just debris, and there was damage to buildings everywhere. Exactly how many people had been killed no one seemed to know, but Megan guessed that the death toll would be high.

And here she was full of self-pity for her own problems. Pull yourself together, woman, she admonished. Get on with it and thank God that you're alive. You're not the only woman whose children are away.

She decided she would go home and write to the twins, and on Monday she would get a couple of postal orders for pocket money to put in the envelope before she posted it off. That would cheer them up.

Heading back home and looking around her, she remembered a time when the river had been a place for fun and recreation: colourful pleasure craft sweeping by, rowing crews gliding past, the waterside full of people.

Now only essential craft used the river and

bomb damage flanked it. As she picked her way through the debris, she realised that her walk had done nothing to raise her spirits. The disappointment of the day was still rampant. It seemed to drag her down physically. But she would put on the performance of her life so that her mother didn't realise it. The poor woman had enough to put up with without her daughter adding to it by going around with a long face.

★ ★ ★

Dolly had plans for a spot of performing of her own. While she accepted the fact that she couldn't actually defeat nature, she could put up a damned good fight. So what if she did have her foot in plaster and her arm in a sling? The rest of her was in good working order, and fortunately it was her left arm that was out of action. She had crutches to help her walk so she wasn't completely incapacitated. She was a tough old bird. It would take more than this setback to put her out of work for long. There was the pain to contend with, of course, but aspirin helped with that.

By the middle of the week she was up and about, and on Friday she had some news for Megan.

'You're going to Wales for the weekend,' she announced gleefully over breakfast.

'Which weekend would that be, Mum?' Megan asked. 'One sometime after the war?'

'This one.'

'Ooh, I wish.'

'Your wish has come true, then.'

'Don't be daft.'

'I'm being perfectly serious,' Dolly told her. 'I am not going to let you wait six weeks to see those kids of yours and risk having something else come up to stop it. So I've made arrangements for you to go this weekend. This way you'll only be a week late.'

'Come off it, Mum,' Megan protested. 'I wouldn't go away leaving you here with only one working arm and leg. It's ever so nice of you to suggest it, and I'm really touched, but you must know I can't go. Even apart from the fact that you need looking after, there's the shop and the dairy to be seen to.'

'All taken care of,' Dolly informed her briskly. 'Mabel will come in early and do the round, and she'll work for as long as I want her to. She's even offered to stay the night to be on hand in case I need her.'

'But Mabel can't do everything.'

'She won't have to,' said Dolly. 'I can serve in the shop. For anything I need two hands for, the customers will help out. Mabel's bringing young Eric with her. He'll help her with the round and will stay for as long as we need him.'

'But . . .'

'I want no more buts,' Dolly stated firmly. 'You really will upset me if you don't do as I say and get yourself off to Wales. The place isn't going to grind to a halt because you're not here. No one is indispensable, not even you.'

'Oh Mum,' Megan said, her face wreathed in smiles. 'I don't know what to say.'

'Don't say anything. Just eat your breakfast, then you can pour us both a cup of tea.'

'I'll have to let Auntie Dil know.'

'I've already done it,' her mother informed her brightly. 'I phoned the pub from the shop while you were in the dairy.'

'Bossy little thing, aren't you?' Megan teased her.

'Well, I am the senior member of the family, remember,' Dolly chuckled. 'I might have a few knocks and bruises but I haven't lost my authority.'

'I'd better do as I'm told then, hadn't I?'

'I should,' Dolly advised her. 'You'll get no peace from me unless you do.'

★ ★ ★

'We haven't told the children that you're coming,' explained Uncle Owen as he drove her from the station to Cwmcae in the farm truck. 'Just in case something happened up in London, like, and you couldn't make it. We didn't want them disappointed like they were last week.'

'Very wise,' Megan said. 'Thank you.'

'How's your mam now?'

'She says she's all right but she's still in a bit of pain, I think,' she told him. 'She's the sort who won't give in. She absolutely insisted on my taking the weekend off to see the children; she practically threw me out of the house.'

'Still bad up your way, is it?'

'Pretty bad.'

'Nice to have a little break then?'

'It certainly is.'

'Looking forward to seeing the kids?'

'Oh yes, Uncle Owen,' Megan said with feeling. 'Oh yes.'

★ ★ ★

Much to her disappointment, the children weren't in when they arrived at the cottage.

'They're out playing,' Hetty explained after greetings had been exchanged. 'We didn't want them getting themselves all worked up just in case; you never know these days what might happen at the last minute.'

'That's true,' said Megan.

'They'll be back in a minute, I expect,' said Dilys, sensing her niece's disappointment. 'They're in and out all the time.'

'The kids all play down on the green by the village hall,' Hetty informed her. 'Ours have got to know some of the local children. There are a few other evacuees too. They congregate there every day.'

'Settled in tidy they have, this last few days,' said Dilys, wanting to ease Megan's mind.

This was bizarre, thought Megan. They were talking to her about her children as though she had nothing to do with them, and she didn't like it one little bit. 'I'll take a walk down there, I think,' she said.

'I'll come with you,' said Hetty. 'It's almost time they came in for their tea anyway.'

They were about to leave the house through the back kitchen door when the children burst in.

150

'Is tea ready?' asked Poppy.

'We're starving,' added Netta.

'Have we got jam as it's Saturday?' George wanted to know.

They were all far too interested in food to look up, so didn't notice Megan standing behind her sister.

'Hey, Poppy and Netta, look who's come to see you,' said Hetty, nudging Megan forward.

They looked up and for one dreadful, heart-stopping moment Megan thought they hadn't recognised her.

'Mummy,' whooped Poppy at last, running up and throwing her arms around her.

'You came,' said Netta, doing the same.

'Yes, I came, and it's so good to see you,' said Megan, breathing in the smell of them and feeling their young skin against her lips as she smothered them with kisses. Intoxicated by their presence, she was unable to stop the tears falling.

'What's the matter, Mum?' asked Poppy.

'Why are you crying?' echoed Netta.

'I'm crying because I'm so happy to see you,' Megan said, 'so very, very happy.'

'Aah,' said Poppy sympathetically, patting her mother in a comforting gesture

'We're pleased to see you too, Mum,' Netta told her.

It was an enormous moment for Megan. She thought there could be no greater joy than she was experiencing now and she was imbued with new vigour.

Then Poppy said breezily, 'Can we go out to play again after tea, Auntie Hetty?'

There was an awkward silence. Then Hetty said, 'Don't ask me, love. Your mum's here now. She's in charge.'

'Can we, Mum?' asked Poppy casually.

'Yeah, of course you can; as long as I get to see something of you while I'm here,' Megan said.

'We're playing a good game, you see, and we want to finish it because our friends from the village can't play out on Sundays; they're not allowed,' explained Poppy.

'In that case you'd better see what you can of them today, hadn't you?' Megan said.

They were children, living in their own enclosed world, she reminded herself. It was a relief to know that they had got used to it here and were obviously happy. But it hurt to know that she was no longer at the centre of their lives. How could it be otherwise? It was bound to happen, and better for them that they had got accustomed to being away from her; she would rather that than have them moping for her. It was a desolate feeling, though, to know that she was losing them.

★ ★ ★

On Saturday afternoon Dolly had a visitor.

'Well, well! I didn't expect to see you behind that counter,' said Audrey Stubbs, coming into the shop. 'I heard you'd been badly hurt.'

'I got a bit bashed about in a bomb blast,' explained Dolly. She was forced to stay behind the counter because it was too difficult for her to

152

come in and out when the shop bell rang. 'But I'll live.'

'I'd have been over to see how you are before this, but I've been working extra hours during the week and it was too late by the time I got home,' Audrey told her.

'That's all right,' said Dolly, who was looking pale and strained from the constant pain and struggle of getting about. 'It's nothing serious, and I'm absolutely fine.'

'You don't look it, girl,' said the forthright Audrey. 'Certainly not well enough to be working.'

'I've got a chair here,' Dolly informed her. 'So I'm sitting down between customers, and I've taken some aspirin.'

'Even so, you shouldn't be out here in the shop,' Audrey opined. 'Megan's busy in the dairy, I suppose.'

'No, she's gone to Wales to see the children,' Dolly explained.

'And left you to cope on your own?' Audrey didn't try to hide the fact that she took a dim view.

'No, of course not,' replied Dolly defensively. 'Our assistant Mabel is here for the weekend helping me, and her brother's come too, so I've got plenty of support. They're both working in the dairy at the moment.'

This didn't dispel Audrey's obvious disapproval and it didn't go unnoticed by Dolly, who had always found Audrey difficult to get on with. She never seemed to have a good word to say about anyone and Dolly wasn't going to have her thinking ill of her daughter, so she said, 'Megan had arranged to go to Wales last weekend but she couldn't go because of the bomb. I was determined that she would get to see the children this weekend. She had no intention of going. It was all my idea. It isn't right for a mother to be parted from her children, and I know she's been fretting, even though she hasn't said anything. So I organised it and wouldn't take no for an answer.'

'Humph.'

'There's no need to look like that, Audrey,' admonished Dolly. 'I'd have thought you'd be pleased about it, seeing as they're your grandchildren too.'

'I'm glad she's seeing them, of course,' said Audrey sharply. 'It just seems a bit hard on you.'

'I'm absolutely fine, so you can stop worrying. If I hadn't thought I could cope I wouldn't have insisted on her going. I'm not that much of a fool.'

'If you say so.' Audrey was thoughtful. 'How are the children settling down in Wales?'

'That's what Megan is going to find out.'

Audrey mulled the situation over. 'Mm, yes, I can appreciate that she would need to go down there to see for herself,' she admitted finally.

'I'm glad you understand. We don't want any bad feeling, do we?' Dolly was surprised by Audrey's volte-face; she wasn't the type to back down. Perhaps there was hope for her after all.

The other woman didn't reply but looked pensive. 'Look . . . how would it be if I were to take over from you here in the shop for an hour

154

or so?' she suggested unexpectedly. 'You really do seem as though you could do with a break.'

'Well . . . ' Dolly was feeling exhausted and would have loved to put her feet up. 'But you don't know the job . . . there are the ration books to see to.'

'I'm not so thick that I can't manage to deal with a few ration books, neither am I thinking of running the place on a permanent basis,' Audrey said in her more usual terse manner. 'I just want to give you some cover so that you can have the rest you so obviously need. What I don't know, the customers will tell me.'

Dolly was too weary to argue. 'Well, if you're really sure you don't mind . . . '

'I wouldn't have offered if I minded, you know me better than that,' Audrey said briskly. 'Now let me help you through to your living room. I'll make you a cuppa while I'm at it. You've got a shop bell, haven't you? I'll rely on that while I'm back there with you.'

'It's very kind of you,' said Dolly gratefully.

'Don't be soft,' Audrey said, as though embarrassed to be thought of in a kindly light. 'It's no more than my duty. We are sort of related, after all.'

So she does have a heart after all, thought Dolly, as she sank gratefully into an armchair with her aching foot resting on a pouffe. That theory was confirmed some time later when, having unintentionally fallen asleep, she awoke and hobbled into the shop to find that it had been given a good going-over with the mop and duster, and that Audrey was preparing to close up.

'There was a bit of a slack period earlier on,' she explained, almost apologetically. 'So I thought I'd make myself useful. Young Mabel says she'll get you something to eat when she's finished in the dairy. She's still busy getting the milk bottled but she won't be long.'

'Thanks ever so much, Audrey,' said Dolly.

'No trouble at all,' she said curtly. 'I'll hand over to you now and get off home to get Jack's tea.'

With that, she picked up her handbag from behind the counter and left the shop. Well, well, I didn't know she had it in her, thought Dolly, feeling much better for the rest.

★ ★ ★

Audrey felt curiously uplifted as she walked to the bus stop; as though she had rejoined the human race after a long and painful absence. It had been such a long while since she'd felt genuine compassion, she'd assumed she must have lost her humanity altogether and would be isolated within her own private hell for the rest of her life. She'd forgotten how rewarding it was to do something for someone else.

She had a weird suspicion that some unknown force outside of herself had been at work this afternoon; something that had inspired her offer of help so that it seemed to happen of its own volition. Whatever the explanation, she felt different to the woman who had arrived at the

156

shop earlier; she had an almost forgotten warm feeling inside. Maybe it was just a glimpse of how things used to be. But it was enough to make her realise that life could be like that again if she made the effort.

*　*　*

'Do you feel a bit easier in your mind now that you've seen for yourself how well the twins have settled?' Hetty asked her sister in the early evening of the same day as they stood on a stone bridge over a shallow stream, leaning on the wall and watching the children paddle nearby.

'I'm glad they're happy, of course,' Megan replied. 'I wouldn't be much of a mum if I wasn't. But I miss them something awful. I want them at home with me.'

'You're bound to feel like that. It's only natural,' Hetty said sympathetically. 'But it's still too dangerous in London, isn't it?'

'Yeah. I wish to God this bloomin' war would end so that I could have them home where they belong.'

'I'm doing everything I can to make it easier for them,' Hetty tried to reassure her. 'I really do try very hard not to treat them any different to George.'

'Yes, I have noticed.'

Hetty threw her a look. 'Look, Megan, I know it must hurt when they ask my permission instead of yours,' she said. 'They've got used to my being the authority figure, that's all it is. It doesn't mean anything. Once they're back at

157

home with you they'll soon revert to normal.'

'I know,' sighed Megan. 'It's just such a peculiar feeling. But thanks for looking out for them.'

'I'm glad I'm here to be able to do it.'

'How are you getting on yourself?' enquired Megan with interest. 'It must be very different for you. Do you get homesick?'

Hetty looked sheepish. 'Not really. I feel awful for saying it, but I just love it here.'

'Why feel awful about it?'

'Because I'm enjoying myself while you're having a hard time at home, what with the bombing and now Mum not able to work at full strength. You must feel as though you're the one who drew the short straw.'

'No,' said Megan without hesitation. 'It could have gone the other way. You could have hated it here and still had to stay. You don't have to wear a hair shirt, you know.'

'I stayed because I couldn't bear to leave George, and I wasn't looking forward to it at all. I didn't expect to like it.'

'You seem to have taken to it better than when we both came during the Blitz,' Megan said thoughtfully. 'I mean, it's a huge culture shock: village life after being used to London. It couldn't be more of a contrast.'

'I just seem to have slotted into it this time,' Hetty explained. 'Maybe because I don't have you for support, I've been forced to join in with village life or never see a single soul besides the children and Auntie and Uncle.'

'We were a bit wrapped up in ourselves and

158

our children when we were here before,' Megan mentioned reflectively. 'They were smaller then and needed more attention. Now they're old enough to enter into village life, which draws you in, I suppose.'

'Obviously I'm an outsider here because I don't speak Welsh, but I join in as much as I can and I am picking up a few words and phrases, through working in the shop mostly. And of course being Dad's daughter helps.'

'He was very well thought of around here, wasn't he, even though he left when he was young?' said Megan.

'Auntie and Uncle are popular too, and that reflects on me. I enjoy the way of life here,' Hetty went on. 'I like the slowness of everything, the fresh air and the freedom. The atmosphere seems to agree with me, and George. He hasn't had so much as a runny nose since we've been here.'

'You'll be sorry to come back by the sound of it,' observed Megan with a smile.

'Don't be daft,' Hetty said firmly. 'London's my home and my life is there. But I can now understand why Dad loved this place so much.'

They chatted for a while longer, then Hetty said, 'Well, I suppose we'd better get these children home to bed. It's way past their bedtime.'

Her sister nodded. 'Netta, Poppy,' she shouted. 'Come on now. It's time to go home.'

'And you, George,' added Hetty.

There was a predictable storm of protest and pleas for another few minutes, to which their mothers agreed.

The air was warm and clean, a quietness seeming to wrap itself around the village, broken only by the joyful sound of the children playing. The green hills were touched by an evening mist beneath the orange-tinted horizon.

'It seems a shame to take them in when it's so lovely out here,' remarked Megan.

'I think that nearly every night,' confessed Hetty. 'It's one heck of a relief to know that they can play out without the fear of getting blown to bits.'

Megan nodded in agreement, smiling. But she actually wanted to weep with the sadness within her, because she felt like a stranger to her own children.

6

Very much the worse for wear, his suntanned face unshaven and shining with sweat, Private Will Stubbs was laid up in a medical tent in a clearing in the Burmese jungle. A bullet wound in his leg was the reason he was here; not a serious enough injury to get him sent home to England, but of enough significance to need medical attention and a brief period of recuperation; brief being the operative word in this battle zone, where every man was needed.

'Oh, so you've woken up at last then, have you?' observed the soldier in the next bed, a lean, unhealthy-looking man who was a stranger to Will. 'I was beginning to think you'd kicked the bucket, you've been asleep for so long.'

'Only the good die young, mate,' riposted Will, 'which means I'll be around for a long time yet.'

'The painkillers they gave you must have knocked you out,' suggested the soldier.

'Sheer exhaustion more like it,' was Will's opinion. 'We've been on the move for days, and awake for most of the time. We daren't sleep because the Japs were everywhere. You need eyes in your arse as well as everywhere else with those slimy sods around.'

'You're telling me.' The man gave Will a studious look. 'I've been hearing nice things about you. The word is that you're a bit of a hero.'

'Don't talk daft. Who told you that?'

'The nurse.'

'What would she know about it?'

'Dunno, mate. Someone must have said something when they brought you in. I suppose the medics would talk about how the injury came about as a matter of course. Anyway, according to her, you got hurt saving someone else's life.'

'Nothing unusual in that, is there?' Will said modestly. 'Soldiers are doing that sort of thing all the time.'

The man puffed out his lips and raised his eyes, looking mildly cynical. 'Oh I don't know so much about that, mate. When I'm in combat I'm always too busy trying to save my own skin to worry about anyone else's. I bet there's a good few more like me too.'

'I just happened to be in a position to help a bloke, that's all,' Will explained. 'It was no big thing.'

'You could have got yourself killed.'

'But I didn't, did I? I didn't even get badly hurt; nothing that they can't put right without too much bother.'

'All right, you modest old bugger. Let's change the subject if it embarrasses you,' suggested the man amiably. 'My name's Gus. I didn't get a chance to talk to you when you came in. You went to sleep as soon as they'd attended to your wound.'

'I'm Will; pleased to meet you.'

'You too, mate,' Gus responded, wiping the sweat from his face with a khaki handkerchief.

'What are you in here for?' enquired Will in a friendly manner.

'Malaria. I got a really bad dose this time, so they had to bring me in,' Gus replied.

'You don't look too good.'

'I'm still a bit weak, but I'm on the mend now so they'll be throwing me out to rejoin my unit soon.' He made a face. 'Worse luck.'

'I don't suppose I'll be here for long either. As long as you've still got your arms and legs, they get you back into battle sharpish,' remarked Will. 'Still, I feel a lot better for getting some kip.'

'It's just my luck to get ruddy malaria instead of a nice deep bullet wound, just serious enough to be my ticket back to Blighty,' said Gus with a wry grin.

The khaki canvas tent was like a large room with a few other beds which were unoccupied. The more serious cases were taken to proper military hospitals. The atmosphere in here was hot and stifling, the fan battling away but barely effective against the punishing tropical temperature.

'At least we're alive to tell the tale,' Will pointed out.

'Yeah, course we are. Take no notice of me. I just enjoy a good moan.' Gus paused, remembering. 'Oh, by the way, there's a letter for you on top of your locker. They came round with the post while you were asleep.'

Will sat up and reached over for the letter, warm with pleasure when he recognised his wife's handwriting. He tore open the envelope and read the contents eagerly. It was mostly everyday news from home. They were all still missing her father; the children had gone to stay with Megan's auntie in Wales. The part that he enjoyed the most was the bit at the bottom, telling him that she loved him and was longing to see him again. He would read this later, again and again, and savour it anew every time.

'You've got a great big soppy grin on your face,' observed Gus as Will put the letter back into the envelope. 'If it's from the woman in your life, I'm very pleased to see that you're smiling.'

'Why wouldn't I be?'

'If you had a letter like the last one I got from the girl I was engaged to, you wouldn't be smiling, I can tell you,' he said grimly. 'Quite the opposite.'

'One of the other kind, then?'

Gus nodded. 'She wrote to tell me that she'd found someone else. An airman she met while he was home on leave. How's that for a kick in the teeth?'

'That's rotten luck. I'm sorry, mate.'

'Not half as sorry as I was,' grumbled Gus. 'I thought the world of her, and she turned out to be just a cheap little tart. You never know where you are with women. You can't trust any single one of 'em. They're all the same.'

'I don't agree with you about that; not at all,' argued Will firmly. 'I trust my wife completely. I know she would never so much as look at another man.'

'That's what I thought until I got the letter,' said Gus, looking doom-laden.

'I'm as certain as anyone can be that my wife

164

wouldn't get up to anything,' stated Will categorically. 'I'm the one who isn't to be trusted in our marriage.'

The other man shrugged. 'That's different,' he said breezily.

'Why?'

'Because you're a man, o' course,' said Gus with an air of authority. 'We're driven by our animal instincts. It's nature's way of making sure the human race continues.'

'I've never been unfaithful to my wife,' pronounced Will with sincerity. 'And I don't intend to be either.'

'But you just said you weren't to be trusted.'

'I didn't mean in that way.'

'Oh, I just assumed . . . '

'Well you were wrong,' Will interjected firmly. 'I would never cheat on Megan. She means too much to me.'

'What's that got to do with it?' Gus asked.

'Everything.'

'Come off it. Just because you love a woman doesn't mean you have to say no to someone else if an opportunity comes along.'

'It does to me. But each man to his own on that subject,' said Will reasonably.

'True. I'm not going to argue with you about it. Live and let live I say. Anyway, you're the one who started all this,' Gus reminded him. 'You said that you can't be trusted.'

'Because there's something my wife doesn't know about my past,' explained Will, his manner becoming grave. 'Not because I've been unfaithful to her.'

Gus considered the matter. 'You're not the only man who's got stuff in his past that his wife doesn't know about. That applies to every other chap on the planet, I should think,' he chortled. 'Anyone with a bit of savvy will make sure he keeps quiet about it.'

'Even if it was something really bad?'

'All the more reason to keep shtoom,' advised Gus.

'Which is what I have done, and it tears me apart every day of my life.'

'What did you do that's so terrible? Get a girl in the family way or something?'

'No, nothing like that. Not everything is about sex, you know,' said Will.

'So they tell me,' Gus agreed. 'So, what did you do then? Nick something off the counter at Woolworth's?'

'If only it was that simple.'

'Robbed your granny of her life savings then?

'Course not.'

'Oh well, I don't know what you're on about then,' said Gus. 'You're getting too deep for me.'

Will fell silent, the nightmare returning. He lay back against his pillows, staring at the ceiling, his clean-cut features gleaming with perspiration, thick lashes curling over his tired eyes.

'Have you ever killed anyone, Gus?' he blurted out suddenly.

'Course I have,' the other man answered in an even tone. 'That's what we're trained for and why we are here.'

'No, I don't mean in the war; this is just a job and we're working under orders. There's nothing

166

personal involved in it at all. We're taught to eliminate the enemy and we get on and do it.'

'It's still killing, though, ain't it? It's still ending the life of a human being, whichever way you look at it,' Gus pointed out, his manner becoming more serious. 'It doesn't bear thinking about too much, I reckon. It could give you nightmares if you let it get to you.'

'I'm not talking about the war,' repeated Will. 'I mean in peacetime.'

'Well of course I ain't killed anyone,' stated Gus with affront. 'What do you take me for?'

'I have,' Will confided.

'Oh come off it, mate. Don't start coming out with a load of codswallop.'

'I wish it was just that,' sighed Will.

'It's those painkillers they gave you; they've done more than just make you sleep,' suggested Gus. 'I reckon they're giving you flaming delusions.'

'No, I'm not having delusions,' insisted Will. 'I killed my brother. And there is only one other person besides you and me who knows about it. A trusted friend.'

Gus looked grave now; worried in fact. 'So why have you told me?' he wanted to know.

'I don't know,' Will confessed, looking bewildered. 'I certainly didn't intend to. Maybe it was because I just wanted to say it out loud instead of hearing it echoing in my mind like toothache day after day.'

'They say it's easier to talk to strangers, don't they?'

'Mm. I suppose that's the reason I blurted it

out,' said Will. 'You and I are just ships that pass in the night. We'll be sent back to our units soon and will never see each other again.'

'You're right about that. But I think you'd be wise to keep your mouth shut about what you've just told me,' Gus suggested solemnly. 'Someone might begin to take you seriously if you say it often enough. You could get yourself into all sorts of trouble.'

'Yeah,' said Will, angry with himself for confiding his dark secret in a weak moment. 'Thanks, mate.'

The conversation came to an abrupt end when the young nurse bustled in.

'Oh, so you're awake then, are you, Private Stubbs?' she said cheerfully. 'I thought I could hear the two of you talking. How are you feeling now?'

'Not so bad.'

'Is the leg causing you any trouble?'

'It's throbbing a bit.'

'I'll get you something for that.'

'What about me, Nurse?' enquired Gus saucily. 'Don't I get any attention?'

'You've had your share while you've been here; you're almost better now,' she told him.

'Aren't you going to give me a blanket bath?' Gus teased her, with a slow grin.

'No, I most certainly am not,' she informed him with a serious face but a smile in her eyes. 'You're quite well enough to wash yourself now.'

'I'd rather you did it for me.'

'Don't push your luck, soldier,' said the nurse. She was used to dealing with men like Gus.

Most of it was just bravado anyway, and they enjoyed a little spirited repartee with the nursing staff. God knows, they deserved cheering up, and it was part of her job to do that.

'Sorry, Nurse.'

'I should think so too,' she said with feigned sternness and a twinkle in her eye. 'Now I'm going to get something for Private Stubbs to help with the pain.'

As she hurried away, Gus said, 'I reckon you're in there, mate. She likes the look of you.'

Will grinned. 'There you go again with your one-track mind.'

Gus gave a half-smile. 'That's me. I'm just an uncomplicated, red-blooded soldier. I take people as I find them and I don't delve too deeply into anything,'

The look that passed between them told Will that the topic of conversation prior to the nurse's appearance would never be mentioned again. He was very grateful.

★   ★   ★

'So, there'll be no more special treatment for me then,' said Dolly when she got back from the hospital, having had the plaster on her ankle removed.

'That's right,' said Megan, teasing her. 'You've had enough spoiling, hasn't she, Mabel?'

'Yep, we're gonna put our feet up and let you do all the work from now on,' chuckled the younger woman.

'We'll sit back and watch you, and have you

waiting on us,' laughed Megan.

They were in the parlour of the dairy house, taking a short afternoon break. It was August and London was still under attack from the flying bombs at any hour of the day and night. There were often long intervals between them, and most people ignored them unless they stopped immediately overhead, but the number of fatalities continued to grow and the damage was pitiful. Megan had heard that south London was the worst hit, but there didn't seem to be any shortage of Hitler's evil weapons around here.

The blown-out windows and door of the dairy house were still boarded up, and although a moment didn't pass without Megan missing her children, she hadn't had time to dwell on it since she got back from Wales.

Her mother had been stoical and had done more work than could be expected of anyone with her injuries. But her capabilities were limited with her arm in a sling and her foot in plaster. She'd soldiered on as best she could, hobbling about on crutches, with Megan and Mabel doing the lion's share of the work.

There had been a number of crises for Megan to deal with since she'd been back, besides her mother being unfit for work. Their milk supplier's depot had been hit by a bomb, so she had had to find a temporary source of supply rather then let the customers down. She'd found one but they couldn't deliver to the dairy, so Megan had had to take the horse cart and go and collect the churns every day herself from a depot in East Acton. She hadn't minded but it had taken up a lot of time she could ill afford.

The bottle shortage that had been growing since the beginning of the war had worsened to the point where they'd had to refuse to deliver to customers who didn't return their bottles, except in genuine cases when they had been broken by bomb blasts. The errant customers came to the dairy to collect their milk in jugs.

Working so closely together had taken Megan's relationship with Mabel to a new and different level. She was a family friend now, rather than just the hired help, a process that had begun when Megan had been in Wales. Mabel had got friendly with Dolly then, and now the three of them were pals.

Mabel was a great antidote to the gloominess of life in their battered city as the war dragged on, and kept them amused with cheery tales of her goings-on outside working hours. Her life had recently been greatly enhanced by a boy called Bob whom she'd met at the Hammersmith Palais and was now seeing regularly. He wasn't yet eighteen so hadn't been called up. Mabel was hoping the war would be over before his call-up papers came.

'I don't want to have him snatched away before I've had a chance to get to know him better,' she'd say dreamily. 'He's gorgeous and he's sweet on me. Fancy that! He's better-looking than any film star, and a proper gent. Not the sort to take advantage of a girl.' She roared with laugher and added, 'Unfortunately.'

He had indeed seemed like a decent type of

boy, Megan and her mother had thought, when he'd come to meet Mabel from work one day. They were both instinctively protective towards her because her openness and generous nature made her particularly vulnerable, even though she behaved as though she was as tough as old boots.

But now Dolly was speaking, still in the same light-hearted mood.

'Willingly would I do all the work so that you two can take it easy, but there's only so much one pair of hands can do.'

'Excuses, excuses,' teased Megan.

'Cheeky,' chided her mother jokingly.

'Just kidding, Ma.'

'One thing I am going to sort out now that I'm properly back on my feet is the bomb damage. It's time they gave us a new door and did something about the windows.'

'We'll just have to wait our turn,' suggested Megan. 'There are so many people waiting in the queue for work to be done. They don't have the labour or materials.'

'We can't live with the windows and door boarded up for much longer,' Dolly went on. 'It isn't healthy. We wouldn't still be waiting if your dad was around, bless him. He'd have found someone to do it for us and paid over the top if necessary. He wouldn't have waited about for the council, even though bomb damage is their responsibility.'

'I don't think even Dad could have got this one sorted any quicker, Mum,' Megan pointed out. 'Anyway, we might upset a lot of people if we were to get ours done before those who have been waiting longer.'

'That's true. But I think we probably get priority as we're a business,' Dolly said. 'I mean, we've our stock to protect. If some villain was intent upon helping himself, it wouldn't be much trouble to get past those boards into the house, then through to the shop. And if we have our stock nicked, it's the customers who suffer.'

'It's a flamin' miracle the shop window didn't get blown out,' remarked Mabel.

'It certainly is,' added Megan.

'We must be grateful for small mercies, I suppose. We've been lucky.' Looking on the bright side was inherent in Dolly's nature and she knew she had a lot to be thankful for. But although she tried never to show it, she didn't feel in the least bit lucky when she was missing Dai. The fact that people were losing sons, and whole families were being wiped out, didn't make her personal loss any less painful. Having her husband taken from her was like having the heart sucked out of her, sometimes to the point where her life didn't seem to have a purpose any more. But she knew she must shake herself out of it because she had daughters and grandchildren she loved and they were now the sole point of her existence. Feeling the black grief descending, she said quickly, 'Anyone fancy going to the flicks tonight? I feel like being taken out of myself.'

'I'll come, Mum,' said Megan with enthusiasm. 'A night out at the pictures will be lovely.'

'I wouldn't mind that either,' said Mabel.

Megan and her mother looked at her.

'What about Bob?' enquired Megan. 'I thought you saw him every night of the week.'

'Not every night. We're not that far gone,' she explained. 'He's on duty at the ARP on a Wednesday.'

'Let's all go then,' suggested Dolly eagerly. '*Fanny by Gaslight* is on at the Gaumont. James Mason is in it, and Stewart Granger.'

'Blimey, we're in for a real treat then, with the two of them to gawp at,' mentioned Mabel. 'I've got some sweet coupons left too, so we can have something nice to chew while we're doing it.'

'We'd better get back to work then, so we can knock off at a reasonable time,' said Megan, finishing her tea in a purposeful manner.

★ ★ ★

'That James Mason's a bit of all right, isn't he?' said Mabel as they came out of the cinema and walked through the Broadway in the warm summer night, the air tinged with bomb smoke.

'I love the way he speaks,' said Dolly.

'Me too,' agreed Megan. 'I just simply melt at the sound of his voice.'

'Stewart Granger ain't too bad neither,' pronounced Mabel, 'though it isn't his voice that gets me going. It's his handsome boat race and lovely physique.'

'Now, now, Mabel,' laughed Megan. 'You're going out with Bob, remember.'

Mabel laughed. 'He probably feels the same way about Betty Grable, but he can't run off with her any more than I can with gorgeous Stewart Granger. That's what film stars are for: for people to worship from afar.'

'What about their acting?' queried Megan.

'They're good at that too,' Mabel said. 'That's all part of what makes your spine tingle.'

'What did you think of the film?' asked Dolly.

'I thought it was good,' replied Megan. 'A well-acted Victorian romantic melodrama.'

'A gripping story,' added Mabel. 'It kept me on the edge of my seat from start to finish.'

There was a murmur of agreement from the others.

'You coming back to ours for a cuppa, Mabel?' invited Dolly.

'Ta very much,' said Mabel. 'I don't mind if I do.'

They walked on in companionable silence, slowly and carefully because of the blackout and also because there were a lot of people about, having just come out of the cinemas.

'Seems as though we struck lucky as regards the air raids,' remarked Dolly as they left the Broadway and got closer to home, their eyes accustomed to the dark now. A cloud had moved away from a slice of moon, giving them a little more light. 'It all happened while we were in the pictures. Plenty of bangs and crashes while we were in there, but it seems to have quietened down now.'

Arm in arm they turned into Blossom Street and headed towards the dairy.

'What the hell is going on?' gasped Dolly as they approached the building to see figures moving about outside; shadows in the dark shifting swiftly and silently. 'What are those people doing?'

'Looting, by the look of it,' replied Megan, peering ahead and feeling her feet crunch on glass beneath her feet. 'The rotten buggers.'

'Oh God, no,' gasped Dolly.

'The shop window has been blown in, I think.' Megan trod on something soft, and on inspecting it found it to be the remains of a squashed biscuit. 'The bomb blast must have smashed the window and blown the lid off the biscuit tins.' She stared ahead of her, straining her eyes and managing to see enough to get an idea of what was happening. 'The stock is all over the road and people are helping themselves. Some are going into the shop through the open window and taking what they want.'

'You ought to be bloody well ashamed of yourselves,' shouted the spirited Dolly, moving forward and standing in front of the shop. 'Stealing from your own neighbours; that's sheer greed. It'll be your fault if we've nothing to offer people when they come with their ration books. Looting is the lowest of the low, and the lot of you ought to be locked up. You will be too when the police catch up with you; you won't get away with it for ever. There's a law against looting, I'll have you know.'

But there was no one left listening. They had all disappeared into the night.

It wasn't like Dolly to be negative, but this blow was just one too many for her to take on the chin.

176

'Now what are we going to do, with a lot of our stock gone and our shop window blown out?' she said, her voice cracked with emotion. 'How on earth are we going to carry on?'

'I don't know yet, Mum,' sighed Megan, putting her arm around Dolly protectively, careful not to show how worried she herself was. 'But we'll do it somehow. I promise you. You're not on your own with the problem. We'll see to it together and we'll win through, don't worry. It'll take more than Hitler's bombs and that bunch of lowlife to get us down.'

*   *   *

The shop was in a terrible state. The floor was littered with various groceries. Broken glass was mingled with flour, lentils, tea leaves, broken biscuits, soda, matches and tins of Spam, to mention just a few.

'At least we haven't lost it all,' said Megan as they pulled the blackout blind across the broken window and turned on the light. 'A lot of the stuff on the shelves is still there: tinned food and things in packets and jars. The looters obviously didn't have time to get to those before we arrived home. And the glass has stayed in the shop door; must be because it was further in than the window.'

'Even so, we'll be well down on what we've got to sell,' said her mother gloomily.

'Mm, but we can put in for a special allocation to cover what we've lost so that we can meet the customers' needs,' Megan reminded her. 'Once they know we've got a genuine case and are not just trying to get more than our share, I should think they'll co-operate. I'll go to the town hall tomorrow to find out about it.'

'The dairy is all right,' Mabel informed them, having been to check. 'The windows are all intact. The blast must have just caught the front of the shop.'

'There doesn't seem to be any structural damage, and the electric is still on,' said Megan.

'The flying bombs don't cause craters; that's why they don't often interrupt the water or electric supply, even though the blast covers a wide area,' said Mabel knowledgeably. 'Bob was talking about it to my dad the other day and I just happened to be listening.'

'That's something to be thankful for anyway,' said Megan. 'At least we can see what we're doing.'

'To think that those people would steal from their own neighbours,' said Dolly in disgust. 'That's upset me far more than losing stock.'

'It wasn't our neighbours or friends, Mum, I'm sure of it,' Megan claimed in a definite tone. 'I know we couldn't see who they were in the dark, but the residents of our street wouldn't do that to us. It was people from outside our area who make a habit of that sort of thing. Word soon gets round to that type of person when there's a chance of getting something for nothing. Anyway, there's no point in brooding about it. We need to concentrate on putting things right. I'm going to make a start right away. You go to bed, Mum.'

'And leave you to deal with this on your own?' Dolly said hotly. 'Not likely!'

'I'll just pop home and let my mum know where I am and I'll be back to give a hand,' said Mabel.

Megan and her mother were too grateful to her to argue. Any assistance was sorely needed.

★ ★ ★

There were certain things that couldn't be done until daylight — clearing up outside and organising the boarding of the shop window — but the three of them worked well into the small hours, sweeping and scrubbing, cleaning all the shelves of their flour coating, getting rid of every last splinter of glass, refilling the shelves with what was left of the stock.

Megan didn't get more than a couple of hours' sleep because she had to get up to do the round. After she'd unloaded the cart of empties and taken Chips back to the stable, she went to the town hall to make a claim for extra food allocation to replace what they'd lost; then to the war damage department to ask for the front of the shop to be urgently made safe from looters and burglars until they could reglaze it. An overworked, weary-looking clerk assured her that they would get a man out to board the window up before nightfall, but her claim for extra supplies would take longer.

She arrived home to find a shop full of people and her mother and Mabel working cheerfully behind the counter in the fresh air. Everyone was

179

talking about the events of the previous night, the customers outraged by the behaviour of the looters and full of praise for Dolly and her team.

The Open sign was on the door and it was business as usual. Megan felt a huge surge of pride in her mother as she went inside to join them. Mum had had a lot to contend with recently and this latest blow had really shaken her. But her spirit had come through for her yet again. Absolutely indomitable was the only was to describe her!

7

One morning a week or so later when Megan was busy sweeping the dairy yard after taking Chips back to the stable, a soldier came out of the house and walked purposefully over to her.

'Wotcha, Megan,' he greeted, in a manner to suggest that they were on friendly terms.

As he approached, Megan noticed the horrific scars on the man's face.

'Er . . . hello.'

'I called in at the shop looking for you and your mum directed me through the house,' he explained.

Megan stared at him blankly, feeling very much at a disadvantage because she simply couldn't place him, even though there was something familiar about him, especially his voice.

After an awkward silence he said, 'Just thought I'd pop over to say hello and see how you're doing after all this time.'

'Doug!' she burst out at last, when recognition finally dawned and she realised that this was her husband's best pal, Doug Reynolds. But what on earth had happened to his face? She attempted to hide her shock and smiled warmly. 'How lovely to see you. It's been a long time.'

'Not half.'

Embarrassed and angry with herself for her initial response to him, she wasn't sure how to proceed. Should she risk humiliating him by mentioning the dramatic change in his appearance, or ignore it which could seem patronising? Fortunately the decision was taken out of her hands.

'It's my fashionable new wartime look,' he told her jokily. 'I was too close to a hand grenade when it exploded.'

'Oh Doug, I'm so sorry you've been injured,' she said with feeling. 'It must be very painful.'

'When I look in the mirror it certainly is,' he told her.

'That wasn't what I meant. I — '

'I know,' he cut in. 'Take no notice of me. I'm just feeling sorry for myself.'

'It doesn't matter.'

'I don't make a habit of it, you'll be glad to know,' he said. 'There are people much worse off than me. But being hideous isn't something you can easily forget. Other people notice it so it's best to bring it out into the open straight away.'

'You're not hideous,' she tried to reassure him. 'You look different, that's all, and I hadn't seen you for a long time. That's why I didn't recognise you at first glance.'

Actually, she was deeply ashamed to find herself repelled by him and desperately wanted to avert her gaze. She took herself firmly in hand. The man deserved respect after what he'd suffered for his country. But it was such a shock. The countenance that had been healthy and handsome the last time she'd set eyes on it was now freakish, the skin pulled tight in places and puffy in others. There were ugly red patches and his flattish nose was odd and unreal. The whole of his face looked so painful, she could almost feel it.

'You're very diplomatic, but there's no need, honestly. I know what I look like and I've learned to come to terms with it.' He looked at her and she remembered his eyes: greyish-brown, often with a resentful gleam back then. Now the flesh around them was so swollen they looked smaller, almost like slits. 'Anyway, enough about me. How are you keeping these days?'

'Oh, bearing up, you know,' she said, forcing a casual air. 'Missing Will, of course.'

'You're bound to.'

'I don't have much time to brood, though. I'm a lot busier than I was before the war, like most other people. We lost my dad in the bombing so I'm helping Mum to run this place. I'm dairy hand and roundswoman-cum-shop-assistant.' She looked towards the broom she was holding and added with a wry grin, 'As well as cleaner and general dogsbody.'

Doug offered his condolences for her father, and enquired politely about her children. She put him up to date.

'I expect you've guessed that the main reason I'm here is for news of Will,' he explained.

'He's still in the Far East somewhere as far as I know, but I haven't heard for a while so he could be anywhere,' she informed him. 'His letters are intermittent. I think it must be difficult to get the mail through from so far away, but the last time I heard, he seemed chirpy enough.'

'Good. I'm glad to hear he's still alive and kicking,' he said. 'You never know these days.'

She nodded in agreement. 'You're on sick leave then?' she assumed.

'Yeah, I'm at home now but I was in hospital for a long time and I still have to go back regularly to see the doctor. They did what they could to patch me up; skin grafts and so on. I don't know when I'll be reporting back for duty.'

'Surely they won't send you back on to active service, will they?' she queried.

'Wounded men do sometimes go back to the front line once they've been put right, but I don't think I'll have to go because the skin on my face isn't up to roughing it in unsanitary battle conditions. Infection could set in and I'd be a liability. They'll probably give me some sort of a desk job,' he explained. 'The army will make use of me somewhere, you can bet your life on it. They won't discharge me on health grounds just because of my face; not while the rest of me is functioning all right.'

'I suppose they need every man they can get.'

'Exactly.'

A silence fell uncomfortably around them. Megan trawled her mind for something to say to be sociable, but it wasn't easy because there was not so much as a flicker of affinity between them. 'Are you still single, Doug?' she managed at last, remembering that he hadn't been married before the war but had had no shortage of girlfriends. He'd been good looking back then. Megan hadn't known him well. The friendship between him and Will hadn't included her. It had been a boy thing: football matches, billiards, a pint of beer and a game of darts at the local and so on. The two men had been friends all their lives, and had gone to the same school. She remembered having the impression that Doug had rather resented the fact that Will had got married and was therefore no longer able to lead the bachelor life. Nothing had ever been said, but she'd sensed an underlying hostility occasionally. Fortunately there was no sign of that now.

'Oh yeah, I'm still single; living at home with Mum and Dad,' he said with an edge to his voice. Then his manner changed and he grinned and added, 'I chose to be a bachelor before I went away. I won't have any choice now, will I? My face is enough to send any woman running for cover.'

Megan didn't know how to respond to this, since she herself was having difficulty not recoiling from him. But it was such an awful fate for the poor chap she wanted to come up with something positive. He needed all the support he could get.

'I wouldn't say that, Doug,' she said. 'I'm sure there's someone out there for you.'

He shrugged. 'We'll see. I'm not worried really.'

Her compassion was such that she wanted to do something practical to help him.

'Look, I have to get on with my work now, but why don't you come round to the house and have something to eat with us one evening, if you're at a loose end,' she suggested, thinking it was the least they could do for her husband's best friend. 'It won't be anything elaborate, given the shortages, but Mum's a creative genius when it comes to wartime rations. It will be nice to have a chat about old times and life before the war.'

He gave a half-smile. 'Thanks. I'd like that a lot,' he said. 'When do you suggest?

'How about tomorrow?'

'Suits me.

'About seven?'

'Lovely.'

'We'll look forward to it then,' she said, and returned to her sweeping as he headed back towards the house.

★　★　★

'That poor bloke,' said Mabel later that morning when she and Megan were working together in the dairy. 'What a bloomin' fine reward he's got for fighting for his country: a face like a squashed tomato. I could have wept for him, I really could, the poor love. But of course you can't show it, can yer? Just in case he doesn't want to be pitied.'

'It is awkward but he's quite open about it, which made it easier for me; he even jokes about it, and admits to feeling sorry for himself, which takes courage in itself.'

'It does,' agreed Mabel wholeheartedly.

'It must have been very painful for him when it happened too,' said Megan, using a stiff, narrow brush to remove some stubborn residue from the neck of a milk bottle before putting it into the washer. 'It makes me shudder to think about it. Anyway, I've invited him round for a bite to eat with Mum and me.'

'I'd do something like that if I knew him better,' mentioned Mabel. 'He seemed so nice. I reckon we all ought to put ourselves out for our heroes.'

'I don't know him very well because he's Will's friend, so heaven knows what we're going to talk about all evening,' remarked Megan. 'But I'm sure I'll think of something. I know Will would want me to be friendly towards him as he isn't here to do it himself.'

'What did he look like before?' asked Mabel, washing a milk churn with water with soda dissolved in it. 'Was he good looking?'

'Yeah, he was rather; a bit of a dish in fact. He didn't appeal to me but he was never short of a girl on his arm.'

'He's still got something about him even now,' observed Mabel. 'I mean, I know his face is no great shakes but he's still a hero. He's what I call a real man and there's something attractive there despite the injuries. He's got a smashing physique.'

'Oh Mabel, I'm beginning to worry about you,' laughed Megan. 'First Stewart Granger. Now Doug.'

'I'm only human,' Mabel said. 'Us women can't help noticing these things, can we? Even if it isn't very ladylike to mention it.'

'In the case of Stewart Granger I can understand it,' Megan conceded. 'But not Doug Reynolds.'

'He's got a lovely pair of shoulders on him,' enthused Mabel.

'I think I shall have to have a word with your Bob,' Megan teased her. 'Tell him that you're admiring other men's attributes.'

'He knows that already and he won't mind; he ain't the jealous type,' Mabel chuckled. 'Anyway, don't try and make me believe that you don't notice a good physique when you see one, because that won't wash with me. Being married doesn't make you blind.'

'Of course it doesn't,' agreed Megan amiably. In all honesty she couldn't see anything at all attractive in Doug Reynolds, and it had nothing to do with his facial disfigurement. She had never thought of him in that light; and as for the shoulders Mabel was so impressed with, Megan hadn't even noticed them. 'But when you see Will you'll know why I don't take much notice of other men.'

'I can't wait.'

'Me neither,' said Megan. 'In the mean time, I've got to think how to keep the conversation going tomorrow night.'

★ ★ ★

As it happened there wasn't a problem, because her mother and Doug got on so well any significant contribution from Megan wasn't really necessary.

'Lovely meal this, Mrs M,' he said, tucking heartily into a corned beef hash.

'Thank you, dear.'

'Megan told me that you're a bit nifty in the kitchen and she's right,' he flattered. 'I don't know how you do it with everything being so short.'

'It just takes a bit of savvy,' Dolly responded, pink-cheeked and enjoying herself. 'We get plenty of tips from the government on how to make things go around but most of us find a good few tricks of our own. Anyway, everyone's so hungry they'll eat anything.'

'I don't know about that,' he said. 'I think you're a ruddy marvel.'

'No more than your mother, I daresay.'

He made a face. 'Mum wasn't much of a cook even before the war, bless her,' he said. 'Now that she's working full time and having to cope with rationing, we're never quite sure what she's gonna dish up. And I'm not saying anything I wouldn't say to her face. Mum has many gifts but cooking isn't one of them.'

Dolly looked misty-eyed. 'She must be very proud of you,' she said warmly.

'Yeah, I reckon she is,' Doug agreed, adding with a wry grin, 'Though she'll never get me married off and out from under her feet now, will she?'

'Don't say that, son.' Dolly frowned, feeling dreadfully sorry for him. 'Someone will come along.'

'Don't get me wrong,' he said, sounding cheerful. 'I'm quite happy to stay single. I enjoy the freedom. I can come and go as I please and do as I like. Until I go back off sick leave, that is.

There's no such thing as pleasing yourself in the army.'

'What would you do if they discharged you?' Dolly enquired with interest.

'There's no chance of that, but if they were to, I'd find myself a job,' he replied. 'I wouldn't want to sit about all day doing nothing, even if I was declared medically unfit for work.'

'That's the stuff, son,' encouraged Dolly. 'I like someone with a positive attitude.'

'That's because you're a very positive person yourself,' he complimented her. 'From what I've heard tonight anyway. You know, carrying on after you lost your husband, opening the shop the day after it was wrecked by a bomb blast. You're the sort of person who tackles life head on.'

'Thank you. But there isn't a choice in wartime, is there?' she pointed out. 'Anyway, a lot of it is down to Megan. She's the one who keeps me going.'

Doug looked at Megan. 'It runs in the family then,' he said. 'Will is a lucky bloke to be a part of it.'

Megan smiled politely.

'We're just hoping he comes back safe to be one of us again,' said Dolly.

'He'll be back, don't worry. Will's a survivor,' stated Doug heartily. 'He's got the luck of the devil, that man. Always did have, even when we were kids. You can take it from me.'

'You knew him before his brother died, didn't you?' mentioned Megan.

190

'That's right; the three of us were always together.'

'They say the twins were very close,' she probed.

'Like butter and bread,' he informed them. 'Or margarine as it is these days. Where there was one, there was the other. That's the way a lot of twins are. You've got twins, so you know.'

She nodded thoughtfully. 'You must have been very upset when his brother died, then, as you knew him so well,' she said.

'Totally gutted,' he agreed, clearing his plate and putting his knife and fork down on it. 'I was always with 'em, you see; tagged along everywhere. They were brothers but I was their mate.' He paused, looking into space. 'I was with them when Ron died, as it happens.' He shook his head. 'Cor, what a tragedy that was. There was nothing we could do.' He paused again, seeming emotional. 'It's traumatic to lose a mate as young as that; and of course poor old Will never got over it, as you probably know. He wasn't the same boy after that. His mother changed too.' He sighed. 'Still, life goes on, and it's a long time ago now. We've all had our share of suffering since then. I've seen mates die in action and that knocks the stuffing out of you. But having your pal die when you're just a kid, that's something else altogether.'

Megan was eager to know more about it because Will had never spoken about the details.

'He fell off Hammersmith Bridge, didn't he?' she said.

'Yeah, that's right.'

'How did it come about?' she asked.

'We were mucking about as boys do; being daredevils, joshing, trying to outdo each other, and things got out of hand. We climbed up on to the rail and Ron lost his balance and fell off. He was there one minute and gone the next. Will and I both dived in after him but we couldn't bring him up.' He shuddered. 'It turns my stomach just thinking about it, even after all this time.'

Megan deemed it wise not to delve further as he seemed so upset, and they fell into silence until her mother said, 'I've made a suet pudding for afters. I don't have any jam to go on it but I can manage a sprinkling of sugar. Will that do you, Doug?'

'That will do me lovely, Mrs M,' he enthused. 'Thanks very much.'

After the meal they had a game of cards. Dolly and Doug were really enjoying it but Megan was tired so she left them to it after a while, explaining to Doug that she had to be up early in the morning to do the milk round.

'It was nice seeing you again,' she said.

'Likewise. See you again sometime I hope,' he said casually, then turned his attention back to the card game.

She could hear the low murmur of their voices as she got into bed. Seems like they're going to make a night of it, she thought, as she turned on to her side and curled up ready to go to sleep. She was glad it had gone well. It was nice to see her mother enjoying herself too.

'What a smashing bloke that Doug is,' enthused Dolly the next morning when Megan got back from the round and they were having a cup of tea together at the kitchen table while Mabel looked after the shop. 'It must take some bottle to make jokes about the way he looks, presumably to put people at their ease. He just seems to take it in his stride.'

'I suppose he finds it easier to bring it out into the open rather than have people feeling embarrassed and not knowing what to say,' suggested Megan. 'After all, he can't hide away for the rest of his life, can he? And why should he anyway? He's every reason to be proud of himself.'

'I still say it takes some courage to do it, though,' asserted Dolly. 'But by the time he left I didn't even notice his face. He was such good company it didn't matter.'

'What time did he leave?' enquired Megan. 'I didn't even hear you come to bed.'

'Must have been nearly midnight,' Dolly said. 'The time just flew by. He's so entertaining; quite a wag in fact. I haven't enjoyed myself so much in ages, especially as the doodlebugs didn't come over last night. It took my mind off your dad for a few hours anyway.' She paused, sipping her tea and looking sad. 'I might not always mention it but I still miss him a lot.'

'Me too, Mum, but it's harder for you obviously.'

'Anyway, young Doug cheered me up,' Dolly

193

said, forcibly brightening her mood so as not to depress her daughter. 'I think I'd only met him once or twice before he went away. I remember seeing him at your wedding. He was best man, wasn't he?'

'That's right.'

'Well he's a best man in my book, wedding or not,' stated Dolly. 'A son any mother would be proud of.' She yawned heavily. 'He must have been good company to keep me out of my bed that late. We're early to bed in this house. We have to be, in our game.' She paused, remembering. 'He was so apologetic about keeping me up late. He's got the loveliest manners. His mother's done a good job in bringing him up.'

'He's really impressed you then,' said Megan.

'I'd be proud to have him as a son. Put it that way,' explained Dolly.

The conversation was interrupted by the sound of the buzzer above the door which meant that Mabel needed help. Dolly took a swig of tea. 'No peace for the wicked,' she said, rising purposefully.

'I must get back to work in a minute too,' mentioned Megan. 'I've the cart to empty and the bottle-washing to get underway.'

'All in a day's work,' said Dolly and hurried from the room.

★ ★ ★

When Megan went to visit her mother-in-law a few days later she found that she was also an enthusiastic member of the Doug Reynolds fan club. Megan had noticed how much more cheerful and easy to get on with Audrey had been lately. It was lovely.

'I always did have a soft spot for him,' Audrey was saying. 'But I'm even more impressed now. It's wonderful the way he's coping with his injuries.'

'Yeah, my mum liked him too,' Megan told her. 'In fact, she thought he was wonderful. I think she wanted to mother him, never having had a son.'

'He was always round here when the boys were kids,' said Audrey wistfully. 'He adored the twins and went everywhere with them. Then, of course, after we lost Ron, he was Will's pal. No one could make up to Will for the loss of his brother, but he was very glad of Doug's company. They both missed Ron so helped each other through it. I don't know what Will would have done without Doug in those early days.'

'I shall have to tell Doug if he calls again that he's a hit with the two of you.'

'He'd sooner be a hit with women of your age, I should think,' suggested Audrey.

'With his positive attitude he will be eventually,' said Megan. 'Once people see beyond the scars to the man beneath, his personality will shine through. Our shop girl Mabel is really taken with him but she's already spoken for.'

'Will will be relieved to know that Doug is still in the land of the living,' said Audrey, 'being that they are such good mates.'

'Yeah, I was thinking that,' mentioned Megan. 'I'll write to him tonight and tell him all about it.'

* * *

Although there were still plenty of doodlebugs about, the war news from abroad was very heartening, and early in September the government was optimistic about an end to the hostilities on the home front quite soon.

But then one evening there was a new kind of explosion: a loud crack followed by the roar of a devastating explosion which shook the whole of west London. There was no official explanation for the noises but it was rumoured to have been a gasworks exploding. When these loud crashes were heard several times a day this seemed to be extremely unlikely.

'Gas explosions my arse,' said Bert, a round-faced, emotional man who delivered the milk to the dairy in churns. 'They're bombs of some sort. That first one was in Chiswick. I know because I live there. You should see the damage it caused.'

'Perhaps it was a particularly loud buzz bomb,' suggested Megan thoughtfully, rolling the churns into the dairy as he lifted them off his cart.

'Never in a million years. They're rockets but different altogether to the doodles,' declared Bert, who was in late middle age and very opinionated, especially about the war. He lifted his cap to scratch his head and revealed a shiny scalp without a hair on it that seemed comically at odds with the white shaving brushes he had for eyebrows. 'You've heard them so you must have realised that. They're much more powerful.'

'Well yes, I have noticed the difference, of course, but there doesn't seem to be any other explanation as we haven't been told anything officially.'

He stopped working and leaned towards her in a confidential manner.

'I get to talk to a lot of people when I'm out doing my deliveries, and I've spoken to someone who's actually seen them. He said they're even more menacing than the others. There's no warning; just a bright flash in the sky and a loud bang and a massive explosion on the ground.'

'There's been nothing on the wireless or in the papers about any new type of bombs,' Megan pointed out

'The government are keeping shtoom about this, for some reason best known to themselves.'

'Probably so that people won't panic.'

'Or because they got it wrong when they told us the bombing was almost over,' he said.

'A bit of both maybe,' she suggested. 'But we've a right to know if there's a new danger.'

'They won't tell us until it suits them; you can bet your life on it.' He was becoming more agitated with every word.

'Well there's no point us getting into a stew about it,' she suggested, hoping to calm him. 'We'll just have to wait and see what happens; there's nothing else we can do.'

'And hope that one of these new things doesn't drop on us,' he said, with a wry grin.

'Don't be so morbid, Bert,' Megan chided good-humouredly. 'You'll get me into a state if you carry on like that.'

'Sorry, love. I was just saying what I think.'

There was no doubt that the man was a purveyor of gloom, but what he said made sense on this occasion. The explosions couldn't all be down to gasworks blowing up or there would be none of them left by now. This never-ending war could tear your nerves to shreds if you let it, Megan thought worriedly.

★ ★ ★

There was always a great deal of excitement among the men in the platoon when any mail came through, and they each hoped there would be a letter for them. Will listened eagerly to the sergeant calling out the names, an ache growing in his heart as his wasn't one of them.

'Stubbs,' said the officer at last, sending Will's spirits soaring, and he tore the envelope open excitedly.

'Is it from your missus?' asked his pal as Will finished reading and put the letter back into the envelope to read again later. The other man hadn't had any mail himself.

Will nodded.

'Everything all right?'

'Yeah, she's fine.'

'Still loves you, does she?'

'Course she does. Why?'

'You're frowning,' the other man said. 'That

usually only means one thing when a bloke's had a letter.'

'No, nothing like that,' explained Will. 'She mentioned that my mate's back home and his face has taken a real battering. The poor devil.'

'Still, he's alive and home,' his companion pointed out. 'There are plenty of men buried on the battlefield who would have given a lot to have that.'

'That's true,' Will agreed. 'But on the other hand, I bet there are some people who would rather be dead than have to walk about like a freak.'

'He could be worse off,' said the soldier. 'What about all those who have lost limbs or their eyesight?'

'I won't argue with you about that,' Will was quick to point out. 'It's just that this pal is a particularly good friend. The sort you can trust with your life.'

'Can you trust him with your wife, though, that's the important question,' chortled the man.

'No question about that,' said Will without hesitation. 'I trust him one hundred per cent with everything.'

'That's all right then.'

Will drifted off into his own thoughts, remembering the huge debt he owed to Doug Reynolds. In all these years Doug had never breathed a word to anyone about the dark secret they shared. This train of thought depressed Will, because it reminded him of the past and his huge loss. Guilt engulfed him.

He would write back to Megan and ask her to

do what she could for Doug until he himself got back. Of course, she had no idea that he owed his friend anything. But she and her mum would do what they could for him anyway; that was the way they were, bless them.

Oh, what he would give to be home.

★ ★ ★

'So what have you been doing today, son?' Ida Reynolds asked when she got home from the factory to find Doug ensconced in the armchair, as usual.

'Nothing much,' he replied in a perfunctory manner.

'Been out?'

'What business is it of yours?'

'Just taking an interest,' said his mother patiently.

'Well don't,' he snapped. 'I'm a grown man and I don't want my mother checking up on me. Just lay off, will you?'

'I wasn't checking up on you, and that's no way to speak to your mother,' Ida admonished. 'What's happened to the manners I taught you?'

He leapt out of the chair and stared at her, his beady little eyes blistering with fury. 'For God's sake, woman,' he seethed. 'I am not five years old.'

'Nobody is suggesting that you are,' she said, his constant hostility towards her wearing her down. Apart from when he'd been a very small boy, he hadn't been an easy child to bring up because he'd always been so discontented with everything in his life. Since he'd been home from the war he'd been simply unbearable and she didn't know how much more she could take. She could understand his being depressed and her compassion for him knew no bounds. But it was she who took the brunt of his anger and it was punishing to the point where it actually made her feel ill. 'Though I sometimes wish you were, because you didn't have quite such a nasty temper then.'

'What do you expect me to be like?' he snarled. 'Should I be dancing around for joy and thanking God for my good looks? Is that what you expect of me?'

'You know very well it isn't.' A tall, weary-looking woman with sad brown eyes, she said in a sympathetic manner, 'Look, son, I know you've been through a lot and it's very difficult for you to come to terms with what's happened to you. No one could be sorrier for you than I am. I'm your mother and your pain is my pain, believe me. But sitting around the house on your own while your dad and I are both out at work isn't helping. All it's doing is making you more miserable and bad-tempered.'

'I'll go out if and when I want to,' he told her impatiently. 'Anyway, where the hell am I supposed to go?'

'You could go out for a walk, or even to the pub for a drink around the middle of the day,' she suggested. 'As long as you don't sit in that chair all day long brooding. The doctors have stressed the importance of facing people.'

'How would you feel if you saw what I do

every time you looked in the mirror?' he challenged her.

'You don't look that bad, son.'

'Stop lying.

'I wasn't.'

'And stop judging me.'

'Oh Doug,' she sighed. 'I'm not judging you, son. I'm just trying to help.'

'You've got a bloody funny way of showing it.'

Ida didn't reply for a moment; just tried not to let his barbs destroy her completely. She knew her son only too well, and was aware that if she allowed it to happen he would grind her into the ground until there was nothing left of her spirit. Standing up to him wasn't easy, but she had to do it.

'Look, I know you have to take your anger out on someone, and I'm the obvious person because you know your dad wouldn't stand for it for too long. That's all right if it makes you feel better, but do you have to be so horrible all the time? Couldn't you give me a break every now and then? You can be nice when you want to. You're perfectly charming to people when you do manage to shift your bum out of the chair and go out. Butter wouldn't melt then. Everybody thinks you're wonderful. I bet no one would believe me if I were to tell them what you're like when you're at home.'

'But you won't tell them, will you?' Doug said nastily. 'Because that would mean you would lose your reflected glory. You like everyone to think that you're the mother of a war hero. It gives you a bit of status round here.'

'I *am* the mother of a war hero,' she stated categorically. 'You're just not a very easy hero to live with at the moment. How you behave towards me doesn't alter my admiration for what you've suffered for your country.'

'This is home,' he told her. 'This is where I can be myself. I don't have to keep up a pretence here. God knows I need somewhere I can just let go.'

'I realise that, but surely you don't have to be so bad-tempered all the time. Don't your father and I deserve a bit of respect?'

'Oh stop moaning and put the kettle on,' he said, sitting down and picking up the newspaper.

It occurred to Ida that it wouldn't have hurt him to have had the kettle on ready for her when she got in. There was nothing wrong with his legs. He knew how hard she worked at the factory and how tired she was when she got home after a long shift. But to even hint at such a thing would send him into a rage, and she didn't have the energy to cope with any more rows. So she just took her coat off and went to the kitchen.

★　★　★

Although Doug appeared to be reading the paper, the print wasn't registering because, as usual, he was thinking about his ghastly fate. Bitterness welled up inside him; it was so strong he felt a choking sensation in his throat and wanted to punch the walls.

He calmed himself with a spot of self-congratulation for the clever way he had learned to use his appalling burden to his advantage. He had begun to realise that if he played the chirpy soldier resigned to his fate and not complaining, only occasionally seeming sorry for himself to make the performance believable, it aroused far more sympathy than allowing his real feelings to show. He could get people eating out of his hand with that sort of attitude. But he couldn't keep it up when he was at home. It was far too exhausting. Here he had to let go and be himself.

All the jokes he made about his appearance in order to seem to be coping bravely were like physical bruises, but they got people on his side to the extent that they couldn't do enough for him. So it was worth it.

But in reality, he was so full of resentment he could taste it like bile in his mouth. Why him? Why had he had to get it in the face so that he was so ugly people shrank back from him? He watched them do it; saw them trying not to look away, struggling to pretend they hadn't noticed anything out of the ordinary. So he made a joke about it; made them think he didn't mind.

Of course, Will Stubbs would come home without a mark on him, you could bet your sweet life on it. He'd always had the luck of the devil; both the twins had had that. Well, Ron's had run out prematurely, of course, but he'd had it in spades when he'd been alive. They'd had each other for a start, and that was the greatest gift anyone could have in Doug's opinion. He had always regretted being an only child. His mother couldn't have any more after him, apparently, the deformed bitch. She irritated the hell out of him.

So Will would come back flashing his good looks around while Doug had to put up with the indignity of people staring at him with revulsion, and his chances of ever getting a woman completely nonexistent. About the only way he was ever going to get any loving was by paying for it. Still, he reminded himself, he did have one hold over Will from the past, so life wasn't all bad.

His thoughts turned to Will's wife, who Doug fancied rotten. She didn't reciprocate his feelings at the moment, but she was sorry for him. So he had something to work on. But first he needed to get his feet under the table with Mrs Morgan and her daughter. He'd stayed away for a while since his last visit deliberately, because absence made the heart grow fonder, and he wanted to make sure he got a warm welcome. But it was time to go visiting again; time to turn on the charm . . .

8

Mr Griffith Jones was the headmaster of Cwmcae village school. Big Griff, as he was known by the children when he was out of earshot, ruled his small school with an iron hand, his time divided between teaching and administration, though the wartime shortage of teachers meant the balance weighed more heavily towards the former.

Nearing retirement age, he was awesome in appearance: big-built and bald, with eyes that seemed to bulge as they peered through the thick lenses of his horn-rimmed spectacles. Dedicated to education and the belief that rigid discipline was essential to the character-building of the pupils in his school, he could be extremely intimidating to those of tender years. One dark look from him was enough to make the whole of the British army quiver, let alone a group of primary-school children.

Whilst Griffith Jones was a strict disciplinarian, he was also a brilliant teacher and an avid champion of a responsive mind. If he spotted so much as a glimpse of potential in a pupil he would go to no end of trouble and time — often his own — to nurture it. As it happened, he saw plenty of it in George, whose hand was always the first to shoot up when the class was asked a question; his written work was first-rate too. And such enthusiasm for learning!

'This boy has saved my sanity,' Griffith Jones boomed to the children one day after George had excelled himself in mental arithmetic as well as reading. 'He's given me back the will to teach. Education is the greatest gift any of you can have and we take it very seriously here in Wales. I was beginning to think I was doomed to spend the rest of my days trying to stuff knowledge into empty heads that don't take in a word I say because their owners are too disinterested to listen. So let him be an example to you all.'

Naturally George was delighted. He had enjoyed school far more since he'd been in Wales than he had at home. The smaller class and personal atmosphere suited him, and it felt good to have his work noticed. Unfortunately the popularity he had found with the teacher wasn't mirrored by some of his classmates. In fact, a couple of them weren't prepared to put up with it. So they put their heads together and decided what was to be done about this incomer to their community who was stealing all the limelight.

★   ★   ★

'Where's George, I wonder?' said Netta after school the next day when she and her sister were waiting at the school gate for their cousin. The children were under strict instructions from their Aunt Hetty to come home from school together, even though they didn't have far to go.

'Dunno,' responded Poppy, 'but I hope he isn't going to be long, because I'm dying to get home. I'm starving hungry and want my tea.'

'So am I, but we'll cop it if we go without him,' Netta reminded her.

'Well I'm not waiting here all day for the little twerp,' declared Poppy after a while when he still hadn't shown up. 'I suppose we'd better go and look for him and tell him to get a move on. He must have gone back for something. We'll go round the back and look through the window to see if he's in the classroom.'

The two girls walked back across the playground towards the school building.

★ ★ ★

'Crawler,' accused one of two boys who were pinning George against the wall at the back of the school, having forced him round there on the way out. 'Crawling round Big Griff and making the rest of us look *twp*.'

'We don't want you round here,' added the other, a dark-haired boy with red cheeks and blue eyes. 'Why don't you go back to England where you belong?'

'I can't,' said the terrified George. 'We've had to come here because of the bombs.'

'Well go somewhere else,' said the boy viciously. 'There must be other places for your sort. You're not wanted in this village.'

'I'll be going home after the war.' Poor George was so frightened he felt sick and wanted to go to the lavatory. Having an overly protective mother hadn't helped him learn how to look after himself. 'It might not be long.'

'The sooner the better,' said the boy.

208

'If you've got to stay, yer you can stop sucking up to the teacher,' ordered his pal.

'I don't suck up to him,' denied George, close to tears. 'I wouldn't do that.'

'Yes you do,' argued the pal. 'You're always calling out the answers to his questions and getting your reading and writing done tidy.'

'I can't help it if I know how to do it.'

'You're not to put your hand up again with any answers at all,' commanded the first boy. 'Right?'

'And you're to stop doing good work in your exercise book,' added his pal. 'Even if you know the answers you must pretend not to, see.'

Although George was a nervous child by nature and was currently scared out of his wits, he wasn't entirely without spirit when it came to something he cared about deeply. He couldn't bear the idea of not being able to do his schoolwork properly.

'No. I won't do as you say,' he said defiantly, though his voice trembled and he had such terrible griping pains in his stomach he could hardly stand up straight.

'If you don't, you'll get plenty more of this,' said one of the boys, punching him in the face.

'And this,' said the other, doing the same.

'Oi you, leave him alone,' shouted Netta as she and her sister rushed on to the scene.

'Who's going to make us?' sneered one of the boys.

'Who do you think?'

'Two dull English girls like you?' he mocked,

cocking his head and blowing out his lips in scorn.

'That's right. You just leave our cousin alone, you rotten bullies,' demanded Netta, pouncing on the boy and dragging him away from George, while her sister took care of the other boy, both lads so taken aback by the bullish behaviour of the dainty little girls that they didn't fight back. 'Just because he's cleverer than you are you're picking on him, and you've no right. You jealous little twerps.'

'He'll put his hand up whenever he wants to and get his work right all the time because he's good at it,' announced Poppy, prodding the boy in the chest. 'If you touch him again, we'll tell Big Griff and you'll be sorry, because you're the dimmest boys in the class and he'll really give you what for.'

Fuelled with courage derived from the support of his cousins, George pushed one of the boys for good measure. 'I shall put my hand up as much as I like and you won't stop me, so there.'

'Good for you, George,' praised Netta, putting her arm around him.

'We're going home for our tea now,' Netta told the boys. 'So you two can clear off, and don't you dare be horrid to our cousin again or you know what will happen.'

Stunned by such temerity from these young members of the opposite sex, and the unexpected opposition from George, the boys went off muttering something in Welsh.

The three children walked home together, united, for once, against George's attackers.

'George is the cleverest boy in the class, Auntie Hetty,' announced Poppy that evening.

'Oh, really?' said Hetty, beaming at her son, her knitting needles clacking. 'Is that right, George?'

'No,' said George, embarrassed. 'O' course not.'

'Yes it is,' Netta chimed in. 'He's so clever that two horrible boys in our class are jealous of him and they tried to beat him up.'

'What?' gasped Hetty, her smile vanishing along with all thoughts of her son's academic success. 'Who are these boys? I'll soon sort them out.'

'We've already done it,' George told her proudly.

'Yeah, we did 'em over good and proper,' confirmed Netta. 'They won't be bothering him again.'

'Tell me who these boys are and I'll go and see the headmaster,' persisted Hetty, riled and ready to do battle, her knitting put aside. 'I'll make sure they are punished for what they've done so that they won't dare to do it again. No one beats my boy up. Oh no! You poor little thing.'

George was thrown into despair at the prospect of his mother turning up at the school. 'No, Mum, don't come, please,' he begged her. 'Everyone will think I'm a baby and a telltale if you do.'

'I should leave well alone, for the moment anyway,' advised Auntie Dil wisely. 'You don't want to embarrass the boy, now do you?'

'Well, no ... but if someone is bullying him ...'

'They're not,' claimed George quickly. 'It was only this one time.'

'Once is one time too many, George.' Hetty wasn't about to be put off when it came to the well-being of her precious son. 'I need to make sure it doesn't happen again.'

'We'll tell you if it does, Auntie,' said Poppy, who could view George's concern from a child's perspective. 'Promise.'

'There you are,' put in Auntie Dil. 'We've got the girls keeping an eye out for him. If it happens again, then you could consider going to see Mr Jones. But I don't think there's anything to worry about at the moment.'

'Mm. I suppose you're right.' Hetty still seemed doubtful, and turned to her son looking grave. 'You're to tell me if anything like this happens again, understand?'

'If he doesn't tell you, the twins will,' Dilys suggested drily. 'I doubt if much goes on at the school that those two don't know about.'

Hetty lapsed into a thoughtful silence for a few moments. 'Cleverest child in the class, eh?' she said, his achievement now fully registering. 'Well, well, isn't that just the best thing? Well done, George. I'm proud of you.'

'The teacher didn't exactly say that I was the best,' he said, blushing.

'He's always saying how good you are at schoolwork. He said you are an example, which means you're best,' said Poppy without a trace of envy. The twins were bossy towards their cousin and sometimes offhand or even spiteful. They would fight with him to the death over the last sweet in the bag, or what game they would play, but they would defend him tooth and nail against anyone else. The absence of jealousy of his scholarly achievements was mostly due to the fact that it wasn't something they aspired to themselves. In fact, they rather enjoyed the reflected glory of being related to the boy at the top of the class. 'Everybody at school knows that George is the best in the class at lessons. He gets all his sums right, and his spelling.'

'You must get your brains from your father,' said Hetty lightly. 'You certainly don't get them from me. I was never anywhere near the top of the class for anything. Average has always been my middle name.'

Suddenly she found herself with an intense longing to share this special moment with her mother and sister. They would be as proud of George as she was, and she felt sad that they were so far away. Oh well, one day we'll all be together again, she thought wistfully, and the men home too.

★ ★ ★

There were fifty prisoners in the hut, in bunks in rows of three, close together, with thin mattresses and rough, itchy blankets. It was after lights-out and most of the men were sleeping. Although Ken was bone weary, he was lying awake listening to the snoring and grunting, wishing they could have some windows open to clear the miasma of male sweat, dust, smelly socks and flatulence. He was accustomed to it, but it was particularly pungent at night.

As always before he went to sleep his thoughts turned to home and his beloved Hetty: her smile, her loving ways and the harmony that existed between them. They'd always seemed to be of the same mind about things. His last image of her was seeing him off at the gate with tears in her eyes and George in her arms. Of course George would have changed a lot by now, and Ken couldn't wait to see what sort of a boy his baby had grown into. But Hetty would still be her same lovely self.

He turned over on to his side and closed his eyes, letting the memories of her flood in until he finally dozed off.

⋆ ⋆ ⋆

'You seem a bit quiet tonight, Megan,' observed Doug, who had been invited round to the house for a game of cards by Dolly when he'd called in at the shop recently. 'Nothing wrong, is there?'

'No, I'm fine,' she replied. 'I'm busy concentrating on the game.'

'She's missing her kids, I reckon,' Dolly put in. 'It's only natural for a mother.'

Megan nodded. 'I can't deny it,' she said, actually aching with the pain of wanting to see them. 'So I'm not very good company at the moment.'

'Couldn't you go to visit them?' suggested

Doug, keen to seem helpful. 'I know it isn't the same thing as having them at home, but it might keep you going for a while.'

'That's what I keep telling her,' said Dolly.

Doug looked at Megan. 'So what's the problem?'

'I don't think it would be fair to Mum,' she told him. 'There's a lot to do here.'

'I had my leg in plaster when you went to see them last time, and we managed,' Dolly reminded her. 'Mabel won't mind doing some extra hours.'

'It means getting her to come in early to do the milk round,' Megan reminded her mother. 'It isn't fair to her. She's got her own life to lead outside of work.'

'She'll be only too glad to help out,' insisted Dolly. 'You know what a willing soul she is, and it isn't as if it happens very often.'

'There is that, but I don't want to take advantage.'

'She'll soon say no if she doesn't want to do it,' said Dolly. 'She isn't afraid to speak out. But I don't think she'll mind at all.'

'Is there anything I can do to help?' enquired Doug, relishing the opportunity to get even further into their favour.

'You're on sick leave,' Dolly reminded him. 'It's hard work in a dairy.'

'It's only my face that's injured, Mrs M,' he reminded her. 'And I'll be happy to come along and give a hand wherever you need it.'

'There you are, Megan, another helping hand,' said her mother, enthusiasm rising. 'You go and

215

see your kids and leave this place to us.'

Megan didn't hesitate for long. Her need to see her children was too great.

'How can I refuse?' she said beaming from one to the other. 'I'll go at the weekend if it can be arranged. Meanwhile, let's get on with the game, shall we? I'm planning on beating you both hands down.'

'A bit too sure of herself, wouldn't you say, Doug?' said her mother jokingly.

'Definitely,' agreed Doug, entering into the spirit of the joke because it enhanced their image of him. 'Maybe we should bring her down a peg or two.'

'Do your worst,' challenged Megan, her spirits high at the thought of the forthcoming weekend. She couldn't wait.

★ ★ ★

Megan's visit to Wales was disappointing. It rained the whole time and the village, which was so pretty in summer, was bleak in the extreme now it had passed; everywhere was wet and grey and swathed in mist. George was in bed with a cold and Hetty was too preoccupied with him to bother much with her sister. The twins seemed to have lost any notion of their mother as a figure of authority, her place having been taken by their aunt's. The process that had already begun the last time Megan had been here was now well established and inevitable, so she decided not to confuse the children by making an issue of it. Their attitude towards her was casual almost to

216

the point of indifference. They hugged her briefly when she arrived, then went off to play. Their life was here now.

Hetty was doing what she always did when George was the slightest bit off colour: fussing over him, feeling his brow at short intervals and muttering worriedly about his temperature being up.

'You'd be better off leaving him alone for a while,' advised Auntie Dil at one point. 'He's got a cold, nothing more, and feeling for a raised temperature every five minutes isn't doing him any good at all. He'll grow up thinking he's ill the whole time.'

But still Hetty nursed him as though he was at death's door. It was in her nature to do this and Megan was used to it, but Auntie Dil wasn't, so found Hetty's constant observation of her child's condition rather worrying, Megan noticed.

Megan and Hetty had a chat on their own after the children were in bed. They were alone in the house because Uncle Owen had gone across to the pub and Auntie Dil was at a ladies' gathering at the chapel. The sisters exchanged news and Hetty reassured Megan that the twins were happy and settled so she could go home with an easy mind.

'Well we didn't get the autumn victory we were expecting, did we?' mentioned Megan. 'The failure of the airborne landing at Arnhem has seen to that. People at home are still hoping it'll all be over by Christmas, though.'

'What's the bombing like up there now?'

'The doodlebugs are still coming over. We've

got these new bombs as well that arrive without warning. Just crash, bang, wallop. No time to hold your breath or take shelter. The government are denying all existence of them. But some people reckon they're rockets and that there are plenty more of them to come.'

'It isn't looking too hopeful, then?'

'Oh I wouldn't say that,' Megan assured her. 'Everyone thinks the end won't be long now, even though it keeps dragging on. Of course, there are signs of normality returning. The half-lighting is a good sign.'

'It's better than total blackout,' agreed Hetty. 'Though it doesn't make much difference to us. It's always dark at night around here since we don't have much in the way of street lighting.'

'We have to revert to total blackout if the siren goes, so the blackout curtains will have to stay up for a while longer,' Megan told her. 'But it's a positive sign, though some people think it's a letdown because they thought the lights would go on properly when they did go on again.'

'I don't suppose that will happen until victory comes,' Hetty suggested. 'Maybe it'll come by Christmas and we can have as much light as we like then.'

'On the subject of Christmas, I desperately want to have the girls home for that, though not if there are still bombs about,' Megan told her. 'We've come this far, it isn't worth taking a chance.'

Just then there was a cry from upstairs.

'Auntie Hetty,' called Poppy, sounding drowsy, as though she had just woken up.

218

'Yes, what is it, love?'

'Can I have a drink of water please?'

'Coming.' Hetty looked at Megan. 'It's only what she's got used to, love,' she tried to cheer her. 'She's half asleep and said the first name that came into her head.'

'I know.' Megan forced a smile. 'I'm not usually around, so there wouldn't be much point in calling for me.'

'You could take her drink up to her, though.'

'Yeah, I'll do it,' she said with a sinking feeling in the pit of her stomach. It was her aunt her daughter wanted, not her mother.

★ ★ ★

In all honesty, Doug wasn't much help at the dairy at a practical level because Dolly was reluctant to ask him to do anything too physically demanding. His contribution came in the form as such tasks as sweeping up, filling shelves and making tea. He even helped in the shop, though she didn't let him loose near the bacon slicer or cheese cutter.

But she enjoyed having him there because she liked his company, and was in a state of constant admiration for the way he coped with his disfigurement. It must be so hard for a young man like him, and her heart went out to him. He was so easy to get on with, she sometimes felt as though he was the son she had never had and always wanted.

'Wouldn't you rather be with people of your own age than spending time with an old codger like me?' she asked when he came round for a game of cards with her on the Saturday night.

'Not at all. Anyway, there's no one around,' he said. 'All my mates are away in the forces.'

'Mm, there is that.'

'And you're not an old codger,' he said in a deliberate attempt to please her. 'Far from it. I enjoy your company, and coming round here gets me out of my mum's hair.'

'It's nice for me to have someone to talk to, with Megan being away,' she told him. 'It stops me getting morbid, and dwelling on how much I miss my husband.'

'Aah, it must be ever so sad for you,' he said, in a manner so sympathetic, her eyes watered.

'Don't let's talk about that,' she sniffed. 'It'll only start me off. Let's talk about you and how to improve your social life.'

'I think we'll have to give that up as a bad job,' he said lightly. 'I expect I'll be going back to camp sometime soon anyway. The doctor indicated as much the last time I went to see him. The wounds are almost healed. The army don't waste any time getting you back on duty once you're on the mend. There's no chance of swinging the lead with that lot.'

'They won't send you back into the fighting, though, will they?'

He shrugged nonchalantly. 'Probably not, but it won't worry me if they do,' he said. 'I am a soldier after all. Fighting is what I'm trained for.'

'It's good that you can look at it in that light,' she said, full of admiration for him. 'Let's hope the war comes to an end soon, and then no one will have to go.'

'The end is in sight. We've definitely got the Jerries on the run. It's just a question of time now, I reckon,' he said knowledgeably. 'But until that time comes, how about you putting the kettle on?'

'Cheeky,' she grinned.

As soon as Dolly's back was turned, Doug's expression darkened into a scowl. This was what he was reduced to by his ugliness: spending Saturday night with someone old enough to be his mother when he should be out with some pretty young woman. Still, Mrs M served a purpose in that she had a very tasty daughter. There was also the fact that he was away from his deadly boring parents, whose every word and mannerism grated on his nerves.

Of course, Will's wife still wasn't interested in Doug in that way — he was fully aware of that. But pity was a very powerful emotion, and a man in his position had to use anything at his disposal to achieve his own ends. He was entitled to that much after what had happened to him for the sake of King and Country.

Some of the men he'd been in hospital with who had had similar injuries to his own had been so psychologically damaged by the way they looked they'd refused to see visitors; just hid themselves away, ashamed of their unsightliness. Doug was determined not to let that happen to him. Why should he? It wasn't his fault he'd lost his looks. If people didn't like his appearance, that was just too bad. They should get down on their knees and thank him for what he'd given for his country.

Anyway, he had a plan to work on; something that would give vent to his anger and make him feel better about everything. He had a little while left before he was taken off sick leave, so he still had time to bring it to fruition.

★ ★ ★

The journey back from Wales was dismal for Megan. The train was overcrowded, smoky and slow. She managed to squeeze in between a soldier and an elderly man, both of whom went to sleep as soon as the train was in motion. Fatigue was general among the population; you could see it everywhere. It had been a long war and people were tired, though most only admitted it in private for fear of seeming unpatriotic.

Megan was still hurting from parting from her children again. It dragged the very heart out of her, especially as they didn't seem to care if she was around or not.

She'd found it difficult to the point where she'd almost brought them back with her. But she'd known she mustn't let her personal feelings jeopardise their safety, so had managed not to give in to temptation. It was still too dangerous here, especially with the new explosions, rumoured to be the V-2 rockets that had been threatened for a long time, dropping out of the sky without warning and destroying everything in their path.

There were cancellations on the tube to Hammersmith so she joined the bus queue and had a very long wait in the rain. By the time she finally arrived home, she was cold, wet, tired and miserable.

'Hello, love,' said her mother, smiling and getting up to greet her as she came into the parlour. 'How did it go? Have you had a nice time? How are the kids?'

The depth of caring in Dolly's voice and the warmth in her eyes was too much for Megan, and she burst into tears.

'Whatever's the matter?' asked Dolly worriedly. 'What's happened?'

'Oh Mum,' Megan sobbed. 'I'm so ashamed.'

'Ashamed?' queried her mother. 'What earthly reason would you have to be ashamed?'

'It's the girls. I miss them so much, and I absolutely hate it that they turn to Hetty for everything like she was their mum, when I should be thanking God that they're happy in Wales with people who care about them.'

'Shush,' said Dolly, putting her arms around her daughter's shuddering body and holding her close. 'That's nothing to be ashamed of. It's only natural you would feel like that. Any loving mother would. But it won't be for much longer, I'm sure. Once they're back home, things will soon get back to normal.'

There was the sound of someone clearing their throat from the doorway.

'I'll be off now, Mrs M,' said Doug.

Megan stared at him in embarrassment. She'd assumed her mother was alone.

'I've been keeping your mum company while you've been away,' he explained. 'But I'll be on my way now. Leave you two alone.'

'There's no need to rush off on my account,' said Megan thickly. 'I'll be all right in a minute.'

He raised his hands in protest. 'Definitely a case of mother and daughter time,' he insisted.

'Thanks for making sure Mum didn't get lonely,' Megan said gratefully.

'And for helping me out in the dairy,' added Dolly.

'A pleasure,' he said and slipped quietly from the house.

'Such a nice boy,' remarked Dolly. 'He's so sensitive to other people's feelings.'

'Yeah, Doug's a good sort,' Megan agreed.

'Now come and sit down and tell me all about your weekend,' said Dolly, leading her daughter to the sofa. 'I'm dying to hear all the news.'

★ ★ ★

Doug was smiling to himself as he walked down the street. The fact that Megan was missing her kids was good news for him because it made her all the more emotionally vulnerable. Added to the fact that she was full of pity for him and thought he was a nice bloke meant that he practically had it in the bag. It was just a question of recognising the right moment when it arrived and seizing it.

★ ★ ★

It wasn't until the tenth of November that the public were finally given an official explanation for the thunderous explosions that had been heard all over London. The Prime Minister admitted that a new enemy weapon — a long-range rocket, the V-2 — was in operation, launched from mobile bases in Holland, and London had already been under attack for some time.

'I told yer, didn't I?' said Bert triumphantly. He was full of it when he came to deliver.

'You certainly did,' said Megan, checking the paperwork while he unloaded the churns.

'I've seen 'em with my own eyes; seen the damage they cause,' he went on. 'The government must think we're all deaf, blind and daft to think we'd swallow that story about gas explosions. It's about time they came clean, especially as these are the most lethal weapons of the war so far. It isn't as if we can take shelter, as there's no warning.'

'You're either alive or dead,' she said. 'There's no building yourself up into a state like before.'

'I suppose some people might prefer it,' he suggested.

'Not much of a choice, though, is it?' said Megan, making light of it because the man was such heavy going. 'Knowing that you might be killed, or not knowing.'

'Gawd knows where it will all end.'

'With us winning the war, of course,' stated Megan brightly. 'And it won't be long either.'

★ ★ ★

Despite Megan's inherent optimism, her hopes of having her children home for Christmas were fading, and when a Woolworth's store in Deptford was destroyed by a V-2 one Saturday morning, killing one hundred and sixty people and injuring many more, she knew she was going to need a pretty big miracle. When news came through of a German breakthrough in the Ardennes, people resigned themselves to the fact that this would be another wartime Christmas.

There were plenty of children around in London — indeed some of those killed by the Woolworth's bomb had been kiddies — but Megan couldn't justify taking such a risk for her own. She was one of the lucky ones who had a safe haven for her children with relatives, so she must let them stay where they were, however painful it was for her personally. There was no possibility of her going to Wales for the holiday because the milk still had to be delivered, every day except Christmas Day, and she wouldn't ask for help outside of the family at the festive season. Anyway, there would be no trains over the actual holiday and the service would probably be much reduced on the days around it.

December was a gloomy month with plenty of ice, frost and fog. Megan lost her way coming home from the post office when she went to post the children's Christmas parcel, then slipped on the ice. She was helped to her feet by a neighbour who was also lost. They teamed up and somehow found their way home.

Not that there was much comfort there. The

place was freezing and full of icy draughts because the windows still had no glass in them, only cardboard and mica. Megan and her mother had to drag themselves around the house in outdoor coats and scarves, saving their precious coal supply for a fire over Christmas. Being constantly cold caused aches and pains in their limbs, and they had to rub their feet to get the feeling back in them.

The festive spirit was absent everywhere, Megan noticed, right up until the middle of December, when crowds lined the main shopping streets in search of something to give as gifts. Anything worth buying needed either coupons or a bulging purse. This year their family was reduced to two for Christmas dinner. It was going to be particularly difficult for her mother; her first without Dad.

She said as much to Doug when he called into the shop a few days before the holiday. She happened to be looking after it while her mother was taking a break and Mabel had gone to the bank for change.

'It will be hard for her, no doubt about it,' said Doug with apparent understanding. 'That's the trouble with Christmas. It's miserable for people who've lost someone. It makes them feel worse.'

'What with her grieving for Dad, and me missing him as well and also pining for my kids, we'll be a right pair of miseries. Still, we'll manage to get through it somehow, I expect.'

'Have a few drinks if you can get hold of any booze,' he suggested.

'We've managed to get a couple of bottles,' she told him.

'That will ease the pain.'

She looked at him thoughtfully. 'Have you got anything special planned for Christmas Day?'

He made a face. 'No. I shall be at home with Mum and Dad all day, worse luck,' he replied. 'We'll probably be ready to murder each other by the end of it.'

'That's not very nice.'

'Well, you know how it is. There's no escape on Christmas Day, is there? Everything's closed so there's nowhere to go. Even the local is shut on Christmas night. And you can have enough of the people you live with when there isn't a break from each other.'

'You're very welcome to come round here for a few hours, if it will stop you and your folks from throttling each other,' Megan offered. 'We'll be in all day. And some company might save us from sinking into the doldrums completely.'

'I may take you up on that.'

'It'll please Mum if you did turn up,' she told him, enthusiasm growing because she knew how much her mother enjoyed having him around.

'That's nice to know.'

'You're more of a card player than I am. I get bored with it very quickly, and you know how Mum enjoys a game,' she went on. 'Anyway, the offer is there if you want it. It won't be a party, but I can promise you a nice fire and a glass of something more interesting than tea.'

'Thanks, Megan, I appreciate it.'

She smiled at him. She and her mother often

228

teased him about his having nothing to do all day while they were always busy.

'So did you come in to buy anything or just to kill some time and watch us work?' she asked in a light-hearted manner.

'To kill some time,' he admitted. 'But while I'm here, have you got any fags?'

'A few.'

'Could I have ten Weights, please?'

She reached under the counter and produced a packet of cigarettes.

'There you are,' he said, handing over a shilling piece. 'Now you can't say I'm not a bone fide customer.'

'It wouldn't matter if you weren't,' she said handing him his change. 'You know you're always welcome here. It's a long day for you without anyone to talk to.'

She liked Doug as a friend, and understood that it was sheer loneliness that drove him round to the dairy so often. All his mates were away and he didn't have a girlfriend, so the dairy house was a bolthole for him. It was an added pleasure for her to know that Will would be pleased that she and her mother were providing his pal with somewhere to go and helping him through his sick leave.

Just then Dolly appeared from the door behind the counter.

'Hello, Doug,' she greeted warmly. 'Are you fed up with your own company again?'

'That's right, Mrs M,' he replied. 'You're getting to know me too well.'

'You're always welcome.'

'I've invited him to call round on Christmas Day if he feels like a break,' Megan informed her mother.

'Good. That will be lovely,' Dolly approved, smiling at him. 'I quite fancy beating you hands down at cards.'

'You'll have a job,' he quipped.

'Don't you be so sure.'

'Never in a million years will you give me a pasting,' he chuckled.

'Let's wait and see, shall we?'

He lit a cigarette as a flurry of customers came into the shop. 'Well, I'll leave you ladies to get on with your work,' he said breezily. 'See you.'

'See you, Doug,' said mother and daughter, turning their attention to their customers as he headed for the door.

Outside the shop, Doug drew hard on his cigarette pleasurably, congratulating himself on his cleverness in having obtained an open invitation for Christmas Day. How to get the old girl out of the way for a while so that he could be alone with her daughter; that was the only problem.

9

Dolly awoke early on Christmas morning to find herself racked by the full gamut of flu symptoms. Her throat hurt, her head throbbed, her legs felt as though she'd just walked ten miles in four-inch heels, and she couldn't get warm even though her skin was burning.

'It's probably just a heavy cold starting,' she suggested somewhat unconvincingly to Megan. Dolly had managed to drag herself out of bed and go downstairs to the kitchen to make the porridge for breakfast, even though she was shivering and sweating simultaneously. 'But oh dear, I do feel rotten. What a bloomin' fine time to go down with something.'

'Aah, it's bad luck,' Megan sympathised as she made the tea. 'But don't stay down here feeling awful. Take a couple of aspirin and go back to bed. I'll bring you up a hot-water bottle and anything else you need.'

'I'll be all right once I get going. I don't want to make a fuss unnecessarily,' insisted her mother.

'You wouldn't know how,' Megan smiled. 'You're obviously too poorly to be up and about so you might as well make the most of the fact that the shop isn't open and take it easy. I'll see to everything down here.'

'I can't spend Christmas Day in bed.' Dolly was appalled at the idea. 'It wouldn't be right.'

'If you're not well, you need to be in bed whatever day of the year it is,' her daughter pointed out. 'Anyway, there's only the two of us, so you won't be missing much.'

'I'm not worried about that. It's just that I don't want to leave you to celebrate the day on your own. Christmas Day is special even if there are only the two of us, and I need to be up and about. A couple of aspirin will soon shake it off.'

But as the morning progressed there was no improvement, and after an alarming dizzy spell at the table as she struggled to eat some of the shepherd's pie Megan had cooked for Christmas dinner, Dolly was forced to admit defeat.

'I'm sorry to desert you today of all days, love,' she said as her daughter tucked her up in bed with a hot-water bottle. 'I'll do my best to get up later on.'

'There's no need,' Megan tried to convince her. 'You stay there until you're well enough to get up, even if that isn't until after we've opened up for business again. Meanwhile, let me pamper you. Would you like anything?'

'Nothing, thanks, love,' Dolly said, shivering and snuggling gratefully under the covers. 'I just want to go to sleep if my aching limbs will let me.'

'The last dose of aspirin should take effect soon and perhaps you'll doze off then. I'll be up again in a little while to see how you are. If you want anything before then, just bang hard on the floor with this shoe and I'll come straight up,' Megan said, taking one of her mother's shoes out of the wardrobe and putting it on the floor beside the bed. 'I won't hear you if you call down with the walls being so thick, and for goodness' sake don't make yourself worse by getting up and coming downstairs to get what you want.'

'You'll probably be fed up of running up and down the stairs after me.'

They both knew that wasn't true. Dolly would never take liberties with anyone, no matter how ill she was. But Megan said jokingly, 'I'll soon tell you if that happens, don't worry.'

★   ★   ★

Back downstairs, Megan washed the dishes and cleared up in the kitchen, then settled in the armchair by the parlour fire with her legs extended so that her feet were close to the flames. She'd been looking forward to sitting by the fire for weeks and it didn't disappoint. Having been cold to the bone for so long, it was sheer bliss to have warm feet again, even though the direct heat made her chilblains itch and throb like mad. The sight of the orange flames rising gently was pleasurable and relaxing, as was the sound of the wireless playing low in the otherwise silent house. The light was already fading fast with the advancing afternoon, and as she sat there in the darkening room her thoughts turned inevitably to her children. She hoped they'd enjoyed the day and wanted to weep with love for them.

She was recalled to the present by a knock at the front door.

'Doug,' she said, surprised to see him standing

there, having forgotten all about the casual invitation. 'Happy Christmas! Come on in.'

'I was feeling a bit stifled at home,' he explained, putting his army cap on the hall stand and following her into the parlour, 'so I thought I'd take you up on your invitation rather than listen to my father snoring in his chair.'

'I'm glad you did,' she told him. 'Perhaps some company will stop me sinking into despair over the absence of my children. Mum isn't feeling well so has had to go to bed.'

'Oh, poor old Mrs M,' he said with feigned concern, though he was hardly able to believe his luck. 'I'm sorry to hear that.'

'Yeah, it's tough luck to be ill on the one day of the year the shop is closed and she could have relaxed and enjoyed herself.'

'Nothing serious, I hope.'

'No, just a touch of flu, we think,' she informed him. 'Knowing my mother, she'll be up and about again tomorrow.'

'Let's hope you're right,' he said, silently offering thanks to Dolly for her beautifully timed absence.

'Anyway, would you like a cup of tea?' Megan paused, looking at him with a half-smile. 'Or something stronger, perhaps, as it's Christmas Day. I know the afternoon isn't really the time for alcohol, but I think it would be acceptable as it's the festive season. We can drink a toast to absent friends.'

'You won't catch me saying no to a drop of booze at Christmas, whatever time of day it is,' he said in a jovial manner.

'I don't have a huge selection, but we did manage to get some gin, though nothing to go with it, some port and sherry and a few bottles of beer for when people call in over the holiday.'

'A drop of gin will do me nicely, ta. I like it neat.'

'Coming up,' she said and went over to the sideboard to pour a gin for him and a sherry for herself.

'Cheers,' she said, raising her glass. 'Here's hoping this really will be the last wartime Christmas.'

'It better had be or we'll all want to know why.' Doug chinked his glass against hers.

'Here's to loved ones who can't be here with us. To Will, to my mum upstairs, all the children, and my sister and her husband Ken.' Her voice broke as she added, 'And last but not least my dear departed dad.'

'Cheers,' he said, swigging his drink with relish.

Megan put her lips to her glass but was suddenly overtaken by emotion which sent tears streaming down her cheeks. 'Sorry,' she said, her voice breaking into a sob. 'Christmas is a terrible time for opening up the floodgates.'

'Don't apologise,' he said with feigned understanding. 'You have a good cry. It might make you feel better.'

'You're so kind, Doug.' She sat down and looked at him gratefully, drying her eyes and composing herself. 'That means a lot to me.'

Like hell I'm kind, you silly cow, he thought, but said, 'I'm glad.' He finished his drink. 'May I help myself to another?'

'Of course. Have as much as you like.'

He poured himself a large one and put the bottle on the table by his chair.

'Are you feeling a bit better now?' he asked, sipping his drink and beginning to feel the soothing effects of the alcohol kicking in.

She nodded. 'Nothing will make the pain of missing Will go away, though. It's something I have to live with; me and millions of other woman. He's everything to me, you see.'

Another gin was poured and consumed at speed. Doug needed it if she was going to start going on about her precious husband. 'I'm sure he is,' he said, pouring yet another drink.

'You'll get tipsy, the way you're knocking them back,' Megan remarked lightly.

He frowned. 'I thought I was welcome to have what I wanted.'

'You are. I was only teasing,' she assured him. 'But I don't want to have to carry you home. I'm not built for it.'

'You won't have to do that, I promise,' he said, downing more drink, confidence growing with every sip.

'Good.' Megan's thoughts were of Will and she wanted to talk about him, presuming Doug would welcome it as her husband was the reason she and Doug were friends. 'If Will was here he could carry you home, no trouble. He was a really strong man.'

'Mm.' Another swallow of gin to kill the pain of her admiration for Will.

'I wonder if he's still the strong man I

remember,' she said in a contemplative manner. 'The hardship's bound to have taken its toll on him.'

'He'll be all right,' Doug said dismissively, nastiness creeping into his tone as the alcohol took control. 'Will Stubbs always falls on his feet. If he was in the middle of the desert with men dying all around him he'd be the one to find water. Everything goes that bloody man's way. It's enough to make you spit.'

'Doug!' Megan exclaimed, shocked by this side of him she hadn't seen before. 'I thought you were supposed to be his best mate.'

He took another swig of gin. 'He only ever had one best mate and that was his twin brother.'

'But his brother died.'

'And precious little good it did me,' he said.

'Why should it do you good? I don't understand.'

'I thought that he'd turn to me when Ron died, but his twin was always still there in his head, even when he was with me.'

'That's only natural; they were twins. He'll always be in Will's thoughts until the day he dies,' she said. 'As his wife I know I have to expect that and not be jealous.'

'It was always Will and Ron when we were kids,' Doug went on, ruled now by inebriation and uncaring of the consequences of this conversation. 'I was always just the hanger-on, the outsider, and I hated them for that.'

'Why did you still go about with them then?'

'I admired them; liked being seen with them. Everyone knew the Stubbs twins; we all wanted to be like them. They were good looking and daring and there were two of them, which made them even more special. I was grateful that they let me tag along. It gave me standing with the others that I wouldn't have otherwise had. But it wasn't enough. I wanted to mean something to them and I couldn't make it happen no matter how hard I tried to impress them. They didn't care if I was around or not because they had each other. The friendship was all on my side. I did all the running.' He paused, draining his glass and pouring another drink. When he spoke, it seemed to Megan almost as though he was thinking aloud. 'When Ron died I thought it would be different and I'd be Will's best mate.'

'And so you were,' said Megan, hoping to placate him. 'You were best man at our wedding anyway.'

'I was still only tolerated by him.' His speech was slow now and full of self-pity. 'No one could take Ron's place.'

Megan was irritated by Doug's pathetic whining but deemed it wise to be cautious, because he was rather frightening in this mood. 'Maybe not, but you've been his best mate since I've known him, anyway.'

'Only because he doesn't have a choice.'

'Oh? Do you have some sort of hold over him then?' she asked, inwardly shaking from this unexpected turn of events but needing to know more as it concerned her husband.

'Yeah, I sure do.'

'What is it, Doug? As his wife I think I should know.'

He didn't reply; just stared ahead as though reliving some past event. 'I was there when his brother died,' he said after a while, still not looking at her. 'I know what really happened, so he has to stay on the right side of me in case I spill the beans.'

'But his brother died in a drowning accident, didn't he?'

'That's the official explanation.'

'Meaning . . . ?'

'He drowned, but it wasn't an accident,' Doug explained. 'Your *wonderful* husband pushed him off the bridge into the river.'

His fist in her face couldn't have had more impact, and she reeled from the shock. 'Are you saying that Will killed his own brother?' she asked in disbelief.

He looked at her, bleary-eyed. 'I'm saying that Ron didn't just slip and fall into the river as people think. I was there so I know, but I am the only other person besides Will who does. That's why he daren't cross me.'

'I'm sure Will didn't mean to kill his brother.'

'Of course he didn't.' Doug was belligerent now. 'They were larking about on the bridge as boys do and Will accidentally pushed against Ron, which caused him to lose his balance and fall.'

'Why didn't Will tell the truth at the time?'

'Because I told him not to,' he said in a boastful tone, relishing the influence he had found over Will. 'We were just kids and he was in a hell of a state. As no one saw what happened I suggested that it would be best not to mention the fact that he was responsible for Ron's fall because he'd have people blaming him for the rest of his life for something he hadn't meant to do.' He smiled horribly. 'He fell for it and for the first time I had power over him. Once he'd gone along with it there was no going back, so I could make him be my mate.'

'That's wicked.'

'Yeah, I know.' He seemed to take it as a compliment. 'It felt really good, especially as he wasn't to blame for Ron's death at all.' He looked at her, his lips curling into a smile. 'It was me. I killed Ron.'

For a moment Megan couldn't speak. 'Are you going to tell me what happened?' she asked at last, lips dry and heart pounding.

'Might as well,' he said drunkenly. 'When Ron fell into the water, Will went in after him to try and save him. I jumped in as well. Will hit the water awkwardly and was under for a while, during which time Ron came up.' He looked into space. 'At last I could see a way I could stop being just tolerated by both twins and be a real pal to one of them.' He paused. 'I pushed Ron under and held him down. I realised I shouldn't have done it and stopped, expecting him to come up to the surface, but he didn't. Will didn't see what I'd done so thought his brother had gone under as a result of what happened on the bridge. It didn't suit me to enlighten him.'

'You've let Will suffer for all these years, blaming himself for his twin's death,' Megan said, appalled, leaping to her feet and staring at him, her eyes blazing.

'He hasn't suffered. The whole thing was written off as an accident. There was no blame attached.'

'Not by anyone else, but plenty from Will himself. He's tortured himself all these years. I've always known he was deeply troubled by Ron's death. I've seen it in his eyes and felt it coming between us. I thought it was just that he was still missing his brother. Now I know the truth. Poor Will. Fancy having to live with something like that on your conscience when there was no need. You murderer; you filthy, rotten murderer!'

'I'm glad I made him suffer. I'd been in his shadow for long enough,' Doug said. 'Anyway, I've got my punishment. A face like mine is more than enough for anyone to bear. Do you know what it feels like to be so ugly people don't want to look at you?'

'I thought you'd come to terms with it.'

'Of course I haven't, you silly cow; that was all just an act to get sympathy,' he told her. 'Which I bloody well deserve for the misery I have to suffer every single day of my life.'

'You're evil,' she rasped furiously, leaning over and slapping him around the head. 'You're only getting what you deserve after what you've done to my husband and his brother.'

'Ooh, nice, I like a woman with spirit,' he said, getting up and grabbing her in a grip from which there was no escape. 'I fancied the look of you as soon as I clapped eyes on you. Why should Will Stubbs have all the good things in life while I have to live with a face everyone turns away from? I want everything he has . . . especially his wife.'

She was rendered helpless against his superior strength as he forced her down on to the sofa. The scream she managed to emit before he rammed his fist into her mouth went unheard in the big old house as her mother slept upstairs.

★ ★ ★

Megan sat by the parlour fire in the dark, looking unseeingly into the flames, feeling sick and shaky in the aftermath of what had happened. It was just as well that her mother was still sleeping, because she would have questioned her daughter's motive in using precious hot water for an extra bath. It was the only thing Megan could think of to do to make herself clean, albeit with only the permissible five inches of water. The effects of the carbolic soap hadn't helped and she doubted if she would ever feel properly clean again.

The callousness of the rape had been astounding. Clinically brutal was the only way to describe it, and it had left her feeling isolated and different; as though she had been separated from normality by the disgusting onslaught which now set her apart from other people.

Seeming to sober up, Doug had stood over her afterwards and warned her of the consequences if she breathed a word to anyone of what had taken place that afternoon.

'If you tell anyone what I told you about Ron's death, I shall tell Will that you slept with me, that you pestered me until I gave in,' he'd threatened, and he had never looked uglier, his skin tight and his beady eyes gleaming with malice in their scarred surroundings. 'You won't be able to deny what happened between us because it did.'

'I shall tell him it was rape,' she'd managed to utter, even though she was terrified and distraught. 'In fact I can have you done for rape this very day.'

'You couldn't bear the shame.'

'I've done nothing wrong,' she'd reminded him. 'Why should I be ashamed?'

'It's the way it works,' he'd told her smugly as she sat shivering and cowering from him in the corner of the sofa, pale with shock, her hair askew but her skirt pulled down firmly over her knees. 'How it happened doesn't matter, only that it did. You won't want people to know because it will change the way they see you. You can go ahead and tell Will, you can tell the police. I shall say you wanted it and it will be your word against mine. You'll be the one with the ruined reputation, not me. It's a man's world.'

'My husband will believe me.'

'You won't take the risk of telling him,' he stated with confidence. 'You know there'll always be an element of doubt in his mind, however much he might want to believe you. It's the way men are; they can't help it. It will eat away inside him until he can't even bear to look at you, let alone touch you. Your marriage will be on the rocks and there won't be a thing you can do

243

about it. For all your brave talk, you won't risk it.'

'If you think I'll let Will go on suffering for something he didn't do, you are mistaken.'

'Do what you like,' he'd said. 'As long as you're prepared to lose your marriage and your good name. Anyway, no one would believe you about Ron's death. I'd make damned sure of it. Everyone would hate you for dragging it all up again and upsetting Will's mother. She's always been very fond of me.'

'Get out and don't come round here ever again,' Megan said.

'I'm going back to the army after Christmas anyway, so I won't be in the area,' he'd told her, and left.

For a long time she hadn't been able to move; just sat there shivering and feeling sick, until she'd at last found the strength to go and run a bath.

She still felt very frightened and never wanted to see Doug again. He'd violated her body to satisfy his need to hurt Will because he was insane with jealousy of him. She'd been used in an obscene and cruel act.

The sound of the telephone cut into her thoughts. It jarred on her shattered nerves and her legs felt weak and shaky as she got up, turned on the light and went to answer the phone in the shop. The operator said she had a long-distance call for her. After a lot of crackling and buzzing Megan heard Hetty's voice.

'Happy Christmas, sis.'

'Same to you, Hetty.'

'I've got the twins here with me.' Megan could just about hear her against the hissing on the line. 'They want to wish you a happy Christmas.'

'Oh, how lovely.' Her mouth was parched and she was still trembling from the effects of her ordeal but did her best to sound normal. 'Put them on.'

'Happy Christmas, Mummy.'

'Happy Christmas, Netta,' she said thickly.

'Love you, Mum.'

'Love you too.'

Then Poppy came on the line and the brief dialogue was repeated. Then Hetty came back on to say that they were in the phone box as the pub was shut. The money was running out and she didn't have any more change, but would Megan pass on her love to their mother.

Megan replaced the receiver and went back to the fire, shivering from the bitter cold in the shop, and with tears flowing uncontrollably. The sound of her children's voices had been the best Christmas present she could have had, but she felt distanced from them; emotionally separated from her children because of the wickedness of Doug Reynolds.

She leaned forward towards the hearth with her elbows on her knees and her head in her hands, mulling things over and trying to find a way forward. There didn't seem to be one. Her life as she'd known it had been shattered here in this very room earlier this afternoon.

Turning it over in her mind, she reminded herself that she had been brought up to believe that you carried on no matter what adversity life threw at you. You didn't whinge and make a fuss; you just put up with it because nothing was sent that you couldn't cope with. She knew in her heart that no matter how terrible she felt, somehow she had to pick herself up and put the awful incident behind her. Women had been doing that over this kind of violation since time began.

Somehow this thing had to be fought; she couldn't allow Doug Reynolds to ruin her life. So — however much she might want to — she would not hide away in a corner licking her wounds. It wasn't possible anyway because she had too many responsibilities. There were people relying on her: her children, her husband, and her mother. They needed her and she wasn't going to let them down just because she didn't know which way to turn.

The sound of banging on the ceiling broke into her thoughts and she hurried upstairs.

'How are you feeling now, Mum?' she asked, noticing how flushed Dolly looked.

'A bit rough, love. But I've managed to have a sleep so that's helped a bit. Sorry to bother you, but would you mind bringing me up some more aspirin?'

'Course I don't mind.' Megan lifted her mother up gently and plumped her pillows, which were warm from her fevered skin. 'What about something to drink?'

'Just water, love, thanks. Tea tastes funny when you're not well.'

'We'll have a few drinks together when you're feeling better,' said Megan. 'Christmas has been

246

postponed this year; not cancelled altogether.'

'That'll be nice. It's a bit miserable for you down there on your own, though,' Dolly said, obviously not having heard anything of their visitor, much to her daughter's relief.

'No it isn't, as it happens. I'm enjoying a day of relaxation,' Megan assured her. 'I had a nice surprise because Hetty rang up and put the twins on the phone. She sent her love.'

'Aah, I'm sorry I missed that.'

'It was a very brief call. I didn't have a chance to say anything to Hetty before the money ran out.'

'Nice that they phoned, though.'

Megan nodded. 'It made my day.'

'Anything else happened while I've been asleep?'

There was only a brief hiatus before Megan said, 'No, nothing at all. I've been toasting my toes by the fire and enjoying the fact that it's warm down there for a change.'

'As long as you're all right.'

Megan knew she wouldn't ever be all right again, but she said, 'Course I am.'

As she made her way back down the stairs, she thanked her lucky stars that the house had thick walls and ceilings. Her mother would be devastated if she was to get so much as an inkling of what had happened to her daughter on Christmas afternoon of 1944. Fortunately there was no reason for her, or anyone else, to know. This was something Megan was going to have to live with on her own.

'Did you have a good Christmas, Mrs Morgan?' enquired Mrs Tucker from across the road. She was a regular customer, a good one too because she had a big family.

'No, not really.' It was a few days after Christmas, and Dolly was feeling much better. 'I spent most of it in bed with the flu.'

'That was bad luck, going down with that when you've got some time off,' said the other woman. 'But it was a funny old Christmas for most of us, I think, with people having sons away, and kiddies evacuated, especially as we'd hoped to have peace by Christmas. We've all had enough of the war; I know I have.'

Dolly nodded in agreement. 'Mind you, I felt so rotten on Christmas Day, I wouldn't have cared if a bomb had dropped on me, to be perfectly honest,' she said.

'You must have been bad then.'

'I was. Poor Megan was all on her own,' Dolly went on. 'It was so different last year. We had a house full then, except for the girls' husbands. This year it was just Megan and me, and I was out of action.'

'Good job Megan had a bit of company on Christmas afternoon then, wasn't it?' mentioned Mrs Tucker.

'Company?' Dolly was puzzled. 'She didn't have any. That's what I'm saying. I was upstairs in bed so she was on her own.'

'That friend of her husband's came to visit, though, didn't he?' Mrs Tucker mentioned. 'The one with the scarred face. I just happened to see him arrive when I went to the window to draw the curtains because it was getting dark.'

'Oh . . . I'd forgotten about Doug,' fibbed Dolly because she didn't want to appear not to know what was going on in her own household. She wondered why Megan hadn't mentioned it and would ask her when she came into the shop from the dairy. 'He did pop in, so that broke it up for her.'

'Anyway, at least we got some extra fat and sugar rations for the holiday,' said the customer. 'So it wasn't all bad.'

'That's true.'

'Roll on peacetime, I say.'

'Hear, hear,' said Dolly. 'Now then, dear, what can I get for you today?'

*　*　*

'Shall I make some tea, Mum?' suggested Megan, coming into the shop.

'Mabel has just gone to do it,' said Dolly, who was wearing outdoor clothes, even a woolly hat and mittens. 'Anything to try and keep warm. It's murder in this shop without the paraffin heater. There are icy draughts everywhere.'

'How long will it be before we can get some paraffin?' Megan enquired.

'At least another couple of weeks,' Dolly told her. 'The fuel ration doesn't last any time in this weather. It isn't much better in the house either. We'll have to go to bed fully dressed again.'

'It is certainly freezing in here with customers

coming in and out all the time,' said Megan, shivering. 'Have you been busy?'

'On and off as usual,' Dolly replied. 'You get nobody, then everyone comes at once, though people were stocked up for the holiday as far as they could be and that keeps them going for a while.' She paused, remembering something. 'Oh, by the way, Mrs Tucker from across the road has been in and just happened to mention that Doug came calling at the house on Christmas afternoon. I was surprised you didn't say anything.'

Megan felt the blood rush to her cheeks. 'Sorry, Mum. It must have slipped my mind with you being ill in bed,' she lied. 'You were asleep a lot and by the time you were feeling well enough to take notice I must have forgotten all about it.'

'I've been wondering why he hadn't called in to see us over the holiday,' said Dolly.

'He sent you his best wishes,' Megan told her. 'He's going back to the army, so he won't be around for a while.'

'Oh, that's a shame. I'd have liked to see him before he went,' Dolly said, looking disappointed. 'Still, never mind. It wasn't his fault I was in bed when he came.'

Megan felt terrible. She'd only been back in the shop about five minutes and she'd already lied to her mother. She was normally a straightforward sort of person and hated dishonesty of any kind. How many more times was she going to have to tell lies to avoid revealing what had happened?

The sooner the truth about Ron's death was

out in the open, the better, and Will must be the first to know. After that it was up to him who else he passed it on to. It wasn't the sort of thing you could say in a letter, though. Would Megan have the courage to risk everything by telling him when the time came?

10

Public morale was boosted somewhat as the new year of 1945 got underway and news came through from abroad of a more cheerful outlook on the Western Front. But nothing much changed on the streets of London as the V bombs continued to be a danger, shortages were still crippling and the weather was freezing.

'I'll be glad when my ol' man comes home to keep me warm in bed,' said one of the shop's regulars, Gertie.

'Me an' all,' added another customer. 'I woke up in the night and my feet were like blocks of ice.'

'A hot-water bottle is no substitute for a warm-blooded man,' said someone else. 'And I don't just mean to warm your feet on.'

The crowd in the shop roared with laughter. It was a busy time of day because housewives usually made the shopping one of their first jobs. This particular group of punters enjoyed some social intercourse while they shopped, and Dolly joined in the fun while she worked. Their lively conversation sometimes got a bit risqué, but she took it all in good part. As a shopkeeper of long standing, she had learned to be very adept at matching her mood to the present company.

'Mind you,' continued Gertie, grinning, 'it's so ruddy cold in my house because of the coal shortage, I have to go to bed in my outdoor clothes — coat, scarf, gloves, hat; the full range — so if my ol' man were to come home and have any ideas, he'd lose interest by the time that lot came off.'

'It would take more than a few winter clothes to dampen my husband's ardour,' said another cheery soul. 'I reckon he could get through a suit of armour in ten seconds flat.'

Another burst of raucous laughter.

'You never know, ladies, it might be summer by the time they come home,' suggested Mabel, who was at the cheese-cutter, slicing someone's cheese ration with the wire. 'You can give 'em a real treat then and wear your very best birthday suit.'

'You saucy young pup,' admonished Gertie laughingly.

'It's working in this shop that's made her come out with that sort of thing,' intervened Dolly, who was weighing up some broken biscuits on the scales. 'She was a proper little innocent when she first came to work here. Until you lot corrupted her.'

'Us corrupt her? That's a good one,' said a woman in a dismal brown coat and matching felt hat with a woollen scarf tied over it. 'I've seen her with that boyfriend of hers when he meets her from work. Cor blimey, I thought she was going to swallow him whole the other night. It looked to me as though he was the one who needed the suit of armour. Innocent my eye!'

'You're only young once,' retaliated Mabel, enjoying the joke. 'He's going away in the army

253

soon so I want to make the most of him while he's here.'

'You were certainly doing that when I saw you,' grinned the woman. 'Phew, not half!'

'With a bit of luck, your young man might miss the fighting,' remarked Dolly more seriously. 'We keep being told it won't be long now, so by the time they've trained him up, it could be all over.'

'I hope so. I can't bear the thought of him getting hurt . . . or worse,' said Mabel.

'He's a nice-looking lad,' remarked someone.

'He's more than just nice, he's gorgeous,' agreed Mabel wholeheartedly. 'Couldn't you just eat him?'

'I'd sooner have a nice hot dinner,' chuckled Gertie. 'That's what comes of not being seventeen any more.'

'You want to make sure you don't end up eating for two, my girl,' one of the others warned Mabel in a light-hearted manner. 'The way you're carrying on.'

At that moment there was an almighty crash that shook the shop and left the people in there whey-faced and trembling. No one spoke as echoing rumbles filled the air in the aftermath. Before they'd had time to gather their wits, an ashen-faced Megan burst in through the door behind the counter.

'Phew, that was close,' she said shakily. 'I've just come to see if you're all right.'

'We're still here,' said Dolly. 'Only just, though.'

'Just when we start talking about it being all

over, we get one of those to remind us that the Jerries aren't quite beaten yet,' observed Gertie.

Megan went to the shop door and out into the street, followed by the others.

'Well, there's no sign of anything in the immediate vicinity, so it couldn't have been as near as it sounded,' she observed. 'I thought it was right on top of us.'

'Bloomin' things. I reckon these V-2s are the most evil bombs of the war,' opined someone. 'As least with the others you had a warning, and time to take shelter.'

A discussion ensued about the rating of the various bombs as they all trooped back into the shop. But Megan wasn't listening. She was thinking that just when she was beginning to feel it might be safe to bring her children home, something happened to change her mind.

★   ★   ★

When news came through in March that British troops had crossed the Rhine, there was a genuine sense of imminent victory. Peace in Europe now seemed within reach, especially as restrictions were gradually being lifted and Union Jacks were on sale on the streets of London. People were still a little circumspect because of the setbacks of the past, but the papers were extremely optimistic and predicted that it was now only a matter of weeks until the final collapse of the Nazis.

Another crop of V bombs and the sudden return of piloted enemy bomber planes was disappointing, but was generally believed to be the Nazis' final desperate attempt to make life as hard as possible for civilians before their inevitable defeat. Yet still Megan didn't feel confident enough to bring her children home. These latest raids might well be the finale, but they were still lethal.

It wasn't until around Easter time that she began to be more positive. It was hard to be otherwise with the sirens falling silent and the papers full of promise that the war years were over and victory in Europe might come at any moment. Even the weather was in tune with the mood of optimism. The streets were shabby, but here and there fresh green shoots were coming up, and the street barrows had daffodils for sale.

Then came the news of the death of President Roosevelt. People were shocked and saddened, even those who were more concerned with getting their evacuated children home than with politics. People stood in the streets staring at the newspaper headlines. Few could forget the darkest days of the conflict, when the President's reassuring voice had come over the radio late at night. The fact that it was so close to the end of the war made his passing all the more poignant, and the last thing anyone had expected.

Despite the crushing blow, the signs of forthcoming victory were everywhere. When Megan saw some workmen pulling down the surface shelters, she knew that it was time to bring the evacuees home. At last she was going to be reunited with her darling children, and they would all be together to celebrate peace when it was officially declared. Thank God!

★ ★ ★

It wasn't the reunion of her dreams, with the twins ecstatic to be home and hugging her as though they never wanted to let her go. Quite the opposite: they seemed bewildered and strained, not particularly pleased to be back either.

A week or so after their homecoming Megan was almost at her wits' end. They were awkward and rude, wouldn't do a thing she told them, and referred to Hetty for everything.

'You're home now,' Hetty constantly reminded them. 'Your mum is in charge. She's the one to ask, not me.'

'I don't like it here,' Netta complained. 'I want to go back to Wales.'

'I want to see Auntie Dil,' wailed her sister.

'There's nowhere to play here.' This was Netta.

'What's wrong with the street?' asked their mother. 'That's always been good enough before, and most of your friends are back from the country now.'

'Our friends are in Cwmcae.'

'Yes, I realise that you made new friends there and you're sad to leave them, but you've got lots here too, and you've got each other. Perhaps we might all be able to go to Wales for a holiday when things settle down after the war,' Megan suggested patiently. 'But this is your home again now. You only went away because the bombing was so bad.'

'Me and Pops would sooner live there,' Netta informed her.

Megan reeled from the pain of the words. She'd longed to have her little ones home again, and the last place they wanted to be was here with her.

'They'll settle down in time,' advised her mother when the two of them were on their own. 'You'll need to be firm with them, though. You're treading on eggshells at the moment and letting them get away with murder.'

'I know. It's just that . . . I don't want to be telling them off all the time when they've been away for so long,' Megan told her. 'I want to make a fuss of them. It seems such a long time since I was able to. I've missed them so much, Mum.'

'I know, love,' soothed her mother. 'I've been looking forward to having them home myself, and a bit of spoiling won't do them any harm at all. But you need to re-establish your authority as well. Be the mum you were before they went away; the one who loved them but wouldn't stand any nonsense. They're bound to be unsettled, having been so disrupted. But they're running rings around you. You need to toughen up a bit.'

Megan knew that her mother was right, but acting on her advice wasn't easy for someone who had been parted from her children and whose whole life had revolved around having them back. She was unnerved to realise that she felt inadequate to the job of discipline. It was as though she'd lost her confidence and skills as a parent.

It didn't help to be told by Hetty on a regular basis how happy and well behaved the twins had been in Wales, once they'd settled down there.

'I had no trouble with them at all,' she had a habit of saying quite often. 'Angels, the pair of them.'

Angels wasn't a word that sprang readily to mind in relation to the twins as they were at the moment, so Megan said, 'Do you mean all the time?'

'They had their moments, of course, like all children, but most of the time they were good; not nearly as naughty as they are when they're here anyway. It's a different environment, you see; a healthier way of life altogether. George thrived on it; he didn't get ill much at all. And of course the twins were in their element with all that freedom and fresh air.'

Dolly was the first to buckle under the constant barrage of enthusiasm for Wales.

'Well you're back here now,' she reminded Hetty one morning when they'd been back a couple of weeks and her daughter was extolling the virtues of country life yet again. They were in the kitchen, where Dolly was making the porridge for breakfast. 'These far-off country places are pretty and all the rest of it, but London has a spirit all of its own, and you're a part of it whether you like it or not.'

'Meaning?'

'Meaning that things haven't been quite so

wonderful for us here, with bombs dropping and us having to keep the dairy going despite everything, so give the green, green grass of Wales a rest, will you, and come back down to earth here in Hammersmith at Morgan's Dairy, our family business, remember.'

'I didn't mean . . . ' Hetty coloured up. 'Look, I had to stay there with the children. I couldn't leave George. I just couldn't do it. You know that.'

'And nobody is suggesting otherwise,' said her mother.

'I've been working while I was there, you know. I didn't sit on my bum all day doing nothing. And I have been looking after the three children.'

'Mum knows that,' Megan intervened. 'But you have been hammering on rather a lot about Wales. It does get a bit tedious after a while.'

'Sorry, I thought you'd be interested,' Hetty said haughtily. 'It is where Dad came from, after all.'

'We are interested, of course we are,' Dolly assured her. 'In reasonable doses. We don't want it for breakfast, dinner and bloomin' tea. Now let's have a bit of normality around here if you please. The girl we took on to replace you is leaving on Friday, so we need you back at work properly, and if we all behave normally perhaps the children will start to settle down.'

Megan had rarely seen her mother so authoritative. She was really beginning to come into her own as Dolly Morgan now, rather than just Dai the milkman's wife. Megan was proud of her. Hetty was much less impressed and commented on it when they were upstairs on their own, making the beds.

'Mum's getting to be a bit stroppy, isn't she?' she said, plumping George's pillows. 'What's brought all that on?'

'Nothing in particular, and she isn't being stroppy. She's learning to stand on her own feet and speak up for herself, that's all,' said Megan defensively.

'You can say that again,' snorted Hetty.

'Don't be like that,' admonished Megan. 'It must be very hard for her without Dad, even though she doesn't make a big thing of it. I'm pleased to see her being so strong.' She gave her sister a meaningful look. 'Talking about people being stroppy, you could win medals for it since you've been back.'

'I don't know what you mean.'

'Oh, I think you do,' disagreed Megan. 'The only time you've had a good word to say to Mum and me is when you've been talking about Wales. Anyone would think you're not pleased to be home.'

'Of course I am,' Hetty snapped. 'I haven't been away on some exotic holiday, you know. You'd think I have, the way you and Mum are carrying on. Now give me a break, will you?'

'I think we all need to calm down and get used to living together again.'

'Sorry, Megan,' Hetty blurted out unexpectedly. 'I shouldn't have gone on so much about Wales when you and Mum have been having a hard time here.'

'You can talk about it as much as you like,' her sister invited her lightly. 'As long as you stop comparing London with it unfavourably.'

'I didn't even realise I was doing it,' Hetty said. 'It wasn't intentional.'

'You got a bit too fond of country life, I think.'

'I liked it, there's no point in my denying it. But the fact that you and Mum are both looking so pale and tired hasn't gone unnoticed. I may not show it but I do feel bad about being away.'

For the first time since Hetty had been back, Megan felt at ease with her sister.

★ ★ ★

The one aspect of the evacuees' return that Megan really didn't like was the departure of Mabel. She was so warm-hearted and entertaining, and the place wouldn't be the same without her.

'I hate to see you go,' Megan told her.

'Me too,' added her mother. 'We're really going to miss you around here.'

'You haven't seen the last of me, don't worry,' Mabel told them when Dolly handed her her final pay packet. 'I shall call in to see you regular. You're my friends and that isn't going to change just because I'm not working here.'

'You're welcome any time,' said Dolly.

'I hope you don't have too much trouble getting another job,' mentioned Megan.

'Don't you worry about me,' Mabel said, sounding upbeat. 'There might not be many jobs about for us girls when the men come home, but

I shouldn't have any trouble at the moment.' She gave one of her wide toothy grins. 'The war's almost over. Everything else can be sorted as long as we have that. The future's bright.'

And off she went with a cheery smile, leaving Megan and her mother wishing there was some way they could keep her on.

★ ★ ★

In the end it was a mixture of frustration and self-respect that put Megan back in control as far as her children were concerned.

'Eat your porridge, please, Netta, love,' she urged one morning.

'Don't want it.'

'Oh, and why is that?'

'Don't like *your* porridge,' Netta declared.

'Nor do I,' chipped in Poppy. 'We only like Auntie Dil's porridge.'

'Gran made the porridge, not me,' Megan pointed out.

'We still don't like it,' stated Poppy.

'I think it's quite nice,' said George, who had finished his.

'Trust you to side with them.'

'I'm not siding with them,' he declared. 'Auntie Dil's was creamy because we had milk on it straight from the farm. This isn't the country, so we can't have it here.'

'As you've finished, George, let's go and get you ready for school,' said Hetty diplomatically.

'I've got to get on too,' said Dolly, also realising that Megan needed to battle this out with her children on her own. 'We'll leave you to it.'

'So,' began Megan, standing up and looking down at her daughters in a way that said she meant business. 'You don't like anything much around here, do you?'

Neither replied. They both stared at her, dark eyes burning with defiance.

'Now, let's see. You don't like your beds, your room, the school, the street, and now you've decided that you don't like the porridge either.' She paused. 'And as well as all that, I get the impression that you don't like me very much.'

Silence.

'What's the matter?' she demanded. 'Have you both lost your tongues? You had plenty to say just now.'

'No,' mumbled Netta.

'We don't like it when you're cross like you are now,' confessed Poppy.

'Another grumble to add to the list,' Megan said. 'Well, I'll tell you something. There are children who would be very glad to have any one of the things you don't like. Children whose countries were occupied by the Germans would be grateful for just a spoonful of porridge because the poor things are half starved. And you have the audacity to complain about this, that and the other. You should be thoroughly ashamed of yourselves.'

Netta bit her lip. Poppy stared at the tablecloth.

'Anyway, I'm going to give you a choice,' Megan announced in a tone that defied argument. 'As you don't like being at home, and are so full of complaints, perhaps you'd like to go back to Auntie Dil's to live for good.'

This made them look up. The rebellion in their eyes wasn't so prominent now.

'You can either stop complaining and being so rude and difficult, or you can go back to Wales,' she told them. 'It's entirely up to you.'

They both stared at their hands.

'If you decide to stay here,' she continued, managing to keep her voice strong, 'you will behave yourselves and treat me and the rest of the family with respect. The first thing you will do is eat your porridge and get ready for school without any fuss or complaint. I'm going to the kitchen to help Gran with the dishes now. That's where I'll be when you're ready to let me know what it is you want to do. Don't take too long about it either.'

She knew she'd taken a huge gamble and was inwardly quaking. There was no way on earth she was going to send her children away again. So if they called her bluff she was going to lose all credibility with them. But drastic measures had been necessary because the situation was becoming impossible.

Dolly had finished the washing-up and gone off somewhere and Megan was drying up when they appeared, each carrying an empty porridge bowl.

'You've decided to stay, have you?' she said.

They nodded in unison.

'You are going to stick to the rules then?'

They nodded again.

'Good. Now off you go and get your things for school. I'll come and do your hair in a minute.' She paused. 'How about a kiss for your mum? I haven't had one since you've been back; not a proper one anyway.'

They came to her, almost shyly, and she hugged them, her throat constricted by a choking sensation.

'Sorted?' asked her mother when she came back into the room.

'I think so. For the moment, anyway,' she replied.

'Well done.'

Megan knew that this small victory didn't mean it would be all plain sailing, since motherhood was a minefield of problems, and discipline had to be maintained however tempting it was to let it slip in the interests of popularity. But with her confidence somewhat restored, she felt one small step nearer to her daughters' affection and awash with love for them. She was beginning to feel as though she really did have her own daughters home again, and not a couple of strangers.

★   ★   ★

When Mr Churchill finally broadcast the news on the wireless that the people had been waiting for for so long, Dolly burst into tears and sobbed all through the National Anthem. Megan wasn't far off herself, and she was sure Hetty wasn't either.

Nobody tried to hide it, not even when they all

rushed outside into the bunting-strung street already crowded with jubilant neighbours. Complete strangers from other streets were hugging everyone in sight; emotion was palpable everywhere, and Megan wanted to laugh and cry simultaneously. It had come at last: the day they had worked and waited for for so long. The war in Europe was over. Hitler was dead, the bombs and blackout finished. The street was brimming with good will.

People were singing, dancing, kissing each other. Children the length of the street were squealing with excitement, some seeming bewildered by it all. Megan had never experienced anything like it before and knew she never would again. When things had calmed down a little, everybody gathered on a bomb site opposite the dairy to plan a street party the children would never forget.

Later on, Megan, Dolly, Hetty and the children joined the crowds in the West End and walked to Buckingham Palace, which was floodlit and glorious. Megan felt so proud of her country. She thought how sad it was that her father hadn't lived to see this, and linked arms with her mother companionably, guessing that she was having similar thoughts. The crowd was dense but there was no rough pushing and shoving. People could move around quite easily.

Some coloured rockets went off quite close to them, then all eyes were on the palace as the King and Queen and the two princesses came out on to the balcony. Everybody waved and cheered and the royals waved back. Some soldiers who were standing nearby put the children on their shoulders so they could get a good view.

The whole of London was lit up. They walked to see dear old Big Ben and waited with the crowd for midnight to strike; at one minute past the hour, the war with Germany was officially at an end. As the final chime rang out, a great cheer went up.

It was a moment that would live for ever in Megan's memory, she was certain of that. The children were tired but she was glad they'd let them stay up to experience this extra-special occasion. Even if they only retained a shred of what they'd seen and heard today, it was something they would take with them into adulthood and treasure all their lives.

They finally arrived home in the small hours, having managed to get a taxi. The children went to bed, and Dolly and her daughters drank a toast to absent loved ones.

★ ★ ★

The next day preparations got underway for the street party. If Megan thought she'd seen community spirit yesterday, today's surpassed even that. Everybody wanted to help. All the neighbours pooled their sweet coupons and collected money. They borrowed trestle tables and chairs from the church, the dairy donated their stock of fruit jellies, blancmange powders and biscuits. The women baked and made sandwiches and the men worked hard sweeping the street, setting up tables and chairs. They even dragged someone's piano out into the street, and a gramophone.

Blackout curtains came down to be made into fancy-dress costumes for the children, and everyone dived into the back of their drawers and wardrobes for anything they could find. Megan and Dolly managed to cobble together flower outfits for the twins, who went as Buttercup and Daisy, the dresses made of old yellow curtain material and a white bed sheet, with some organdie provided by one of the neighbours. Hetty made George a cowboy outfit out of some blackout material and an old felt hat of her father's.

After a wonderful tea, they had three-legged and egg-and-spoon races, followed by games such as musical chairs and pass the parcel. As darkness fell they lit a bonfire. The adults indulged in something stronger than tea, and people danced to the music from the gramophone.

Attempting a jitterbug with the twins while Hetty danced with George, Megan was imbued with thoughts of Will. The troops would be coming home soon, but she didn't know when she would be reunited with her husband because the war with Japan had yet to be won.

It was a sobering thought, but she had no intention of spoiling the fun by showing it. The party went on until the small hours, with a sing-song around the piano to end the celebrations. The children were too tired to stay up for that, so their mothers took them home to bed.

Listening to the singing outside, Megan thought she had rarely heard a sweeter sound. Music instead of air-raid sirens. The joy was indescribable. Even the horror of last Christmas that had haunted her ever since and the nightmares she'd suffered because of it were put to the back of her mind at this moment.

★ ★ ★

'Who do you reckon will get in then?' asked one of Dolly's customers, referring to the forthcoming general election; the first for ten years, following the resignation of the wartime coalition government. The whole country was caught up in election fever as the opposing campaigns got underway.

'Who knows?' Dolly deemed it wise not to discuss politics with those on whom her living depended.

'There's a lot of talk about people who don't usually vote Labour doing so this time,' said the customer, a long-term regular whose name was Flo.

'Surely they won't reject Mr Churchill after he's brought us through the war,' blurted out Dolly. She was a great admirer of Mr Churchill and wouldn't hear a word said against him.

'I dunno so much about that,' said the other woman, whose own allegiance was blatantly obvious. 'People want decent homes to live in and a fair deal for all, not just for the toffs. We won't get that with Churchill's lot. They'll just look after their own; those who've already got plenty like themselves.'

'We'll just have to wait and see what happens, won't we?' said Dolly diplomatically.

'We will indeed,' agreed Flo. 'It'll cause some excitement, I reckon. Good job too. It's all gone a bit flat since the victory celebrations finished.'

Dolly nodded in agreement. Nothing could spoil the pleasure of living in peace, but life had gone on much the same as in wartime; without the bombs, but with shortages as bad as ever.

'Anything else, dear?' she asked.

'That's all for now, ta.' As Dolly handed back her ration books, Flo said, 'I wonder how much longer we're gonna be needing these bloomin' things for.'

'I suppose it'll take a little while for things to get back to normal,' said Dolly.

'As long as they don't take too long about it,' said Flo. 'Let's hope the new government gets things moving.'

'Indeed,' agreed Dolly.

'Still, at least we can go to bed without fear now, and the kiddies are back home,' Flo said. 'I bet you're glad to have your grandchildren back.'

'You bet.'

'They need their dads home now to make it complete.'

'Yeah.'

As Flo left, Dolly was aware of a dull ache in the pit of her stomach. The men would come back to their wives but Dai would never come home again to her. She wouldn't tell the girls, because she didn't want to worry them, but she still missed him to the point of desperation at times. She would have loved to have shared the end of the war with him. She had people around her all the time and she loved her family to death. But nothing felt whole or right for her without him. Maybe it never would.

★ ★ ★

Flo was right in her prediction about a change of government. The Labour Party had a landslide victory in the general election, and for the first time in Britain's history there was a Labour government in power, promising a new era and claiming that 'Labour can deliver the goods'.

People hoped ardently that they were right, because the shortages and rationing seemed set to continue well into the future, with no prospect of any change. The housing shortage was simply appalling. But amid the shabby war-torn streets where bomb sites were such a part of the landscape they seemed to have been there for ever, colourful welcome-home banners began to appear as the gradual return of the fighting men began. One day in July there was one strung across the front of the dairy house. On it was emblazoned in big blue letters: WELCOME HOME KEN.

★ ★ ★

Hetty was expecting her husband home towards the end of July but she wasn't sure exactly when he would arrive. For several days her stomach churned with excitement, and she waited up late every night to greet him.

'Anyone would think he was already home by the amount of yawning you're doing,' said one of the cheekier customers. 'You should get some sleep while you can, girl. There'll be precious little of it when he does get here.'

Hetty took it all in good part. Nothing could spoil the joy of knowing Ken was coming home at last. She wanted to see him so much it was almost a physical pain. George didn't remember much about him, but he was infected by the excitement in the house and entered into the spirit with his mother.

They had changed the sleeping arrangements to accommodate the men's return. The attic room had been cleared out and made into a bedroom for the children, to allow Megan and Hetty privacy with their husbands.

Determined yet again to wait up for him, for the seventh night running Hetty sat alone in the parlour in the small hours. She had dozed off in the chair when she was awoken by a tap at the front door. Leaping up and patting her hair into place she went to answer it, heart racing.

There he was on the doorstep, a tall soldier with a kit bag slung over his shoulder and his cap in his hand, still in uniform as he hadn't yet been officially demobbed. She couldn't take her eyes off him because she was so shocked by the change in his appearance. He looked so different to how she remembered, she could hardly believe it was him. He was thinner and older. The warm amber eyes she knew so well were sunken in his lean face, his features appearing sharper because of the dramatic loss of weight. He seemed like a stranger, not the man she had married at all. Seeing him again was so different to how she'd imagined.

'Well, do I get to come in?' he said, smiling at her on the doorstep. 'Or are you just going to stand there staring at me all night long?'

She opened her arms to him. 'Hello, Ken,' she said.

'Hello, Hetty.'

As she put her arms around him, she was struck with a terrible sense of panic. She didn't feel the same about him. That special magic had gone. She wanted to run away.

Oh my God, what was she supposed to do now? Her husband had come back from the war looking weary and half starved, and she had fallen out of love with him. There was only one thing to do. She'd have to fake it and hope the feelings came back.

'It's so good to see you, Hetty,' he said with tears in his eyes as they went inside. 'I can't tell you how much I've longed for this moment. It's all I've thought about for all these years; the only thing that's kept me going.'

'Me too, Ken,' she said, adding silently, 'But I certainly didn't expect to feel like this. Please God, let me learn to love him again somehow.'

★ ★ ★

'This is your dad, George,' said Hetty the next morning when the boy came wandering into the bedroom while she and Ken were still in bed. It had been previously agreed that she wouldn't work on her husband's first day home so that she could spend time with him, and the schools were closed for the summer holidays, so the morning routine could be more leisurely.

''Ello,' said George, staring at his father curiously.

'Wotcha, son,' said Ken, and Hetty knew she would never forget the look on his face as he looked at his son, who was quite different to the small child he had left behind. Ken seemed at first bewildered, then full of wonderment. He was obviously feeling emotional but struggling to hide it in typical male tradition. 'My, how you've grown. You'll be as big as me soon.'

George looked at him, weighing him up. 'You don't look like a soldier,' he stated.

'That's because he hasn't got his uniform on,' said Hetty anxiously, getting out of bed and pulling on her dressing gown. She hadn't realised she would be this worried about how the two of them would get along, and her protective instincts towards George were on full alert.

'I won't be a soldier much longer, I hope, son,' said Ken, sounding ill at ease. 'I'll be handing my uniform in soon.'

'Did you kill many Germans?' asked George, staring at his father in a most disconcerting way.

'George,' admonished Hetty. 'What a question to ask. Your dad doesn't want to talk about things like that when he's just got back after years away.'

'It's all right, love,' Ken said to her. Turning to the boy he added, 'It's what soldiers are trained for.'

George nodded, then said in a matter-of-fact tone, 'Please can I go downstairs now, Mum?'

'Yes, I'll be down in a minute.'

As the door closed behind him, Ken said, 'He's a fine boy. You've done a good job bringing him up on your own.'

Hetty flushed with pleasure. 'Thanks, Ken,' she said. 'He's very bright and is doing ever so well at school. He's streets ahead of the others in his class.' She paused, her expression becoming serious. 'He isn't a strong child, though.'

Fear leapt into Ken's eyes. 'Is there something the matter with him?' he asked.

'He's sickly and gets ill a lot,' she explained. 'I have to be very careful with him.'

'So there's nothing in particular wrong with him?' he said, sounding relieved and remembering what a worrier Hetty had been when George was little.

'No, nothing specific.'

'Thank God for that. You had me worried for a minute there.'

'He's very delicate, though, Ken,' she made clear. 'He needs special care.'

'You'll have me to help now, and take some of the strain off you,' he offered warmly. 'I'll give you plenty of moral support.'

She bit her lip. 'Er . . . you'll have to give him a chance to get used to your being around. It might take a bit of time.'

'He'll probably adapt quicker than I will,' he said cheerfully. 'I'm clueless as regards being a dad. He was only little when I went away; not old enough for me to be involved to any real extent. But I can do all sorts of things with him now.'

'He's very sensitive.' She cleared her throat, feeling awkward but knowing she must speak out. 'The thing is, Ken, it's been just the two of us for so long, he isn't used to sharing me.'

'Oh . . . oh, I see. I'll take it slowly, don't worry,' he assured her. 'I've no intention of barging in and upsetting things.'

That was typical of Ken. He'd always been kind-hearted and self-effacing. That was what Hetty had loved about him. She was imbued with guilt for wanting to escape from him; from the situation. What was the matter with her? He was a good man and she was lucky to have him returned to her all in one piece.

'Do you think George looks like me?' he asked.

Not at all, Hetty thought. George was Morgan through and through. But she said, 'I can see something of you in him.'

This obviously delighted him. 'That makes me feel very proud,' he told her.

'I'm sure,' said Hetty, wishing she could conjure up some genuine enthusiasm instead of having to pretend. She'd got so used to managing without him, she felt as though he was encroaching on her life and she resented it. 'Anyway, I must go downstairs and see to

George's breakfast. I'll bring yours up here for you. On your first day back you deserve a bit of spoiling.'

'Thanks. I'll enjoy that.'

When she returned with a tray of porridge and toast for one, he asked, 'Aren't you having yours up here with me?'

'No.' She looked sheepish. 'I have to go down to see to George,' she explained. 'I'll leave you to enjoy the peace and quiet. Make the most of it while you can, because there's precious little of it downstairs, I can promise you that.'

'George will be all right with the others, won't he?' suggested Ken. 'You don't need to rush down there, surely, if all the others are there.'

Umbrage simmered and Hetty knew there was trouble ahead. She was accustomed to a free hand in bringing up their child, and she didn't welcome interference, even from his father; in fact especially from his father.

'I usually have my breakfast with him. It's a part of our daily routine,' she said, managing to curb the impulse to tell Ken to mind his own damned business and let her live her life in the way she was used to. She was his wife, for heaven's sake, and George was his child as well as hers. She was going to have to learn to adapt, but the prospect was a daunting one. Forcing a softer tone, she added, 'He's going to have enough new things to get used to now that you're home. I don't want to push them all on to him at once. He needs time to get used to your being around.'

'I thought it might be nice for the two for us to

have breakfast together as it's my first morning home.'

'I won't be long,' she told him, putting her hand on his. 'You just enjoy the rest and relaxation. You deserve a lie-in after what you've been through. I'll be back before you know it.'

'All right then,' he agreed, and looked down at the tray in front of him.

★   ★   ★

'Are you enjoying the party, Ken?' asked Megan the following Saturday. At the dairy house Ken's welcome-home party was in full swing, drinks flowing, a neighbour playing the piano against a chorus of boozy singing.

'Yeah, I'm having a good time, thanks,' he said, puffing on a cigarette, a glass of beer in his other hand. 'It's very nice of you all to put on a do for me.'

'It's the very least we can do after what you boys have done for us,' she assured him. 'We'll do it all over again when Will finally gets home. Please God that he does. That flaming war with Japan isn't over yet.'

'I'm sure it won't be long,' he said in a comforting manner. 'I'm looking forward to seeing Will again myself, as it happens. He was a real mate; always good for a laugh. It'll be nice to have some male company around here.'

'I've been without that man of mine for quite long enough,' Megan chuckled, though she was having to put up a cheery front because the incident with Doug still shadowed her life,

279

despite all her attempts not to dwell on it. She was angry with herself for trusting him enough to welcome him into their home. If only he hadn't seemed so nice. 'I shall probably lose control and ravage him when I do get my hands on him.'

'Lucky man.'

'I hope he thinks so.'

'He will, believe me.' Ken forced a smile but it wasn't sincere. His homecoming hadn't lived up to expectations at all. He felt like a lodger here among the Morgan family, despite the fact that they were all very welcoming to him. He needed to provide a home for his wife and son, but how could he do that when the housing shortage was so acute?

The worst thing was suspecting that Hetty was happy to stay here indefinitely. She didn't seem to want to be alone with him at all. She seemed to prefer being with the crowd, and she certainly wasn't going to let him get a look-in with George. Even more worrying: did he really want one?

He didn't have the faintest idea of how to go about being a father. It had been different before he'd gone away because George had been small then and all that was required of Ken was the odd word or two in kid's talk. Now George needed more than that; he was an intelligent child and expected proper conversation. Ken needed to get to know him and he hadn't a clue how to do it because he felt so awkward with him and never knew what to say. The lad probably thought his father was a fool. But despite all that, Ken had an ache inside which he recognised as love, and yes, he did want to play a part in his son's life. Very much!

Yet at the same time he felt hemmed in and longed to escape from all of it: the house rules, the strained atmosphere with Hetty, and his own inability to communicate with his son. He was used to living rough, in dire hardship, to being in male company twenty-four hours a day. He'd seen things on the battlefield and in the prison camp that he could never share with anyone; things that haunted his dreams as well as his waking moments. He could never forget the grinding fear and the death and degradation that he wouldn't have believed possible before the war. Like every other soldier who had been in action, he wasn't the same person who'd gone away.

Now he looked across the room to where Hetty was jigging around to the music with George and the twins, having a whale of a time by the look of it. He wanted to be a part of her life again, and make her happy, but so much time had passed. Not only did he have to get to know his son; he had to get to know his wife all over again.

'I suppose it takes some getting used to, being back, after army life?' said Megan in an understanding manner.

'Yeah, it does feel a bit strange. It's such a complete change to what I've become accustomed to,' Ken said.

'I shall bear that in mind when Will comes home,' she remarked, 'and try not to expect too much of him.'

'He'll appreciate that.'

'Let me get you another drink,' she suggested as he drained his glass.

'Thanks, Megan,' he said gratefully. He needed something to cheer him up. Guilt consumed him. How could he have such thoughts when he was out of that hellhole he'd been in for five years? A lot of his mates hadn't made it past Dunkirk. He was one of the lucky ones. Give it time, he told himself. Give it time.

★ ★ ★

'Well isn't this nice?' said Dolly the next day. 'All of us sitting round the table for Sunday dinner: a proper family occasion.'

'Yes, it's lovely, Mum,' said Megan supportively.

'Once we get Will back, we'll have a full house.' Dolly paused, lowering her eyes. 'Well, we'll never have that again without your dad, of course, but it's nice that things are beginning to get back to normal. It's so good to have you home, Ken.'

'It's good to be back, Ma,' said Ken, feeling trapped and hating himself for it because his mother-in-law was such a good-hearted soul and he was fond of her. 'It's a lot for you, though, having us all here. You must be longing for a bit of peace and quiet.'

'Not me, Ken. I love having you all here,' she

said, then added quickly, for fear of seeming clingy, 'Of course, you and Hetty will be looking for a little place of your own as soon as things pick up. But I expect you'll still come for Sunday dinner.'

'We'll be living here for a while yet, Mum,' said Hetty assertively. 'There are no places to rent at all.'

'The housing situation is bad in London,' agreed Megan, 'what with so many homes being bombed and everybody coming back from the forces and the country. The council waiting list is a joke. Unless you're actually homeless and have about five or six kids, you don't stand a chance of getting housed; not the way things are at the moment anyway.'

'We'll just have to keep our ears to the ground,' said Ken in a definite tone. 'We can't stay here for ever.'

'We're all right here for the time being, though, aren't we?' Hetty said, and her reluctance to move out was obvious to him.

But he nodded and they passed on to other things. By the time they got to dessert and Dolly brought in a huge rice pudding straight from the oven, the children were bored with the adult talk and beginning to get fidgety. Inevitably the bickering began.

'Stop pushing me, Poppy,' objected George.

'I didn't touch you.'

'Yes you did,' he said, flushing with temper and rubbing his arm. 'You poked my arm really hard. Keep to your own chair.'

'I can't help it if the chairs are close together,'

283

Poppy came back at him. 'I don't wanna sit next to you anyway.'

'And I don't want to sit next to you either,' said her cousin vehemently.

'Fat face,' she said.

'Bighead,' added Netta, joining in on her sister's side as usual.

'You two are the bigheads around here,' George retorted, giving Poppy a sneaky prod under the table that made her wince. 'You think you know everything.'

'Oi, you,' she said, retaliating to his prod by slapping his arm.

'That's enough, all of you,' intervened Megan with authority. 'You girls will be sent from the table without any pudding if you don't behave yourselves.'

'It's always our fault, never his,' complained Netta. 'We always get the blame.'

'That's because you usually deserve it,' said Hetty, who hadn't noticed George's furtive action.

'See,' said George, looking at his cousin triumphantly.

'Shut up you,' said Netta.

'Twerp,' added Poppy.

'Right. That's it,' blasted Megan. 'I've had enough. You two girls can both go and stand outside the door until you learn to behave yourselves. When you're ready to apologise to your cousin you can come back in.'

Ken, who had spotted George's sly prod, was appalled at the lack of discipline from Hetty. As far as he could see, George had been equally to blame.

'Didn't they all ought to go outside?' he suggested. 'George was doing his share of pushing and poking. I saw him.'

There was a deathly silence. Megan held her breath as she waited for her sister's reaction. The children stared from one to the other. George didn't look any too happy at the intervention from his father.

'Don't you dare question my judgement as regards my son,' objected Hetty, her cheeks flaming. 'I won't have it, do you understand?'

'Our son . . . '

'All right, our son,' she conceded, her voice rising almost to a shriek. 'But I'm the one who's brought him up. I'm the one who says what goes. So keep your nose out.'

Ken gave her a cold look, then turned to Dolly and said, 'Excuse me, Ma, I'm sorry about this when you've cooked us such a lovely meal,' and got up and marched from the room.

Red-faced and close to tears, Hetty went after him.

The tense silence the couple left in their wake was broken by Poppy, who got a fit of nervous giggles. Megan knew she didn't mean to be rude, so said simply, 'Well, let's have our pudding, as your Gran has been kind enough to make it. We'll put some aside for the others to have later on.'

'I thought we had to go outside,' said Netta, while her sister shook with silent laughter and tried to hide it by staring at her lap.

'There'll be no one left to eat your grandmother's pudding if you go as well,' Megan pointed out. 'We'll let it go this time. But I might not be so lenient if it happens again.'

'Sorry for pushing you, George,' Poppy said.

' 'S all right.'

Noticing how anxious George obviously was, Megan said, 'Don't worry, love. Your mum and dad will be down in a minute. They'll be making it up as we speak.'

'It's all my fault, isn't it?' he said.

'Of course not,' said Dolly. 'What on earth has put that idea into your head?'

'It's me they're arguing about, so it must be my fault.'

'It isn't your fault, George, so stop worrying. All mums and dads fall out from time to time,' said Dolly. 'You're not used to having your dad around, so it's all new to you. Your mum and dad have to get used to each other, and when they do it will be better.'

'I did poke Poppy,' he admitted, turning a fiery red. 'Should I go and tell them?'

'No. You stay down here with us, son,' replied Dolly without hesitation. 'Leave them to fight it out. You'll see them when they come down and you can tell them then.'

'Meanwhile let's have some pudding,' suggested Megan. 'It'll be time for you children to get ready for Sunday school soon.'

Dolly served the pudding and Megan could see from the red blotches on her neck that she was upset by the altercation between Hetty and Ken.

Megan was worried about it too. She'd seen it coming and predicted plenty more ahead. It was second nature to Hetty to be overprotective towards George, and that wasn't going to change just because his father was around. Whereas a lot of men were quite happy to leave the raising of the children entirely to their wife, Ken had shown today that he wasn't one of them and wanted to be involved with George. Hetty wouldn't take kindly to that. Heaven knows how it would all work out. It certainly wouldn't happen overnight. If it was like this now, what would it be like when Ken was demobbed and home for good?

★ ★ ★

Upstairs in the bedroom, they were at it hammer and tongs.

'Don't you dare speak to me like that in front of the whole family,' objected Ken angrily. 'Humiliating me like that.'

'Don't undermine my authority, then,' Hetty snapped back at him furiously.

'George was just as much to blame as the girls,' he insisted. 'He shouldn't be allowed to get away with it. Without discipline he'll become a spoilt brat.'

'If I'd thought he needed telling off, I would have done it, but he didn't.'

'I saw him push Poppy,' Ken told her, his voice rising. 'He gave her a right hard prod under the table.'

'You're just jealous because he takes up my time and you want all of it,' Hetty accused.

'I don't like the fact that you never have time

for me, I admit,' he said, 'but that has nothing to do with the fact that I think the boy should be properly disciplined.'

'I do discipline him when it's necessary,' she informed him haughtily, 'and it wasn't necessary just now.'

'I completely disagree.'

'The twins are always trying to shove him around. They're little devils. Everybody knows that. You can ask Megan if you don't believe me. She admits it herself.'

'She seems to be doing a pretty good job, from what I've seen since I've been home,' he responded. 'They're nice kids, the twins; a bit boisterous perhaps, but there's no harm in them. She's got the measure of them and keeps them well in order.'

'Don't compare me to my sister.'

'I'm not. I wouldn't do that,' he denied. 'I was just saying things as I see them.'

'You know nothing about any of it,' she raged, the words flowing almost of their own volition. 'You haven't been here, so how can you? I've done the best I can for George and you come home and start being critical.'

'Perhaps you'd like it if I got sent to the Far East to finish things off out there, and left you to get on with your life with George without me,' he said grimly. 'That's what you want, isn't it?'

'Don't be so ridiculous.'

'That's what it feels like to me,' he said, speaking from the heart and with no prior intention. 'I feel like an interloper between you

288

and George. It's obvious you don't want me around.'

His words registered with a terrible clarity and she reeled from the cruelty of her own behaviour, her anger changing to contrition. 'Oh Ken, I'm so sorry,' she said, her tone almost humble. 'I shouldn't have screamed at you like that in front of everyone. It was unforgivable.'

'Apology accepted,' he said at once. He'd never been one to bear a grudge.

Calmer now, she was able to speak rationally. 'I suppose I've got so used to it being just George and me, I don't quite know how to handle this new situation.'

Ken was standing with his back to her, looking out of the window. 'Me neither,' he said, turning to look at her. 'When I was away at the war, it was as though everything back here was frozen in time in my mind, just as I remembered it. I imagined coming back and finding it all the same. But life doesn't stop just because you're away. People move on, get on with their lives and change with the passing years. It's the natural way of things and can't be otherwise.'

'We can work it out, Ken,' Hetty said, going over to him and taking both his hands. She was deeply saddened by the situation she found herself in and wanted so much to make it right. 'We go back a long way; we can make things better between us.'

'I'd like that,' he said, putting his arms around her.

'Me too,' she said, and meant it with all her heart. But she wasn't sure if it was going to be possible. Maybe too much time had passed; perhaps they had both changed too much. As much as she wanted it, she wasn't sure if she could rearrange her life and her feelings to include Ken, given her new-found independence and the strength of her feelings for George.

11

Japan finally surrendered on the fourteenth of August, and the government declared a two-day holiday for the VJ celebrations. To Megan's eye, there didn't seem to be as much excitement about as there was on VE Day back in May, maybe because for most civilians, victory over Europe had ended the war. There was also a general feeling of horror at the use of the first atomic bombs, which had wreaked devastation on Hiroshima and Nagasaki, killing thousands of civilians.

There was no shortage of street parties, fancy-dress parades, bonfires and so on, but the Blossom Road festivities were definitely less exuberant and emotional than the earlier ones. It just wasn't the same the second time around. For the men in the services, however, it was a huge relief, because it meant that the risk of being sent to fight in the Far East had now been removed and they could look forward to demob, as could the men already serving out there.

For Megan personally, the end of the war with Japan was very significant indeed, because it meant that her husband would be coming home at last.

★   ★   ★

It was a cold and frosty January day; breathlessly still and brilliant with sunlight beaming down from a clear blue sky on to the shabby London streets. Here and there little twists of chimney smoke hung in the air above the rooftops, and skeletal winter trees stood out like pencil sketches on the skyline.

But Megan was almost oblivious to the weather and her surroundings as she stood at the front door of the dairy house, walked to the corner of the street and back, then went inside and peered out of the window, repeating the process over and over again. She didn't know what time to expect him; just that it would be sometime today. Such was her febrile anticipation, no one expected any work from her. Ken had taken over from her in the dairy anyway, after being demobbed, and she and Hetty now shared the shop duties with their mother, so time off wasn't such a problem. As the children were at school she was free to indulge her restlessness.

Warmly clad in a grey winter coat and scarlet knitted hat with a matching muffler around her neck, she watched, walked and waited, imbued with a plethora of emotions. She was happy, excited and more than a little frightened too. It had been five and a half years; what if things weren't the same between them?

She was standing on the corner by the main road, stamping her feet to stop them going numb with the cold, when she saw him get off the bus, a tall figure bounding towards her. As soon as she set eyes on him she knew that her feelings for him hadn't changed; perhaps they were even stronger. He was absolutely gorgeous and she was just as nuts about him as she'd ever been.

'Hello, darlin',' he said, putting his kit bag down and looking at her, love exuding from every pore as he opened his arms to her. 'You look beautiful.'

There in the street, she hugged and kissed him, uncaring of passersby, tears of joy rolling down her cheeks. People around only smiled anyway. This sort of reunion was happening everywhere, and everyone thanked God for it.

'You don't look so bad yourself. The sun tan suits you,' she said, drawing back and feasting her eyes on him, trying not to show how shocked she was at the amount of weight he had lost. He was still incredibly handsome, his sparkling dark eyes as compelling as ever against his tanned skin. He'd always had a chunky look about him before, being square-jawed and solid, but now he looked tall and lean, despite his clean-cut features. 'But we definitely need to get some meat on your bones.'

'That comes later. For now, just let me look at you,' he said, his warmth melting her heart. 'I was beginning to think this moment would never come.'

'Same here.'

He looked around at the bombed streets. 'The old place has taken a pasting, I see,' he remarked.

She nodded. 'We've had our share.'

'Thank God you came through it. I was sad to hear about your dad, though. I'm really sorry, love.'

'Thanks, Will.'

He put his arm around her and they walked home, happy to be together.

'I'm feeling quite nervous,' Will admitted later as he and Megan walked to the school to meet the children. 'It's such a long time since I last saw them.'

'After what you've been through this past few years, I would have thought you'd be fearless.'

'War doesn't make you immune, you know. Anyway, this is a different sort of nervousness to the fighting-for-your-life sort of fear. It's playing havoc with my insides.' He took a deep breath, puffed out his lips and looked at her worriedly. 'Do they know I'll be here?'

'They know you're coming home sometime today,' she replied. 'But they don't know you're going to be waiting for them when they come out of school. I didn't know if you would be home in time so I didn't mention it.'

'Supposing they don't like me?'

'Don't be daft, Will, of course they'll like you,' she assured him. 'The question is, will you like them?'

'Course I will, I'm their father. I love them.'

'I know that, but liking them is a different thing altogether,' she pointed out 'They are the most wonderful little girls and I love them to bits, but they are not the quietest of children or the most well behaved.'

'Sounds as though they take after their dad.'

She looked towards the school. 'Brace yourself. They're coming out,' she said as a trickle of home-going children became a great noisy stream.

He had his eyes fixed anxiously on the school gate. 'You'll have to point them out to me,' he said, with a tremor in his voice. 'They'll have changed so much I might not recognise them.'

'There they are,' she said, waving to them. 'Poppy . . . Netta. Over here.'

Up they rushed, both clad in navy-blue school raincoats, hoods down and hair flying, their cheeks pink from the cold. Their huge brown eyes studied Will carefully. George made a diplomatic exit and said he was going to walk on and would see them at home.

'Hello, you two,' Will said shakily.

'Are you our dad?' asked Netta.

'That's right,' he replied, barely able to speak for emotion. 'You've changed a bit since I last saw you. You're so much alike, I don't know which is which.'

'I'm Netta and she's Poppy,' she announced as her sister stood beside her. They were both looking up at him with unnerving childish scrutiny.

'Are you going to live with us?' Poppy enquired.

'Yeah, that's the plan,' he told her thickly.

'Well, we have roast dinner on Sunday, cold meat Monday and stew on Tuesday,' she informed him, slipping her hand into his with instant trust. 'And you have to come to the table as soon as it's ready or Gran gets cross. She says it's bad manners to be late when someone has taken the trouble to cook the food.'

'And you're not allowed to be too long in the bathroom if there's a queue,' added Netta, taking his other hand. 'Or make a noise when the news comes on the wireless.'

'There you are,' said Megan, smiling. 'Now you have a full set of house rules.'

'Thank you, girls,' he said, smiling at one then the other, overwhelmed by the change in them and the depth of his feelings for them. 'But the first thing I have to learn is how to tell one of you from the other.'

'You'll soon learn to tell them apart,' Megan told him with a wry grin. 'You'll have to or they'll play wicked tricks on you.'

'Our teacher has to ask which one is which even though she knows us,' Poppy informed him. 'But we don't dare to play tricks on her in case we get into trouble.'

'Since when have you two ever worried about getting into trouble?' said their mother.

Neither of them replied to that.

'We've just learned to do handstands against the wall,' Netta told her father proudly. 'We'll show you when we get home if you like.'

'Yeah, that would be nice.'

'It's their latest craze,' explained Megan.

'I can see that I've got a lot of catching up to do,' said Will. 'And I'm going to enjoy every single moment.'

★ ★ ★

'Well?' said Will later when the children had gone to get changed out of their school clothes and he and Megan were snatching a few moments alone in their bedroom. 'How did I do?'

'You were brilliant.'

'I felt like some tongue-tied goon,' he confessed. 'I didn't know what to say to them. I don't know the first thing about little girls.'

'You'll soon get the hang of it,' she reassured. 'Anyway, Poppy and Netta are never lost for words. They do enough talking for everyone else, so you've no need to worry.'

'I feel such a raw beginner at being a dad,' he admitted. 'They weren't much more than babies when I went away. Now they're little people in their own right. So I must get it right.'

'Nobody gets it right all the time, least of all me, so stop worrying about it,' she advised him. 'You'll be great once you get over this initial shyness.'

'They're such beautiful children,' Will said effusively. 'I thought I was going to disgrace myself by bursting into tears when they held my hands. I was so proud.'

'Yeah, they are a couple of smashers,' agreed Megan, adding jokingly, 'But that isn't really surprising when you take note of who their parents are.'

'Especially their mother,' he said, looking into her eyes.

'Well yeah, I'm glad you've noticed that,' she returned with feigned conceit. 'But as it happens, they are like you to look at: the same dark eyes and hair.'

'I did notice that,' he said, taking her in his arms, the air filled with romance and passion. 'But even so, they do have the most beautiful mother.'

'Ah, that's nice.' Her voice was soft and lyrical. 'I can take any amount of flattery.'

'I'm only saying it because it's true,' he said.

He was about to kiss her when there was a knock on the door, followed by a cry of 'Mum!' from outside the room.

'Yes, Netta, what is it?' Megan said, opening the door just a little. Will was standing behind her.

'Poppy's pulled my ribbons off and I can't tie my bunches,' Netta replied. 'She's been yanking at my hair.'

'She pulled my ribbons off first; that's why I did it to her,' claimed her sister hotly. 'Can you do them for us, please, Mum?'

'Yes, of course I will, but I'm talking to Daddy at the moment,' explained Megan, deciding that her husband had the first call on her attention today of all days. 'I'll come and do them for you in little while. Run along and I'll see you in a few minutes, there's good girls.'

But the twins weren't that easily put off.

'Netta wants to know why we can't come into your bedroom without knocking, like we usually do,' claimed Poppy.

'Ooh, you fibber,' objected Netta. 'It's you who wants to know. It's her, Mum, not me, honest.'

Megan turned away from the children and looked at Will, spreading her hands in a gesture of defeat. 'Well, are they still the most beautiful children who ever walked the earth?' she asked.

'Most definitely,' he grinned. 'We might have to get a lock fitted to the door, though.'

'It's the novelty of your being back,' she told

him. 'They don't want to miss anything.'

She opened the door wide and they both peered in, as though expecting to see something out of the ordinary.

'Right, you pair of nosy parkers. The reason you have to knock now is because Daddy and I might want some time together.'

'Without us?'

'That's right.'

'Why?'

'Because I say so.'

'Are you going to do kissing?'

'I bet they are,' added her sister.

Megan touched her nose. 'Never you mind what we are going to be doing. But just for the sake of peace and quiet, let's get this hair sorted out now. Give me the ribbons.'

'Are you coming to watch us do handstands now, Dad?' asked Poppy as her mother fixed her hair. 'Only we'll have to do it before we have our tea. We're not allowed to do it after we've eaten because Mum says it will make us sick.'

'Of course I'll come and watch your handstands,' he said, exchanging a glance with his wife that spoke volumes. Their love was stronger than ever but it encompassed their daughters too. Their private time could wait.

★   ★   ★

Will went to see his parents that evening and was rather taken aback when his mother burst into tears at the sight of him. She was usually quite cool towards him.

'Blimey, Mum,' he said with a wry grin. 'Am I that much of a depressing sight?'

'Of course you're not,' sniffed Audrey. 'Can't a mother shed a few tears when her son comes home from the war?'

'Your mother's just pleased to see you, son,' said his father, shaking his hand vigorously and slapping him on the back. 'Welcome home. It's good to see you.'

'I'm glad to be back,' declared Will. 'How are you both keeping?'

'Not so bad,' replied his father, his dark eyes warm with pleasure to have his son back safe and sound. 'We've had a good few worried moments about you, though, especially back awhile when the news from the Far East was so bad.'

'You know me,' Will said lightly. 'I'm a survivor.'

The instant he'd said it he regretted it. He looked at his mother to see the same old sad look in her eyes, and it gave him the familiar ache inside that had been absent in all the excitement and joy of being back.

'Thank God you are,' she said. 'We couldn't bear to lose you as well.'

'Now, Audrey, don't start getting morbid,' said Jack in a tone of good-humoured admonition. 'Will's home and that's the best reason I know of to be happy. We don't want anything to spoil it.'

'Yeah, you're right. Welcome home, son,' she said, giving him a rather restrained peck on the cheek. 'Have we got anything in to drink his health with, Jack?'

'There's a drop of port in the sideboard left over from Christmas,' he said. 'We'll use that, then I'll take him down to the pub for a proper drink.'

As they chinked glasses, Will noticed how much more cheerful his mother seemed. He wondered if she might ever get over the loss of her other son. On the surface she was fine now and made him feel that she was genuinely pleased to have him home. But did Ron's death still cast a shadow over her? He fancied he could see it in her eyes, and in turn it affected him.

He had to choose which way to go. Did he move forward to a bright new future with Megan and the twins, or did he allow his corrosive guilt to ruin his life and his wife's along with it? The uneasy conscience would always be there, and so it should be, but could he stop it from dominating his life as it had before he'd gone away? He'd been through a war and seen good mates die by his side. It was time to let go.

Being back with Megan had made him realise just how much he had to lose if he couldn't keep his compunction under control. It had come between them before; he didn't want it to happen again. He didn't want to hurt her; she meant too much to him. It was his guilt, not hers. So it was up to him to make sure it didn't spoil their life together.

Sometimes he wondered if he should confess to his mother. But although that might salve his conscience it would devastate her. One son dead; killed by the other. It would be too much for her to bear, and he couldn't do it.

Now that his daughters were older and he could relate to them as people, he could empathise with his mother more strongly than before. The parental tie was all-consuming, and he couldn't begin to imagine how he would feel if he lost one of his children. But to find out that the other child was responsible — how could any parent cope with that?

'Have you got any plans for the future, son?' his father enquired. 'As regards employment.'

'Yeah, I've got one or two ideas running around up here,' Will said, putting his head to one side and tapping it with his forefinger. 'But nothing definite yet.'

'A spot of wheeler-dealing, eh?' the other man surmised.

'You know me. Clocking on and off isn't my style.' Will grinned wryly. 'I'll have quite a lot of back pay to come from the army; enough to set myself up doing something gainful, I hope.'

'As long as it's legal,' warned his mother.

'Don't worry, Mum. I'll stay this side of the law.'

'You're entitled to some time off to think about it before you do anything,' she said.

'I'm still only on leave at the moment anyway,' he explained. 'I'll have to wait my turn for demob.'

He stayed for a while longer, chatting to them both, then went to the pub with his dad. He stayed rather longer than he'd intended and left feeling pleasantly relaxed. It was while he was walking back to the dairy from the bus stop, through the shabby streets, that he realised suddenly what he wanted to do in civvy street, and he couldn't wait to share his idea with Megan.

★ ★ ★

Everyone had gone to bed when he got in except for Ken, who was sitting in the parlour smoking.

'You're pushing your luck, aren't you, mate?' remarked Ken. 'Staying out past your wife's bedtime on your first night home?' He shook his head with an air of gloom. 'Not a good idea. I wouldn't want to be in your shoes.'

'It isn't all that late.'

'Not by normal standards it isn't, but they turn in very early in this house. Early risers, you see,' he explained. 'I can't get to sleep at all if I go to bed too early, even though I'm up at the crack of dawn to do the round.'

'I had to go and see my folks and spend some time with them, after being away so long,' explained Will. 'Megan understands that and doesn't mind.'

'I shouldn't bank on it,' warned Ken gravely. 'You know what women are like. They say one thing and mean another.'

'You sound to me like a man who's well in the doghouse,' observed Will.

'That's a permanent state for me since I've been back,' Ken told him miserably.

'It isn't going too well for you then?' suggested Will.

'That's one way of putting it,' Ken replied. 'But never mind that now. If I were you I'd get up those stairs sharpish or you'll be in the same boat.'

'We'll talk another time,' said Will, heading across the room in the direction of the stairs. 'We'll go for a pint one night soon.'

'I'd like that,' said Ken.

'Me too.'

'It's good to have you home, mate. I could really do with some adult male company around here.'

'See you tomorrow and we'll arrange a trip to the pub,' said Will, and disappeared through the door.

Alone in the room, Ken stared ahead of him into the pall of smoke he was exhaling. He felt lonelier now than he had done in the prison camp.

★ ★ ★

'Sorry I'm so late back, love,' apologised Will, relieved to see that the light was still on in the bedroom even though his wife was in bed, and that she appeared to be in good humour. 'I went for a pint with my dad.'

'I guessed you would. I didn't expect you to spend just half an hour with your parents after being away for such a long time,' she told him.

'I'm not in trouble then?'

'Of course you're not,' she assured him cheerfully. 'I didn't wait up because I didn't know what time you'd be back. I got so used to going to bed early when I was doing the milk round it's become a habit. Anyway, how are your folks?'

'Pleased to see me,' he said, unbuttoning his battledress. 'In fact Mum was quite emotional, which is most unusual. She cried her eyes out and that isn't like her at all. I thought she'd used all her tears up on Ron.'

'You're her son too, Will,' Megan pointed out. 'It's a long time since they've seen you, and there were probably times when you were away when they didn't think you were going to make it back.'

'I think it would have finished Mum off if I hadn't; you know, after losing Ron.'

'I quite agree.'

Fleetingly she saw the old pain in his eyes and her heart twisted. She knew why he was so troubled, and was aware of the fact that she could make it better in an instant if she were to tell him what she knew. But now that the time had actually come, it wasn't so easy to do it as she'd planned. Not only because of her fear of losing him — though that was a major factor, of course — but also because of the emotional upheaval the truth would cause him. There was no doubt in her mind that Doug would carry out his threat if she were to speak out. Would it not be kinder to leave things as they were, especially as Will seemed so happy to be home and positive about the future?

'Anyway,' he said, shivering as he got undressed, 'I've had this terrific idea and I can't wait to tell you about it.'

'Ooh, it sounds exciting. What is it?'

'Well, walking home through the streets tonight and seeing all the bomb sites and everywhere looking so scruffy and broken made me think that there must be a huge demand for painters, decorators and jobbing builders.'

'There is. Nobody can get anything done.'

'I want to set up my own business,' he burst out with enthusiasm. 'All legit. I'd keep proper books and everything. I've got a lot of back pay to come from the army, so that will give me a bit of capital to start with. The ultimate aim would be to build us a house to live in, but I'd start off painting and decorating, and learn about building as I go along; might even go to night school. I've done up a few houses and worked on building sites in the past when I was stuck for cash, so I should be reasonably competent.' He paused, mulling it over. 'Of course, there'll probably be a lot of other ex-servicemen with the same idea, but I think there'll be enough work for anyone who does a good job at a reasonable price. By the look of things out there, what doesn't have to be rebuilt will have to be done up.'

Megan sat up in bed, her face alive with enthusiasm, the electric light shining on her golden hair. 'That's a smashing idea, Will,' she approved wholeheartedly, determinedly pushing his brother's death and Doug Reynolds to the back of her mind. 'I could help you.'

He gave a wry grin. 'I know you women have been doing men's jobs during the war, but do you actually fancy going out stripping wallpaper?'

'Not really, no, though I'd do it if you were

really stuck,' she told him. 'But I meant the office work. If you're going to do this thing properly, you'll need someone to answer the phone and look after your paperwork. Do the estimates and invoices and so on. I worked in an office for a while when I left school. I'm only a two-finger typist but I'm sure I can improve.'

'In that case, you're hired,' he chuckled. 'The future is looking good for us.'

'The here and now is quite promising too,' she said, reaching out for him as he got into bed beside her.

★   ★   ★

Megan's love for Will was deep and reciprocal; even better than before he went away, with the benefit of maturity and the girls to add to it. She had some difficulty with the intimate side, though, because the rape had left her fearful, even though she tried to cast it from her mind. She managed to hide her feelings from Will, but he had noticed that she was tense and was very gentle, bless him. He thought she was nervous because he had been away for so long.

Despite his rather apprehensive start at fatherhood, it took Will no time at all to win the hearts of his daughters. He teased them relentlessly and they couldn't get enough of it; they would giggle until their sides ached. He played Snap and Ludo with them and walked to the corner every day to meet them from school. He and Megan took them to the park and to the river and to the West End to see the sights.

He was no pushover, though, and Megan didn't interfere when he was being firm with them. He was their father and as such needed their respect. Although he played the clown a lot of the time, they knew when they had gone too far.

'Pack it in, you two,' he would say gruffly when they were larking about after being put to bed. 'There's a time for play and a time for quiet and the quiet time is now. One more peep out of you and there'll be no park and no Ludo for a good long time. I'm not mucking about. I mean it. Now settle down and go to sleep.'

Megan wasn't naive enough to believe that they went straight to sleep. She guessed there was a lot of whispering and giggling under the covers before they finally settled down, but they did stop making a noise. She welcomed the support and embraced the involvement Will had in raising his daughters.

★ ★ ★

'I don't know how you get away with it, Will, I really don't,' said Ken over a pint in the local one evening. 'My missus goes berserk if I so much as raise my voice to George. Yet you keep your girls in order without a peep out of Megan.'

'She likes me to be involved. I think she finds it a help.'

'I daren't even look at George the wrong way,' said Ken, inhaling on a cigarette.

'I have noticed a bit of a chill in the air

between you and Hetty sometimes,' remarked Will.

'It's below freezing point most of the time,' Ken told him sadly. 'She's changed while I've been away. Sometimes I think she wishes I'd never come back.'

'Oh Ken, I'm sure that isn't true.' Will was seriously troubled to see his pal so unhappy. 'You just need time to adjust, that's all. I'm sure there are couples all over the country having the same problems, having been apart for so long.'

'You and Megan don't seem to be having any trouble at all,' observed Ken.

Will smiled. He hoped he didn't seem smug but he couldn't hide his happiness. 'Yeah, it's better than ever for us, as it happens.' He paused. 'But all couples have their difficult times. Things were a bit shaky before I went away. I was moody; couldn't put the past behind me. There were lots of rows. I came home knowing that I had to change if my marriage was going to survive. The thing about being away in action, you get plenty of time to think, in the long, boring periods between the actual fighting.'

Ken nodded in agreement. 'I had plenty of time to think in the prison camp,' he told Will. 'But most of it was about getting home to Hetty. The last thing I expected was trouble. Things were absolutely fine before I went away. We had a happy marriage; rock solid, or so I thought.' He paused, peering dismally into space over the top of his glass. 'It never occurred to me that we wouldn't just carry on where we left off.'

'I'm sure things will work out in time,'

suggested Will hopefully.

'It isn't all Hetty's fault,' Ken went on, obviously needing to unburden himself. 'I've changed too. The things you see and do when you're out there fighting or locked up in a prison camp stay with you and make life's trials and tribulations at home seem trivial after the inhumanity at the front. But you could never talk to the wife about it, or anyone come to that. I expect it's the same for you, isn't it?'

'Not half.' Will sipped his beer. 'What we saw, what we had to do for our country is best put to the back of the mind. Those things will stay with us till our dying day, but they're best kept private.'

Ken agreed and the men drank their beer in silence for a while, each busy with their own thoughts.

'You don't think Hetty met someone else while I was away, do you?' said Ken, his face creased with worry. 'There were lots of servicemen in London: Americans, Polish; all sorts. There must have been opportunities.'

'Never in a million years,' Will assured him without hesitation. 'The Morgan sisters are the most loyal women on earth. Surely you're not seriously harbouring those kind of suspicions?'

'No, I'm not really,' Ken confirmed. 'But she doesn't seem to like me very much, so I can't help wondering if it's perhaps because she's found someone else. These things happen. You hear about it all the time.'

'You're barking up the wrong tree with that one, mate,' stated Will. 'I'd put money on it.' He

310

looked at his companion. 'The only other man in Hetty's life besides you is young George.'

'Mm, I suppose you're right.'

'What you've got to remember is that while we were away, the women got used to doing things their way and looking out for themselves,' Will went on. 'Then we come home wanting everything to be the same as before we went, when it can't be because they've learned to be independent.'

'Perhaps that's what it is, then.'

'I'm sure of it,' said Will. 'Why don't you take her out for an evening; have some time on your own? Megan and I will look after George.'

Ken gave a dry laugh. 'Leave George while we go out to have fun?' he exclaimed. 'Wild horses wouldn't get her to do that. Let alone a husband she's none too fond of.'

'Oh well, each to their own,' said Will diplomatically, since it wasn't his place to criticise another man's wife. 'But I'm sure it's just a question of time.' He thought of something. 'Perhaps it'll be better when you get your own place.'

'I've had that thought too,' mentioned Ken. 'But Hetty seems quite happy the way things are. She likes having her mother and sister around, I think.'

Will was at a loss to know how to help his friend. It wouldn't be wise to offer advice on the subject; in his opinion other people's marriages were too personal for outsiders to enter into. He was no expert, but he believed that interference, no matter how well intentioned, could make matters worse. 'Fancy a game of darts?' he suggested. 'To take your mind off things?'

'Yeah, all right.'

'I mustn't be too late home, though,' mentioned Will. 'I don't want to upset Megan.'

'I reckon I'll upset my wife if I get home too early.' Poor Ken was at a very low ebb.

'I'll go and get the darts,' said Will.

★ ★ ★

'Come on, George!' shouted Megan as the young boy dribbled the ball across the grass towards the makeshift goal in which Will was standing. 'Whack it in.'

'Yeah, come on, love,' cheered his mother from the other side of the pitch.

He kicked the ball and it went in, deliberately missed by Will, to a hail of cheers from the two women, who were acting as linesmen, with the men in goal and the three children playing to see who could get the most goals. The fact that football was traditionally a male game didn't put the twins off in the slightest. They entered into the spirit of most things with gusto.

It was a cold winter Sunday afternoon, but clear and dry, and they were in Ravenscourt Park. Not the sort of weather to stand about in, though, so Megan and her sister were running up and down with the game to keep warm. Megan thought it was great fun and was glad to see that Hetty and Ken seemed to be enjoying themselves for a change. It was heartbreaking to watch them moving inexorably towards disaster;

to feel the atmosphere between them worsen and to listen to hushed arguments coming from their bedroom. Through it all Megan could somehow sense a spark remaining between them, but it was as though they couldn't recapture what they'd once had because they'd grown too far apart.

Now the game was progressing and Netta was tearing up the field with the ball; a bit too enthusiastically as it happened, because she crashed into George and they both went flying.

'Are you all right, kids?' asked Will, who was first on the scene, followed by Ken and the women.

'I banged my arm,' said Netta, wincing as her father helped her up.

'Aah, let me rub it for you,' said Will. 'There you are, the magic Stubbs touch. All right now?'

She nodded.

Ken had helped George up and was checking him over. 'Any cuts or bruises anywhere, son?' he asked.

'I grazed my knee,' George said, bending down and rubbing the affected area.

His father inspected it and saw that it was only a minor scrape. 'Do you want to carry on playing?' he asked in a kindly manner. 'Or have you had enough?'

'I'll carry on,' said George immediately. He was having a lovely time.

'Good boy,' said Ken, tousling his hair affectionately. 'Would you like to go in goal?'

'Are you stark raving mad?' shrieked Hetty, glaring at her husband. 'Of course he can't go on playing. He's hurt himself; he needs to go home.'

'He's all right,' said Ken. 'It's only a scuff. It's barely broken the skin.'

'I'll be fine, Mum, honest,' George assured her. 'We're having such a good game.'

'You are certainly not all right,' argued his mother. 'There's a nasty graze on that knee that needs seeing to. You're coming home with me.'

'But Mum, I want to stay.'

'Don't take him home, Hetty,' said Ken at his peril. 'He wants to stay and play. He's enjoying himself.'

'He's coming home with me.'

'You can't mollycoddle him over every little scrape and bump,' said Ken, losing patience. 'It's part and parcel of childhood.'

Wisely, Megan and Will moved away with the girls, out of the firing line.

'How many more times must I tell you not to question my judgement and interfere in the way I bring George up?' Hetty shouted, her voice quivering on the verge of tears. 'Now come on, George. We're going home to put a dressing on your knee.'

'But Mum — '

'Don't argue. We're going.'

She stormed off towards the park gates, dragging a reluctant George by the hand, and leaving Ken white with anger.

'You're not going after her then?' said Will quietly, when the girls went off to play.

'No. It's best if I don't because I'm feeling much too angry,' replied Ken, his voice deep with emotion. 'I won't be able to hold my tongue and it'll end up in another row, and I don't want to argue in front of George again. There's far too much of that as it is. She'll not want me anywhere near her anyway, the mood she's in.'

'I'll go after her,' said Megan, deeply concerned about her sister. 'You two bring the girls home when you're ready.'

★ ★ ★

Megan caught her sister up and walked home with her, but she waited until Hetty had dealt with George's knee and he was in the parlour reading a comic with his grandmother before she got her on her own in the kitchen with the door firmly shut.

'What's making you so unhappy, Hetty?' she asked. 'And I don't just mean the incident in the park.'

'Mind your own business.'

'I've minded my own business for long enough, watching you get more and more miserable each day.'

'It's nothing to do with you.'

'Strictly speaking that's true. But you're my sister and I care about you.'

'Keep your nose out of my affairs.'

'There's obviously something wrong between you and Ken and it's having an effect on George,' Megan went on, undaunted. 'That's when it becomes my business. He's my nephew and my godson. It's my duty to look out for him.'

'You're bound to take Ken's side,' Hetty grumbled. 'You've always thought I'm overprotective of George.'

'You were this afternoon, that's for sure,' stated Megan. 'It was little more than a scratch on his knee and the lad wanted to stay in the park because he was having fun. It certainly didn't warrant him being dragged home to be smothered in Germolene and have a ruddy great bandage put on. You'll have a hypochondriac on your hands if you carry on like this.'

'Do I tell you how to bring up your girls?'

'No, and neither do I tell you how to raise George,' retorted Megan. 'You make the occasional criticism of the way I do things, and I am doing the same thing now because I'm worried about the three of you. That incident in the park was completely uncalled for. It upset George and Ken. But most of all it upset you.'

'Leave me alone, will you?' And with that Hetty burst into tears.

Megan held her close while she cried her heart out. Then she made some tea and they sat at the kitchen table to drink it.

'I take it things are really bad between you and Ken?' said Megan eventually, when she judged the time to be right.

Her sister nodded. 'Oh it's all such a mess,' she said thickly. 'The poor man has been in a prison camp for all those years and I should be being kind to him. Instead I'm horrid and I can't help myself, and I'm permanently racked with guilt, which makes me even more bad tempered.

316

As hard as I try, I can't stop being irritable with him.'

'You're not expected to be kind to him all the time because he's been locked up in a prison camp,' Megan pointed out. 'That's too much to expect of anyone, and the last thing he would want. Life goes on and the war is over now.'

'But I can't seem to be pleasant to him for more than five minutes at a time,' Hetty confessed, sounding desperate. 'As hard as I try, he always does something to annoy me and I start going on at him and hate myself for it. I don't remember being irritated by him before he went away.'

'I'm sure you must have been at times.'

'Not like this. Now I'm permanently on edge,' she said. 'I'm used to doing things my way and being solely responsible for George. Ken doesn't have a clue how to handle the boy and he will keep on interfering.'

'He *is* George's father,' Megan reminded her. 'He's entitled to have a say in things.'

'He knows nothing about looking after children. Nothing at all!'

'He seems to have got the general idea,' Megan pointed out. 'All right, so his way of doing things might not be the same as yours, but that doesn't mean his way is wrong. You can't blame him for wanting to be a part of his son's life. Plenty of men leave it all to their wives, so you're lucky. It isn't as if he's trying to take control away from you; he just wants to be included in George's life.'

'You're right, of course.' Hetty paused,

cradling her teacup and looking thoughtful, her eyes swollen from crying. 'This is going to sound really terrible, and you are the only person I would admit it to, but I sometimes feel as if I don't want Ken in my life at all; that I was better on my own when it was just George and me. I did as I pleased then and made my own decisions.'

'Are you saying, then,' Megan began tentatively, 'that you don't love Ken any more?'

'I don't know what I mean.' Hetty looked tortured. 'I'm totally confused about my feelings. All I do know is that when I saw him standing on the doorstep looking so thin and different, I felt as if I was looking at a stranger, and it frightened the life out of me. I felt very sorry for him, but at the same time I wanted to run away. That special loving feeling has gone and I can't get it back.' She leaned on her elbows with her head in her hands. 'I just want everything to be how it was before he went away. We were happy then.'

'Nothing will be the same for any of us,' Megan said slowly. 'The war changed everything. The men have been through hell and we've got used to managing without them. Now that they're home we have to let them back into our lives. It will be a gradual process for a lot of people.'

'You don't seem to have had any difficulty letting Will back into yours,' Hetty mentioned. 'The two of you seem blissfully happy together.'

'We are, but it wasn't something I could have expected. Over the years he was away, I wondered if it would be different. I remember telling you my thoughts on the subject years ago. But as it happens, I needn't have worried, because as soon as I set eyes on him I knew I was still in love with him, and he with me. Everything else can be sorted as long as we have that,' she said. 'Will and I had our problems before he went away, because his dark moods made him uncommunicative, and I don't suppose it'll be all plain sailing in the future, because it isn't for anyone. But at the moment we are very happy and I'm making the most of it.'

'It was the exact opposite for me,' confessed Hetty. 'It never even occurred to me that anything would have changed between Ken and me when he came home. I just took it for granted that we would carry on where we left off. So I was quite unprepared.'

'Do you still have any feelings for Ken at all?' ventured Megan. 'Or can you simply not stand the sight of the man?'

'I still have feelings for him, and I want my marriage to get back on track,' Hetty said. 'But . . . there are times when I don't want him anywhere near me.'

'We all feel like that about our other halves from time to time,' said Megan. 'That's just human nature.'

'No. This is more than that. It's really strong,' Hetty said. 'I'm particularly resentful as regards his relationship with George. Oh, kid, what shall I do?'

Megan sighed, thinking what a terrible situation her sister found herself in.

'I can't tell you what to do or how you should feel. No one can manufacture feelings. But I will say that whatever happens between you and Ken personally, you'll have to learn to trust him with George. You can't keep the boy all to yourself. It wouldn't be fair to George for one thing. He needs you both, and he's been deprived of his dad for long enough.'

'And if I can't do it?'

'You'll have to force yourself, Hetty,' Megan advised. 'It might help if you keep it in your mind that Ken's a smashing bloke and you had a good marriage once.'

Hetty nodded.

'I hope you can make it work, kid,' said Megan. 'I hate to see you so unhappy; both of you. I'm fond of Ken too.'

'I have to make it work,' declared Hetty. 'What choice is there? I married Ken until death us do part.'

'Yes, you did.' Megan could hear voices outside. 'I think the others have arrived back, so if you want to put things right, now's your chance to make a start.'

But she knew it wasn't that simple. If it was, Hetty wouldn't be in this miserable state. Knowing how possessive her sister was towards George, Megan couldn't see a solution. She did know for certain, though, that Ken was showing the strain, and that he, like any other man, could only take so much.

12

'Well . . . what do you think of the new gear?' asked Will, sashaying around the parlour in his navy-blue pinstripe demob suit with a trilby hat worn at a jaunty angle. He lifted the hat and swept the air with it, bending over into an exaggerated bow. 'How's that for a titfer?'

'Ooh, very snazzy,' approved Megan.

'The hat's all right, but the suit doesn't fit you at all,' observed Hetty. 'It's all skew-whiff.'

'I've been to the demob centre, not Savile Row,' grinned Will, taking it all in good part. 'It'll do me for the time being.'

'The army are consistent, I'll say that much for them,' Ken expressed waggishly. 'Yours fits about as well as mine and every other ex-serviceman's I know.'

'Ken's would look better on a kangaroo than it looks on him,' Hetty chuckled. 'It's short in the arms and the trousers are as baggy as bell tents.'

'They're kitting out a lot of people, so you can't expect tailor-made clothes,' Dolly reminded them. 'Anyway, I think you look very handsome, Will. You'll turn a few female heads in that get-up.'

'Not if I'm anywhere near,' laughed Megan. 'In fact, I think I'll pin a notice on his jacket saying 'Hands off; already spoken for.' '

'They might think you mean the suit and stick a label on him saying 'You're welcome.' '

This raised a laugh.

'You won't rattle my cage today, no matter how much you take the mick,' pronounced Will, smiling. 'Nothing will upset me today because I'm a free man. Demobbed at last! Oh, what a lovely feeling!'

The shop was closed for the dinner hour, the children were at school and the adults were about to sit down to eat.

'I can remember feeling very chuffed with myself on demob day too,' recalled Ken thoughtfully. 'I thought, right, that's it, the government have had more than their money's worth out of me, now I've got my life back.'

'The sweet taste of freedom,' said Will. 'You can't beat it.'

'You're bound to feel like that after what you've been through,' said Dolly.

'You deserve to feel proud of yourselves as well,' added Hetty, who'd been doing her very best to be nice to Ken ever since she'd poured her heart out to her sister and been told a few home truths.

'That's all in the past,' said Will breezily. 'This is a time to look forward, not back.'

'Hear, hear!' said Megan.

'And looking forward in the short term to tonight, if my wife isn't too embarrassed to be seen out with me, I'd like to take her out to celebrate my demob.'

'Embarrassed is the last thing I'll be, you twerp,' Megan tutted good-humouredly. 'Every other man you see is wearing a suit that doesn't fit.' She paused. 'There is a slight snag, though.

322

We have two children we can't just go out and leave.'

'I was coming to that,' he explained. 'Any offers on the baby-sitting front?'

'Yeah, of course we'll do it,' Hetty agreed at once. 'You go out and enjoy yourselves.'

'I'll be here too,' offered Dolly.

'Ta very much, all of you.' Megan looked at her sister. 'We'll do the same for you with George if you two want to go out on your own one night.'

'Thanks,' said Hetty, knowing for certain that she wouldn't take them up on it. She wasn't going to leave George for any reason other than an emergency. Ken had suggested they go out on their own several times since he'd been home, but she'd made some excuse so he'd given up asking, and sometimes went down to the pub of an evening without her. She thought the poor man probably needed a break after putting up with her all day. She was trying so hard not to be irritable with him and not to come between him and George, but her adverse feelings towards him were so strong she couldn't always manage it. Criticism and annoyance consumed her at the slightest thing, causing a barrier between them as she struggled not to show it and suspected that she was failing miserably.

'So get your best clothes out, darlin',' said Will now to Megan, 'because tonight, my beautiful wife, you and me are going to paint the town.'

'Smashing,' enthused Megan.

★ ★ ★

Painting the town proved to be something of an exaggeration on Will's part, but they did go to the West End to the cinema to see a Hollywood spectacular with lots of singing and dancing. To make the evening a bit special they had a drink in a pub first and a sausage-and-mash supper afterwards.

Although the only new clothes around were utility ones, and they were still on ration, Megan could usually manage to make herself look smart from the most limited of wardrobes. Tonight she was wearing a light blue jumper with a chiffon scarf tied jauntily at the neck, a straight black skirt and high-heeled court shoes. A light dusting of powder and rouge with a pink lipstick added a subtle touch of glamour.

'I'm having such a lovely time, Will,' she told him over supper in a side-street café near Leicester Square. 'I love our girls to bits, but it's nice to be on our own occasionally. They don't give us much privacy, do they?'

'They certainly don't.' He smiled affectionately. 'They're little smashers, though, and a constant source of fascination to me,' he told her, looking misty-eyed. 'I could watch them all day. I wish I hadn't missed so much of their childhood.'

'Mm, it's a shame about that, but there's no point in dwelling on it because you can't change what's gone. All you can do is make the most of the present.'

'And look forward to the future,' he added, his voice rising with enthusiasm. 'Now that I'm free of the army at last, I can start to turn my plans into reality. Oh love, it's going to be so good. I'm going to make you so proud.'

'I am already.'

'I'll make you even more so,' he promised. 'I'll have to start small, of course, and materials won't be easy to get hold of. But I'll get stuff somehow. Where there's a will there's a way, so they say. People are desperate for a spruce-up to their homes, and there are a million and one small building jobs that need doing in the London area. I shall go out knocking on doors to find work if necessary.'

'Good for you.' She looked at him searchingly. 'I don't know if it's just my imagination, but you seem to be different in your attitude since you've been back; more positive about everything.'

'Do I? Maybe it's because I've realised how lucky I am to have come back, and that sort of puts things into perspective,' he said, seeming to lapse into thought, a frown furrowing his brow as though remembering sadder times. 'Living so close to death changes you. A lot of my army pals didn't make it, the poor devils. Young men with their lives ahead of them; gone just like that.'

She nodded sympathetically but didn't make comment. The men must have suffered unimaginable traumas at the front. But Will never spoke about what life had been like, beyond the odd humorous anecdote concerning his army pals.

'I find it difficult to be pessimistic about anything too,' she told him. 'I know that food is shorter than ever, and we still have to queue for every single thing, but there are no more bombs and you are home safe, so life has to be good even if it's going to take a while for everything else to get better. I genuinely believe that the future is bright for the people of this country. I don't see how it can be otherwise when the war is over.'

'It'll be bright for you and me and the girls. I shall make damned sure of it,' he told her. 'Whatever the state of the economy.'

She reached over and took his hand. 'I'll be beside you all the way,' she said.

'That's my girl.' He squeezed her hand. 'On a practical note, the first thing I have to do is to ask your mum if I can put the dairy phone number on my advertisements. So with a bit of luck, you'll be answering the phone for me while I'm out working.'

'Exciting, eh?'

'Very.' He looked at her across the table, her clear blue eyes brimming with trust for him. She was so unconditionally encouraging about his new project, wanting to help, willing him to do well and never once doubting his ability to do so, and he felt a sudden piercing stab of compunction. Would she feel the same way about him if she knew what he'd done and what a coward he was not to own up to it?

Should he tell her the truth so that she could judge for herself? Didn't she have a right to know the sort of man she was married to? Then she smiled into his eyes and he knew he wasn't going to do it. He couldn't take the risk of losing her. Once again he had shirked it; once again he'd not been man enough to come clean.

'What's the matter, Will?' she asked. 'You look all worried suddenly.'

'Nothing,' he said, forcing a smile. 'I'm all right.'

She knew some dark thought had come into his mind, and she had a pretty good idea what it was. Until now she had thought he had managed to put it behind him. But it was still there, lurking in the shadows of his memory, surfacing and tormenting him every so often. Her heart sank as she knew that she must tell him the truth, even if it meant the end of their marriage. It was her duty as his wife. She couldn't let him go on punishing himself for something he hadn't done. It wouldn't be right.

Then he gave her a melting smile and said, 'You mean the world to me, Megan. Everything is worthwhile because you are there in my life and in my heart. There wouldn't be any point in making plans for the future if I didn't have you and the girls.'

She was lost, all resolve gone. She knew she wasn't going to tell him, and was ashamed.

★　★　★

Although rationing continued and the food queues grew ever longer, weeds flourished on the untouched bomb sites and shabbiness prevailed everywhere, there was an underlying spirit of optimism in the air. People were fed up with seemingly endless hardship and vociferous in their complaints about it, but the majority of them had faith in better times ahead.

Megan and Will certainly had cause to be cheerful as requests for work came in thick and fast. Off he went every day on his bike and when he got home there were usually some new enquiries, so he was kept busy either going out looking at jobs or actually working. With spring around the corner he expected to be even busier.

'You can do this place up if you get a slack patch and need something to keep you going,' Dolly told him one evening when they were all sitting around in the parlour before bedtime. She cast her eye over the room. 'It's looking very tatty. The business will pay you for it. But you get yourself established first and keep that as a standby.'

'Thanks, Mrs M, I'll bear that in mind,' he said.

'You must be making a fortune, all the hours you put in,' remarked Ken. He wasn't maliciously jealous of Will but he couldn't help noticing that everything seemed to go Will's way, at work and in his private life. Ken couldn't help wishing he himself had fared better as regarded the latter.

'No one makes a fortune painting walls, mate. I'm making a decent living through sheer hard graft and hours worked. I'm not looking to get rich at this stage, especially not from people who can't afford high prices.'

'Why burden yourself with all the worry of working for yourself, then?' Ken was curious to know.

'I'm just doing the groundwork for my long-term plans,' Will explained. 'I won't always be going off with my ladders on my bike. Building is the thing to get into at the moment and that's what I intend to do when the time is right. That's when I'll make some real money, with a bit of luck. But it won't be right away and it won't just fall into my lap. I've got a good bit of hard work ahead of me. But I'll need to use my savvy, too, for the business side of things.'

'I think I'd sooner work for an employer,' said Ken. 'Let him find the work and do the worrying.'

'I enjoy working for myself,' Will explained. 'I like a challenge and it's good not having a boss breathing down my neck. You can't beat it, mate.'

'You do have a boss,' Megan reminded him laughingly. 'You have me.'

He raised his eyes, grinning. 'And you're scarier than any official guv'nor.'

'I can see you trembling,' she joked.

'So you wouldn't fancy trying something new then, Ken?' asked Will with friendly interest.

'I'd like to make more money, the same as anyone else, but as long as I can support my wife and child and get us a place of our own eventually, you won't hear me complaining.' He looked at Dolly and winked. 'Besides, I wouldn't want to desert Mrs M.'

'We managed while you were away,' Hetty reminded him. 'We could do it again if you wanted to try your hand at something else.' She gave him a warning look. 'As long as it was something with a regular income.'

'Self-employment isn't my sort of thing at all. I'm all right as I am.'

Dolly cleared her throat. 'Actually, there is something I've been wanting to talk to all of you about,' she began hesitantly, looking solemn, 'and now is as good a time as any, while we're all here together and the children are in bed.'

'That sounds ominous,' said Megan. 'Have you fallen for a man or something?'

'Don't be flippant, dear,' Dolly said in a tone of mild admonition. 'It's a serious matter.'

'We're all listening,' said Megan, worried by her mother's grave tone.

'I've had a letter from Capital Dairies,' Dolly announced. 'They want to buy us out.'

There was a shocked silence, as they all just stared at her.

'They've bought out most of the small independent dairies in London. Isn't that enough for them?' Megan burst out eventually.

'It's a very generous offer.' Dolly had her own reasons for wanting to present the facts without bias. 'They would pay me a lump sum for the dairy premises and the round, and if we wish, we could continue to run the dairy for a wage, and stay on in the house. We'd have to pay them rent, of course.'

'And do things their way,' Ken chipped in.

'Well, yes, of course. It would be their business, so that goes without saying,' responded Dolly.

'They'd probably want to make all sorts of changes,' predicted Ken gloomily. 'They'd control what you stocked in the shop; probably even set new shop hours.'

There was a brief hiatus before Dolly caused a

330

sharp intake of breath all round by announcing, 'The shop would cease to exist. They want to use that space to extend the dairy; they would install new equipment, much more modern and expensive than ours. They're a big company so they can afford it. I get the impression that they want to go into other dairy products too, cheese and butter and so on, when the wartime restrictions are lifted. To deliver to the customers along with the milk.'

'You're not seriously considering the offer, are you, Mum?' asked Megan, aghast at the idea.

'I'm not dismissing it out of hand, put it that way,' she replied. 'But what I do about it depends on all of you. I want this to be a family decision.'

'Dad would turn in his grave if you were to sell out,' Megan proclaimed.

'Times are changing,' Dolly pointed out. 'There isn't as much call for small independent dairies these days as there was when your dad started this one.'

'I disagree entirely,' argued Ken. 'There's a huge need for a small business like yours where the customers get personal service. If the shop closed it would be a blow to the locals as well as to you. They rely on it.'

Dolly's eyes were clouded with worry. She hated arguments within the family. 'Look, I've had a fair offer and I have done nothing about it yet. I wanted to discuss it with you all before responding.' She paused, her eyes turning to them all in turn. 'I should explain that when this offer came in, I saw the chance to set you all up.

I would split the lump sum three ways equally between myself and my daughters. This would benefit you boys too, because what's theirs is yours as far as I'm concerned. There should be enough for you both to put a deposit down on a place of your own when more houses become available.'

'I can't speak for Hetty, but I wouldn't take a penny of your money,' declared Megan at once. 'You and Dad built the business, so anything you get for it would be yours entirely.'

'That goes for me too,' added Hetty.

'You'd be having your inheritance early, that's all,' Dolly pointed out. 'You'd get it now, when you need it, not later on, after I die. It'll make things easier for you.'

'I still wouldn't take it,' said Megan.

'Nor me.'

'Don't forget that they are promising me paid employment with them, so I would still be able to earn my living, and have a tidy sum put by,' Dolly said.

'But you'd be stuck in the dairy all day instead of working in a friendly little shop where you know all the customers,' disapproved Megan. 'I don't think you'd like that one little bit.'

'I'd manage.'

'But we don't want you to just manage.' Megan was ardent about it. 'We want you to do something you enjoy. You love the shop, and you'd be lost without it.'

'That's beside the point,' Dolly persisted, 'This is a chance to get you set up at a time when you really need it.'

Will made a timely intervention. 'If you do decide to go ahead and accept the offer, Mrs M, Megan's share of the money would stay hers. I wouldn't take a penny of it. I want to make my own way and provide for my wife and children myself. I feel very strongly about that.'

'Hear, hear!' said Ken.

Dolly sighed. 'All right, let's take a vote on it,' she suggested. 'Those in favour of selling?'

Not a hand was raised.

'Those in favour of keeping the dairy and carrying on as we are?'

All hands shot up.

For a moment Dolly couldn't speak. 'Thank you,' she said at last, her eyes brimming with tears and her voice quivering. 'I really appreciate your loyalty. I'm so proud of you all.'

'We're just scared Dad will come back to haunt us if we let you sell his precious dairy,' said Megan in a light-hearted manner to ease her mother through an emotional moment.

'He might just do that if I were to sell up,' Dolly responded, dabbing at her eyes with a handkerchief. 'I'll write and tell them that I'm not interested in their offer. And they can't steal our delivery customers because the government is keeping the wartime law as it is as regards each dairy having its own territory. So our milk round is safe.'

'The big boys are just after running the milk trade for the whole of London, I reckon,' suggested Will. 'There won't be any small dairies with corner shops left if they have their way, and people will be the worse off for it.'

'There aren't as many as there used to be. Lots have been taken over already,' Dolly told him. 'But thanks to you lot, this one is here to stay.'

'Morgan's for ever,' said Will, raising his arms, and a cheer went up.

Dolly was awash with warmth towards her lovely family, and that included her sons-in-law. She had just offered them a substantial sum of money and they had turned it down because of love for her and for family tradition. The loss of her husband, who had been her soulmate, best friend and lover, had left her with a permanent sense of desolation, no matter how many people were around. The expression of family devotion she had just witnessed lessened the feeling and gave her the strength to carry on.

★　★　★

It was a beautiful spring Sunday afternoon and Will, Megan and the twins were taking a leisurely stroll along the riverside. Will was only there under protest. He didn't much care for the riverside. Megan was hoping that coming here might drive out his demons.

'There are plenty of other places we can take the girls on a Sunday afternoon,' he grumbled as the children went on ahead, skipping and running. 'The park, for instance. There's much more space for them to run about there.'

'They go there all the time, so this is a nice change,' Megan said. 'I'm hoping you might learn to like it again.'

334

'They could have had a go on the swings at the park.'

'There are no swings,' she reminded him. 'They were taken away for the war effort and haven't been replaced yet.'

'Oh yeah, that's true, but we could have had a game with the ball . . . Oi, come away from the edge, you two. Careful; now watch where you're going, both of you.'

'Calm down, Will,' Megan chided. 'They'll be all right, I promise.'

They walked on, but Will was tense and had his eyes glued to his daughters.

'It's nice to see people out in pleasure boats, isn't it?' Megan remarked chattily, hoping to take his mind off the children so that he could relax and enjoy himself. 'The riverside is a place to have fun again after the long war years.'

'It's a mess,' he complained, glancing with disapproval to the side of them, where there was a large bomb site, untidy and littered with rubbish and weeds. 'It's about time they got things smartened up and started building.'

'People say that they are not going to put anything up in this area. It's going to be public gardens with lawns, flower beds and benches,' she mentioned.

'I'll believe that when I see it.' Will's mind was still on his daughters.

'It will be rather nice when it does happen, don't you think?' persisted Megan, ignoring his negative attitude. 'To have somewhere quiet where we can sit and enjoy the river and the fresh air while we watch the boats go by.'

But her words fell on deaf ears. He had darted forward and grabbed hold of Poppy, who had been walking slightly nearer to the edge of the towpath, though not dangerously so.

'You mustn't go that close to the bank,' he reprimanded her, so sharply that she collapsed into tears. 'It's far too dangerous. You could have fallen in.'

'I wouldn't have fallen in, Daddy,' wailed the child. 'I know I'm not allowed to go too near the edge and I didn't.'

'That water is very deep when the tide's in.'

'Sorry, Dad,' she sobbed.

'All right,' he said, wiping her eyes and putting his arm around her. 'Just make sure you're careful when you're near the river, and that goes for you too, Netta. Understand?'

'All right, Dad.'

Megan held her tongue because she didn't want to undermine his authority in front of them. But when the girls went on ahead she said, 'Go easy on them, Will. She wasn't too near the edge and neither of them will be because I've taught them not to. They've been brought up living near the river and they know the rules. Keep an eye on them, by all means, but don't scare the living daylights out of them.'

'She could have missed her footing and gone over the edge just then,' he insisted, his voice ragged with emotion. 'The Thames isn't just a gentle little stream, you know. It's a powerful river, and it shows no mercy to its victims. It's taken no end of lives.'

'I know all that, but it isn't fair to make the

girls nervous of the water because of what happened to your brother,' she told him firmly. 'We live in a riverside town. Of course they like to come down here. I did at that age and so did you. Children have always enjoyed rivers, and we are privileged to live so close to the Thames. It's part of our heritage. Don't spoil it for them.'

'You wouldn't say that if one of them fell in.'

'Of course I wouldn't. I'm not some sort of an idiot,' she responded crossly. 'But they never come here without an adult.'

'They will when they're older unless they're discouraged now,' he said.

'It doesn't work that way. They'll be even more drawn to the place if we stop them coming here now,' she said.

'Mm, maybe you're right.'

'The world is full of danger, Will, and we won't be able to protect them from everything when they're old enough to go out on their own,' she pointed out. 'We mustn't instil fear into them so that they grow up being afraid of everything. During the air raids, when terrible danger was all around us, I tried to protect them from fear by never showing mine.'

When he didn't reply, she turned to him and saw that he was pale and trembling slightly. She glanced ahead to see that the girls were a safe distance from the bank, and took hold of his arm in a reassuring gesture.

'They'll be fine. You mustn't worry so much. I've kept them safe so far, haven't I?'

'Yeah, course you have.'

'And I'll keep on doing that, and so will you,' she said gently. 'But they have to be allowed to be children. I know you're nervous about the river, and any parent worth their salt would keep a close eye on their offspring near water of any kind. But you're really frightened for them and it shows. I don't want them to pick up on it.'

'Sorry.'

'There's no need to apologise. Being a parent means being constantly vulnerable,' she said. 'But we mustn't let them know that.'

'I'm not making a very good job of being a dad, am I?'

'You're making a brilliant job of it,' she said with ardour. 'The kids love you despite the fact that you're firm with them when you need to be. You've got the whole thing right except for this phobia about the river.'

'I just can't bear it here.'

'Oh come on, Will, you've fought in the war, I'm sure you're not going to let a strip of water faze you.'

'I'm scared for them, not for myself,' he explained. 'I know how easily it can happen. You can be larking about one minute and dead the next.'

She didn't respond at once, and when she spoke she chose her words carefully. 'It's time to put it behind you, Will,' she advised him gravely. 'You're a father now. It wouldn't be right to pass on your personal fears to your children.'

'You're right, I know,' he sighed. 'I'll try and

338

keep it in check in the future.'

She reached up and kissed him on the cheek. 'You'll do it,' she said. 'You can do anything you set your mind to.'

'What did I do to deserve a wife like you?' he said, smiling at her and trying not to show how riddled with guilt he was for not being the man she thought he was.

'You don't need to do anything other than be yourself,' she told him, slipping her arm through his. 'Now come on, we'd better get along and catch up with those daughters of ours before they get into some sort of mischief.'

They walked arm in arm along the towpath, the river gleaming patchily in varying shades of green, brown and grey, the familiar sight of Hammersmith Bridge in the distance outlined against the clear blue sky.

On the surface all was well, but Megan was uneasy and shaky inside, which she realised was a lingering reaction to the mention of Will's brother's drowning.

Will obviously still wasn't over it and she had the power to help him here and now. He probably never would recover entirely from losing his twin, but he could be freed from misplaced guilt. So why didn't she just speak out? Was she so shallow she was allowing her own selfish fear of losing him to restrain her? It was partly that, she was ashamed to admit. She hated herself for her cowardice, but the price was simply too high.

★ ★ ★

Megan decided that her mother needed a night out, so she booked tickets for the Shepherd's Bush Empire, where her parents had been regular patrons when her father was alive.

Hetty, who refused to go out and leave George, stayed at home with the children. Dolly wore her best hat — a navy-blue one with a feather — and a jacket and skirt in the same shade. They spent all their sweet coupons on toffees and fruit drops, which they started on as soon as they were settled into their seats for an evening of variety entertainment. People were pouring into the auditorium and the familiar sound of the orchestra tuning up against the warm and vibrant roar of conversation added to the excitement.

'It's very good of you to organise this for me, Megan,' said Dolly.

'It's the least I can do after everything you've done for me over the years,' Megan responded.

'I'm very grateful anyway,' Dolly made clear. 'I must admit I do miss having a night out every now and again. I used to enjoy going out occasionally of an evening with your dad. It was something to dress up for.'

'Whenever you fancy it, you tell me and I'll arrange something,' promised Megan.

The orchestra struck up and the curtains opened. For the next few hours they sat back and allowed themselves to be enthralled by a rich diversity of performers. The show opened with dancing girls high-kicking across the stage; then there was a female singer with a saucy repertoire, a woman with performing chickens, a troupe of acrobats, various other novelty acts, and at the top of the bill the famous comedy duo Flanagan and Allen, who closed the show sentimentally with their well-known ballad 'Underneath the Arches'.

'A good show, wasn't it?' remarked Megan, as they walked home in the spring night, still revelling in the fact that they could be out on the streets without fear for their lives.

'Smashing,' was her mother's response. 'I enjoyed every minute.'

'Me too.'

'It's a pity Hetty didn't come with us,' Dolly went on chattily. 'George would have been all right with the men. A night out would do her good.'

'You know Hetty. She won't go anywhere without George, and I don't think the Empire is quite the thing for a little boy except at pantomime time.'

'She's a very diligent mother and I'm proud of her for that,' proclaimed Dolly. 'But everyone needs a bit of a break occasionally, and there's no harm in going out for an evening with your mum and sister so long as you know that your kiddie is being properly looked after.'

'She won't even leave George to go out with Ken,' mentioned Megan. 'So we stand no chance.'

'Is everything all right with those two?' Dolly enquired. 'There always seems to be a bad atmosphere between them, and you can't help but hear them arguing in their room.'

'I think they're having a bit of trouble

adjusting to each other after such a long separation,' replied Megan. 'I expect they'll come through it in time.'

'They'll have to, won't they?' Dolly looked worried. 'They're married with a child. Their personal feelings must come second to George.'

'I'm sure they'll work it out,' said Megan, hoping to reassure her mother, but she wasn't at all confident herself, because Hetty and Ken bickered endlessly. 'Don't you spoil your evening by worrying about them.'

'Thanks again for tonight,' said Dolly as she drew the key through the letter box on the end of a piece of string and put it into the lock. 'You're a good daughter to me.'

'It was a pleasure.'

Megan followed her mother into the hall and they took their coats off and hung them up. The sound of male voices coming from the parlour was loud and exuberant; talking interspersed with raucous laughter.

'The men are a bit lively tonight,' remarked Dolly.

'Perhaps they went to the pub and had one too many.'

Dolly opened the door to the parlour and called out, 'Coo-ee, everyone. We're home.'

'We've got a visitor for you, Mrs M,' Megan heard Will say. 'Ken and I found him propping up the bar in the local and brought him home to say hello to you.'

'Doug!' exclaimed Dolly, her voice rising with pleasure. 'How lovely to see you again. It's been ages.' She went into the room. 'Come here so I can give you a hug.'

'Sorry I've left it so long, Mrs M,' Megan heard him say. 'I should have come to see you before. I just haven't got round to it somehow.'

'Don't you worry about that, son,' she assured him warmly. 'We're pleased to see you whenever you turn up. Come and see who's here, Megan.'

Outside the door Megan felt as though all the blood had drained from her and her legs had turned to water. She'd known this moment would come at some point but had pushed it to the back of her mind. Doug Reynolds was Will's best pal, so it was obvious that sooner or later the two would have got together again. Bracing herself and taking a deep breath to try and calm herself, she walked into the room.

'Hello, Doug,' she said, struggling to keep her voice steady. 'How are you?'

'Mustn't grumble. Yourself?'

'I'm fine, thanks,' she replied. 'All the better for having Will home, as you can probably imagine.'

'I'm sure.'

'You two are very formal with each other tonight,' remarked Will, squinting at them and half smiling. 'Anyone would think you were complete strangers. But Megan, you told me in your letters that Doug used to come to visit when he was home on sick leave. Your husband's best pal who you haven't seen for ages: I should have thought you could do better than that. A peck on the cheek at least.'

With tension drawing so tight her breathing was short, Megan moved robot-like towards him and briefly brushed his cheek with her lips, feeling nauseous as she did and glad to move away.

'That's better,' said Will. 'Now I feel as if we're all friends together here.'

Throughout this whole charade Megan had been studiously avoiding Doug's eyes. But her gaze moved inexorably in his direction and she was chilled at what she saw there. He transmitted a threat as plain as if he'd announced it to the room, even though he had his mouth arranged convincingly into a smile.

'Have they given you a cup of tea or anything?' enquired Dolly, ever the diligent hostess.

'We haven't got around to that yet,' replied Doug 'We've been too busy talking about old times and swapping army stories. Ken's missus was driven to bed out of boredom.'

'I'll put the kettle on, Mum,' offered Megan, desperate to escape. 'You stay here and chat. I know how fond you are of Doug.'

In the kitchen Megan was shaking so much she had to hold on to the table to steady herself for a moment, her hands trembling as she made the tea. Just the sight of Doug made her skin crawl. How was she going to cope with seeing him on a regular basis? Now that they had got together again, Will's friendship with him would probably resume, which would inevitably mean him dropping in from time to time.

It was essential she didn't allow him to see how intimidated she was by him. There was no time like the present to get her message across, she thought as she carried the tea into the parlour wishing she didn't feel so shaky and hoping the cups and saucers wouldn't rattle on the tray.

★   ★   ★

The worst thing for Megan was the way they were all making such a fuss of Doug as he played the brave, uncomplaining hero, self-effacing and humble.

'No point in moaning about it, is there?' he said in the way he had of inducing sympathy that Megan knew so well and could see right through. There was no sign of the anger and bitterness she guessed were still simmering away inside him. 'There are plenty of chaps with worse injuries than I've got. It's just a question of putting up with it and getting on with life.'

'Ken and I got off scot-free in comparison,' observed Will. 'I've had a few bullets removed but no long-term damage. We're all scarred, of course.'

'You're right there,' said Ken, rising. 'But as much as I'm enjoying your company, folks, my bed is calling me. It's an early start in the morning for us milkmen. G'night, all.'

'I bet you're glad you don't have to do the milk round now, aren't you, Megan?' remarked Doug when Ken had gone. 'When I last saw you, you were the one up early and out on the streets at the crack of dawn.'

'I didn't mind it actually,' she told him, waiting for the opportunity to leave this gathering without Will sensing anything was wrong. 'There's something very special about being out so early in the morning. Though, naturally, the actual getting out of bed wasn't much fun.'

Her chance to go came at that moment, when Dolly said she was going to bed.

'Me too,' said Megan, rising.

'Stay a minute, will you, love?' Will requested.

'Why?'

'I need to answer a call of nature. Could you stay and talk to Doug while I'm gone? It isn't much fun for him to sit here on his own when we've not seen him in such a long time. I'll only be gone a minute.'

Megan's heart did double somersaults now that she was alone with Doug. She perched on the edge of the sofa and stared at the floor. She didn't want to speak or even look at him.

'So . . . how have you been?' Doug enquired.

'You've already asked me that and I've told you, so don't bother to ask again to make conversation,' she said.

'Ooh, pardon me for breathing.'

'Look, I've told Will I'll stay here until he gets back, but I don't want to speak to you,' she made clear. 'I don't want to have anything to do with you.'

'That's not very nice.'

'Neither was what you did,' she snapped. 'So don't bother to keep the act up with me.'

'I don't know what you mean,' he stated. 'Have I upset you in some way?'

'Oh stop playing silly games, for goodness'

346

sake, you stupid man,' she said angrily. 'You are Will's pal so you're going to be around and I shall have to be polite to you in front of him, unfortunately. But that's as far as it goes.'

'I don't know what you're talking about . . . '

'Now you're just taking the mick. Shut up or I just might lose my temper, and you wouldn't want me to do that, would you?' she said through gritted teeth. 'You never know what I might blurt out if that were to happen.'

'I think I must be missing something here,' Doug said, spreading his hands and looking at her as though genuinely baffled. 'I really don't know why you're so angry, or why you might lose your temper on my account.'

It was sinister the way he was pretending that nothing had happened. She wasn't sure if it was because it was nothing much to him, or if it was all part of the way he operated, to perplex and unnerve her. He was so convincing, it was almost enough to make her wonder if she had imagined the whole thing.

Mercifully, Will came back into the room at that moment.

'I thought I heard raised voices,' he said, looking from one to the other. 'I hope you two haven't fallen out.'

'Of course we haven't,' lied Meg. 'Why would we?'

'Exactly,' added Doug. 'Your wife and I are the best of friends, aren't we, Megan?'

She was forced to look at him, and now she saw such evil in his eyes, she knew he was having a wonderful time playing mind games with her.

'Yeah, that's right,' she said.

'Good,' said Will.

'But I'll leave you two to talk about old times if you don't mind. I'm feeling a bit tired.' Megan went over to Will and kissed him on the lips. 'Good night, darling.'

'I'll be up in a few minutes, love,' he said.

'Good night, Megan,' said Doug.

'Night,' she said without looking at him, and hurried from the room.

What a ghastly trap she was in, and the consequences of escape were awesome. But she daren't let Doug break her spirit. Seeing him had brought the whole thing to the front of her mind again, though: the dilemma of whether or not to tell Will the truth. She had to do what was best for him. It wasn't just a question of the risk of losing him; there was also the anguish he would suffer knowing that his best friend had betrayed him in two of the most terrible ways.

Whatever else, she must keep her head and act normally for the moment, for Will's sake. He was the one who mattered most in all this.

13

A veil of sadness fell upon the dairy one Saturday in early summer when the family's beloved horse Chips became ill while out on the round and subsequently died. He'd had a heart attack and nothing could be done to save him, despite Ken's frantic dash through the town to get the vet. They were all devastated, but the children were inconsolable, especially George.

'We won't see him again ever, will we?' he said soulfully. They were all gathered in the parlour, where Ken had just broken the news after his distressing ordeal in the street with the sick horse. 'He's gone, just like Grandad.'

'I'm afraid we won't see him any more, son,' said Ken. 'But we must remember that he had a good life with people who loved him.'

'Why did he die?' asked George.

'He got sick, son,' explained Ken. 'We wouldn't want him to soldier on in pain and feeling poorly, would we?'

'No,' chorused the children sadly. Even the twins were subdued.

'Is he in the same heaven as Grandad?' George was curious to know. 'Or do animals go to a different one?'

'I don't know the answer to that,' replied Ken. 'But I should think they'll be together, the same as they were here. I'm sure wherever they are, they'll look out for each other.'

'Poor Chips,' said Netta, sniffing.

'I hope he isn't hurting,' said George.

'He won't be now, son; he's at peace,' Ken assured him. 'I know we all want that for him.'

'Yeah, we do,' agreed George. 'But it's just so awful that he's gone.'

'We're all going to miss him; there's no doubt about that,' said Dolly thickly. 'He's been like one of the family. Your grandad loved that animal.'

Megan was as shocked and saddened as everyone else, but she thought the children needed a diversion before they sank any deeper into morbidity.

'We're all very sorry to lose Chips,' she began, 'but I think you children need something to give you a bit of a lift. I know you'll be thinking of him — as we all are — but it isn't necessary to go around with your chins on the ground all day. Chips wouldn't be happy with that at all. You might just make the Saturday morning pictures if you hurry. You know how you hate to miss that.'

'I don't feel like goin' this week,' said George miserably.

'It might cheer you up, George,' suggested Will hopefully. 'A nice big helping of cowboys and Indians or Laurel and Hardy is just the thing when you're feeling a bit down.'

'No. I don't want to go.'

'All right, son.' No one was going to force him.

'What about you two?' Megan asked the twins.

'We might as well go, I s'pose,' said Poppy, and her sister nodded in agreement.

'Are you sure you don't want to go with them,

George?' his mother enquired.

'No thanks.' He was very disconsolate.

'I tell you what, son,' began Ken, 'I'll have to go and finish the deliveries and collect the money as it's Saturday. When I've done that I shall go to the livestock market to get another horse.' He looked across at Hetty with overt defiance, as though challenging her to oppose his suggestion, then turned his attention back to the boy. 'Would you like to come with me to choose one?'

George brightened a little. 'Could I?'

'I don't see why not, if you fancy it.'

'Cor, yes please.'

'Right. I'd better go and finish my work, then, so that we can be on our way.'

'How are you going to move the cart?' Will wondered.

'The stables have loaned me a horse just for today.'

'I'll come and give you a hand,' offered Will.

'Thanks, mate, I'd appreciate that.'

'Are you coming with us to choose the horse, Mummy?' asked George excitedly.

There was a brief hiatus while Hetty thought it over. 'No, love, I'll be busy in the shop,' she said at last. 'You go with your dad. I trust you to choose a good one.'

Megan and her mother exchanged glances. It was unheard of for Ken to be allowed to take his son anywhere without Hetty present. This was promising indeed!

★ ★ ★

'I think you were a real star today, Ken, having to cope with Chips being taken ill and dying like that,' praised Hetty that night in the bedroom. She was brushing her hair at the dressing table; Ken was already in bed. 'It must have been awful for you.'

'It was pretty grim.'

'I thought it was wonderful the way you dealt with George too,' she added.

'Oh!' Ken was completely taken aback. A genuine compliment from Hetty was such a rare thing, and he'd expected to get a roasting from her for taking the initiative with George. 'I'm glad you were pleased with the way I handled it.'

'George is very sensitive to that sort of thing,' she went on chattily. 'Chips was such a large part of his life; a part which included Dad and was very special to him. He adored his grandad, and was always the favourite of the three children, even though Dad would never admit it. Going with you to choose a new horse helped him a lot today. It made him feel important, I think.'

'He was good company, and took a real interest,' said Ken, who was lying back against the pillows with his hands behind his head. 'We now have a lovely grey horse called Smoky.'

'You let him choose the name, I hear?'

'Yeah, he was chuffed about that.'

'It seems a bit callous, doesn't it? You know, out with the old and in with the new.'

'It does seem hard, but it's just the way it is with working horses,' was Ken's response. 'We had to get a replacement right away so that I can do the round tomorrow. It doesn't alter the fact that we were all very fond of Chips.'

'None of us will ever forget him,' Hetty said sadly. 'I feel absolutely shattered by his death.'

'A milkman's horse is his best friend, so they say.' Ken pondered on this for a moment. 'Not for too much longer, though, according to what I've heard.'

'Really?'

'Yeah. The day is coming when horse-and-cart deliveries will be a thing of the past for the milk trade. The battery-electric milk float is the thing of the future, apparently. I was reading an article about them in a trade magazine recently. I remember seeing one at an exhibition before the war. It'll be a while before they come into general use, but it'll happen eventually.'

'It will make the round a lot easier for the delivery men, won't it?'

'Not half.'

'Wouldn't one of those be too expensive for a small firm like ours, though?' she queried.

'When things get back to normal and stuff is plentiful again so that the business makes a decent profit, it might be possible, though that will be up to your mum, of course. When they become generally accepted in the milk trade, the price of them will go down. Anyway, we shall have to move with the times when they become the usual way of delivering milk and replace the horse altogether.'

Hetty laughed. 'You big kid. You just can't wait to have a ride on an electric truck, can you?' she teased him. 'That's why you're so interested in them.'

'I'm just a little boy at heart,' he admitted in a jovial manner. 'Though they don't exactly go at speed, so I'm not likely to have the thrill of a lifetime.'

'It feels like the end of an era, with Chips going,' she said wistfully. 'He was synonymous with Dad somehow.' She sighed. 'Still, life moves on and times change.'

She realised in that moment that for the first time since Ken had been back she'd experienced a glimpse of how things had once been between them. They'd talked and laughed together as they had in the old days, and she'd felt easy with him. It was a warm and precious feeling but too delicate to mention somehow.

'It was nice just now when you said you were pleased with how I'd handled things today,' Ken told her.

'Was it?'

'Yeah, it made me feel good, especially as I don't often manage to please you these days.'

It was an innocent enough remark, but it was misunderstood and the tenderness in the air vanished in an instant.

'Anyone would think I was some awful harridan, to hear you speak,' Hetty heard herself snap.

'No . . . I didn't mean that — '

'It sounded like it to me,' she interrupted crossly. 'It was a nasty little dig about me being hard to please.'

'You heard it wrong, then — '

'I do my best for you, Ken,' she cut in.

'And I do my best for you,' he came back at

354

her, angered and disappointed by her attitude just when things were going so well. 'But it's never good enough.'

'That isn't true, you're just nit-picking.'

'You're the one who's doing that,' he retorted. 'There was no need for you to take it the wrong way just now. I was *not* having a go at you. You chose to think I was because it suited you; it gave you another stick to beat me with.'

Silence fell like a stone, tension drawing right.

'All right, I'm sorry. Let's just forget it, shall we?' Hetty said ungraciously, tears pricking at the back of her eyes because she was so saddened to have lost that loving feeling, and so powerless to get it back.

'If that's what you want,' he said, and turned on to his side with his back to her. 'Anything to stop you complaining.'

'Look . . . I've said I'm sorry; there's no need for you to go all sulky.' She just couldn't do what she knew she should and put her arms around him and show him how sorry she was, because such actions wouldn't come from the heart.

'Just leave it, will you, and let's get some sleep.'

The blame for this latest altercation was all hers, she accepted that. She could go through the motions every day and fulfil her duty as a wife, but she couldn't re-create the feelings she had once had for him and wanted again so desperately. She knew that at least a shred of them still existed because — however small — something had been stirred in her just now. But it was elusive and didn't remain, and this made her bad tempered and unhappy.

Turning off the light, she got into bed and lay on her side with her back to Ken. It was up to her to make the peace, but she couldn't bring herself to do it because part of her still resented his presence in her life. So she just lay still feeling miserable and at a loss to know how to make things better between them.

★ ★ ★

Ken was feeling depressed too about this latest row. It had been a bugger of a day. The death of the horse had upset him more than he'd let on. Maybe he hadn't been as emotionally tied to Chips as Hetty and the others because he'd been away for so long, but he'd been fond of the animal and it hadn't been pleasant watching the poor thing suffer and die like that. The horror of active service and imprisonment had thickened Ken's skin but had not made him impervious.

Something good had come out of it, though: it had brought him closer to his son. He'd enjoyed that time alone with George more than he'd enjoyed anything in a long time. He was an intelligent boy, and seemed bright beyond his years. He certainly didn't take after his dad in that respect. Ken had been a right little toerag at that age; always full of devilment and getting into scrapes. George was quieter and more serious altogether. He was the sort of boy he himself would probably have derided for being a swot at that age. But now Ken was older and wiser and he saw good things ahead for his son. He would do everything in his power to encourage George in his education and help him to reach his potential.

Ken had been hopeful of better things with Hetty, too, when she'd encouraged him to take George to the horse market on his own. And for a while back there she'd been softer and nicer, more like the woman he had married. Then it had fallen apart; gone in a second, and they were sniping at each other again.

It wasn't all her fault. He knew that he wasn't as easy-going now as he'd been before the war. He was more inclined to overreact and take umbrage these days. Could be something to do with the lingering effects of the prison camp, he supposed, but he was at a loss to know what to do to put his marriage back on track. He wasn't the romantic type, but he suspected anyway that that wasn't what Hetty wanted from him. If he were to ply her with flowers and pretty speeches she would probably ridicule him or accuse him of having a guilty conscience.

He was beginning to think he simply didn't possess what it was she wanted. He was just an ordinary bloke and it wasn't in him to be different. He worked hard but he didn't have ambition and charisma like Will. Hetty had never wanted that from him; she'd liked the fact that he didn't strive for the limelight. But she had matured while he'd been away and seemed to need something else now, which made him feel inadequate.

Just a few minutes ago, though, he'd felt something from her that had given him hope. It was nothing more than a fragment, but he would cling to it. It wasn't much but it was all he had.

★ ★ ★

'Are you still feeling upset about Chips?' enquired Will as Megan got ready for bed. 'You seem a bit down.'

'Yeah, I am actually,' she replied. 'I can't shake it off, though there's no point in moping, I know.'

'The girls coped with it better than George, didn't they?' he remarked thoughtfully. 'The poor lad seemed heartbroken.'

'That's George for you. He gets himself into more of a state about these things. The twins are sad, of course. Chips had always been around in their lifetime. He'd been like a family friend. But our daughters are resilient little things,' she told him. 'I think perhaps it's got something to do with them being twins. No matter what disaster arises, they always have each other; that might be the reason, though you'd know more about that than me, being a twin yourself.'

'Mm.' He did know how it felt; he also knew the feeling of utter devastation when that other wasn't there any more, and was very afraid for his daughters suddenly. 'Do you think we should encourage them to be apart more; to have different friends and so on, so that they are not quite so dependent on one another?'

'I've often wondered about that. When they first started school I spoke to the teacher about it. She sat them apart but they were so miserable she had to put them back together because it was upsetting their school work.'

'I seem to remember them trying the same thing with Ron and me but it didn't work,' Will confessed. 'Though in the end I did have to learn to get along without him.'

'Yes, you did, and that's what the girls will do if it's ever necessary. It would be cruel to try and part them at the moment. They'll find their own way as they grow up.'

'I expect you're right.'

Turning the light off, Megan got into bed and Will put his arm around her, her head resting on his shoulder. They lay together in comfortable silence, each engrossed in their own thoughts. Megan was thinking of her father, because losing Chips seemed very much connected to him. She still missed her dad but tried to concentrate on the many happy memories she had of him.

Will was thinking about his brother and knew that he would never feel really complete without him. Being a twin made you vulnerable, and he hoped his daughters never had to go through what he had at such a tender age.

'A penny for them,' said Megan.

'I was thinking about my brother, as it happens.'

'I was thinking about my dad,' she told him. 'He was such a personality. I often smile when I remember him.'

'It's good that you can do that.'

'Can you do that about Ron after all this time?'

He longed to unburden himself; to tell her

everything. But he just said, 'Sometimes.'

'Good,' she said, yawning.

They lay there quietly and eventually drifted off to sleep in the same position.

* * *

Mabel was in the Saturday shopping crowds in King Street, Hammersmith, when she saw a familiar face.

''Ello there,' she said, smiling broadly. 'Remember me? I used to work at Morgan's Dairy during the war.' She paused before giving him a reminder. 'Mabel White.'

'I remember you,' said Doug Reynolds.

'So . . . how have you been this long time?'

'Mustn't grumble. Yourself?'

'I'm getting by.'

'I expect you're married by now,' he said conversationally. 'You were courting strong if I remember rightly.'

A shadow fell across her face momentarily. 'It didn't work out,' she said. 'He found someone he liked better.'

'Sorry to hear that,' sympathised Doug. 'He must need his brains testing.'

She shrugged. 'These things happen and it's water under the bridge. How about you? Married?'

'No, still footloose and fancy-free,' he replied in a breezy manner. 'I think my poor mother despairs of ever getting me out from under her feet.'

'I find that hard to believe,' she said lightly.

'She probably enjoys spoiling you rotten. Mothers and sons, eh! The boys get all the attention in our house.'

He shrugged and changed the subject. 'So, what are you doing with yourself these days?'

'This and that, but nothing special. I work in an office now,' she told him. 'I'm only a dogsbody, filing and running errands and that, but at least I get Saturdays off.' She paused, looking pensive. 'I enjoyed working at the dairy with Dolly and Megan, but when Megan's sister came home from the country they didn't need me.'

'You don't sound all that struck on this office job.'

'I'm not,' she confirmed in a definite tone. 'I miss the direct contact you get with people in a shop. I used to enjoy a chat with the customers; taking an interest in them and that. Still, it's a job so I'm not complaining. Are you working?'

'Yeah, I've got a job in the stores in an engineering factory over Acton way,' he said.

'Good.' Mabel looked at him. 'Did they send you back into action when you went back?'

'No. They gave me a home posting.'

'I should think so too,' she approved. 'You'd done your bit.'

The conversation came to its natural conclusion and they fell quiet.

'Well, I'd better get on with my shopping,' she said, with the idea of making a timely departure before the silence became an awkward one. 'It was nice to see you again.'

'You too.'

'Ta-ta.'

'Cheerio.'

Mabel turned and strode off into the crowd. Doug stood there for a few moments, then went after her.

'I was wondering,' he began, catching her up and tapping her on the shoulder. 'I was wondering if you might fancy going out sometime. The pictures, perhaps.'

'Yeah, I'd like that,' said Mabel, who was so lacking in guile it didn't even occur to her to hold back so as not to seem too eager. 'That would be lovely.'

'When are you free?'

'Most evenings,' she said.

'Tonight?'

'Suits me.'

'Shall we say seven o'clock? Outside the station?'

'Lovely,' she smiled.

'See you later then.'

*   *   *

Watching her swing away, a small, slim figure with shiny brown hair worn in a pageboy, Doug felt extremely pleased with himself. Things were definitely on the up for him now. He'd got a job; his best mate was back from the war, their friendship intact; and he had a date for tonight. Mabel was no oil painting but she was presentable.

She'd made it clear that she liked the look of him despite his ugliness. In fact she didn't even

362

seem to notice it. He had to accept the fact that no stunner would want to go out with him so he had to make the most of what came his way. It had been so long since he'd been out with a woman, he was feeling quite nervous. He didn't want to make a mess of it because opportunities like this didn't come his way very often. This might be the only one he ever had.

Looking back, he remembered how friendly Mabel had always been towards him when he used to call in at the dairy. Even though she'd had a boyfriend then, she had seemed to take a shine to him, but he'd been too preoccupied with his plans for Megan to take much notice.

Although the prospect of going out with someone new was rather daunting, it was thrilling too, and he felt truly alive for the first time for years. He'd better hurry home and make sure he had a clean shirt to wear. Maybe he'd be allowed to have a bath if he talked to his mother nicely, though once a week was the house rule. There was a spring to his step as he made his way home. Suddenly he felt as though he had rejoined the human race. He'd show Will Stubbs he could still get a woman!

★ ★ ★

One evening a week Will met his mates at the pub. On this particular occasion Ken went with him, Dolly had gone to visit a neighbour who hadn't been well, so the sisters found themselves alone, with the children asleep in bed.

'It's rather nice being just the two of us for a

change, isn't it?' remarked Megan. 'Good to have a bit of peace and quiet together. We can listen to the wireless without a racket in the background. There's usually so much noise in this house, you can't hear yourself think.'

'Can we turn the wireless off and talk?' requested Hetty.

'Course we can,' said Megan, going over to the set and turning the knob to off. 'So what's on your mind?'

'You can probably guess.'

'You and Ken?'

Hetty nodded.

'I was hoping perhaps things might have got a little better,' suggested Megan. 'You don't seem to be at each other's throats quite so much as you were. Or is it just that you're more careful to stop us from hearing you?'

'Partly that and partly because we're often not speaking at all,' Hetty explained.

'Oh dear.' Megan was really worried. 'Is there nothing that can be done to put things right?'

'There are brief spells of improvement, but they're so short-lived they've vanished before we have a chance to work on them. He claims that I'm too critical of him, but I think he picks me up on every little thing and sees criticism in everything I say when it isn't there at all. I've reached the stage now where I dread waking up next to him in the morning. If it wasn't for George I think I'd go out of my mind altogether. I feel even guiltier, too, because I know that Ken is troubled by what happened abroad; sometimes he screams in his sleep. That's strictly between

364

you and me, though.'

'I won't say anything,' said Megan. 'Will does that sort of thing too sometimes. I reckon they'll be scarred for life by what they went through.'

Hetty nodded.

'Anyway, you seem to have been a lot better about George as far as Ken is concerned,' mentioned Megan. 'You're a bit less possessive about him. I couldn't help noticing that you let Ken spend time with him now.'

'It's hard for me to let go, but I am trying,' Hetty told her. 'Ken has become George's hero ever since the drama with Chips, so my hand has been rather forced. I like it, anyway, now that I've got used to it, that they get along so well. George is so different to his father — so serious and studious — I thought Ken might have been disappointed. You know how men like their sons to be tough and outgoing. But he absolutely adores him; thinks he's a genius in the making.'

'Well, that must please you.'

'Yeah, it does, but it doesn't change the way things are between Ken and me,' Hetty explained. 'I don't want us to be one of these couples who stay together just because of the children even though they grow to hate the sight of each other.'

'It's not that bad, surely?'

'It feels like it sometimes.'

'Oh Hetty, that's awful,' exclaimed Megan. 'Have the two of you talked about it?'

'In a reasonable manner? Of course we haven't,' she replied. 'You know what men are like when it comes to talking about their feelings.

He just won't do it. If I try to bring the subject up he just says I'm nagging and goes off in a huff.'

'Seems to me as though it's six of one and half a dozen of the other,' expressed Megan.

'It probably is, but I feel as though it's my fault entirely because I didn't feel the same towards him when he first came home, and I am irritable with him, I admit it. But he's not the man he was either. I don't know how he feels about me any more. He might hate the sight of me by now. Who knows what's going on in his mind?'

'You could always ask him.'

'It will only start a row.'

'If you can't get him to talk about it, I don't know what else to suggest.'

'Sometimes I get it back, that old feeling,' said Hetty, looking into space thoughtfully. 'It never lasts long, though.'

'That must be a good sign.'

'It's very fleeting.'

'But it hasn't died a death completely, which sounds heartening to me,' Megan said. 'Though it isn't my opinion that matters. The only people who can put this right are yourself and Ken.'

'Yeah, I know, but it's a relief to talk to you about it.' Hetty paused thoughtfully. 'I read in the paper the other day that there are thousands of couples getting divorced because of the war.'

'Oh Hetty, don't even think about that,' urged Megan, her brow furrowed.

'I'm not in any serious way. It might not be quite such a dirty word any more but people like us don't divorce, we put up with it, no matter what,' said her sister.

Megan nodded in agreement. It was true that divorce had become more common since the war, but it was still very much frowned upon in their circles.

'But I want my marriage to be more than just a legal document forcing us to stay together because it's the done thing,' Hetty went on.

'Then you're going to have to bring it out into the open,' Megan advised. 'You can't carry on like this.'

Hetty brushed a hand across her brow wearily. 'Oh, I'm tired of worrying about it. Let's have the wireless on for a bit of light relief.'

Megan went over to the set and turned it on. She felt sad and powerless to help two people who meant a lot to her.

★ ★ ★

'Well, did you enjoy yourselves, as if I need to ask?' enquired Megan later on when the men returned, flushed and hearty.

'Yeah, it was all right,' replied Will.

'It was only an hour down the pub for a chat with a group of blokes,' said Ken, sharply defensive. 'We haven't exactly been out hitting the high spots.'

'All right, Ken, keep your hair on,' snapped Hetty, throwing him a look. 'No one is suggesting you've been out chasing women at the Hammersmith Palais or anything.'

'Now, now, you two,' intervened Dolly, hoping

367

to nip a full-blown row in the bud. 'Don't start getting at each other and making the rest of us feel uncomfortable.'

'Sorry, Mum,' said Hetty.

'Sorry, Mrs M,' added Ken.

'We've got a bit of gossip for you, girls,' said Will in a deliberate diversion.

'Oh yeah?' said Megan. 'What is it?'

'Doug's got himself fixed up with a woman,' Will informed them. 'He was full of it tonight; chuffed to bits.'

'Oh, how lovely,' was Dolly's instant reaction. 'I'm so pleased for him. He needs someone by his side.'

'It can't be easy for him to get a girl, the way he looks,' remarked Hetty. 'I know it shouldn't matter — and it's very cruel that it does — but it's one of the harsh facts of life that appearance is important to a lot of people.'

'Let's hope this woman is nice,' remarked Dolly. 'I wonder if he'll being her here to meet us.'

'You already know her, apparently,' Will informed them casually. 'She used to work at the dairy during the war.' He paused as though trying to remember. 'What did he say her name was?'

'Mabel,' said Ken helpfully. 'I'm surprised you've forgotten, considering the number of times he mentioned her name in the pub. We've had a right ear-bashing, I can tell you. I think he'd given up hope of ever finding anyone to go out with him.'

'Oh no,' Megan blurted out before she could

stop herself. 'Not Mabel!'

'What on earth is the matter, dear?' asked Dolly, glancing curiously at her daughter, who was looking pale and disapproving. 'Mabel is perfect for Doug. She's a decent girl. She won't let him down.'

'Doesn't she . . . doesn't she already have a boyfriend?' stuttered Megan, struggling to explain her reaction without giving the game away. 'She was courting strong the last time we saw her.'

'She obviously isn't now or she wouldn't be going out with Doug,' decided Dolly. 'She isn't the type to be deceitful. We haven't seen her for quite a while. It's obviously all off with the other chap.'

'I suppose it must be,' said Megan shakily. She felt physically sick at the idea of Mabel and Doug. The girl was like a lamb to the slaughter. God only knew what suffering he would inflict upon her. 'I just can't see her making a go of it with Doug, that's all.'

'Why not?' asked her mother.

'Well . . . ' Megan scoured her mind for a plausible reason. 'There's an age difference for a start. Mabel can't be more than about eighteen now, and he's a good bit older than that.'

'He's the same age as me, twenty-eight,' said Will. 'So yeah, there is a few years between them. But it isn't that big a difference. It isn't as though he's middle-aged or anything.' He paused. 'Anyway, it's very early days. I don't think he's been going out with her for long. But I hope it works out for him.'

'Me too,' said Dolly. 'He deserves some happiness after what he's been through.'

It was as much as Megan could do not to scream the truth about Doug at them all, and tell them that Mabel's relationship with him would end in disaster. But how could she do that when there would be such terrible consequences?

'Your mum is right, Megan,' said Will. 'It's no fun for a man of his age to be single.'

'No, I expect you're right,' she said with a feigned air of casualness, though she was actually wondering frantically how she could warn Mabel about Doug. Maybe it wouldn't come to anything. It didn't sound as though it was serious yet. But she couldn't just let it go; that would be too cruel. She had to do something to protect her friend.

★ ★ ★

'So . . . ' began Will when he and Megan were alone in the bedroom with the door firmly closed. 'What's the matter with this girlfriend of Doug's then?'

'Mabel?' she said, shocked at his misinterpretation of her response to the news. 'There's nothing the matter with Mabel; nothing at all. She's a smashing girl.'

'Oh.' He looked at her quizzically. 'I thought she must be your arch-enemy and a right old tart, the way you reacted to the news that she's going out with Doug. I'd rather you told me if she's a flighty piece so that I can warn him. I don't want to see him made a fool of. He's a mate of long standing.'

If it wasn't so serious, Megan would have laughed out loud at the way he had misunderstood so completely.

'Mabel won't make a fool of him,' she told Will. 'I can promise you that.'

'Why are you dead set against it then?' He looked at her, narrowing his eyes thoughtfully. 'Oh, now I get it. You think he might mess her about?'

She looked at him, hating herself for being deceitful but seeing no other way. 'She is quite young,' she said lamely. 'And she's got a lovely nature. She'd do anything for anyone. She's a good friend and I wouldn't want to see her get hurt.'

'I shouldn't think Doug would mess any woman about because he isn't in a position to do so, is he?' said Will. 'I mean, it isn't as though he's got them queuing up to go out with him, is it?'

'No, there is that, I suppose.'

'Anyway, as far as I know he's decent enough when it comes to women.'

Oh Will, she cried silently. How little you know about the man you call a friend.

'We'll just have to see what happens,' she said, careful to keep her voice steady.

'It's none of our business anyway,' he reminded her. 'We have to leave them alone to get on with it.'

'I know that, Will.'

But she felt that it was very much her business because of what she knew about Doug. Her only hope was that Mabel wasn't taking the affair seriously.

★ ★ ★

Her hopes were dashed as far as that was concerned a few days later when Mabel called at the shop to see them. The girl exuded happiness from every pore and looked positively radiant.

'I suppose you've heard about Doug and me,' she said after initial exchanges had been made and she'd apologised for not calling in to see them for so long.

'Yes, we have, and we're very pleased for you,' said Dolly, who was weighing up some loose tea for a customer. 'He's a nice boy. You won't go far wrong with him.'

'You don't have to tell me that.' Mabel was bubbling with enthusiasm. 'He really knows how to treat a girl, I can tell you. Not like boys of my own age, who haven't got a clue how to carry on. He knows what he's doing and he's got such lovely manners.'

'You seem very keen,' said Megan, who had just finished serving and was free temporarily.

'I'm absolutely ecstatic,' she said with a dreamy look in her eyes. 'We get on so well it's as though we were made for each other. I saw something special in him the minute I clapped eyes on him, when I was working here and he used to come visiting. Of course, I've gone well past just liking him now.'

'Aah,' said Dolly's customer, smiling warmly.

'It's lovely for you, Mabel,' added Dolly. 'I'm

so pleased. You deserve someone nice like him.'

It's heartbreak in the making, thought Megan, but out loud she said, 'You're really serious about him, then?'

'I'll say I am,' Mabel confirmed eagerly. 'I've fallen for him hook, line and sinker, and I'm almost certain he feels the same about me.' She lifted her shoulders excitedly, in the manner of one who was full of joy. 'Ooh, I feel like a million dollars.'

She looked it too, thought Megan. Her eyes were bright, her skin blooming, her hair shiny, and she was looking very feminine in a floral summer frock.

'Anyway, that's enough about me. How have you all been this long time?' Mabel asked.

'We're all right,' said Dolly and went on to put her up to date.

The conversation became general, and when the shop got busy Mabel left, leaving Megan desperate with worry for her.

★ ★ ★

The next day, Dolly received a letter.

'It's from your Auntie Dil,' she announced, opening the envelope at the breakfast table.

'Oh, how lovely. How are they all?' enquired Megan with interest, spreading margarine on her toast.

'Fine,' Dolly replied. 'Owen is busy on the farm with the silage but it should be finished soon.' She paused, reading on. 'Oh, she says that they don't only want to see us in wartime, and that we're very welcome to go and stay when there aren't bombs falling here. So if anyone fancies some country air with the school holidays coming up, just let her know. 'As long as you bring your ration books, you'll be more than welcome',' she read from the letter.

'That's so sweet of her,' said Megan.

'They're lovely people,' added Hetty.

'Can we go, Mum?' asked Poppy excitedly.

'Can we, Dad?' begged her sister. 'Will you take us?'

'As much as I'd like to say yes, sweetheart, I can't at the moment,' Will told her. 'I've got too much work on. We'll go another time, when I'm not so busy.'

'Promise?'

'I'll do my best.'

'I'd like to go to Wales again,' announced George. 'Can we go, Mum? You, me and Dad if the others can't.'

'Daddy is busy with the dairy,' replied Hetty. 'So I'm afraid the answer has to be no.'

'That's the trouble, isn't it?' remarked Dolly. 'We're all too tied up here to get away. Still, it was very kind of her to ask us. I'll thank her when I write back.'

'Maybe at some time in the future we could arrange something,' suggested Hetty hopefully.

'I think we should make an absolute point of it,' agreed Megan. 'They are our relatives, after all, and I doubt if we'll be able to persuade them to come here.'

She could feel a germ of an idea beginning to form. But there was something more pressing on her mind that she had to take care of before she could give the plan serious attention.

★   ★   ★

After Megan had put the girls to bed that night, she told Will that she needed to go out for a short time.

'I won't be long,' she assured him. 'I'm only going local to see an old schoolfriend. The girls have settled down so you shouldn't have any trouble with them.'

'Don't you worry about that,' he said in his usual amiable way. 'I'll soon sort them out if they give me any bother. You go and have a nice long natter. A break from here will do you good.'

'Thanks, love. I'll see you later then.'

His complete trust in her had her reeling with guilt as she hurried from the house and walked down the street. The trouble with secrets was that they bred lies.

★   ★   ★

Mabel answered the door to Megan and asked her in.

'I'd rather talk out here if you don't mind,' said Megan, hating herself for what she was about to do.

'Just as you like, it is a bit noisy inside,' Mabel said cheerfully, stepping outside and pulling the door to behind her. 'So what's up? You got a problem?'

Megan took a deep breath and cleared her

throat. 'It's about Doug,' she began nervously.

'Doug!' Mabel's eyes widened with fear and her cheeks turned scarlet, indicating her depth of feeling for him. 'What's happened to him? Is he ill? Has he been hurt?'

'No, no, nothing like that,' said Megan, putting a comforting hand on her arm.

'Thank Gawd for that; you gave me the fright of my life.' Mabel had her hand clutched to her upper chest. 'So what about him then?'

'Er . . . ' Megan bit her lip. This was so difficult. 'I feel that I have to warn you.'

'Warn me? What of?'

'Doug isn't the man you believe him to be,' she replied. 'There's a side of him you don't know about and you'll get hurt if you carry on seeing him.'

Mabel's eyes narrowed on her friend with anger and suspicion. 'Oh yeah, and what exactly has he done to make you say that?'

'I can't tell you, but I'm asking you to trust me,' Megan said earnestly. 'He's no good for you, Mabel, believe me.'

'Why are you doing this, Megan?' the younger girl asked, two angry spots of colour staining her cheeks. 'Why are you trying to spoil things for me? I thought you were my friend.'

'I am. That's why I'm trying to stop you getting hurt.'

'You come round here trying to make trouble for me and Doug and you won't even tell me what it is he's supposed to have done,' said Mabel, angry tears threatening. 'Can't you bear to see me happy, is that it?'

376

'Of course it isn't that.'

'I'm surprised at you, Megan,' she said, her voice shrill with fury. 'You've got a good husband and two lovely kids, yet you're too mean-minded to want me to be happy.'

'You know me better than that, Mabel.'

'I *thought* I knew you . . . '

'You do. I hate to hurt you like this, but as your friend I feel duty-bound.'

'You're no friend of mine, not any more. Just go away and do your meddling somewhere else,' Mabel sobbed, tears flowing. 'I love Doug and you won't come between us. Sod off and don't come back.'

'Mabel . . . '

'You heard what I said: clear off and don't come knocking on my door again.'

Mabel went inside and slammed the door behind her. Megan stood where she was, trembling. The only way she could make Mabel listen was to tell her the whole sordid truth about Doug, and that wasn't possible when Will was still in the dark. What a dilemma, she thought as she began walking home.

14

Considering the fact that Megan and Hetty lived in the same house, it was surprisingly difficult to have a private conversation because there was always someone else around.

Megan finally managed to get her sister on her own the following day when the children were at school, her mother had popped out to the bank and Ken was busy in the dairy. The sisters were taking the opportunity of a quiet period in the shop to unpack an order from the wholesaler.

'I've had an idea,' mentioned Megan, removing tins of peas from a cardboard carton and stacking them on the shelves. 'Something that just might give you the chance to try and get your marriage back on track.'

'Oh yeah, found someone who dabbles in magic, have you?' was Hetty's tart response.

'I didn't say I'd found a solution; just the possibility of a chance to try.'

'It'll take a flaming miracle to put my marriage right.'

'Or . . . ' began Megan tentatively, 'perhaps a holiday in Wales might do the trick.'

Hetty squinted at her, deeply puzzled. 'How exactly will that help?' she wanted to know. 'If we can't get along here, we certainly won't do any better there, being with each other for twenty-four hours a day and no work as a diversion. Not to mention having to pretend that

378

everything is fine and dandy between us in front of Auntie and Uncle.'

'I'm not saying it's the answer, I just thought maybe a change of scenery was worth a try, especially as you love it so much there,' Megan said.

'I don't know if it would appeal to Ken, though. He's a townie through and through.'

'It would be away from here, that's the important thing,' Megan pointed out. 'Perhaps the two of you might relax more without us lot on top of you all the time. I know Auntie and Uncle will be there, but Uncle Owen will be at work all day and Auntie is involved in village activities a lot of the time. Anyway, you could go out for country walks, that sort of thing, to get some privacy. Maybe you could persuade Ken to talk about it if you were both calmer and in different surroundings.'

'George would be with us so there would be no question of privacy.'

'He'll want to go off and play with his friends in the village, I should think,' said Megan. 'It'll be the summer holidays, so the other kids will be around.'

'Mm, you've got a point.' Hetty was thoughtful. 'But Ken would steer clear of an in-depth discussion if we were alone together on a desert island.'

'You never know,' suggested Megan. 'A change of environment might make you see each other in a different light.'

Hetty paused in her work, mulling it over and gradually warming to the idea. 'It's worth a try, I suppose, and I would love to go back to Wales.' She sighed. 'But as we discussed yesterday, we're all tied up here.'

'I wouldn't have suggested this if I hadn't got all that side of it worked out. This is the plan,' Megan explained. 'I'll do the round for Ken and the rest of the dairy work, and Mum and I will look after the shop between us.'

'It'll be far too much work for just the two of you,' Hetty was quick to point out.

'We managed during the war,' Megan reminded her.

'There were three of you when Mabel came, and that extra pair of hands makes all the difference.'

'Now you're just looking for excuses,' said Megan in a tone of friendly admonition. 'Yes, it would be too much work in the long term, of course. But I'm only suggesting you go for a week or two at the most. Mum and I can scrape by for a limited time.' She grinned. 'Anyway, I shall rope Will in to help when he's around.'

'It's a smashing idea.' Hetty was full of enthusiasm now. 'I adore Cwmcae, and George would be in seventh heaven.'

'Talk to Ken about it then, and if you do decide to go, you can rely on me to see to things here.'

But Hetty had thought of another potential snag. 'What if it doesn't help my marriage and you and Mum will have been put to all that extra work for nothing?' she queried.

'It doesn't matter,' Megan assured her. 'At least you will have tried. Anyway, if nothing else, a holiday will do you all good.'

'It's a lovely thought, but what about the rest of you?' Hetty asked. 'You deserve a holiday just as much as we do.'

'We can go another time, and you can look after things for us then,' Megan told her. 'The war's over and we have to start thinking in terms of better things ahead. When rationing ends and the shop's profits start to go up, perhaps we'll be able to pay somebody to provide cover for holidays.'

'You're so good to me,' said Hetty.

'No more than any other sister,' Megan responded simply.

'I really envy you,' Hetty said. 'You are so practical and uncomplicated.'

Once that might have been true, Megan thought. Her sister couldn't possibly know about the complications that plagued her life now and the state of abject despair she was so often plunged into. It was all far too dark and horrible to burden Hetty with, as much as she would welcome someone to talk to about it.

'You just concentrate on that marriage of yours,' she advised, glossing over the moment.

'Thanks, Megan, you're a good sort,' Hetty said.

'You're not bad either, as sisters go,' grinned Megan.

Just then the shop door opened and let in a flood of customers and the conversation came to an end.

★ ★ ★

'I hope you all realise that I'm a woman of independent means as from today,' Megan announced to the family during the evening meal a few weeks later.

'That's right. I can give up work now that she gets the Family Allowance,' joked Will.

Megan turned to him with a smile in her eyes, and as he looked at her she put her hands flat on his cheeks and tapped them playfully. 'All mine, honey bunch. All mine,' she teased him. 'Five shillings a week, every week; paid to Mrs Megan Stubbs at the post office.'

'It's supposed to be to help with the housekeeping,' he reminded her jokingly.

'Get away,' she said with good-humoured sarcasm. 'And there was me all ready to blow it on booze and the horses, putting on bets with Syd the butcher.'

'Shush,' warned Dolly, joining in the fun. 'Walls have ears, remember, and what Syd does is illegal.'

'Has no one told you that the war is over?' chuckled Will. 'We don't have to watch what we say any more.'

Ken steered the conversation back on course. 'It's all very well, this new Family Allowance,' he began, 'but Hetty doesn't qualify because we only have one child.'

'There's only one answer to that,' grinned Will. 'It's easily done, mate. You're going away to Wales on holiday at the weekend. All that fresh country air should do the trick.'

'Don't be so vulgar,' tutted Hetty.

'Yeah, behave yourself, Will,' supported Megan,

but it was very much tongue in cheek.

'I don't know why the government doesn't give it for the first child,' remarked Hetty. 'It doesn't seem fair to me.'

'I suppose they have to work within a budget, and they think you don't need it so much if you only have one child,' suggested her mother. 'The idea behind it is to benefit large families, and to make sure the father can't claim the money and fritter it all away, by paying it directly to the mother.'

'Who do you get it for, Mum?' asked Poppy. 'Me or Netta?'

'Me because I'm the youngest,' said Netta.

'Only by ten minutes,' her sister reminded her.

'Officially I get it for Netta,' Megan explained. 'But it all goes into the family pot, so you both get the benefit.'

'I suppose it's a sign that the government are doing something for the people,' Ken mentioned. 'There's still a lot more for them to do, though. They need to get the housing crisis sorted; that should be a priority.'

'I wonder if this free medical treatment for everyone they are talking about will ever come in,' mentioned Will.

'It seems a bit ambitious to me,' opined Dolly. 'I can't see it coming off myself. It sounds too good to be true.'

The conversation became general until Megan said, 'Are you looking forward to your holiday, George?'

'Yeah, it'll be smashing,' he replied, his soulful features lit with excitement. 'I can't wait to get there and see them all again.'

'Lucky thing,' said Poppy. 'I wish we could come with you. Can we come, Auntie Hetty?'

Hetty exchanged a look with her sister. 'Not this time, love; perhaps your mum and dad will take you one day.'

Megan was glad Hetty had taken her advice, and hoped that she and Ken returned from Wales happier people. If not, she couldn't see much hope for them.

★ ★ ★

Smoky was a most lovable animal. A docile dapple-grey shire horse, he had a white mane and huge dark eyes that always seemed to have a hint of sadness about them. Megan could quite understand why. It couldn't be much fun having to drag a milk cart around every day.

Megan made a great fuss of him when she was out on the round with him in Ken's absence, fondling his head every so often and talking to him in the natural way she had always had with Chips. It was nice to have the opportunity to spend time with him.

She was loading some empties on to the cart and thinking how much she enjoyed being out on the round again when she found herself under verbal attack from a stranger who happened to be passing by, a middle-aged man in a dark suit and a trilby hat, even though the weather was warm.

'I thought we'd seen the last of you women muscling in on men's work. I thought all that finished with the end of the war,' he said aggressively. 'Don't you think our boys deserve their jobs back after fighting for their country? Don't you think it's their right to be able to earn a wage?'

'Of course I do.'

'Well, get back to the home where you belong and leave the men to do the work outside of it. It's nothing short of a disgrace, and most unpatriotic.'

'I haven't taken a man's . . . ' she began, but he wasn't prepared to listen and was already marching off up the street.

'Well, Smoky, I don't think I can let him get away with that,' she said, giving the horse a gentle pat on the head. 'Be back in a minute.'

She caught the man up as he was about to turn the corner and planted a firm hand on his back to detain him.

'What the . . . ' he said swinging round. 'Don't you dare accost me.'

'And don't you dare accuse me of something without knowing the facts,' she came back at him, and went on to explain why she was doing the milk round.

'Oh . . . oh, I see.'

'It might be an idea for you to remember that women kept this country going during the war while the men were away. They were making shells, working in transport, as plumbers, electricians and engineers, to name just a few of the jobs they took on. I was up at four o'clock every morning — in all weathers — making sure people got their milk. So don't you dare to call me unpatriotic!'

'It seems that I — '

Now it was her turn to cut him short. 'Yes, our boys were brave beyond measure, and I am so proud of them I could weep. But us women did a good job too, under dangerous circumstances. We did the jobs when we were needed and we've given them up now.' She glared at him. 'Right!'

At least he had the grace to look sheepish. 'It seems I owe you an apology. I'm sorry.'

'Thank you,' she said. 'I should get your facts right before you attack any other unsuspecting woman.'

And with that parting shot she turned and marched back to the milk cart, thinking how out of touch the man was with the general situation. Women had stepped back from their wartime jobs for the homecoming soldiers, but workers were now needed for the industries and services that were vital to economic recovery, so jobs were gradually becoming plentiful for both sexes, a trend that was expected to grow over the next few years.

Although interesting and fulfilling employment had been lost by women at the end of the war, new opportunities were beginning to appear with the expansion of office work, and the demand for them to train as teachers, nurses and social workers, which meant that the days when they were forced into the drudgery of domestic service for want of any other employment were over. Married women had gone back to domesticity in droves, but they had learned new skills and tasted independence, and nothing could ever be quite the same again. Oh well, it takes all sorts, she thought, and dismissed the bigoted man from her thinking.

As other personal problems started to creep into her mind, she deliberately turned her thoughts to Hetty and Ken and wondered how things were going for them in Wales. The weather was glorious here and it was a beautiful morning: warm and soft, with the sun coming up and the sweet scents of late summer spicing the air. Here's hoping the Welsh rain manages to stay away while they are there, she thought as she took a full carrier of milk from the cart and prepared to cross the road. Let's hope that sister of mine and her husband are able to rediscover what they once had in abundance.

★ ★ ★

It was the second week of the holiday and they had woken to clear skies every day so far. Ken was enchanted with the place and had struck up an instant rapport with Uncle Owen, George had renewed friendships with the village children and Hetty had enjoyed the afternoon sunshine in the garden with Auntie Dil and caught up with people she knew locally. It had been very relaxing and Hetty felt all the better for it.

The strain of pretending that all was well between herself and Ken hadn't been such a trial as she'd imagined, mainly because she hadn't seen much of him since they'd been here. The farmer for whom Uncle Owen worked had had a sudden staff crisis because one of the labourers had broken his leg, so Ken had stepped in to help out and went to work with Uncle Owen every day.

'Not much of a holiday for you, is it, bach?' remarked Auntie Dil one evening over supper. 'You're probably working harder here than you do at home.'

'It's so different to what I usually do, it doesn't really feel like work. A change is as good as a rest, so they say.' Ken gave a wry grin. 'Though my muscles are telling me different.'

'I'll tell the boss not to pay you then, shall I, if you're enjoying it so much?' said Owen waggishly.

'It isn't that much of a rest,' laughed Ken.

'I thought you'd say that,' smiled Owen. 'You'd be a fool if you hadn't.'

In actual fact Ken would have gladly worked at the farm for nothing. Apart from the fact that he enjoyed being out in the sunshine and fresh air all day, it saved him from being alone with Hetty, especially as Owen usually invited him to go over to the pub with him after supper of an evening. It wasn't that he didn't love his wife and want to be with her as such; it was just that he couldn't bear the criticism he had come to expect when they were together, especially on their own.

He hadn't wanted to come on this holiday; had dreaded it in fact, mainly because Hetty had told him that the idea of it was to get their marriage sorted out. They would get a chance to talk things over, she'd said. That had scared the

388

living daylights out of him, because he was afraid of what she was going to say; terrified she was going to tell him that she didn't love him any more and wanted them to go their separate ways. So he avoided any sort of confrontation with her. It was spineless of him, but he was a coward when it came to the prospect of losing Hetty. Here in Cwmcae he had been given the perfect excuse to avoid the much-dreaded conversation.

One thing that he and Hetty were in agreement about was the place. She'd told him many times how lovely it was and he'd always thought she was exaggerating. But he'd fallen in love with it the instant they had come down the hill and seen it nestling in the valley. As well as the beautiful scenery, he liked the feel of it: the people, the way of life; everything.

Hetty had seemed different since they had been here: gentler and more easy-going. There had been fewer snide remarks and less snapping at him. He couldn't help thinking — somewhat cynically — that the fact that he wasn't around much obviously pleased her.

George seemed to thrive in the country environment too. He'd got pals in the village, and had developed a keen interest in nature, of which there was such an abundance here: wild flowers, insects, birds and animals, he showed an intelligent curiosity in them all.

Ken was recalled from his reverie by Auntie Dil, who was saying, 'You have a very patient wife, Ken. Some women would play pot with you for going off to work all day and leaving her when you're on holiday together.'

He looked at Hetty warily. 'You don't mind, do you, love?' he asked.

'No, of course I don't mind,' she assured him. 'These things happen. I'm glad we were here so you were able to help the farmer out.'

'What a devoted and well-matched couple you are,' judged Auntie Dil. 'It's a treat to see it.'

'Aye, it is,' agreed Uncle Owen.

If only you knew, thought Hetty, feeling like a fraud.

★ ★ ★

'Is Ken not with you today?' asked Doug when Will arrived at the pub for their usual pre-prandial pint on Sunday lunchtime.

'No. He's still away on his holidays,' explained Will.

'Lucky devil,' said Doug with unveiled envy. 'I wouldn't mind a week or two at the coast myself now that the beaches are open again to the public. Margate or Clacton would do me nicely. I wouldn't fancy Wales, though. It's all coal mines down there, isn't it?'

'No, of course it isn't, you ignorant sod,' corrected Will. 'A lot of it is agricultural land. It's beautiful countryside where they've gone, according to Megan.'

'Dead as a doornail, though.'

'I don't know because I've never been there, and neither have you, so you're not in a position to say what it's like,' said Will, irritated by Doug's tendency to judge things he knew nothing about. 'Obviously it will be quiet in the country parts, the same as any other rural area. But there'll be livelier parts too, I expect. Anyway, not everyone wants a seafront like Margate, lined with pubs, chip shops and amusements. Some people like the countryside. Megan and Hetty certainly love it there.'

'You'll be the next one to be dragged off, then,' observed Doug, making a face.

'Megan doesn't drag me anywhere,' snapped Will. 'If we go we'll go by mutual agreement.'

'All right.' Doug frowned darkly. 'There's no need to bite my head off. Who's rattled your cage anyway? Has your missus upset you or something?'

'No, not at all.'

'Well, you don't seem very amiable.'

Will had been feeling on fine form when he'd walked into the pub, but Doug's company had soon depressed him. Maybe it was because there was only the two of them today. Doug on his own was a bit stifling these days. He never seemed to have anything of interest to say and tended to be somewhat possessive of Will, reminding him of their long-term friendship rather too often.

Perhaps being in his debt was beginning to pall after all this time, thought Will. Maybe it was making him overly sensitive and inclined to find fault. He knew he couldn't seriously upset Doug because the price was too high. But sometimes the urge to break away was almost unbearable. Gratitude and guilt made a burdensome combination. Nothing was ever said directly, but it was implicit in Doug's constant references to

391

the length of their friendship.

'Sorry, mate. I must have got out of bed the wrong side or something.' Seeing that Doug's glass was almost empty, he said, 'What are you having?'

'The usual, please.'

'So what have you been up to this week?' asked Will of his pal as the barmaid drew the pints.

'I've seen Mabel most nights.'

'Blimey, you are keen, Doug. When is the engagement party?' Will joked.

'It's a bit too soon for that yet,' responded Doug. 'You won't have to dip into your pocket for a present just yet. But I reckon it's on the cards at some point.'

'I'm pleased for you, mate,' said Will. 'I'm glad you've found a nice girl.'

'So am I,' Doug said heartily. Having a girlfriend boosted his ego and made him feel less inferior to Will Stubbs. 'It means a lot to me to know that you're pleased for me and approve of Mabel. There's nothing like old mates, is there? You and I go back such a long way, your opinion is important to me.'

Doug was being sickeningly cloying today and it was as much as Will could do not to make his excuses and leave. He was immediately consumed with guilt. The poor bloke had a lot to contend with, looking the way he did. It must be awful for him, and the least Will could do was give him some friendly company.

'I'm flattered, mate,' he said, paying for the drinks and taking a sip of his. 'I mustn't stay too long. Megan and I are taking the kids out this afternoon as it's such a nice day. The summer will be over soon enough.'

For a moment Will thought he saw an objection in Doug's eyes, but it was so fleeting he guessed he must have imagined it, especially when Doug said in an amiable manner, 'I'm meeting Mabel later on, so I can't stay too long either.'

'Sunday afternoons as well,' approved Will, teasing him. 'I think I'd better start saving up for a wedding present, never mind an engagement one.'

'You never know.'

'Good luck to you, mate,' Will said warmly. 'I hope everything goes well for you.'

★ ★ ★

In contrast to the sunshine of London, it was a wet Sunday afternoon in West Wales and bleak in the extreme. The village was deserted and silent because everyone was either at chapel or indoors. Dil and Owen were in the former category, their visitors in the latter: Hetty and Ken in the living room, George upstairs in the bedroom. There was a steady drizzle outside, running down the windows, causing condensation to cloud them over and a mist to rise across the fields.

'What's George doing up there, I wonder,' mentioned Ken.

'Studying his pet beetle, I expect,' Hetty suggested. 'He's got one in a matchbox and calls it Bob. I tell you, Ken, if he gets a pet spider, I shall have to leave home.'

They both laughed, the atmosphere between them friendly and comfortable.

'It's nice to have the place to ourselves while Auntie and Uncle are out at chapel, isn't it?' Hetty said pleasantly.

Ken nodded, but his guard was up, his eyes resting on her warily. Her tone of voice indicated that she might suggest they take this opportunity to have the much-feared discussion.

'Didn't you say you would get the tea ready for when they get back?' he reminded her tactically. 'Maybe you should start preparing it. I'll give you a hand if you like.'

'It's much too early,' she said, her mood darkening because of his blatant attempt to avoid a significant conversation.

'Oh. Right.' He got up and walked over to the window, clearing a patch in the steaminess with his fingers and looking out at the rain-soaked landscape. 'It's a pity about the weather. Still, we've been lucky up until now.'

'Oh for goodness' sake,' she responded sharply. 'Are we reduced to talking about the weather because you won't talk about things that really matter?'

'Don't start again, Hetty,' he said, without turning round to face her. 'Don't ruin the holiday. It's been so good.'

'Yes, it has. But it is just a holiday, a temporary thing. We have a long-term issue to resolve.'

'Leave it.'

'What are you planning on doing, Ken?' she

asked, her voice becoming shrill with frustration. 'Are you aiming to ignore the situation permanently and let things get worse and worse until we hate the sight of each other and just stay together because of George?'

He wanted to stay calm but she always managed to inflame his temper because she affected him like no one else could. He swung around. 'Are you sure things haven't reached that stage already?' he shouted.

Smarting from his comment, she hit back at him in a loud voice. 'Well they obviously have as far as you're concerned. Why don't you just leave? George and I will manage perfectly well without you. We got along just fine before you came home.'

'That's what it is with you, isn't it, Hetty? You want it to be just you and George,' he boomed. 'I don't come into the picture as far as you're concerned. I'm just a nuisance to you. I saw it in your eyes when I arrived back from abroad and I've seen it there every single day since, so don't try to deny it.'

'If that's what you thought, why didn't you just bugger off and leave us in peace?' she shrieked, beside herself now, the words pouring out of their own volition.

'Because . . . because . . . ' He turned back to the window. 'You wouldn't understand.'

'How can I when you refuse to talk to me about anything that matters?'

'There are some things that are best left unsaid,' he came back at her.

'And our marriage isn't one of them.'

Ken put both hands to his head as though in pain. 'Well bugger it, I will go. I've had enough of being your whipping boy; of living in hope of a smile or a kind word from you. You've finally worn me down, so I'll give you what you want and leave as soon as we get back to London.' He stared at her, his eyes dark with pain and rage. 'But you won't stop me seeing George, if that's what you're after. You won't stop me seeing my son.'

'Don't you dare lay the law down to me.'

'And don't you dare speak to me as though I'm the dirt under your feet,' he ground out, his voice distorted with emotion.

'I don't. You're making things up,' she said, her voice so high with fury it was almost a scream.

'Shut up, woman,' he roared. 'Just stop your yelling and give me a break.'

'I'll yell as much as I like.'

And so it went on: shrieking, shouting and sniping; terrible and hurtful things being said by them both. The situation was completely out of control.

★   ★   ★

Upstairs George was sitting on his bed trembling as the voices downstairs grew louder. Whilst feeling a natural instinct to strain to hear what was being said, at the same time he wanted to blot it out, especially when he heard his own name mentioned again and again. It made him feel physically ill when they quarrelled; he felt sick and had a tummy ache. It was horrid to

396

know that he was the cause of all the trouble. He put his fingers in his ears, which stopped the sound but not the agony of knowing he was to blame. If he wasn't around, his mum and dad would be happy together.

Putting the matchbox containing his pet beetle into his trouser pocket, he crept noiselessly down the stairs past the closed living-room door where the argument was still raging and out of the back door, shutting it firmly behind him because of the rain, tears running down his cheeks as he tore down the garden and out of the back gate.

★ ★ ★

The sound of the back door closing produced instant silence in the living room.

'What was that?' wondered Hetty in a hushed tone.

'Must be the others back from chapel.'

'It wouldn't be them already,' she said.

'George?' suggested Ken worriedly.

'He's upstairs in the bedroom.'

Ken tore from the room and up the stairs.

'He isn't there,' he told her breathlessly. 'He must have heard us and gone out.'

'Oh God,' cried Hetty. 'It must have upset him so much he's gone off in the rain.'

'None of his pals will be out playing in this weather,' said Ken.

'They're all at chapel. They don't play out on a Sunday anyway,' she informed him. 'He'll have just gone to get away from us. Oh Ken, what have we done?'

Of one mind they rushed to the back door and out into the garden calling George's name, the rain soaking them, neither having stopped to put on a coat. There was no reply to their calls as they headed out of the back gate into the lane in the driving rain, guessing the direction he might have gone in.

★ ★ ★

George slipped over in the mud as he ran blindly along the narrow hedge-lined lane, scrambling up quickly and hurrying on, his plimsolls sodden, his clothes dripping and his knee hurting from the fall. He'd been too distressed to stop to put a coat on, so was wet through to the skin.

He had no idea where he was going. He didn't care as long as he was away from the sound of his parents' angry voices. His tears mingled with the rain pouring down his face, blurring his vision. His rubber soles had no grip and he went down again, his clothes plastered with mud as he pulled himself up.

It was then he realised that he wasn't alone in the lane. There was a cow coming towards him. Having no fear of animals whatsoever, he walked towards it.

''Ello, old girl. You'll be in big trouble when the farmer finds out you've got out,' he told the beast. 'But it's his fault, not yours; he should check his fences more often.'

He put his hand out to the cow in a friendly

gesture, in much the same way as he would to the carthorse at home. But the animal took fright and kicked out.

'It's all right, I won't hurt you,' George said gently.

But the cow panicked and charged at him, knocking him over and trampling on him in its hurry to get away. George knew nothing more after his head hit the ground with a thud. He didn't hear the frantic cries of his parents as the cow went over him.

★　★　★

Tearing along the lane in pursuit of their son, Ken and Hetty saw the whole thing but weren't near enough to stop it happening.

'Oh my God!' cried Hetty.

'Bloody hell,' gasped Ken.

'Oh Ken,' she sobbed as they ran towards the small figure lying still on the ground in the rain. 'Please don't let him be dead.'

'He's alive,' said Ken, down on his knees, feeling for a pulse. 'But we need to get him to hospital right away.'

'The hospital's miles away,' Hetty told him, her voice heavy from crying as they both knelt on the ground beside their child. 'It'll take ages for an ambulance to come.'

'We'll have to get him there ourselves then.'

'George,' she said, leaning over and stroking his face tenderly, though her hands were trembling. 'It's Mummy. Please wake up, son, please. Please God let him be all right. I'll do anything . . . anything you want . . . just bring him through this.'

'Come on, Hetty love, up you get,' said Ken, gently helping her to her feet. 'Let me get to him.'

'I can't bear it, Ken, I can't bear to see him like this,' she cried, her body racked with sobs. 'I'm so scared.'

Ken took hold of his wife firmly by the arms and looked into her tear-stained face.

'You'll have to bear it for the moment, love, but it'll be all right, you'll see. You stand back and I'll take care of everything,' he said, calm and in control.

Hetty was shivering so much her teeth were chattering as she said, 'Thanks.'

Ken went back on his knees to George. 'I know you're not really supposed to move an injured person, but it'll be more risky not to in this case, so I'm going to pick him up,' he told his wife. 'You go to the village to get help, and I'll bring the boy along. We need someone with transport to take us to the hospital.'

Hetty couldn't move. She stood rooted to the spot watching while Ken picked up their son with infinite gentleness.

'Go on, love, hurry. Don't just stand there.'

'I can't move.'

'Yes you can. It's just nerves making you feel that you can't. I used to get the same thing myself when I was in combat. But your legs will carry you even if they do feel like jelly, I promise you,' he assured her. 'If you could run on ahead sharpish and find someone with a vehicle, it'll save some time. I'll follow on. I'll have to take it more slowly with George.'

Suddenly she could move. His strength gave her courage and she tore off up the lane and reached the village just as they were coming out of chapel, umbrellas up, the women in their best hats, the men in their Sunday suits.

'Please . . . please can someone help us.' She was breathless from running and drenched to the bone, her hair flat to her head and dripping, clothes sticking to her skin. 'Our boy's been hurt. We need to get him to hospital.'

Help was there in an instant; every single person in that crowd was full of concern and wanting to be of assistance. Owen's boss had his station wagon parked in the village and immediately gave Owen the keys and said he would walk home from chapel.

While the worried villagers stood looking on in the relentless rain, the station wagon rolled out of the village with Hetty and Ken in the back, the unconscious child in Ken's arms. Neither of them had ever been more frightened in their lives.

15

'Why are they taking so long to examine him?' fretted Hetty, pale and anxious.

'I don't suppose it is really all that long in terms of medical examinations,' suggested Ken with amazing sangfroid for one so worried. 'It just seems that way to us because we want news so badly.'

'How can you be so calm when our boy could be dead in there?' She was frantic.

'Don't say that word, please, Hetty,' he entreated. 'Don't even think it. I know it isn't easy but you must try to keep a grip and stay positive.'

'Sorry.'

'Don't apologise, for goodness' sake,' he expressed with feeling. 'That's the last thing you should feel you have to do at a time like this. You've enough on your plate.'

'Well . . . you're being so strong and there's me practically in pieces.'

'I'm feeling pretty shaky too, and we'd both be a bit peculiar if we weren't,' he told her, 'but one thing I did learn in the prison camp was how to keep panic at bay in a crisis. It was the only way to stay sane back then.'

'I'm sure it must have been.' She was so subdued her voice was almost a whisper. 'I wasn't accusing you of being unfeeling or anything.'

'I know.'

They were in the waiting area of the hospital. George — still unconscious when they arrived — had been taken away on a stretcher and Owen had gone outside for a cigarette.

'It's our fault that George has been hurt, isn't it?' Hetty said, the gravity of the situation forcing her to examine her own behaviour with an unsparingly critical eye. 'If we hadn't been yelling at each other he wouldn't have been out in the lane at all.'

'I can't get that off my mind either.'

'I feel so ashamed.'

'Same here.'

'Who knows how many other times he's heard us?'

'Plenty I should think, since we've been at each other's throats ever since I got back.'

'We do usually try not to quarrel in front of him, though,' she pointed out, in an effort to assuage her guilt.

'Yeah, but the way we've been carrying on lately, they can probably hear us in Shepherd's Bush, let alone in another room of the same house.'

'Oh dear, have we really been that bad?'

'Afraid so.'

'You're right,' Hetty was forced to admit. 'It's taken something as awful as this for me to realise just how badly we've been behaving. We've been so wrapped up in our own feelings, we've not been careful enough of George's.'

'Exactly.'

'What's happened to us, Ken?' she asked in a

sad rather than confrontational manner.

'I dunno, love.' He gave an eloquent sigh. 'We changed, I suppose; the war altered us.' He didn't try to retreat from the subject as he had in the past. He'd been doing that for long enough, and their boy's life was in danger because of it. 'I suppose the separation was just too long and we couldn't cope when we were finally reunited. We had both changed as we matured. You'd got used to doing things your way, and I'd got out of the habit of family life. It just didn't work any more.'

'I've been horrible to you, haven't I?'

'I won't argue with you about that,' Ken replied with candour. 'But I don't suppose I've been the easiest bloke to have around. Everything seemed trivial, somehow, after the prison camp. It was a bit of an anticlimax after looking forward to coming home for so long. The worst thing, though, was the powerlessness of knowing that you'd fallen out of love with me.'

'I've never said that, Ken.' She was horrified at his words.

'You didn't need to,' he told her in a definite tone. 'The way you behaved towards me did that for you. I knew the instant I saw you again that you didn't feel the same. I knew it but I didn't want to face up to it so I refused to allow the subject to come into the open. If I had done, we'd probably have gone our separate ways and our boy wouldn't have had to listen to all the rows which finally landed him in here.' He paused, looking at her somewhat warily. 'There's one thing I feel I must ask now that we are on the subject.'

'Fire away.'

'Did you meet someone else while I was away? Is that the reason why you changed towards me?'

'No, of course not!'

'Oh.' Such was his relief, his eyes moistened and a pink flush suffused his cheeks.

'But I did feel differently about you when you got back, there's no point in my denying it,' she admitted frankly. 'You didn't seem the same man that I had waved off to the war. You were like a stranger to me. You looked frail and older and I panicked because I wanted you to be the same as before. The more I tried to get that old feeling back, the more elusive it was and the more miserable I became. I took it out on you, always nagging and criticising, hating myself for it but not able to stop. Looking back on it, I think I must have expected too much too soon. Because our marriage was so brilliant before you went away, I thought we'd just take up where we left off as soon as you came back.'

'I suppose I did too.'

'I'd lived for your homecoming for so long, I suppose I expected it to be magical, with stars going off in my head and stuff like that. But it wasn't like that. It was just so ordinary.'

'I'm an ordinary bloke.'

'That isn't what I meant, Ken,' she told him. 'The homecoming was ordinary but you're not. You're a hero, and I don't only mean in the war.' She took hold of his hand and held it in both of hers. 'I couldn't have got through what happened today without you. I fell apart but you were magnificent. You were so calm and strong;

405

you coped with George and with me being a nervous wreck. I got that old feeling back in bucketloads today.'

The warmth exuding from him at that moment was something she would never forget.

'Whatever we have to face now, Ken, I need you beside me. I *want* you beside me,' she went on, squeezing his hand and putting her face close to his. 'If you'll have me after what I've put you through, I think we should put the last year out of our minds and start again.'

'Of course I'll have you,' he assured her. 'Having you in my life means everything to me. That's why I've been so afraid of losing you.'

'You deserve someone better than me.'

'There isn't anyone better,' he told her. 'You and George are all I want.'

'Likewise,' she said, managing a half-smile. 'Please God that our boy comes through this.'

'Stay positive, Hetty,' Ken said as a doctor appeared from a corridor and headed in their direction. 'Whatever he has to say, we'll face it together.'

★   ★   ★

It was almost bedtime in the dairy house, and Dolly, Megan and Will were sitting in the parlour listening to the wireless when the telephone rang. They were all startled because it was too late for a social call and wouldn't be business at that time of night.

Dolly was up and on her way to the phone before anyone else had a chance. Megan followed her because a late call was synonymous with trouble.

'Oh, Hetty, it's you,' said Dolly in a nervous, staccato manner, after the operator had put the long-distance call through. 'What's happened for you to ring this late? . . . George? Oh no, the poor little thing . . . Taken unconscious to hospital? Oh my Lord!'

There was a silence while she listened. Megan put a steadying hand on her mother's arm, feeling her trembling. Her own heart was racing fit to bust and her legs were threatening to give out.

'Oh, he's come round, thank goodness for that,' said Dolly, brushing her brow with her hand. 'A broken leg . . . and badly bruised . . . Oh dear, poor George . . . Concussion too? Good gosh alive.' She tutted worriedly. 'But thank God he's going to be all right . . . Mm, yes. Oh, I see . . . Yeah, that's the best thing for him, to stay in hospital for a day or two under observation.'

She listened again.

'Yeah, I can understand that. You'll have to stay on in Wales for a few extra days because he won't be well enough to travel, but Ken can come back earlier if we're desperate. No, it's all right, love, we can manage; you'll need Ken there with you. Don't worry about anything here. You just look after that grandson of mine and give him a kiss from me. Thanks for letting us know. Ta-ta, now.'

She replaced the receiver.

'George got kicked and trampled by a cow,'

she told the anxiously waiting Megan. 'He's taken a real pasting by the sound of it, but he's going to be all right.'

'The poor kid,' said Megan sympathetically. 'Thank goodness he's come through it all right.'

★ ★ ★

'Poor George,' Megan said to Will after Dolly had gone to bed and they were relaxing in the parlour on their own before they went up.

'It must have given the lad one hell of a fright.'

'Goodness knows how he managed to get himself hurt by a cow,' she said. 'We'll hear all the details when they get back.'

'George will be full of it; you know what kids are like when they've had a brush with danger.'

She nodded. 'I suppose all the worry of George will have put paid to any chance of Hetty and Ken trying to put their marriage right.'

'Not necessarily,' Will suggested hopefully. 'They might have had a chat before it happened.'

'I hope they get something sorted out,' she said. 'They can't go on for much longer as they are, at each other's throats the whole time. They need to be honest with each other about their feelings instead of hedging round it and sniping at each other. I think honesty is essential in a marriage. If you're not straight with each other, sooner or later things will turn sour.'

Even as she spoke, her own hypocrisy pierced her conscience but was pushed to the back of her mind by the look on her husband's face.

'What's the matter, Will?' she asked, peering at

him. 'You've turned a bit pale.' She grinned and made a joke of it. 'I hope you don't have any skeletons in your cupboard.'

Immediately the words were out she regretted them, because of course Will did think that he had something bad hidden away in his past.

'Don't be daft.' He brushed it aside. 'You know me. What you see is what there is.'

'I was talking about being honest about feelings for each other anyway,' she made clear, 'and you and I know where we stand as regards that, don't we?'

'We certainly do.' He turned to humour to relieve the sudden tension. 'We both know that we can't stand the sight of one another.'

'Oh Will, you are a fool,' she smiled.

But they were both fully aware that a dark shadow had been cast over the atmosphere, despite their efforts to laugh it off.

★   ★   ★

On their way into the ward at visiting time a few days later, the doctor called Hetty and Ken into his office.

'Nothing wrong, is there, Doctor?' asked Hetty worriedly. 'George seemed a lot better when we came to see him yesterday. Apart from a few aches and pains from the bruising, and the broken leg of course.'

'Physically we're very pleased with his progress . . . '

'Good. So you're going to let us take him home with us, are you?' surmised Hetty when the doctor paused. 'Is that what you wanted to talk to us about?'

'No, we'll be keeping him in for a while longer.'

'Oh.' Ken perceived a problem. 'Is something the matter?'

'He seems very low in spirits, distressed in fact, and we're rather concerned,' explained the doctor, a thin, dark-haired man with a neatly trimmed moustache and spectacles worn low down on his nose so that he peered over the top at them. 'We care about the mental well-being of our patients as well as their physical condition.'

'He would be fed up, being stuck in hospital,' was Ken's response. 'That's why he's down in the dumps. No disrespect, Doc, you do a good job, but it isn't like being at home with his mum and dad, is it?'

'That's just it,' said the doctor, leaning back in his chair and stroking his chin while he looked from one to the other. 'He doesn't seem to want to go home. He's said as much to the nurse on several occasions.'

They both stared at him in disbelief.

'But he loves it here in Wales,' Hetty pointed out. 'We'll be going home to London in a few days anyway.'

The doctor leaned forward and tapped the edge of his desk with a pencil, his lips set in a grim line. 'The location doesn't seem to be the problem.' He paused as though choosing his words carefully. 'It's the situation he doesn't want to face up to. You're going away, I understand, Mr Scott?'

'No. Of course not.'

'Oh? George seems to think that you are leaving home.'

Hetty and Ken exchanged glances.

'Oh my God,' muttered Hetty, casting her mind back and remembering painfully what had been said by herself and Ken in anger.

'I'm afraid there's been a terrible misunderstanding, Doctor,' Ken cut in quickly. 'We need to go and see him so that we can put it right.'

'I hope you can, for his sake.'

'Thanks for your concern, Doctor,' said Hetty. 'It's nice to know that he's in good hands.'

'Thanks, Doc,' echoed Ken, and he and Hetty rushed from the room and hurried down the corridor.

★ ★ ★

'Your dad and I need to have a chat with you, George,' announced Hetty, after greetings had been exchanged and they'd given him a copy of this week's *Beano* and a bag of toffees.

'Do you?' He looked worried, as though fearing the worst.

'We know that we've made you unhappy lately because of our quarrelling, and we're both very sorry.'

George stared at his hands, which were folded together on top of the bed sheet.

'All of that's going to stop,' put in Ken. 'We can't promise that we'll never have another cross word, because everybody has those from time to time. But we're going to do our best to stop

411

being so nasty to each other all the time.'

George looked up and stared at his father coldly.

'You're leaving us,' he said accusingly, voice ragged with emotion and cheeks flushed. 'I heard you say it, so don't pretend everything's going to be all right.'

'I'm not going away, son.'

'You are. You're going away because of me.'

'You?' said Ken, stunned. 'What on earth has put that idea into your head?'

'When you quarrel, it's always about me,' he replied. 'I hear you saying my name . . . over and over again.'

'No, son,' Hetty assured him. 'It's never been about you. We would have mentioned you because you are so important to us. But our quarrels have always been with each other.'

'Oh.' George looked at his father, his eyes brimming with tears. 'Anyway, you're going away, so it doesn't matter now.'

'I'm not going anywhere, except back to London with you and your mum,' said Ken.

'But you said . . . '

'We all say things we don't mean when we're angry,' explained Ken. 'I was very angry then but I didn't mean what I said. I'm not going anywhere, I promise.'

George looked at his mother. 'You told him to go,' he accused her.

'I didn't mean it either,' she assured him, taking his hand and looking into his face. 'Honest.'

'Oh.' The boy's gaze moved from one to the

412

other. 'Really?' He was still wary.

'Yes, really,' his father replied. 'Your mum and I have had a long talk and got everything sorted out, so things will be a lot happier for all of us from now on.'

George didn't seem convinced. 'I hate it when you are angry with each other,' he said, his voice quivering on the verge of tears. 'It scares me, and makes me feel all funny inside.'

Hetty felt very ashamed. 'Sorry, darling. We've been very selfish. We know that now.'

'I'm sorry too, son.'

'I didn't like you at first when you came back from the war, Dad,' George confessed unexpectedly. 'Because Mum was always cross then and she didn't used to be before you came to live with us. I wanted you to go away then, but not any more. I want you to stay with us now.'

Father and son smiled at each other, cautiously at first, then with heart-warming grins. The love flowing between them was so palpable, it brought tears to Hetty's eyes.

'Come on then, give us a toffee,' joked Ken, who wasn't comfortable with sentimentality.

'I'm the one who's in hospital,' said George, entering into the bantering spirit. 'I thought the toffees were supposed to be for me.'

'They are, but I'm sure you can spare us just one after we've come twenty miles along bumpy roads with your Uncle Owen driving a farm truck. Cough up, you little skinflint.'

George offered the bag to them both.

'No, I was only kidding, son,' explained Ken, ruffling his hair. 'We brought the toffees for you.

413

You keep them. Your sweet ration is little enough.'

'I want you to have one,' George said, holding the bag closer to his father.

'What about your mum?'

He handed the bag to her.

'Thank you, George,' she said thickly, taking a sweet because she knew that was what her son wanted.

But she couldn't enjoy it, because she was so sick with self-disgust at causing such pain to both her husband and her son. How could she have done that to them because of her selfish longing for something more than she had with Ken? How easy it was to get so caught up in your own emotions that you could make other people suffer without even realising it — until the damage was already done.

★ ★ ★

'Anything wrong, love?' Will asked Megan one evening when they were in the bedroom. She had just washed her hair and was sitting at the dressing table drying it with a towel. Will was relaxing on the bed, having just been to say good night to the twins. Megan and Will often took refuge in the bedroom if they wanted some time away from the family.

'Why do you ask?'

'You seem a bit quiet and preoccupied,' he replied. 'Which means that you are either worried about something or have got the needle with me and are sulking.'

414

'I'm all right, really.'

'You're not very convincing; not to me anyway, because I know you so well,' he told her. 'If I've done anything to upset you, for goodness' sake tell me so that I can put it right.'

'It's nothing you've done, honestly,' she assured him, rubbing her hair vigorously with the towel. 'I'm a bit worried about a friend of mine, that's all.'

'Why? Is she ill?'

'No. She's in love with a man who is wrong for her,' Megan answered. 'He's bad news.'

'She obviously doesn't think so.'

'She doesn't know what he's really like.'

'And you do?'

'Yeah.'

'How's that?'

'These things get round. You know how it is.'

'Is your friend anyone I know?' Will asked chattily.

'No, she's just someone I was with at school,' Megan lied.

'And you don't know whether to tell her about his misdeeds?'

'Something like that.'

'I should steer well clear if I were you,' he advised her, drawing in his breath and shaking his head. 'She'll only want to shoot the messenger if you try to put her right.'

How right he was, Megan thought. Out loud she said, 'Mm. That's what I thought.'

'Anyway, it's never wise to interfere in other people's private business, especially affairs of the heart,' opined Will. 'It's best to leave them to sort it out for themselves.'

Normally she would agree with him, but he didn't know the gravity of the situation.

He got up. 'Well, I'm going downstairs to listen to the wireless and read the paper,' he said.

'I'll be down in a minute.'

'See you later then.'

Alone with her thoughts, Megan was full of compunction about all the lies she kept being forced to tell. One led to another and there was no end to it. She was still very upset about the falling-out with Mabel but couldn't put it right without hurting Will and risking her marriage.

★ ★ ★

Hetty, Ken and George returned from Wales in high spirits. Megan had never seen her sister looking happier. Ken was looking pleased with himself too. The years seemed to have dropped off him and he looked almost handsome.

'There's no need to ask if the plan worked,' Megan said to Hetty on the quiet.

'It didn't, at least not in the way I expected,' Hetty told her. 'But yeah, we had a long talk and got the problems out into the open, and hopefully we have put things right. It feels so good between us now. Thanks for suggesting the holiday, sis, and covering for us here. It might have gone on and on if we hadn't had the break. It took poor George's accident to get us talking, but at least we cleared the air and we've promised each other not to let things get so bad again.'

416

'I'm so pleased for you.'

'Whatever the outcome, it's best to have these things out, don't you think?' Hetty said. 'It could have gone the other way — and thank God it didn't — but at least we would have known where we stood, instead of all that awful bickering without really knowing why we were doing it. We've wiped the slate clean; given ourselves a fresh start.'

Her sister nodded.

'I suppose that's why you and Will get on so well, because you're so straight with each other.'

Megan winced and hoped it wasn't noticeable. Every day her conscience took a battering because of what she was keeping from Will. It was wearing her down.

★ ★ ★

George was enjoying all the attention he was getting from his cousins.

'Cor, I wish I had one of those,' said Poppy, inspecting the plaster cast on his leg.

'And me,' echoed her sister, examining it closely and tapping it with her knuckles.

'It's very itchy,' George informed them, frowning and poking one of his grandmother's knitting needles down the side of the hard casing.

'Having a cow attack you is really special, George,' declared Poppy. 'Were you scared?'

'It didn't attack me, it just ran over me because it wanted to get away, and I wasn't scared because it was only a poor frightened

417

cow,' said the soft-hearted boy. 'Anyway, I don't remember anything after it kicked me over because I was knocked out.'

'Phew, getting knocked out is even better than fainting,' said Netta, breathless with awe.

'A broken leg at the same time is really amazing,' added Poppy, looking at the plaster cast with admiration.

'I wish I could faint,' mentioned Netta in a matter-of-fact tone.

'Why would you want to do that?' enquired George.

'Because people make a big fuss of you of course,' she explained. 'When someone faints at school, there's always a lot of excitement.'

'Yeah,' Poppy chipped in. 'Everybody treats you like you're a film star or something.'

'Can we have a go with your crutches?' requested Netta.

'Help yourself.'

The twins being as they were, the crutches soon became purveyors of enormous entertainment. They were taking it in turns to clonk around the room swinging their legs when their mother walked in, followed by their father.

'Oh no, I might have known you two would make toys of the crutches,' admonished Megan. 'They are for people who have been hurt and need them to help them walk, not for children to play with. You'll break them the way you're carrying on.'

'No we won't, Mum,' said Poppy.

'It's just a bit of fun,' added Netta.

'I do believe that you two girls must be the

most mischievous children in London,' chastised Megan. 'Give the crutches back to George this minute and thank your lucky stars it's us who caught you and not your Auntie Hetty. You'd really cop it if she knew you were messing about with them.'

'I don't mind them playing with them, Auntie Megan,' said George good-humouredly.

'I don't suppose you do, George, because you're a very sweet-natured boy. But I mind and so does their father.' She turned to Will. 'Don't you?'

'Yeah, yeah, of course I do,' he said supportively, not daring to let his wife see that he was struggling not to laugh.

'Sorry,' chorused the twins.

'I should think so too,' said Megan.

'Netta wants to faint and have a fuss made of her, Mum,' announced Poppy. 'How do you do fainting?'

'You don't. It does it to you and isn't at all pleasant, so you can get that idea out of your head right away.' Megan raised her eyes, tutting and forcing herself to keep a straight face. 'I really don't know where you girls get your ideas from.'

'The toy counter at Woolworth's,' said Netta, giggling.

'That's enough of your cheek,' warned her mother.

All three children found the Woolworth's joke hilarious and became helpless with laughter.

Megan turned and left the room quickly so as not to lose her authority. Outside she shook with silent mirth. Will was already out there doing the same.

'Never a dull moment with those two, is there?' she said when she'd recovered sufficiently to speak.

'Thankfully no,' he agreed. 'We don't need to go to the Shepherd's Bush Empire to see a comedian to make us laugh. We have our own resident comic act right here in this house.'

★ ★ ★

It was the last Sunday of the school holidays and you could barely put a pin between the people on Southend beach as the sun beamed down from a clear blue sky. The promenade wasn't as bright and dazzling as in prewar summers, when it was overflowing with rock shops, candy-floss sellers, cockle and whelk stalls and brightly painted amusements. Now, in contrast, the town was shabby and battered, the signs of war still here and the greyness of postwar Britain very much in evidence.

But Londoners still flocked here in their thousands, delighted to have access to their favourite day trip again after the beaches being closed to the public during the war years. Southenders used their initiative to provide entertainment for their visitors in various ways, including pleasure-steamer trips to the anti-aircraft forts in the estuary. They couldn't yet remove the wartime blots on the landscape, so they exploited them. They had, after all, lost their livelihood for the duration of the war, so no one could blame them for using any resource they could find until the resort got back to normal again.

The shortage of seaside rock was not matched by the high spirits which resounded the length of the sea front: in the pubs and cafés, on the sands; everywhere.

'Will you help us to dig our castle moat, Dad?' asked Poppy. 'It's taking us such a long time on our own.'

'Course I will,' he said, getting up from his deckchair and kneeling on the sand, where his daughters were busy with buckets and spades.

'Ooh, I say,' joked Dolly from her deckchair, casting her eye over her son-in-law in a pair of navy-blue woollen swimming trunks. 'You'll have all the girls after you in that get-up, Will.'

'I'll soon chase them off, so they'd better not get any ideas,' warned Megan, also in a deckchair and wearing a short-sleeved blouse and summer skirt, the latter hitched up above her knees to expose her legs to the sun.

'See what I have to put up with, Mrs M,' grinned Will. 'Three women bossing me around all the time. I'm definitely outnumbered among them.'

'I can see that you look hard done by,' kidded Dolly, who was dressed in a summer frock with the skirt pulled down modestly over her knees. 'You've got a browbeaten look about you.'

Megan chuckled at that. 'That'll be the day, when he allows anyone to browbeat him.'

'See what I mean, Mrs M?'

They had caught an early train from

Fenchurch Street station so were here in time to get a place on the sands. Ken and Hetty were looking after everything at the dairy, which they could manage as it was Sunday and there was only the round to do and a few shop hours. They couldn't go far anyway with George's leg still being in plaster, so had suggested that the others have a day out.

Here in this hedonistic atmosphere, with the sun warm on her face and body and the sound of people enjoying themselves ringing in her ears, Megan could put her trauma and the worry of things left unsaid to the back of her mind and enjoy the time with her family.

'Is the moat deep enough for you?' Will enquired of the girls.

'Yes thanks, Daddy,' replied Poppy. 'We need to get some water to put in it now.'

'Give me your buckets then, and I'll go down to the sea and get it for you,' he offered.

'We'll come with you.' Dressed in a red swimming costume the same as her sister's, Poppy squinted towards the sea, which was quite a distance away because the tide was going out. 'Can we go in the water?' she asked, becoming animated at the idea. 'We can finish the sand castle later.'

'Yes, can we, Dad?' squealed Netta, jumping up and down with excitement. 'Let's go in. Are you coming, Mum?'

'Yeah, I'll come for a paddle.'

Leaving Dolly in her chair, content to stay and look after the things, the four of them picked their way through the crowds to the sea's edge, where the two girls immediately ran in splashing and screaming with delight.

'Don't go out any further,' their father warned.

'They're only in an inch of water,' Megan pointed out, holding her skirt up to stop it from getting wet.

'That's all they need for paddling.'

'They want more than just a paddle. They want to splash about and get themselves wet,' Megan informed him. 'They're not babies any more.'

'Just a bit further, Daddy,' said Poppy, wading into slightly deeper water.

'We want to practise swimming,' said Netta.

Knowing from past experience by the river how uncomfortable Will was when the girls were anywhere near water, Megan said to him, 'They'll be all right, love. It's only up to their knees and they can't do much if it's any shallower. They had swimming lessons last term at school, and anyway, no harm will come to them while we're here.'

'A second is all it takes.'

'Take it easy, love, for their sakes,' she urged him quietly so the girls couldn't hear. 'They'll get to be frightened of water if you carry on like this, and that's the last thing we want. I want them to learn to swim. Every child should be able to do that.'

'Ron could swim and it didn't help him, did it?'

Only because he was pushed under the water, she thought, but aloud she said, 'You go off and

423

have a proper swim. I'll look after the girls here.'

'No. I'm not taking my eyes off them while they are in the sea,' Will stated firmly. 'I'll go and have a splash about with them. Coming?'

'I'm right behind you,' Megan said and waded out after him, reminded once again of how deeply his brother's death had affected him.

★ ★ ★

The day was an unqualified success despite Will becoming panic-stricken every time the twins went near the water. They stayed on the sands most of the day, eating fish paste and tomato sandwiches for lunch, then taking a stroll along the prom, queuing for ages for an early fish supper before catching the train back to London in the evening.

The twins fell asleep with the motion of the train, Dolly dozed off too, and Megan sat with her head resting on her husband's shoulder.

'It's been such a brilliant day,' she told him. 'I've enjoyed every minute of it.'

'Me too,' he responded. 'One day we'll do better than a day trip to Southend. I'll take you on a posh holiday somewhere warm and sunny.'

'I'll always want to go to Southend for the day in the summer, whatever else there is in my life. It's a tradition,' she told him. 'There's something about the place that's very special to me. It'll be even better when everything is up and running properly again.'

'We'll go to Southend as well then,' he said.

'I'll hold you to that.'

'But my aspirations are for more than a day trip,' he explained, his voice rising with enthusiasm. 'It might take me a few years but I'm going to make a better life for us and the children. I'll work my backside off to get a bit of money behind me, then I'm going to look for a plot of land and build us a house.'

'That will be lovely, but — '

'Things are a bit slower than anyone expected getting back to normal after the war, I know,' he went on, too caught up in his plans for the future to take notice of her interruption. 'But everything will improve soon; rationing will eventually end and things will be plentiful again. With the war behind us, this is a time of recovery and renewal for our country. There'll be opportunities for anyone with a bit of savvy, and I shall make sure I spot them.'

'I'm sure you will. Not much passes you by.'

'I'm going to go to night school when it starts again in the autumn to learn something about building. I want to know what I'm doing.'

'I admire you for your ambitions, Will, and I want to share them with you,' Megan said.

'Good.'

'But I don't need all the fancy stuff you seem to set such store by,' she went on. 'I would like a place of our own, of course, the same as every other young couple in the country, but I don't need expensive holidays and all the rest of it. As long as I have you and the girls, I'm perfectly happy.'

He squeezed her hand and fell silent, feeling unbearably moved by her unquestioning love for him. He was so lucky to have her. She was far too good for the likes of him.

★ ★ ★

That same evening Doug walked Mabel home from the cinema in the warm balmy air. Her arm was linked in his.

'Will and the others struck lucky with the weather, then,' he mentioned casually. 'He was taking the family to Southend for the day. They'll be back by now, I should think.'

'Ooh, the kids will have loved that,' Mabel responded. 'I enjoy a day trip to Southend myself.'

'We can go if you like,' he suggested.

'The season is nearly at an end,' she reminded him, the scent of incipient autumn perceptible in the night air. 'Summer is almost over.'

'Not quite over yet, though,' he pointed out. 'We'll go next weekend if you like. There should still be some sunshine about then, and if not we'll enjoy ourselves anyway.'

'That would be smashing.'

'That's settled then. We'll get an early train so that we get a nice long day there.'

'You're so good to me, Doug.'

Of course he was good to her; it was in his own interests to keep her happy. She was useful to him. It gave him confidence to have a woman on his arm, and no one else would look at him,

426

so Mabel would have to do. He didn't want to go back to the awful loneliness that had plagued him before they'd got together, so he made sure he kept her sweet. 'No more than you are to me, Mabel,' he said, squeezing her hand.

16

As it was only a short train journey from Southend to London, Megan and the others were home by mid-evening, content with their day and pleasantly exhausted. Having given Hetty and Ken a brief description of the outing and put the girls to bed, Megan and Will went to their own room.

'I don't know about you, but I shall be asleep as soon as my head touches the pillow tonight,' said Megan, dressed in her nightdress and smelling of soap and toothpaste, having just returned from the bathroom. 'It must be all that healthy fresh air.' She brushed some lingering sand from between her toes. 'I reckon I've brought half of Southend beach back with me. The bloomin' stuff gets into everything and defies soap and water.'

'Mm.'

'Still, it's a small price to pay for such a smashing day out, don't you think?'

Silence.

'A penny for them,' she remarked casually, noticing that Will seemed preoccupied with his thoughts.

'You can have them for free,' he said, getting into bed. 'I fact, I want to talk to you about what's on my mind. Do you think you can stay awake long enough to listen?'

'It'll keep until tomorrow, won't it, love? Only

I really am dead tired so I can't promise anything,' she said, yawning. 'It's about your business, is it?'

'No, it isn't about business and it can't wait until tomorrow,' he replied, sounding stern suddenly. 'I have to talk to you now while I feel the need so strong. I don't want to put it off any longer. I've avoided it for long enough already. I wouldn't bring it up at this time if it wasn't important to me.'

'All right, keep your hair on.' Megan looked at him and her mouth dried with nerves at his grim expression. 'As you're so set on talking, I'll have to make sure that I do stay awake, won't I? What is it that's so urgent it has to be discussed after a lovely day out?'

'Could you turn the light out and get into bed, please, love?' he requested.

She did as he asked. 'Right, let's have it then,' she said, snuggling up to him.

'We were happy together today, weren't we?'

'Ecstatically,' she said lightly.

'At one with each other, wouldn't you say?' he said.

'Very much so.' She was growing ever more anxious as it became increasingly likely that this might be leading up to a confession.

'The feeling between us was so good and you are so precious to me, it set me thinking that it's time I wiped the slate clean and told you something you don't know about me, so that there are no secrets between us.'

'I know all I need to know about you,' she said quickly, eager to deter him from going further.

'Let's just leave it at that.'

He began talking about the war. 'Like every other soldier, I'll never forget the things I saw and had to do in battle,' he said. 'But I can blank it out; most of the time anyway.'

'It's a good thing you can,' she said, relieved that the subject matter wasn't what she'd feared it might be. 'You'd drive yourself mad if you dwelled on it.' She paused. 'You can always talk to me about it if it'll help.'

'I appreciate that,' he said. 'But this isn't about the war. I only mentioned that to illustrate a point. This concerns something I've done that I can never blank out — unlike the war — and it's time I told you about it. It's wrong for me to keep something as important as this from you, being that we are so close.'

Now she knew for sure what he was going to tell her, and panic rose, because it meant she would be forced into disclosing the truth, and God only knew what would happen then.

'I don't expect to know every little thing about you.' She was desperate now to discourage him from continuing. 'You are your own person as well as my husband. We didn't stop being individuals when we got married.'

'This isn't a little thing,' he explained. 'This is something that any wife is entitled to know about her husband.'

'I've told you, I know all I need to know about you,' she said, frantic to curb his flow. 'Whatever it is, I should forget about it and go to sleep.'

But there was no stopping him.

'Ron didn't die because he fell in the water,'

430

he blurted out. 'I pushed him. I killed my own brother.'

The echo of his statement seemed to rumble on in the terrible silence.

'Well, say something,' he urged her at last.

Megan got out of bed and turned on the light at the switch by the door, looking down at Will from her side of the bed and seeing his handsome face creased with worry. She knew that the moment of truth had come and could not be put off. He had taken an agonising decision out of her hands.

'You didn't kill your brother, Will,' she stated categorically.

He sat up, looking at her. 'There's no point in your refusing to believe it, Megan,' he said sadly. 'You have to face up to it. It happened, and pretending it didn't isn't going to make it go away.'

She went round to his side of the bed and sat down, looking directly into his eyes. 'You did not kill Ron, and that's not just me in denial; it's a plain fact.'

His face slowly rearranged itself into a puzzled expression. 'Oh yeah, and how would you know anything about it?' he asked.

'I know that you and your brother were joshing on the bridge and the two of you climbed up on to the parapet, mucking about as boys do, and you accidentally pushed him in.'

'How do you know that?' He was staring at her, his brow furrowed. 'No one besides me knows . . . well, except Doug, and he wouldn't have said anything.'

431

'He would and he did,' she informed him through dry lips. 'I know exactly what happened that day on the bridge. Doug was boasting about it to me; he was pleased with himself for fooling you into believing that you owed him a favour all these years.'

'Go on . . . '

There was absolute stillness in the room as she related what Doug had told her; every painful word repeated in a voice hoarse with nerves. 'He'd always resented the bond between you and Ron apparently,' she said in conclusion.

There was pause, then — like a man possessed — he leapt out of bed and dragged on his clothes. He was whey-faced and shaking; still too deep in shock to wonder about the circumstances by which Megan had obtained this information. That would come later; when he calmed down, she thought with dread.

'I'll kill him,' he muttered, pulling on his shirt. 'You wait till I get my hands on him.'

'No, Will, no,' she cried, clutching hold of his arm. 'They'll hang you if you do. Ron lost his life because of Doug. Don't lose yours too. You can't, Will. You can't let him do it to you.'

'Get out of my way, Megan, please,' he urged, removing her hand from his arm. 'I'm going to see him.'

'I'm coming with you.' She was already getting dressed.

'No.'

'I'm not letting you go anywhere on your own while you're in this state,' she insisted, her voice breaking. 'I'm not going to let my children lose

432

their father to the hangman's noose.'

'You stay here with the girls.'

'They'll be all right with Mum and Hetty,' she said. 'You're not going without me and that's definite.'

He was far too distressed to argue any further and left the room with her on his heels. Stopping only to tell her mother — who was in the parlour listening to the wireless with Hetty and Ken — that she had to go out, she followed her husband into the street and started the long walk to the Reynolds house, since Will was too agitated and eager to get there to wait for a bus.

★   ★   ★

When they learned from Mrs Reynolds that her son was out with Mabel, Will immediately wanted to go to Mabel's house. He guessed that Megan knew where she lived so she couldn't plead ignorance in the hope of avoiding bloodshed.

'They probably won't be there anyway,' she pointed out. 'They'll have gone out somewhere.'

'Then I'll wait outside until they get back, because I'm not leaving this overnight,' he stated categorically. 'He's bound to see Mabel home for a spot of canoodling.'

He was right, as it happened. Doug and Mabel were in a clinch at her front gate. Without any warning, Will marched up to them and dragged Doug away from the startled girl.

'Murderer,' he ground out, pushing Doug against a nearby wall and putting his face close

433

to his. 'You're a murderer and a liar. You're rotten through and through.'

'What . . . what are you talking about?' Despite the front he was putting up, Doug was obviously taken aback by this unexpected development.

'You know what I'm talking about,' Will shouted, beside himself with rage. 'You pushed Ron under the water and held him down. You killed my brother and let me think it was me.'

'I don't know what you're going on about.'

'Yes you do, so don't insult my intelligence by denying it.'

'I suppose that tramp of a wife of yours has been putting stupid ideas in your head,' Doug muttered breathlessly.

'Don't you dare use that word in relation to my wife,' warned Will, lifting his fist.

'Ask her what she was doing on the afternoon of Christmas Day 1944,' Doug put in quickly. 'Ask her what she was doing while her poor mother was ill in bed upstairs.'

'I was shaking, being sick and crying mostly,' Megan intervened, knowing the truth must be told before Doug gave his own version. 'After he'd raped me.'

'Rubbish,' snorted Doug as Will stared at him in shock and disgust. 'She came on to me. I couldn't stop her. She'd been asking for it for weeks. This is her way of getting revenge because I rejected her, the cow.'

Dumbstruck, Will lowered his fist but maintained his grip on Doug's arm.

'It isn't true, Will, I swear.'

434

'She couldn't get enough of me,' Doug went on. 'That's why she's lying through her teeth now. What they say about a woman scorned is true. Open your eyes, mate, and see the sort of woman you're married to.'

'It's all lies, Will,' said Megan, managing to sound calm. 'He did what he did to me to have one over on you, because he's been jealous of you all his life.'

Will finally recovered sufficiently to speak. 'So not only are you a murderer and a liar, you're a rapist too,' he roared before punching Doug on the jaw and, as the man reeled back, knocking him to the ground, whereupon the two of them rolled around in the road fighting, despite Megan's desperate pleas for Will to stop.

'I can't believe what I've just heard,' said Mabel, who was crying softly. 'Is it true, Megan? Did he really do those things?'

'I'm afraid so,' she replied.

'Oh, how awful. Why didn't you tell me?' Mabel wept. 'You knew I was serious about him.'

'I tried to warn you, but I couldn't tell you the truth,' Megan explained. 'I was trying to protect Will and my marriage.'

'And it didn't matter about me? Some friend you turned out to be!' Convulsed with sobs, Mabel ran towards her house and disappeared inside.

The men were still fighting on the ground under the lamppost. Will got the upper hand and knelt astride Doug, pinning his arms to the ground.

'I'm not going to kill you, because that would

435

be too easy for you. Neither will I tell the police what you did to my brother,' he said, sounding short of breath but in control. 'Firstly because I don't have any proof and secondly because if it was all dragged up again it would cause my mother and father a great deal of pain. But I don't need proof to know that you did it. You're scum, Reynolds, the lowest of the low, and I never want to set eyes on you again. If you ever come near me or any member of my family, you'll wish you'd never been born.'

'So you believe her rather than your oldest mate, then,' snivelled Doug.

'You're no mate of mine,' Will made clear, his voice gruff with rage. 'You never have been, except in your own mind. Ron and I used to put up with you because you didn't have anyone else to hang out with; not because we enjoyed your company. You were always a whining little sod without an ounce of bottle. And my brother died because we took pity on you and let you go around with us. That mess of a face you've ended up with is a punishment, not enough of one in my opinion, but a small justice for what you've done. Now stay out of my life.'

Leaving Doug sprawled in the road, Will got up and walked over to Megan.

'Well done,' she said.

'Just a job that needed doing,' he responded coolly.

The atmosphere hung heavy between them as they walked home. Neither of them spoke. Conversation of any sort didn't seem appropriate, so Megan stayed silent. When they got to the dairy Will said, 'I'm not coming in just yet. I need to be on my own for a while. If that's all right with you.'

'Of course it is,' she assured him. 'But where will you go at this time of night?'

'Just for a walk; to clear my head.'

'Fair enough,' she said sadly, understanding how betrayed and wretched he must be feeling, and sensing that it would be wrong to try to explain anything at the moment. 'I'll see you later then.'

'Don't wait up.'

'Okay.'

As she watched him stride off down the street, tears began to flow. She wiped them dry, took a deep breath and went inside to thank her mother and sister for listening for the girls.

★ ★ ★

As Megan lay in bed waiting for Will to come home, she recalled how after the rape she had tried to push it out of her mind. She'd vowed not to allow it to ruin her life and her children's.

There were many more women violated than the ones you heard about. The victims probably did what she'd done: picked themselves up, prayed they hadn't got pregnant, tried to put it behind them and got on with their lives as best as they could. There had seemed to be no other option. The only person Megan might have confided in immediately afterwards had not been available at the time: her sister had been away in Wales. There was no way she would have worried her mother with it, especially as Dolly had been ill in bed.

So she'd kept it locked inside, eating away, causing her bad dreams and frightening thoughts behind her brave face. She'd been tormented and made to feel disgusting, but she hadn't been able to show it.

Now she needed to talk about it to the only other person it really mattered to.

★ ★ ★

When Will eventually got back, he didn't switch on the light and was very careful getting into bed.

'I'm not asleep,' whispered Megan.

'Oh.'

'As if I could sleep with you out roaming the streets.'

'Sorry about that,' he apologised. 'I was in such a state, I had to cool down and sort my head out.'

'Do you feel better now?'

'Not really,' he said. 'It'll take more than a walk to do that.'

'Yeah, I understand.'

'You should have told me before,' he admonished. 'I've been home for months.'

'I intended to tell you that you weren't responsible for Ron's death as soon as you got home, but I kept putting it off,' she explained. 'You'd changed when you came back; you were happier and less moody. I thought you must have put Ron's death behind you so I decided not to upset you by dragging it all up again.' She paused. 'Of course I knew that if I told you about that, the other stuff would all come out too, and I just couldn't bring myself to do it.'

'I should have been told everything,' he told her sternly. 'I'm your husband, for heaven's sake.'

'Surely you can understand why I didn't want to talk about what happened to me that afternoon,' she said. 'It hurt me to think about it, let alone talk about it. I didn't tell a soul.'

'I'm sorry you had to go through that on your own,' he said. 'But you've got me now. I'm here for you.'

'I need to tell you about it,' she said, immensely relieved that he hadn't turned on her. 'I want you to know exactly what happened that afternoon. How there was nothing I could do to stop him. Mum and I were sorry for him, that's why we encouraged him to come to the house, as a break from his own four walls. He seemed so nice — '

'Not now, Megan,' he interrupted. 'It's very late.'

'But — '

'Another time,' he cut in. 'I think we've both had enough for one night.'

'Oh. All right. G'night, then.'

'G'night.'

She leaned over to kiss him but he was already turning over with his back to her.

'It wasn't my fault, Will,' she said.

'I know that.'

'Why are you punishing me, then?'

'I'm not,' he denied. 'I'm just very tired and I'm sure you are too. We'll talk tomorrow.'

Megan lay there in the dark, feeling rejected and alone. What had she expected? A comforting cuddle? An outpouring of sympathy? It was only natural he would feel traumatised, having learned of not just one but two major betrayals by someone he'd thought was a friend. She must see it from his point of view and be patient.

'Oh, and by the way, Megan . . .'

'Yes, Will,' she responded, spirits rising.

'As far as anyone else is concerned, Ron still died in a drowning accident. It will be easier for my mother if the truth never comes out; Dad too. I don't think they could cope with what really happened. There's no point in bringing it all back again if we don't have to.'

'I agree with you,' she said. 'I'll have a word with Mabel; make sure she keeps shtoom.'

'Thanks.'

Everything might seem different in the morning, she thought hopefully, but she had a terrible suspicion that she had lost a part of Will the instant he had learned about the rape.

★ ★ ★

Mabel prided herself on being straight with people even if they didn't show the same respect for her. So the following evening she called at the Reynolds house and said she needed to see Doug in private. They went down to the riverside and sat on a bench in a quiet part near a willow tree.

He looked worse than usual, she thought, with

an ache in the pit of her stomach. His eyes were bloodshot and puffy, making his scarred face look grotesque. She'd never thought of him in that way before and was ashamed of her shallowness. Whatever terrible things he had done, he couldn't help his physical appearance.

'I didn't think I'd ever see you again,' he said.

'I don't like leaving things unfinished, that's why I'm here,' she explained. 'I want to let you know exactly where you stand with me and tie up a few loose ends.'

'I see.'

'Megan called round to my house earlier on and asked me not to tell anyone the truth about what happened to Ron Stubbs. They want the story to stay the same because of Will's parents, so you're in the clear as far as that's concerned.'

'Yeah, Will said as much last night,' he told her. 'Er . . . and about last night, Mabel, I'm really sorry that you had to witness the scuffle and all that went with it.'

'Not half as sorry as I am. But it's just as well that I was there,' she said sharply. 'I might never have known the truth otherwise.'

'Look . . . I was just a kid when Ron Stubbs died. It was a boyish prank that went horribly wrong,' he defended.

'You weren't a kid when you raped Megan, though, were you?' she pointed out tersely. 'So what's your excuse for that?'

'It wasn't rape,' he denied. 'She instigated it. She'd been all over me for weeks. Surely you believe me? You know I wouldn't do a thing like that.'

She stared ahead at the Thames, glinting in the last of the day's sunshine. A rowing crew glided by towards Hammersmith Bridge, their coach riding a bicycle along the towpath and calling out instructions through a megaphone. She found herself wondering how everything around her could be so normal when her life was in ruins.

'I thought I knew you,' she said.

'You do know me,' he tried to persuade her. He didn't want to lose the only woman who would look at him. 'I would never do anything to hurt you. You're the best thing that's ever happened to me in the whole of my life. We're good together.' He paused. 'I love you, Mabel.'

'I thought I loved you too.'

'Thought?'

'Yeah. Until last night you were everything to me,' she explained. 'I wanted to marry you; longed for you to ask me.'

'I will ask you,' he burst out, desperate to keep her so that he wouldn't be alone. 'I'll do it now. Please will you marry me, Mabel?'

'No, Doug, I can't marry you,' she said, her voice heavy with regret. 'Not now.'

'Why not?' he implored her. 'I've done wrong in the past, I admit that, but you bring out the best in me. I'm a changed man since you've been in my life.'

'If you really love someone you want to share your life with them as they are, with all their faults, and no matter what bad things they've done,' she said. 'I've given it a lot of thought and come to the conclusion that I don't want to be with a man who has done the things you've done. Whatever I feel for you, it isn't strong enough.'

'It all happened before you and I got together, so why can't you just forgive and forget?' he asked.

'It isn't for me to forgive; that's for Will and Megan,' she pointed out. 'I don't feel strong enough to commit myself to you for the rest of my life, knowing what I know.'

'I was just a boy when that happened with Ron. I was a different person then,' he said pleadingly. 'As for all that stuff with Megan, it was lies.'

'I don't believe you, Doug,' Mabel stated.

'You believe her rather than me?'

'Yeah, I do, as it happens,' she said. 'And I would respect you a lot more if you would be man enough to admit it.'

'All right, I admit it,' he snapped impatiently because he couldn't make her do what he wanted. 'It was wrong and it was a mistake. I wasn't thinking straight. I've told you, I've changed since you and I have been together.'

She winced because it was painful to hear him admit to such a heinous act.

'Happy now?' he asked bitterly. 'Is that why you dragged me down here; just to hear me admit it?'

'No. I needed to speak to you in private because I wanted to tell you to your face that I won't be seeing you again.'

'Oh no, please don't say that,' he begged, turning to her and grabbing hold of her hand in

443

a desperate effort to make her change her mind. 'I'd be good to you, I promise, Mabel.'

'I've no doubt you would, Doug. But it would always be there at the back of my mind, what you've done, and it would come between us. I can't trust myself not to throw it back at you every time we have a row. As much as I want to be with you, I just don't have it in my heart to let something like that go. I'm so sorry,' she said, wrenching her hand away. 'Please don't contact me again.'

'Mabel . . . '

She got up.

'Ta-ta, Doug,' she said, and walked away along the towpath.

Even when she'd almost reached Hammersmith Bridge and was about to turn off towards the town, she still couldn't trust herself not to go back to him. Whatever it was she felt for him, it was very powerful indeed. Even when she'd known the awful things he'd done, she still felt sorry for him. He deserved everything he got, but she still felt as though she'd deserted him.

★ ★ ★

Doug didn't move from the bench. He just sat there staring unseeingly at the river, lost in his thoughts. Now that Mabel had gone, he was agonisingly aware of how much he would miss her. He'd lost the only person who enjoyed being with him and he knew instinctively that there was nothing he could do about it, because the past was irreversible.

If he thought there was even a fraction of a chance, he would move heaven and earth to get her back, because the alternative was loneliness. But he knew that there wasn't. Mabel would have given the matter serious thought before making her decision, and she was a woman who knew her own mind.

With envy so strong it made him feel violent, he watched the couples walking along the riverside, laughing and talking together. He'd had that with Mabel until last night, and knew instinctively that he would never have it again with anyone. People like Mabel, who weren't fazed by ugliness, were few and far between.

An outsider was what he was; a loner. He always had been when he thought about it, and not just since his disfigurement. He'd never felt a part of things; had never felt liked by anyone, though he'd always craved the limelight. Even the Stubbs twins hadn't really wanted him around, it now transpired. His parents were normal enough and seemed to get along with people, so he hadn't inherited his perverse nature from them. They irritated the life out of him, but he supposed that was just because they were of a different generation.

Oh well, they were all he had now, he thought miserably, getting up and heading for the nearest pub. He needed something strong enough to dull the pain.

★ ★ ★

All was not well between Megan and Will. After that dreadful night of drama and truth, Will behaved as though nothing had happened, and refused to talk about it or to allow Megan to tell him about the events of that terrible Christmas afternoon. Her attempts to unburden herself were always greeted in the same way: 'Not now, love' or 'We'll talk about it when we've got more time.'

On the surface he was his usual self: laughing, joking, joshing with the girls. He was as kind and thoughtful as ever towards Megan; more so if anything. But since that night their relationship had become practically platonic. A brief good-night kiss on the cheek was the limit of physical contact between them.

As day followed day, Megan felt increasingly hurt, especially when she spotted him looking at her with a question in his eyes, which made her suspect that he was wondering about Doug's version of what had happened between them. When she confronted him about it, he said she was being paranoid.

She knew in her heart that nothing would be right between them until they faced up to what had happened and talked about it. But as he refused to do that, the future was looking bleak indeed. Her feelings alternated between anger because he wouldn't let her explain about something that hadn't been her fault, and fear of losing him that led to vulnerability so acute it all but broke her. Supposing the doubts she sensed he might be having became so overwhelming he began to believe Doug's version of events? She knew he would never desert his children, but things couldn't go on as they were between the two of them for much longer. One way or the other, a solution had to be found.

When he came home with the news that he had the opportunity of doing up the inside of a factory at night while it wasn't in use, she could see the beginning of the end.

'There's no need to go to such extreme lengths to avoid sharing a bed with me,' she said, when they were alone in their room getting ready to turn in.

'Don't be so ridiculous,' he retorted.

'I'm not.'

'Look, I'm keen to do this job because it will be good money for us,' he explained. 'Whatever I earn will go into the pot; help to build the business and boost the cash flow ready for when I want to move on to bigger things. You do the paperwork, so you know how well it's coming on. I'll be able to afford to rent a yard soon and do things properly. Instead of having my phone calls here, and paperwork all over the place, we'll have a little office.'

'If you're working all day and all night, you probably won't live to see your ambitions reach fruition.'

'Now you're just being dramatic,' he retaliated. 'I'll sleep when I can during the day. I'm young and strong. I can stand up to hard work. It isn't as though it will be for ever. It's just a short-term thing.'

'What will you do when the job is finished to get out of sleeping with me?' she asked coolly.

447

'Oh, I'm not listening to any more of this nonsense,' he said irritably. 'You're creating a problem where there isn't one.'

'There is — '

'If you carry on like this there will be,' he interrupted crossly. 'I really will want to find a bed away from you if you don't give it a rest.'

This whole situation was making Megan feel ill, and worthless as a woman. Knowing that her husband was no longer interested in her in that way had a destructive effect. It wasn't just the sex that was missing, but the general tactile nature of the way they used to be: the hand-holding, a casual arm slipped around her shoulder, a brushing together as they passed; all now carefully avoided by him, as though he couldn't bear to touch her. All of which left her with a dreadful sense of rejection. It wasn't a normal marriage at the moment, and how long could it last without that essential element?

But the atmosphere between them was so explosive that if she continued along these lines he was likely to lose his temper and walk out, and that was the last thing she wanted.

'Perhaps I am overreacting. I'm sorry,' she said, just to keep the peace for the present time.

'That's all right, love,' he said, never one to bear a grudge. 'This factory job will give us a terrific boost. We could have a house of our own a lot sooner than we expected.'

This was the odd part about it. He always referred to his business as theirs and not his, and always spoke about the future as though they would be spending it together. He obviously

448

wasn't thinking in terms of them splitting up. So what did he have in mind, because Will was a normal healthy man?

Perhaps he would find someone else, she thought, with a piercing stab of fear so strong it made her tremble. No, he wouldn't do that. Not Will. Not while he was married to her anyway. What if it went on too long, though? He was only human after all.

She was still convinced that the answer lay in them bringing the rape into the open and facing it together so that it no longer stood between them, forcing them apart. Unless they did that, there seemed to be no way forward for them. As long as he refused to do this, their future seemed very uncertain.

★ ★ ★

Lying with his back to Megan in bed, Will was thinking about his marriage and castigating himself for causing his wife such pain when she'd already been through so much. He was agonisingly aware of the missing element between them; he wasn't just being forgetful about his duty as a husband.

The fact was, he was filled with love and longing for her but couldn't erase the images of her and Doug Reynolds together. The pictures in his mind disgusted him and made him so angry that every time he went to touch her he backed away because he couldn't bear it and tried to stay away from her in the physical sense. He tried to make up for it by being extra caring towards her. His protective instincts had been heightened anyway, so he wasn't being insincere when he made a special effort to take care of her.

It wasn't that he didn't believe her about the rape. He did, of course he did. Not even for a fraction of a second did he doubt her, because his trust in her was so strong, and he now knew that Doug Reynolds was capable of anything. It was the fact that it had happened at all that was causing him such torment. It was still the ultimate intimacy whatever the circumstances, and it had happened between his wife and another man.

Telling himself that it was not the same thing at all made no difference whatsoever. His intellect accepted it but his heart could not. So everything had changed. It was as though a blanket of sordidness had fallen over his marriage. It had been a shiny, wholesome thing before; untouched by anything squalid or dirty. Now it was tainted by the filthiest thing of all.

He wanted to put the whole thing behind him and have everything back to normal, but he just couldn't make it happen. As for talking about it, as Megan wanted, he certainly couldn't cope with that. Every syllable of description would be like a knife in his heart.

Why didn't he just forget it and enjoy his married life as before if he couldn't confront it? It was up to him to put things right. He was the one who was creating the divide, not her. She was the victim, for the second time.

He knew that she was still awake. Why didn't

he just reach across and hold her in his arms? He wanted to so much; to feel her close to him again. But although he loved her and would give his life for her, he couldn't reach out to her. So he lay there in the dark feeling miserable and alone.

17

Ironically, as Megan's marriage headed inexorably for disaster — with Will working all night and a large part of the day, and living on an unhealthily small amount of sleep — Hetty's went from strength to strength.

Having had such serious problems initially on Ken's return from the war, the couple were blissfully happy again. Megan wasn't envious; just relieved for them and encouraged that a marriage that had seemed destined for the rocks had beaten all the odds and recovered.

One morning in the autumn Hetty was late down for breakfast. When she did finally appear everyone had finished and gone their separate ways. Megan was on her own in the kitchen washing the dishes.

'What's up with you?' she asked, glancing at her sister. 'You look like death warmed up.'

'I feel it too,' she muttered, sinking down gratefully on to a chair at the kitchen table with her head in her hands. 'I've been stuck in the lav throwing up. I thought I'd never stop.'

'Oh, you poor thing. You must have picked something up.'

'Yeah, I have, in a manner of speaking.' She smiled weakly. 'I got it from Ken.'

'I don't remember him being poorly . . . ' Megan paused, looking at her sister, half smiling with the tea towel in mid-air. 'Oh, I see, you mean you're pregnant?'

'That's right, kid,' Hetty confirmed. 'I feel really sick but I couldn't be more delighted.'

'Oh Hetty, I'm so pleased for you,' beamed Megan, going over to her. 'Are you up to a hug, or are you feeling too delicate?'

'Course not,' Hetty said, standing up and returning her sister's embrace warmly. 'I'd forgotten how ghastly morning sickness is, though, and this is just the beginning.'

'It'll ease off further down the line.'

'I bloomin' well hope so. I can't stand the thought of another six or seven months of this.'

'Is Ken pleased?'

'Not half. He's like a dog with ten tails, never mind just two,' she replied.

'I take it George doesn't know yet?' remarked Megan with a wry grin. 'We'd all have known about it if he had. He's always wanted a brother or a sister, hasn't he? It's with the twins having each other, I suppose.'

Hetty nodded in agreement. 'We didn't dare tell him until we were ready for you all to know, and we wanted to wait until we were sure, which we are now that I'm feeling so ill in the mornings. We'll tell him after school and after that it can become common knowledge.' She paused thoughtfully. 'Of course, there'll be too much of an age gap for them to be company for each other early on, but it will be nice for them when they're older and the age difference doesn't matter so much. That's the war for you. You can't increase your family if your husband isn't around.'

'No.'

'What about you, sis? Do you have any plans in that direction?' Hetty enquired with sisterly interest.

Any pregnancy Megan had would have to come about by immaculate conception, she thought, given the state of her marriage. But she said, 'We're not planning on having any more children at the moment.'

'Well, you got two for the price of one, didn't you?' grinned Hetty. 'So you can quit while you're ahead.'

It said something for the performance Megan and Will had put on lately that no family member seemed to suspect that anything was amiss between them. If anyone had noticed something they'd kept quiet about it, and this was the sort of family that didn't normally hold back. It was a blessing that they had managed to keep up the pretence, because their problem was so private and delicate, the last thing they needed was any sort of outside pressure.

★   ★   ★

The Morgan family might not have noticed that all was not well, but Will's mother had.

'What's up, son?' she asked of him when he called in to see her one day, something he never failed to find the time for, no matter how busy he was.

'Nothing . . . Why?'

'Something's wrong, I can tell,' she stated. 'Are you sure all this extra work isn't taking its

454

toll on your health? It can't be doing you any good.'

'I thrive on it, Mum.' Never more so than at the present time, he thought gloomily. While he was out at work, the abysmal situation between himself and Megan could be avoided. 'Everything is hunky-dory, so stop worrying.'

'Give over,' admonished Audrey. 'I'm your mum. I know when there's something wrong. Call it a sixth sense if you like, but a mother always knows.'

A new warmth for him seemed to exude from her lately. Was it new, though, or was it just that he'd not been aware of it before because his perception of her feelings for him had always been distorted by his own wretched compunction? Nowadays he could look her straight in the eyes knowing that it hadn't been him who had robbed her of her beloved son.

'You don't always get it right,' he teased her, just to distract her from the subject and with no other meaning.

But much to his surprise she picked up on it. 'I know that,' she admitted. 'I got it very wrong for a long time and I don't think I'll ever forgive myself for that.'

He threw her a look. 'I was only kidding, Mum,' he assured her. 'I didn't mean anything by it.'

'I know you didn't, son, but there are things that should have been said a long time ago and I didn't say them, so now is as good a time as any.'

'What are you on about?'

'Looking back, I realise that I wasn't there for

you as much as I should have been when you were growing up, after Ron died,' she began, her voice quivering slightly. 'I was so caught up in my own grief I think I might have neglected your feelings. I was devastated by Ron's death and not thinking straight for a long time, and I know I wasn't easy to get along with at that time. I was so full of sadness, you see, son, it made me bitter, and I shouldn't have been when I still had you.'

'Mum, it's all right.' He hated to see her upset, and wanted to make her feel better. 'There's no need to do this. It's all in the past and best forgotten.'

'There's every need for me to say what I have to,' Audrey insisted, her voice ragged with emotion. 'It's only this last couple of years I've got to thinking about Ron's death from your point of view. It might have seemed to you as though Ron was the only one who mattered to me. But he wasn't. I loved you both equally; always have. It was the loss of him that made him such a prominent force in my mind. If I'd lost you in the war, I think it would have finished me off. I'm sorry, son, if I haven't always been the mother you deserve.'

'Don't be daft, Mum,' he said thickly. 'I knew how hard Ron's death hit you. Anyway, you know me. I don't take things to heart.'

'That's what you like people to think,' she said. 'But I know different. I know that there's a lot of sensitivity under that cheery strong-man act you live out day after day. Because I'm your mother I know that you're a very troubled man

456

at the moment, and I'd like to help if I can.'

Will was unbearably moved by her confession and her confirmation of her love for him. There had been something missing between them for a long time. Now he felt her reaching out to him, and the bond was so strong it was almost physically painful. He wanted to pour his heart out to her but knew he couldn't. Even apart from the fact that he wouldn't want to burden her, his problems were private, between himself and his wife, and it was up to him to deal with them without advice from anyone.

This conversation made him even more convinced that his mother must never know the truth about Ron's death. After all these years she had finally come to terms with it, and she deserved some peace. It was his job to protect her.

'Thanks, Mum, but it's nothing I can't deal with.'

'I'll respect your privacy and I won't press you then,' she told him. 'But you know where I am if you need me.'

'Thanks,' he said gently, then, reverting to his light-hearted persona, added, 'There is one thing you can do for me.'

'Anything; you just name it.' She looked serious.

'Put the kettle on, will you, Ma, please,' he grinned. 'I'm dying for a cuppa. All this talking has given me one hell of a thirst.'

She was laughing as she got up. 'You really had me going there,' she told him.

Will smiled as she hurried off to the kitchen,

pleased by the improvement in their relationship. But his smile soon faded when he thought of going home to play out the charade he and Megan were caught up in. What was he going to do about that? He was blowed if he knew the answer.

★ ★ ★

It was Sunday lunchtime at the dairy house and the family was gathered around the table for roast lamb. Even Will was able to take time off for this. The portions were small because of the rationing, but they had all become used to that. The subject under discussion was Hetty and Ken's happy event; everyone was buzzing with it.

'Can Poppy and I take the baby out in the pram, Auntie Hetty?' asked Netta.

'I'm sure there will be times when I shall be very glad of that,' replied Hetty.

'Will it be coming soon?' asked Poppy.

'Not until next summer,' replied Hetty.

'Oh, that's ages ahead.' Poppy was disappointed. 'Why do we have to wait so long?'

'That's how long babies take,' explained George knowledgeably. 'Everybody knows that.'

'All right, bighead,' retorted Poppy. 'I did know but I forgot.'

'It'll be lovely having a baby around the place,' enthused Dolly, who was delighted at the prospect of being a grandmother again after such a long time.

'I shall be its brother,' George informed the twins in a superior manner. After being an only child for so long, he could at last glimpse a degree of equality with Poppy and Netta. 'You two will just be its cousins.'

'Mm, that's true.' Netta thought about this for a moment, then looked at her mother. 'Can we have a baby of our own, Mum?' she asked, as yet innocent of the facts of life. 'It would be nice for Poppy and me to have a new brother or sister.'

Keeping her eyes fixed on her daughter, Megan said, 'You already have each other. Be content with that.'

'Oh go on,' wheedled Netta, turning her attention to her father. 'Can we, Dad? Please?'

Megan's steely gaze moved towards Will's and held it, their difficulties appearing to be on show for all to see.

'Dad?' said Netta again.

'For goodness' sake stop wanting everything you see or hear about, Netta,' Megan burst out crossly, looking away from Will. 'A baby is a human being, not a toy. It's want want want with you two girls lately. I want this, I want that; it's neverending.'

'I only asked if we could have a baby,' said Netta, her bottom lip trembling.

'I heard what you only asked and I don't want to hear it again, thank you,' Megan interrupted, her cheeks suffused with an angry pink. 'I'm fed up with this constant barrage of requests from you and your sister.'

The ensuing silence was broken only by the sound of cutlery on crockery as everyone turned their attention to their food to hide their embarrassment.

Will finally tried to put things back on an even keel by saying, 'It's a lovely meal, Mrs M.'

'Smashing bit of lamb, Mum,' added Hetty. 'Very tender and sweet. The roast potatoes are delicious too.'

But the atmosphere was ruined for them all and Megan was ashamed. Heart pounding and cheeks burning after her unreasonable outburst, she decided there and then that the situation between herself and Will could not be allowed to continue. Not now that it was beginning to affect the way she behaved towards her children and upset the rest of the family. It must be brought to a head one way or another. Whatever the outcome, she would have it out with him before another day had passed.

★   ★   ★

That Sunday evening in the living room of the White family home, rain was running down the windows, which were steamed up on the inside. Mabel was sitting on a well-worn sofa, squashed between her two younger brothers and well away from the fire, so she was feeling quite chilly. Her three married brothers had come for Sunday tea with their wives and would probably stay until late in keeping with family tradition. On a Sunday night you couldn't think straight in this house because of the crush and everyone talking loudly at once.

Usually a cheery and positive soul, Mabel was thoroughly fed up and contemplated her future with gloom. There didn't seem to be anything to look forward to without Doug in her life. No more outings or feeling chosen and special; no more warm glow inside. She hadn't wanted to end it but there hadn't been a choice. Who would have thought he would turn out to be such a monster? He'd seemed so sweet-natured when he was with her; she'd felt safe and had trusted him completely.

Try as she might, she couldn't convince herself that he hadn't cared for her, which meant that he was probably feeling as miserable as she was. It hurt her to think that; made her feel as though she'd been too hard on him, and maybe she should have given him another chance. After all, he had done her no harm and those awful things were in the past. But that wasn't the point. The man was a murderer and a rapist and definitely to be avoided. If he'd been a burglar or con man, maybe she could have coped, but trust her to fall in love with a wrong 'un of the worst kind.

Still, looking on the bright side, she'd probably get over it in time. She'd been brought up to be resilient. Anyway, she was young and not bad-looking; someone else would come along. Somehow that line of thought didn't help. It wasn't someone else she wanted.

A worm of unease began to nag in the pit of her stomach. What if her ending it with Doug caused him to do something terrible to someone else out of anger and resentment? Oh God, she did hope not.

These worrying thoughts were interrupted by the probing tones of one of her elder brothers.

461

'Haven't you got yourself fixed up with another bloke yet, Mabel?' he asked.

'I wouldn't be sitting here with you lot if I had, would I?' she came back at him indignantly. There was no such thing as privacy in this house. Everybody seemed to think that her life was their own personal property. 'I'd be out enjoying myself.'

'You're slipping, girl,' he teased her. 'You want to get out there on the lookout. Why don't you go up the Palais? There'll be plenty of spare blokes there just waiting for a girl like you.'

'I don't want to. I've got no one to go with anyway,' she told him. 'All my friends are courting.'

'Aah, you poor thing, get the violins out, someone,' said her brother, to the amusement of everyone else.

'You've been a right little misery since you fell out with that last bloke,' said her mother, a scruffy woman with curlers in her hair and a cigarette in her mouth. 'Why don't you try and patch things up with him?'

'He probably dumped her, not the other way around like she told us,' said her fifteen-year-old brother, who was sitting beside her enjoying himself enormously at her expense.

'Oh, I've had enough of this madhouse,' Mabel announced, wriggling her way off the sofa. 'I'm going out.'

'Good. There'll be more space for us now,' said the brother nearest to her.

'Where are you going?' asked her mother.

'Dunno,' she replied. 'Just out anywhere for a

breath of air and to get away from all the questions and mickey-taking.'

'It's chucking it down with rain out there,' said her mother. 'You'll get soaked.'

'It won't hurt me to get wet,' Mabel said, leaving the room. She knew that she would come under discussion as soon as she shut the door behind her.

Her mother was right about the rain: it was beating down on everything when she went outside in her navy-blue raincoat and a headscarf. It felt good to be out of the house and away from all the family scrutiny, though, even if she was soaked to the skin within seconds and there were puddles up to her ankles that she couldn't avoid walking through. The rain gave her a glorious feeling of privacy because the streets were practically deserted.

Without any prior intention, she found herself heading for Doug's place; for some reason she felt inexplicably drawn there. Getting back with him was not what she had on her mind. That wasn't even an option. But she wanted to see him suddenly with such a feeling of urgency it couldn't be denied.

★ ★ ★

Doug cleared a patch in the condensation on his rain-soaked bedroom window with the net curtain and looked out on to the wet street, the pavements gleaming in the light from the lamps. By God, it was miserable out there, and he was grateful for that. Sunshine depressed him even

463

more because it made everyone else cheerful when he wasn't. It brought out the courting couples, walking along all over each other and making him feel even more alone.

Mabel's departure from his life had left a gap, but the initial regret had soon turned to blind fury. She was just like all the rest: only cared about herself when put to the test. He was no angel, he admitted it, but he'd never done anything bad to her. On the contrary, he'd been good to her, spending all his money taking her out, being polite and caring, and taking an interest in her.

And how had she thanked him? She'd chucked him at the first sign of trouble. It wasn't as though his misdeeds had any relevance to her. They had happened before he'd been with her. His past was none of her damned business. What right did she have to judge him? If the truth be told, she'd probably done a good few things she regretted; the same as everyone else.

Did he regret what he'd done, though? In all honesty, he didn't think he did, because both acts had given him a sense of power; for a while, anyway. It had all gone now, but having one over on Will Stubbs had felt magnificent while it lasted. So the lengths he'd gone to to obtain that feeling had been worth it.

Recalled to the present, he realised that he was shivering. It was bitterly cold in his bedroom, and damp. There was only one fire in the house and his parents were sitting by that. He'd sooner get pneumonia than listen to their boring conversation, and have them make snide comments about him missing his young lady. Ugh, his life was so awful it wasn't worth living. There was absolutely nothing for him. No girlfriend; no mates. No looks and no hope.

Angry with the world in general, he took his raincoat and trilby hat off the hook on the back of the door, put them on and went downstairs and out of the front door into the driving rain without a word to his parents. He walked briskly down to the river and went into the warm and welcoming atmosphere of the Dove, where he ordered himself a double whisky. He knocked it back in one go then ordered another, which received the same treatment. Ah, that was better. He felt more cheerful with every sip he took, so he ordered more; one after another.

Suddenly the answer to his problems came to him and he knew what he must do. It seemed so obvious he couldn't imagine why he hadn't thought of it before.

★   ★   ★

After the twins had gone to bed that night, Megan got her husband alone in their bedroom and told him that they were going out for a walk. When he started muttering excuses and pointing out that it was raining, she said, 'I'm fully aware of that and I'm sorry to drag you out in bad weather, but it can't wait I'm afraid. We need to be on our own to have a serious talk and that means going out, because it's the only way we can be really private. It must be done, Will. I've asked Hetty to listen for the girls. You're not

465

working tonight, for a change, so I need to take this opportunity.'

'You're expecting me to go out for a walk in the pouring rain because you want to have a talk?' he objected, dreading what the subject matter of the talk might be. 'What's the matter with talking here where it's dry?'

'Too many listening ears,' she said.

'This building is old. The walls are thick.'

'Not thick enough for what we've got to talk about. We're going, Will, and I won't take no for an answer,' she said in an authoritative tone that was so unusual for her he was somewhat taken aback. 'Get your coat on and let's go.'

Complaining bitterly, he followed her down the stairs.

★ ★ ★

Mrs Reynolds answered the door to Mabel.

'Hello, stranger,' she said, looking pleased to see her. 'Don't stand out there in the rain, girl. Come on in.'

'I won't stay long,' explained Mabel, stepping into the hall.

'Take your coat off and I'll make some tea.'

'Thank you, but I won't if you don't mind,' said Mabel, eager to get to the point of her visit and leave. 'Is Doug in?'

'No, I'm afraid he isn't, luv,' replied Mrs Reynolds. 'He's gone out. You've only just missed him as it happens.'

'Did he say where he was going?'

Doug's mother gave a dry laugh. 'Are you

kidding? He never tells us anything. We heard the front door slam, that's how we know he's gone out.' She thought for a moment. 'He's probably gone for a drink somewhere.'

'I see.'

Mrs Reynolds liked Mabel; she'd taken a shine to her the first time Doug had brought her home. The girl had a warm heart and an easygoing manner. Polite and respectful of her elders but not without spirit, she was the sort of young woman any caring mother would want to welcome into her family.

'Between you and me, luv,' she began in a confidential manner, 'he's my son and I love him but he isn't an easy person to get on with; never has been. He's always been a miserable sod; even as a little boy he was difficult. But he's been unbearable ever since he came back from the war.'

'It's understandable,' said Mabel, instinctively defensive of him. 'His disfigurement is a terrible thing to have to live with.'

'I know that, and God knows I've tried to be patient,' Mrs Reynolds told her. 'But he creates a living hell for himself and all the people close to him. That's why his dad and I were so pleased when he started going out with you, because he was like a changed man.'

'Really?'

'Oh yes,' she confirmed. 'You were so good for him. It was lovely for us because he was cheerful around the place, had a civil tongue in his head for a change. When you stopped coming round and he stayed in of an evening we guessed you'd

467

parted and were really disappointed. But we daren't risk asking him for fear he would fly into a rage, he's been that bad tempered.'

'Oh dear. Poor you.'

'Is there any chance of the two of you patching things up?' asked Mrs Reynolds. 'Is that why you've come to see him?'

'No. I'm afraid not,' Mabel said sadly, thinking how devastated his mother would be if she were to know what her son had done, and knowing that she would never tell her.

'Oh, that's a shame.' The older woman looked downcast and shook her head sadly. 'He needs someone like you: someone cheerful with a big heart who won't take any nonsense from him. You would have been the making of him if you'd stayed together. I've never seen him so happy as when he had you in his life.'

'He made me happy too and I was sorry it had to end. It's just one of those things that happen I'm afraid, Mrs Reynolds. Things don't always work out as you hope,' said Mabel, who ardently wished things could be different. She found herself wanting that more with every passing moment. 'Anyway, as he isn't here I'll be on my way.' She didn't want to worry the other woman with the sense of urgency that was still bothering her. 'It wasn't anything important. I just wanted to know that he was all right.'

'You'll probably find him in the Dove or the Black Lion. I think that's where he usually goes.'

'Thanks, Mrs Reynolds, but I'm sure he doesn't want me trailing after him when he's gone out for a drink.'

The older woman shrugged. 'As you like, dear,' she said. 'I think he would be pleased to see you, but it's up to you.'

★ ★ ★

'So what's all this about?' Will wanted to know as he and Megan headed for the river in the driving rain, she wearing a bright red mac with a hood, him in a dark raincoat with the collar pulled up.

'It's about you and me, Will,' she told him as they reached the towpath and took shelter under a tree, the light from the lamppost shining on the fallen leaves all around them.

'Surely this isn't the time or place . . . '

'It isn't ideal, I admit. But there never will be a right time and place for us because we have such limited privacy and you are determined to ignore the issue for as long as you can get away with it.' She looked at him; his face and hair were soaked with rain and he looked achingly handsome in the dim light. 'Here and now is as good as anywhere. You're feeling as miserable as I am, so why pretend everything is all right?'

'I don't know, Megan,' he said grimly, his hands sunk deep into his pockets. 'Maybe I'm hoping it will blow over.'

'No chance! It's far too serious for that,' she responded, her face wet, the rain dripping off her hood and running down her neck. The tree offered little protection because it had shed many of its leaves.

'Yeah, I suppose it is,' he sighed.

'There's no doubt about it. Well, I've reached

the point where I feel as though I can't take any more of the way things are between us,' she went on, determined for this dreadful business to be resolved one way or the other. 'I would do anything in the world to put things right, but it isn't in my power to do so.'

'No?'

'Don't act the innocent, Will,' she warned. 'You know as well as I do that only you can do that.' She braced herself to say the words she knew she must utter to bring matters to a head. 'Unless you can accept the fact that I was raped and learn to live with it instead of treating me as though I have some particularly revolting and infectious disease, you'd better pack your things and leave.'

He looked as though she'd struck him, and it tore at her heart to see him standing there looking so forlorn, the rain flattening his hair to his head. But she had to do this.

'Surely you don't mean that, Megan?' he said thickly.

'I'm afraid I do,' she said, her voice breaking. 'I don't want you to leave. I love you more than anything in the world, but I can't allow you to destroy me, which is what you're trying to do at the moment even if you don't realise it. I can't let that happen because I have two daughters to raise and they need their mother to be able to face the world with confidence, not hanging her head in shame, which is what you seem to want.'

'Destroy you?' he exclaimed, looking genuinely shocked. 'I would never do that. And as for you hanging your head in shame . . . that's the last

470

thing I would ever want.'

'Day after day you're punishing me by pushing me away, and it stops now, Will.' She had to stand firm for all their sakes. 'If you can't help yourself, then you must go. It's as simple as that and the only fair thing to do. It's up to you.'

'But I look after you,' he said lamely. 'I try to be a good husband and father.'

'You're a good man, Will, I wouldn't dream of saying otherwise. But the way you are at the moment you are no good for me. The rape happened and nothing can change that. It was not about Doug and me; it was about Doug and you. It was a power game and there wasn't anything I could do to stop it. He did it to get one over on you, and he's succeeding wonderfully because you're allowing it to ruin our marriage.'

Will bowed his head. 'It's just that . . . I can't bear to think of his hands on you,' he said gruffly. 'I'm sorry.'

'*You're* sorry? How the hell do you think I feel? I was the one who lived through the most hateful and degrading thing of my life and you're making me suffer all over again.' Megan was angry now, and desperate to make him understand. 'It isn't fair, Will, and I'm not having it. How dare you make me feel guilty when I've done nothing wrong? When I've been used as a pawn for Doug Reynolds' long-standing jealousy of you. That was why he couldn't resist boasting to me about his part in Ron's drowning. He got a kick out of telling me and then threatening me with what he'd do if I told you. He had us both under his control and he absolutely wallowed in it.'

'Yeah, I realise that.' Will's tone was grim.

'I know it's an unwritten law with you men that a woman is asking for it whenever something like this happens, and that it's never the man's fault,' she said angrily.

'Now you're not being fair, Megan,' he objected, raising his voice. 'I've never suggested anything like that. Not for a single moment. If I had, I wouldn't still be around.'

'All right. Perhaps I was being overly sensitive,' she conceded, sounding more subdued. 'I'm sorry.'

'Thank you.'

'But you're still prepared to let some disgusting incident for which I was not to blame wreck what we have — what we had.'

'That's the last thing I want to happen,' he told her. 'You and the girls are everything to me.'

'So why can't you bear to touch me? Tell me that. Does what happened make me unclean in your eyes?'

'Of course not.'

'That's what it seems like to me.'

'It isn't a straightforward thing,' he told her. 'I don't understand it myself, so how can I explain it to you?'

'What happened was bad, but not bad enough to let it ruin both our lives as well as the children's,' she interrupted, deeply emotional and almost in tears now. 'We've both lived through the war. You've seen mates die, I lost my father and thought my end had come many

472

times during the bombing. Hundreds of thousands of people lost their lives and many were seriously injured, and here we are both alive and fit and healthy. We were spared, Will, and we should make the most of every second. What happened to me was nothing compared to what happened to a lot of people. Doesn't that put it into some sort of perspective?'

'You're not telling me anything I don't already know,' Will told her. 'I'm not a fool. Neither am I the sort of person who would deliberately set out to hurt you.'

'Then don't throw what we have away by letting some past incident of no real significance come between us,' she said, tears mingling with the rain on her face, her words distorted with anguish. 'I'm trying to understand, Will. I've tried to put myself in your place and I know it's hard for you. But it's difficult for me too and I can't take much more of the way things are. I'm sure we can find a way through this but I can't do it without you. So make up your mind what you're going to do, and if you can't behave normally towards me . . . just stay away from me.'

He looked at her and braced himself to say what he knew he must, in all fairness to her. 'I'll move out and stay at Mum's place,' he said, every syllable torn from him. 'I'll come back and pick up a few things later on.'

She couldn't speak so turned away and walked back along the towpath in the driving rain, her head down and her body convulsed with sobs.

So deeply was she immersed in her own

emotions, she didn't notice a drunken man come out of a pub and walk unsteadily towards the bridge.

★ ★ ★

Will stood by the river's edge, staring unseeingly into the dark, rain-dappled river, a haze misting the glow from the riverside lights that shone on to the water in yellow splinters. The rain fell steadily and his clothes were drenched right through to his skin. But physical discomfort was nothing to him; it was the other kind that caused the pain. He was no stranger to hardship and anguish; he'd had to do things in the war that would haunt him for the rest of his life. But letting his wife walk away just now had taken more courage than anything before.

What else could he have done? He couldn't trust himself to do what she wanted; what she deserved. He couldn't guarantee that he wouldn't freeze up the instant they touched because his feelings were so irrational. Everything she said was true and he wanted to run after her and take her in his arms and tell her that things were going to be all right. But he couldn't be sure that they would. He couldn't stop the thoughts. So he'd had to let her go.

Staring into the river with his back to the towpath, he didn't even see the drunk who staggered past him.

★ ★ ★

Mabel hurried along the towpath towards the Dove with a new urgency to her step. Since leaving the Reynolds house she'd been thinking things over very seriously and as a result had had a change of heart towards Doug.

He did have an evil streak in him; there was no doubt about it. But he'd always treated her right, and people could change. He'd done those awful things because he was depressed. If he had her in his life, keeping him happy and content, maybe he wouldn't feel the need. Anyway, he was a human being; one of God's creatures. Someone had to love the rotten apples.

Outside the pub she paused nervously. In the circles in which Mabel moved it wasn't done for a decent woman to go into a pub alone, even though women had made such strides forward during the war. But she had to see him so must take her courage in her hands and do it. She opened the door into a fog of cigarette smoke and a roar of noise, mostly male voices.

People looked curiously in her direction but she paid no attention. She scanned the bar for him. Deeply disappointed that there was no sign of him, she went up to the counter and asked if anyone of his description had been in. She was told that he had left about five minutes ago.

Back outside in the rain, Mabel decided that there wasn't much she could do tonight. As it was still quite early he'd probably gone to another pub, and if he was out on a pub crawl he'd be in no mood for a serious discussion. She wanted him sober when she talked to him. It was a serious decision she had made.

The important thing was that she'd made up her mind to have him back, and felt a lot better for it. She could wait until tomorrow to tell him.

Feeling happy and positive about the future, she started to walk back along the towpath, unaware of the fact that the man she wanted to see was just a few hundred yards away on Hammersmith Bridge.

★　★　★

The copious amount of whisky he'd consumed had taken effect, and Doug felt strong and extremely pleased with himself, if a little muddled-headed and unsteady on his feet. He stood on Hammersmith Bridge looking over the rail into the distance, the riverside lights cloudy from the rain mist, the water only visible because of the splashes of light on it. There was hardly anyone about. Occasionally a car or a cyclist went by on the road, and the odd pedestrian walked past him, head down against the rain.

Most people were inside on a filthy night like this, and very sensible of them too. Only outcasts like himself were driven out into the rain to get drunk because they had no decent company at home and no friends to go anywhere nice with.

He'd show Will and Mabel what they'd done to him and make them sorry for turning against him instead of supporting him when he'd sustained such hideous facial scars in the service of his country. It was their turn to suffer now, holding things against him from the distant past. Neither of them would have an easy conscience ever again after tonight, and serve them damn well right.

He started to laugh drunkenly as he tried to climb up on to the top of the barrier, but the railing was quite high and the rain had made the iron slippery, so he kept sliding back down. There was a time when he'd have been up there in one go. Probably still could if he was sober. But why would he want to be sober with his life in the state it was at the moment?

As last he'd done it. He'd managed to get his legs over the top and was sitting on the rail looking down into the river, feeling calmer but depressed as the effects of the whisky moved from the euphoric to the melancholic stage. A passing cyclist had stopped and was trying to persuade him to come down, but Doug was oblivious to all but his own thoughts.

Suddenly it didn't seem to be such a good idea to be up here in the pouring rain. It was one thing thinking about throwing yourself to your death off the bridge, and quite another actually doing it. What was he doing up here in the cold and wet when he could be in the pub in the warm with another whisky in his hand?

Trying to lift his leg up with the idea of swinging it over the rail and getting back down on to the walkway, he lost his balance and his grip. Too drunk to gather his wits sufficiently to try to save himself, he hurtled towards the murky waters of the Thames at high tide.

18

Although there weren't many people about on this wet and stormy night, a small crowd gathered in response to the cyclist's frantic cries for help which resonated along the riverside.

Breathless from running, Will, Megan and Mabel appeared almost simultaneously.

'This bloke jumped off,' the man was saying, his voice ragged with distress. 'I tried to get him to come down off the rail but he didn't seem to be listening. Then he just . . . sort of went. Must have been determined to do himself in, the poor devil. I can't swim or I'd have gone in after him.'

Will was dragging off his jacket even as the man spoke. 'Could you call an ambulance, mate?' he requested.

'Will,' said Megan worriedly, 'it's dangerous down there in the river in the dark.'

'I'll be all right. I can't just leave him, whoever he is, can I?' responded Will, who had no fear of water for himself; only for his loved ones. 'I've got to do something.'

She knew he would go on whatever the danger to himself. It was the way he was. As the cyclist, swathed in oilskins, pedalled off towards the phone box, Will dived off the bridge.

'Don't worry,' said Mabel, putting a comforting arm around Megan. 'Will's a strong man. He'll be fine.'

The water was ice cold and Will was breathless from the shock and shivering violently. As his eyes got used to the dark, he could see enough from the lights from the bridge and the riverside to know that there wasn't anyone else down here. Treading water to stay afloat, he peered around. Then he heard splashing and a spluttering sound.

'You'll be all right, mate,' he said as he swam over to the struggling man and tried to get a hold on him. 'I'll get you out. Try and relax and leave it all to me.'

'Will bloody Stubbs,' came a gasping voice he knew only too well. 'It would have to be you.'

'Oh not you, Reynolds,' Will responded, and he could smell the alcohol on the other man's breath. 'If I'd known it was you I'd have stayed on the bridge and let you rot.'

'You're the one who's going to rot. Time for you to join your brother,' choked out Doug, somehow managing to push Will down.

'You evil sod,' muttered Will, coming to the surface. 'I ought to make you pay for that.'

The cold water had sobered Doug up a little but he was still muzzy with drink, his movements slow and clumsy, hampering his ability to cope with being out of his depth in the water, even though he could swim.

'You're the one who's gonna pay,' said Doug, pushing and wrestling drunkenly with Will and sending them both under.

With every ounce of strength he could muster,

Will swam to the surface, coughing and spitting out the filthy water. When Doug reappeared he was making choking noises and went back under, bobbing up only briefly before he sank again.

A part of Will wanted to swim to the bank and leave the other man to his fate. But it wasn't in his nature to let a man die, even a murderer like Reynolds.

So he took a deep breath and went under again, finding Doug and pushing him to the surface in a mighty effort that challenged his strength to the limit. Having done a life-saving course in the army, he knew the basic procedure. He put an arm around Doug's neck from behind and with his free arm began to swim to the bank. Ominously, Doug didn't speak or struggle.

★ ★ ★

The small crowd on the bridge moved down to the river bank when the ambulance arrived, Megan and Mabel with them. They hadn't been able to see what was going on in the water; had just been able to make out some movement down there. Megan was worried sick about Will. He was a good swimmer, but jumping into the river in the dark was dangerous. He could have hit his head on some heavy piece of litter, knocked himself out and drowned.

Such was her relief when she saw him climb out of the water she ran up to him and burst into tears. Mabel stood back so as not to intrude.

'Are you all right?' Megan asked, keeping her

480

distance because of the way things were between them.

'Yeah. Cold, shattered and out of breath, but all in one piece.' Shivering, he turned towards the bank, where resuscitation work was in progress by the medics. 'It's not looking too good for him, though.'

'You did your best,' she assured him. 'That's all anyone can do. You need to get into a hot bath and some dry clothes before you catch your death.'

'Don't worry about me.' He looked across at Mabel. 'She's the one who's going to need looking after. The bloke they're trying to bring back to life is Doug, and I don't think there's much chance.'

'Oh my God,' Megan exclaimed, reeling from the shock and turning to go over to Mabel. 'Can you tell them at home what's happened and say I'll be back as soon as I can?'

'Will do.'

⋆   ⋆   ⋆

'Maybe he wouldn't have done it if I hadn't given him the push,' said Mabel tearfully as Megan walked her home. 'I was gonna give him another chance too. I was out looking for him to tell him; that's how I happened to be near the river. I know he was bad, but even bad people need to be loved.'

'Don't go blaming yourself,' said Megan. 'Doug jumped off the bridge of his own accord with no thought to how much it would hurt his

481

mother and father. Selfish, if you ask me.'

'Yeah, there is that.'

Frankly Megan was amazed that Doug had taken his own life and couldn't bring herself to believe that he'd meant to do it. He was far too fond of wallowing in self-pity and planning revenge to commit suicide. Her guess was that he'd had a few too many, climbed up on to the railing in the hope of gaining attention and fallen into the river accidentally. But to save Mabel's feelings she would keep her thoughts to herself.

'I suppose I've had a lucky escape,' said Mabel unconvincingly. 'I wouldn't want to be with a quitter.' She started to cry. 'It's just that I did love him so much.'

'I know you did,' said Megan kindly, putting her arm around her. 'None of us can choose who we fall in love with. But you can choose your friends, and I'll be here for you whenever you need me.'

Mabel cried all the way home. Megan went into the house with her and explained to her mother what had happened.

'Oh, love, you poor girl,' said Mrs White, opening her arms to her daughter. 'Let's get your wet clothes off and you can tell your mum all about it.'

'You can have this chair if you like,' offered one of her younger brothers kindly.

Another brother went to put the kettle on. No one was teasing her now.

Having delivered Mabel into the bosom of her family and stayed for a while to add her support,

Megan made her way home to face her own problems.

It had stopped raining when Will went back to the bridge and stood looking out over the river, his hands sunk deep into his overcoat pockets. It was still cloudy but the lights of the town shone bright, creating a prettier landscape than in daytime because the bomb damage wasn't visible.

He hadn't moved out as he'd said he would. He'd just explained the situation about Doug to the others, bathed and changed and come out again, having felt drawn back here.

Doug's death had affected him far more than he cared to admit, mainly because he couldn't remember a time when Doug hadn't been around. It was the end of an era, and made Will feel as though a chunk of his childhood had been wiped out; a link with Ron obliterated. He couldn't grieve for a man who had caused him such suffering, but he did feel sorry for the waste of a life.

Leaning on the rail, he stared into the waters flowing under the bridge. The Thames had always played a large part in Will's life. He'd always enjoyed that sudden rush of openness when you stepped out of the town and on to the towpath. Despite the dirt and the foul stench of the mud banks that the low tide exposed, there was a constancy about it that soothed him. Even though he'd grown to hate it because of its association with the most traumatic event of his life, at the same time he'd never stopped loving it.

It evoked painful memories, though, especially on this bridge where the waters below had claimed his brother's life and now also that of his killer and the perpetrator of Will's own anguish. He decided that there was no need for anyone else to know about Doug's last murderous attack. No good would come from passing it on. The man couldn't hurt anyone else.

Suddenly Will felt exhausted. He'd been working day and night lately and it was beginning to take its toll. For what exactly? he wondered now. Why was he working every hour God sent if Megan would no longer be in his life? It had been for her and the girls he'd been doing it; to strive for the best for them and give them a golden future. He could provide for them to a reasonable standard by just working normal hours and to hell with his ambitions.

Standing there alone in the damp night, he experienced a sudden moment of clarity. The issue that was tearing Megan and him apart seemed insignificant suddenly. It was in the past, swept away like the rubbish in the river. If his wife had the courage to try to put it behind her, then so should he. She had been through it, not him; what gave him the right to punish them both?

He turned away from the rail, pulled his collar up and walked purposefully towards the town.

★ ★ ★

Megan was feeling tired and dispirited as she walked home, barely even noticing that it had stopped raining. She'd been concentrating entirely on Mabel until she'd left her. Now her own failing marriage hit her and she felt weak, helpless and alone. The worst thing was being powerless to put things right. If it was another woman coming between them she could fight for him. But what she was up against couldn't be fought by her. She couldn't get inside Will's head and make him feel differently about what had happened. Only he could do that, and he obviously wasn't able to or he would have done it.

When she got home everyone was in bed so she went straight upstairs. She was about to get into bed when she heard someone coming up the stairs and the bedroom door opened.

'Will . . . er, have you come for your things?' she asked hesitantly, hardly daring to look at him for fear she would collapse into tears. He'd made his choice and she didn't want to make a scene.

'Not unless you want me to leave, and I wouldn't blame you if you did, the way I've been behaving,' he said, looking sheepish. 'Sorry, love. I've been a fool. If you can get over what happened, so can I.'

The room was suddenly filled with warmth and light. It was going to be all right. The agony was over. Megan leapt out of bed, her face lit with a huge, beaming smile, and went towards him with her arms outstretched.

485

We do hope that you have enjoyed reading this large print book.

Did you know that all of our titles are available for purchase?

We publish a wide range of high quality large print books including:
Romances, Mysteries, Classics
General Fiction
Non Fiction and Westerns

Special interest titles available in large print are:
The Little Oxford Dictionary
Music Book
Song Book
Hymn Book
Service Book

Also available from us courtesy of Oxford University Press:
Young Readers' Dictionary
(large print edition)
Young Readers' Thesaurus
(large print edition)

For further information or a free brochure, please contact us at:
Ulverscroft Large Print Books Ltd.,
The Green, Bradgate Road, Anstey,
Leicester, LE7 7FU, England.
Tel: **(00 44) 0116 236 4325**
Fax: **(00 44) 0116 234 0205**

Other titles published by
The House of Ulverscroft:

IN THE DARK STREETS SHINING

Pamela Evans

After Rose Brown's husband is killed at Dunkirk in 1940, she is determined to pick herself up and start again. Wanting to help the war effort, she begins life as a postwoman on the Blitz-torn streets of London. And when she rescues a young boy from a bombed-out house and takes him back to the family home in West London, she finds a new sense of purpose. Traumatised from losing his mother and being trapped in the ruins alone, seven-year-old Alfie is rebellious and withdrawn. However, he touches the hearts of the family whose patience and special insight from Rose win his trust. But then a stranger, Johnny Beech, turns up on the doorstep looking for his son, and everything changes . . .

LAMPLIGHT ON THE THAMES

Pamela Evans

Since the end of the war, when Bob Brown had taken over the car workshop on Fulworth High Street in London, Frank Bennett had been trying to get his hands on it. With his unscrupulous business methods, Frank was determined to get the prime site — whatever the cost. Bella was drawn to the river, and to the house on the promenade where she had first met Dezi Bennett. Despite disapproval from both families, the child and the young airman had become friends. Years later, their love blossomed and it seemed that nothing, not even the feud between their fathers, could prevent their marriage. Until Bob's tragic death and his last request to Bella . . .